Special EDITION

Believe in love. Overcome obstacles. Find happiness.

The Bachelor's Matchmaker
Marie Ferrarella

Her Fake Boyfriend
Heatherly Bell

T0363328

MILLS & BOON

THE BACHELOR'S MATCHMAKER
© 2024 by Marie Rydzynski-Ferrarella
Philippine Copyright 2024
Australian Copyright 2024
New Zealand Copyright 2024

First Published 2024
First Australian Paperback Edition 2024
ISBN 978 1 038 91745 4

HER FAKE BOYFRIEND
© 2024 by Heatherly Bell
Philippine Copyright 2024
Australian Copyright 2024
New Zealand Copyright 2024

First Published 2024
First Australian Paperback Edition 2024
ISBN 978 1 038 91745 4

This is a work of fiction. Names, characters, places, and incidents are either the
product of the author's imagination or are used fictitiously, and any resemblance to
actual persons, living or dead, business establishments, events, or locales is entirely
coincidental.

Published by
Harlequin Mills & Boon
An imprint of Harlequin Enterprises (Australia) Pty Limited
(ABN 47 001 180 918), a subsidiary of HarperCollins
Publishers Australia Pty Limited
(ABN 36 009 913 517)
Level 19, 201 Elizabeth Street
SYDNEY NSW 2000 AUSTRALIA

MIX
Paper | Supporting
responsible forestry
FSC
www.fsc.org   FSC® C001695

Cover art used by arrangement with Harlequin Books S.A.. All rights reserved.

Printed and bound in Australia by McPherson's Printing Group

The Bachelor's Matchmaker

Marie Ferrarella

MILLS & BOON

USA TODAY bestselling and RITA® Award–winning author **Marie Ferrarella** has written more than three hundred books for Harlequin, some under the name Marie Nicole. Her romances are beloved by fans worldwide. Visit her website, marieferrarella.com.

Dear Reader,

Well, we're back, this time with a brand-new series revolving around the Sterling Brothers (and their father), five men born between eighteen months and two years apart. Shortly after the youngest was born, their mother died as a result of a car accident. At a loss, their father, with the help of his late wife's best friend, found a nanny to help care for the boys as if they were her own. She helped raise them and educate them (rather than just indulge them). Consequently, the boys grew up smart and educated as well as able to do things (they cooked as a way of honouring their mother, who loved to cook).

Their father, Sanford, was lost without his beloved wife, Shirley, but he found a way to keep going and make sure that his sons grew up educated and provided for. Thanks to their nanny, Randi, the boys never sat on their hands. The oldest, Samuel, is a veterinarian; the next in line, Simon, is a very serious divorce lawyer who does not believe in love because of what he has to deal with; Scott, the middle son, is an investment counsellor and takes care of the family's finances; Sebastian, the next to youngest, is brilliant, having gotten his degrees in literature and become a college professor before he turned twenty; and Sean, the youngest and most likely the handsomest of the lot, managed to talk their father into taking him on as his partner despite not wanting his son to be part of a construction business.

The theme behind the books is getting his sons matched up so they could enjoy the sort of happiness that he, Sanford, did.

I hope I succeed in entertaining you, and from the bottom of my heart, I wish you someone to love who loves you back.

With all good thoughts,

Marie Ferrarella

DEDICATION

TO

My Editor,

Patience Bloom,

Who Is the Living Embodiment

Of Just That,

Patience,

With a Dose of Love

Thrown In,

I Will Always Be Eternally Grateful

We Crossed Each Other's Paths

Prologue

Sanford Sterling sat in the trailer he had parked at the newest construction site he had set up. He felt incredibly lost and alone. This sensation was nothing new. It came whenever he was alone with his thoughts, looking at the framed photograph he kept on his desk of his late wife. He was contemplating what his life had become in the years since Shirley had died as a result of a car accident, which had left him with their five sons to raise—two of whom were too young at the time when she died to even remember what she had been like.

"Oh, Lord, Shirley, you have no idea how much I wish you were here," he told the woman in the photograph. "Our boys need to settle down, to get married and start their own families. They need your help— *I* need your help. I lucked out when I found you."

He sighed deeply, remembering the day he first saw her. She had walked into his second-period English class on a Tuesday morning in eighth grade. He fell in love with her right then and there—and they had been together ever since. Until the day she had been taken from him. The resulting wound was still fresh even after all these years.

"I want our boys to feel that sort of luck coursing through their veins, but how on earth do I manage to do that for them? I need your help, Shirley. I really, really need you next to me. I don't want to guide our sons into making a mistake, marrying the wrong woman. Otherwise, they'll be sorry for the rest of their lives. I've never been able to even get them to find time for any serious dating." Sanford sighed, shaking his head. "They've always been too focused on getting their degrees and starting their careers. That much I've accomplished." He had a feeling that had been because Shirley was looking down at her sons and guiding their every move.

But this was too much to hope for—and how could he even be able to get all five of his sons to pair up with the right women? The best dating advice he had to offer was "follow your heart."

Sanford combed his fingers through his hair, frustrated and at a complete loss. "Oh, Shirley, I need you now more than ever. The *boys* need you," he whispered into the shadows.

And then suddenly, just like that, it came to him. The answer. From out of the past.

Maizie.

Maizie Sommers had been Shirley's close friend in high school as well as her maid of honor at their wedding. And, just as important, she had been the one who had helped him find a nanny to watch over the boys so he was able to go back to work, to earn a living and provide for his family.

That hadn't been easy, either, but Maizie was right there beside him, despite her busy schedule, weeding out potential candidates for the position of the boys' nanny, promising him he was going to get through this, assuring him that he *had* to get through this for Shirley's sake. And ultimately telling him that if there was absolutely *anything* she could do for him, she would.

For Shirley's sake.

And that was when he suddenly remembered. Aside from being a successful real estate agent, on the side, Maizie also ran a matchmaking service with two of her best friends. She took no money for it, instead gathering a sense of pride and feeling of accomplishment from the matchup.

That was his answer, Sanford realized.

"Matchmaking service," he said out loud, happy for once that his youngest son and business partner was not on-site with him. "Of course. Boy, talk about being thick," he murmured, shaking his head.

The first opportunity he got, he planned on paying Maizie a visit and laying this new dilemma he found himself facing at her feet. He needed help, and he didn't mind admitting it. This needed a woman's touch, he thought.

"Brace yourself, Sam," he said to his firstborn,

the one he was planning on matching up first. "Your fancy-free days are about to come to an end."

He was that confident that Maizie was about to find someone for Sam.

Now that he thought about it, he had heard good things about the enduring matches that Maizie and her friends had made in the last fifteen years. It gave him hope.

"My sweet boys," he said to the image he had in his heart of his sons. "Your lives are about to change— for the better," he said with certainty.

He decided that Sam, as his oldest, was going to be first. It only seemed fair to go that route. He had a feeling that Shirley would definitely approve of this move.

As soon as he was alone—and able—he placed a call to Maizie. It turned out to be the following day. Since she was successful in both her real estate business and this matchmaking, he had a feeling that he would need an appointment to see Maizie in a timely fashion.

Not that the woman would put obstacles in his way, but he wanted to pay her the courtesy of going to her on her timetable rather than his own, even though he was exceedingly busy 24/7.

Maizie picked up her phone on the third ring. "Maizie Sommers, how may I help you?"

He would have recognized that bright, chipper

voice anywhere. "Maizie, this is Sanford Sterling. Would you be available to meet with me tomorrow?"

It had been several years. "Sandy, is that really you?" she cried, clearly stunned. And then she immediately asked, "Is anything wrong?"

The last time they had spoken was at Sean's college graduation. To her credit as a good friend of both parents, Maizie had attended all five of their sons' college graduations, which was why he felt he could count on her to help him to successfully match up his sons.

"No, as a matter of fact, there isn't," Sanford told her. "But once again, I find myself in need of your very unique services."

He imagined Maizie making herself comfortable. "I'm listening. What can I do?"

He took a breath, launching into the reason for his call. "You once told me that you and your two friends had dipped your toes in matchmaking waters. Are you still treading water?"

"Not for a while now," she admitted. "But the girls and I are ready and eager to get back into it. You're not looking, are you?" she asked incredulously.

No one loved their late wife as much as Sandy loved Shirley. "No, not me, but it's time for the boys to find their soulmates. I hear you're really good at that sort of matchup."

He could hear the smile in Maizie's voice. "As a matter of fact, we are. Why don't you come down to the office the first opportunity you get, and we'll discuss the particulars?" she suggested.

"Tomorrow morning too soon?" he asked her.

"Tomorrow's perfect, Sandy. I look forward to seeing you," she told him. "How about ten?"

This was going to be good. "Sounds perfect," he told her.

"I certainly hope so" was Maizie's response.

The shopping center where Maizie's real estate agency was located had changed somewhat since Sanford had seen it last. It had been built up over the years, even though it continued to maintain its warm, friendly, welcoming appearance.

As he pulled into the lot, he felt as if he had butterflies in his stomach, a strange feeling for a grown man to have, he thought. But this was important. Very important, he told himself. If this visit went well, the ones that would follow would, too.

Parking his vehicle, he made his way over to the recently renovated real estate building. It looked inviting, he thought. That was a good sign. Taking a deep breath at the front door, he knocked once, opened it, then went inside.

There was one person inside. It wasn't a client. He flashed a quick smile in greeting, then nodded.

The woman came straight for him, her arms outstretched. "Sanford?" she asked.

"Maizie, you haven't aged a day since I last saw you at Sean's graduation," he told her.

"And you are still spreading it as thick as you ever did," Maizie said with a laugh, planting a kiss on Sanford's cheek. "How have you been, Sandy?"

"Busy." And then he admitted, "Lonely."

"Do you still have Sunday dinners at the house the way you all used to?" she asked him.

He nodded. "It's a tribute to Shirley."

Maizie smiled broadly. "She would have been very proud. Come, sit," she urged. "So are the boys ready for something serious?"

"Absolutely," he answered. "And I realize that I'm just not any good at matchups. But word on the street is that you and your two friends are extremely good at it."

"Well, I don't mean to get your hopes up," Maizie confessed, "but so far, my friends and I have been batting a thousand."

"I'd say that's pretty damn good," Sanford told her. "Do you think you could do it a few more times?"

Her smile all but lit up the room. "Absolutely," she told him. "I just need to ask you a few preliminary questions. But first, how is everyone?"

"Busy," he said again. "That's the problem. The boys are too busy at the moment to do the ordinary things that men their age normally do. That's why I need you, Maizie. They just don't seem to be able to find the time to sow their oats, wild or otherwise.

They seem obsessed with laying the foundations of their various careers. Sam is a veterinarian, Simon is a divorce lawyer, Sebastian—"

Maizie held up her hand, stopping Sanford mid-sentence. "You don't have to go through all their vocations. I was there at each of their graduations, remember?" she reminded her late friend's husband. "I can take it from here," she assured him. "Are they happy in their chosen fields?"

"They never gave me any reason to doubt that they were very happy," he told her.

Maizie frowned. "Not exactly a ringing endorsement."

"They're not exactly a talkative bunch, at least not around me," Sanford told her.

"Boys have trouble making their feelings known around their father, especially when he sacrificed so much for them," Maizie pointed out. She made a notation on her folder, then looked up. "Are they still as handsome as ever?"

He felt the usual fondness whenever he thought of his boys. "I'm sure that their mother would say that they are."

Maizie flashed a warm smile at him. "Just like their father," she pointed out.

Sanford gave her a look. "I'm not fishing for a compliment."

"I know that," the potential matchmaker told him. "You were never that vain. That was one of the things that Shirley liked about you. She would have approved of you trying to match up your sons to their potential soulmates. So, is Sam dedicated to his vocation?"

"If he could, he would care for animals for free," he told Maizie.

"Selfless and dedicated. There's a lot of his mother and his father in him," she told Sanford.

"But I know my limitations, which is why I've come to you for help," he told her.

Maizie nodded. "Tell me, do I have a time limit on this?"

"Just sometime before I die would be nice, although I need to tell you that I would like to be able to enjoy my grandkids," he told her.

Maizie smiled, probably thinking of her own grandchildren. "Oh, they are just the very best," she assured him. "You get to play with little people and enjoy them without worrying that you're doing things wrong. Because you know you're not." She patted her friend on his broad shoulder. "Smile, Sandy. It's going to be all right, I promise," she said, leaning over the desk and squeezing his hand. "Are there any physical preferences? You know, blonde, brunette, tall, short, that sort of thing."

"Only that she's breathing," Sanford specified.

Maizie nodded, lips pursed as if to keep from laughing. "Definitely breathing," she agreed. She leaned back in her chair, reviewing the notes that she had taken. "Well, I think I have everything I need. I take it you want to match up all of your sons?"

"Most definitely yes," he answered.

"In order?" She knew him well.

"Well, I think that would only be fair," he pointed out.

Maizie nodded. "Wouldn't want any of the boys to think that you're playing favorites," she said, "putting one above the other."

"Just like doing things in their proper order, that's all," Sanford said. "I always have. Will that be a problem?"

"Not for me," she answered. "If we find someone more suited to one of the other brothers, I'll just make a note to get back to the woman at a later date—unless, of course, there's a danger of losing the woman, and if we come up against that, then we'll take the proper precautions."

Sanford smiled. "That's why I came to you, Maizie. You know how to juggle things and keep all the balls up in the air at the same time. If you need anything to make this happen, just let me know," Sanford said. "Also, that goes for any payments."

"Payments?" she questioned, looking at him oddly.

"For possibly the initial outlay," Sanford specified.

She was still confused by his meaning. "Such as?"

"I'll leave that to your imagination," Sanford told her.

She flashed a smile at him. "Not to worry," she answered. "I have plenty to work on in my notes. Let me talk to my friends Theresa Manetti and Cecilia Parnell. We'll put our heads together and see if we can come up with a good candidate for Sam. There'll be a good backstory—all true," she specified. "And once we find the proper candidate for Sam, we'll go from there."

"She needs to be an animal lover," Sanford told her.

"Most assuredly. I wasn't born yesterday, Sandy. This is for my friend's son—as well as my godson," she said. She saw the look on Sanford's face. "You forgot that part, didn't you? Well, I didn't. I remember how he wiggled and wriggled as I held him while he was being baptized. Out of all the matchups I plan to make, Sam will be my very best," she promised. "You have my word on it."

Sanford took heart from the look on Maizie's face. "You've made me very happy, Maizie," he told her as he rose to his feet.

"Good. Then I'll get in contact with you once all the pieces come together," she told him. "My advice to you is to prepare for a wedding."

"You can be that sure of the outcome?" Sanford questioned.

Maizie flashed a bright smile at her friend. "Oh, I can be that sure," she told him with unshakable certainty.

Sanford smiled at Maizie. "Then I'll go home and wait for your call."

Her eyes sparkled. "You do that," she encouraged her friend.

She couldn't wait to call her friends with the news. They were going to be thrilled.

Chapter One

Theresa Manetti and Cecilia Parnell were already waiting next to Maizie's front door when she pulled into her driveway. Both women had expectant expressions on their faces when they saw her approaching.

"You're early," Maizie called out to her friends as she walked up to them.

"You're late," Celia countered with her hand on her hip. "Okay, we're here. So what's up?"

Maizie didn't answer the woman immediately. Instead, she waited until she unlocked the front door, pausing for dramatic effect. Theresa and Celia were used to her behavior. They had known each other for years.

Maizie, Theresa and Celia had a friendship that dated all the way back to the third grade. It was a continuous, lifelong friendship. The three of them had gone through absolutely *everything* together over the years. That included weddings, the births of their children and, sadly, the deaths of their husbands.

They had also, in desperation and unbeknownst to their children, played matchmakers for their children. The secret romantic matches involved Maizie's pediatrician daughter, Nikki; Celia's private investigator daughter; and Theresa's son and daughter, who were both attorneys-at-law. As a matter of fact, their matchmaking efforts had gone so well that after discussing the matter at length, the three friends had decided to branch out and undertake making further matches.

But due to extenuating circumstances, things had slowed down of late, and the friends had been forced to pay more attention to other aspects of their lives.

Until, Maizie thought with a smile, Sanford Sterling had walked into her office today.

Closing the door behind Theresa, Maizie paused once again, then announced, "Ladies, I am happy to tell you that we are finally back in business."

Celia looked at her friend, puzzled. "What do you mean, 'we're back in business'?" she asked as she unbuttoned her sweater and took it off. She placed it over the back of her chair. "We were never out of business, not in all these years."

It was true. Since they had each begun their separate business endeavors, their businesses had been growing steadily. And there was a reason for that. While other people were going on vacations and eventually contemplating the benefits of retirement, that sort of thing never crossed the three friends' minds. Never once. They far preferred working and reaping the fruits of their labors.

Bemused, Theresa tapped Celia on the shoulder. When her friend turned to look at her, Theresa told her, "I don't think that Maizie is talking about the kind of business that yields a monetary profit. I think that she is talking about an emotional one."

Maizie laughed. "Give that lady a cigar," she said, going to the kitchen. She took out the refreshments from the refrigerator that she had previously prepared during her lunch break.

Celia didn't bother attempting to mask her surprise. "You're kidding. Considering the last few years we have all gone through, I was beginning to think we had all just moved on when it came to dealing with people's romances. Nice to know that the matchmaking dream continues."

"Yes, isn't it?" Maizie said, delighted. Picking up the tray, she carried it into the family room and set it on the card table where they usually played their very low-key poker games.

"So, tell us," Celia urged. "Who is it? Anyone we know?"

"As a matter of fact," Maizie told them with a wide smile, "it is."

"Considering the number of people we know when you combine all our various acquaintances together, that does account for an awful lot of people," Theresa noted, her eyes sweeping over her two friends.

Since having someone come to them for their matchmaking services was such a rare event these days, Maizie decided that she could be forgiven for stretching this out just a little more. "This is someone from a long time ago."

Celia shook her head. "Still not narrowing it down enough," she told Maizie. She gave her friend a scrutinizing look. "Are you going to make us play twenty questions?"

Maizie smiled warmly at Celia. "Only if you want to."

The two other women exchanged looks, then simultaneously said, "We don't want to."

At which point Celia followed up their declaration with one of her own. "Give," she ordered Maizie, "or things just might have to get ugly."

"Heaven forbid," Maizie said. "All right, do you ladies remember Sanford Sterling?" she asked, giving each of her friends a scrutinizing look.

"That poor man who lost his wife and was left with five little sons to raise?" Theresa asked. "Of course we remember him. We all went to school together back in the day. You were Shirley and Sanford's maid of honor."

"I can remember those boys used to just love playing with the train sets that I gave them," Celia recalled fondly.

"Well, the boys are not playing with trains anymore," Maizie informed her friends.

Theresa's eyes opened wide as she clearly realized

what Maizie was telling them. "Oh my God, do you mean to tell me that that much time has gone by?"

Maizie nodded. "I mean to tell you that that much time has gone by," she confirmed.

"Wow," Celia said in disbelief. Reaching across the table, she picked up a homemade mint fudge brownie that Maizie had made on her lunch break. It turned out to be the perfect way to celebrate this piece of unexpected good news.

"My sentiments exactly," Theresa agreed, responding to Celia's "wow."

"How could they have possibly gotten so much older? I certainly haven't," Theresa maintained with a smile.

Celia laughed. "You keep telling yourself that, Theresa."

"Why shouldn't she?" Maizie asked, feigning surprise. "We haven't."

"Deal," Celia instructed, pointing to the deck in front of Maizie. She waited until full hands were distributed all around. "So, when do we get together with Sanford so we can pin down all the particulars?"

Theresa asked another pertinent question: "Which son does Sanford want us to find a soulmate for?"

"I got the impression that Sandy wanted to do these matchups in order. You know, not putting one son in front of the other because he didn't feel it was right." Maizie thought that was exceedingly fair. "He mentioned that he wanted us to find a wife for Sam first."

Theresa nodded her approval. "Sam," she repeated. "Did he happen to tell you what Sam is doing these days?" That was a usual question that they asked for matchups, but admittedly it had been a while since they had done this.

"He didn't have to. I know what Sam's field is," Maizie said as she put down three cards and held up the corresponding fingers for Celia's benefit.

Theresa sighed. "Of course you do," she said, rolling her eyes. "What was I thinking?"

"Don't crack wise, Theresa," Celia reprimanded their friend. "You know Maizie doesn't like you getting ahead of her story until she's ready." Celia's smile widened until it all but took in the entire room, lighting it up. "I can't tell you how good this makes me feel," she confided. "It feels like it's been forever since we brought love into someone's life."

Theresa frowned ever so slightly. "Don't jinx it, Celia."

Maizie looked at Theresa over the top of her cards. "Since when did you get so superstitious?" she asked.

"Since we've never had a single failure in all the time we've been bringing couples together. I mean, think of the odds. I have to admit that I'm afraid it's just a matter of time."

"What I would rather think is that the next matchup is going to be our next big success," Maizie said.

Celia laughed as she shook her head. "I guess you really are an optimist, aren't you, Maizie?"

Maizie just smiled at her friend. "I find that being an optimist is the only way to survive in this world," she responded.

Theresa closed her eyes and nodded. "Amen to that."

"So." Celia looked from one friend to the other. "Do we have any idea what Sam's type is?"

"Quite frankly, from what Sandy told me during the course of my interview, he's been too busy working and building up his veterinary business to focus on a type," Maizie answered.

"But he is an animal lover," Celia said, making the assumption.

"Oh, that's putting it mildly," Maizie confirmed.

Theresa nodded, clearly organizing her thoughts. "So, we look into pairing him up with another animal lover."

"It couldn't be just that simple," Celia said. "There has to be more to it than that."

Theresa laughed. "I'm not suggesting that the perfect match has to be able to swing through the trees and hang upside down from one to qualify as Sam Sterling's love match."

Maizie smiled at the simplistic description. Things were never that easy. "Did I mention that Sam has a soft spot in his heart for dogs and cats, with the occasional exotic bird thrown in?" she asked, her eyes crinkling as she grinned at her two friends.

"You did now," Celia replied.

"Sandy also mentioned that, in his opinion, Sam was somewhat overworked, devoting all his spare time to treating and caring for the animals, whether or not their owners are able to pay for his services immediately. As a matter of fact, as far as I know, the only time he does take off is for Sunday dinners."

"Sunday dinners?" Celia repeated, curious for more information.

Maizie nodded. "That was something Shirley started because Sandy was so busy building up his company he hardly had any time for his growing family. She insisted that he take a few hours off at least on Sundays so that the family could have dinner together. From what I gathered, Sandy complained about it, but the truth of it was, he could never say no to Shirley when it came to anything." She didn't give in to the sad feeling that was washing over her. "Sandy told me," she continued, "that after his wife passed away, he and the boys continued the Sunday dinner tradition in order to honor Shirley."

"I think that's really sweet," Theresa told her two friends.

Maizie nodded again. "That gives you some insight into the kind of young men we're dealing with. Apparently none of the boys have ever skipped out on Sunday dinners. They obviously know how much those dinners used to mean to their mother."

"Good for them," Theresa said, nodding her head in approval. "All right, for now we are going to be on the lookout for a bright young woman who has a weakness for working with animals and is in the market for a job. What do you think?" she asked.

Maizie laid out her winning hand on the table, smiled and declared, "Right."

Celia frowned. "How do you do that? Keep your mind on the conversation and still manage to win the hand that you're playing?" she wanted to know. "It doesn't seem very fair."

"It's called *multitasking*," Maizie told her friend.

"Don't feel bad," Theresa told Celia. "Maizie used to drive her husband crazy with that particular little talent of hers."

"I can see why," Celia said. "You know, I think I might have a candidate for this little matchup of ours." She smiled broadly at her friends. "As a matter of fact, I am sure of it. Give me until tomorrow to check this out." Her smile grew decidedly more pronounced.

"Oh, by all means, Celia, check away to your heart's content." Maizie looked first from one friend, then to the other, her heart all but glowing. "Ladies," she happily announced, "we are definitely back."

She could see that her friends agreed.

Chapter Two

"Good thing you don't expect me to just drop everything and cook for you," Sam Sterling said to the overly eager German shepherd shadowing his every step from the moment they walked in the house together. The large dog was dancing from one side to the other. "God, Rocky, I wish I had at least half of your energy. Well, actually," the veterinarian said, reconsidering his words, "I did. But that was much earlier this morning."

Sam sighed as he stopped in front of his refrigerator and took out a number of items packed away in plastic containers. He would combine several of them to create Rocky's evening meal.

The dog's name had been Rocky ever since she was a little thing at the local animal shelter almost four years ago. She had turned out to be a female, and Sam was all set to change her name when he adopted her, but he had reconsidered, thinking that changing her name might be confusing for the German shepherd. So he had, as his mother had been so fond of saying years ago, "left well enough alone."

Rocky's name was the first thing about her that strangers remarked on in surprise, and occasionally disbelief. It also allowed Sam to easily segue into stories about the dog's life, stories that he used to his advantage when it came to treating other ill pets.

But right about now, Sam just wanted to prepare Rocky's food, set it out on the kitchen floor, watch her polish it off and put the bowl in the sink. Right after that, he intended to stumble off to bed, with any luck, headfirst. Plans to eat dinner and catch a program that had aroused his curiosity earlier today had simply faded away. Sam really wasn't hungry any longer, and all he wanted to do was go to sleep and not have his mind challenged or even teased the slightest bit.

The vet paused for a moment to affectionately rub the shepherd's fur along her head and face. Rocky took this as a sign that her master wanted to play, but after the day that Sam had put in, nothing could have been further from the truth. She attempted to nip his hand and get him to chase her, but Sam didn't budge.

"Sorry, girl. I just don't have the strength to play with you tonight. Maybe we'll have more luck this Sunday. Or at least you will," he told the frisky dog.

If he didn't get her food ready, he was going to fall asleep right here where he stood, Sam thought. Forcing himself to move, he opened up the container of pumpkin filling, another container of boiled shredded chicken breasts, as well as shredded cheddar cheese and a small helping of dry dog food. He mixed it all together with a very small helping of the chicken broth he had used to prepare the chicken breasts.

"You realize that you're spoiling that animal," his brother Simon had accused more than once while observing him mixing a meal for Rocky.

Sam had not been moved by the accusation. Simon was a high-powered divorce lawyer who, as far as Sam was concerned, had shut his heart to everyone and everything except for their immediate family—and at times Sam wasn't all that convinced that Simon even allowed his family in.

"You know, it might do you some good to get yourself a pet and spoil it a little, too," Sam told his brother.

"And why would I want to do that?" Simon asked, keeping his distance from Sam's very animated pet.

"Might remind you to be human," Sam had told him.

But Simon had only shaken his head. "Being reminded of that fact only creates pain and disappointment. Trust me," he said wearily, "I know. Dealing with the people I deal with, I really know."

"Maybe you would have been happier if you became a farmer," Sam had quipped, even though he knew that wasn't really true. Sam knew that Simon was good at his chosen career.

"I'm plenty happy." Simon had all but growled his answer.

"Uh-huh," Sam had said, sounding sarcastic even to his ear.

Simon had frowned and then just sighed. "I take it you don't believe me."

It was hard for Sam not to laugh at that point. "So tell me, brother, what was your first clue?"

Simon waved his hand at his older brother, made a disparaging noise and then just walked away to join Sunday dinner, ending that conversation for the time being.

Recalling that now, Sam half smiled to himself.

For the most part, he got along well with all his brothers. He always had—as long as they weren't packed too tightly together and could make room for their differences. Otherwise, they could and most likely would get on each other's nerves. But he supposed when everything was all said and done, there was nothing really unusual about that among brothers.

Given any sort of emergency—*any* sort—all the brothers were there for one another. They always had been ever since they were very young. He realized, as time went on, being there for one another was a way to cope with the fact that their mother could no longer be there for them. Of course, they certainly couldn't make up for the fact that Shirley Sterling was gone, and she was never coming back. What really did help them deal with the situation was the memory that she had created and left behind for them in her wake.

Sam instinctively knew that if his mother were here right now, she would fuss over him, and he would be subjected to a kindly lecture that he needed to take care of himself and should not allow himself to get so worn out. But he couldn't back away from his work. Being dedicated to caring for animals usually yielded this sort of result, he thought. And truth be told, Sam wouldn't have it any other way.

With a strong wave of affection, Sam looked down at the German shepherd.

"C'mon, Rocky, time to eat your dinner so I can get some sleep, or I am going to leave you home tomorrow, and you can spend the day in the backyard, staring at the fence," he told her.

Whether or not his dog understood what he was saying—and if she did, whether she believed what he was saying to her—Sam knew it was just an empty threat. He would no more leave his dog alone in the backyard than he would drop her off in the forest for the day. He was merely talking so that Rocky would respond to the sound of his voice.

Mashing her dinner together, he placed the dog dish in front of her. He had barely pulled his hand back when the German shepherd made short work of what he had set before her.

"Maybe I should count all my fingers just to be sure I still have them," he quipped, looking down at his hand.

Rocky made a noise and looked up at her master

quizzically before very quickly polishing off the remainder of that evening's dinner.

As much as he pretended to be stern about this feeding ritual, seeing Rocky enjoy her food warmed Sam's heart. Almost four years had passed since she had accidentally come into his life and he had taken her into both his heart and his home, but he could remember meeting her as clearly as if it had all taken place just yesterday.

One of the people who ran the shelter had called and asked him to come by. There was an aging spaniel with a growth on his neck that needed to be looked at. Sam had treated the dog the way he always did, charging the shelter only what it cost him for the medication. He hadn't charged for his time, saying that his reward was the satisfaction he derived from seeing the animal get well.

While he was working with the spaniel, a floppy German shepherd had somehow gotten out of her cage and began to follow him around. When one of the caretakers caught her and returned her to her cage, the shepherd had cried so much trying and failing to get to him that she was virtually impossible to ignore. So when he finished sewing up where the spaniel had managed to injure himself, Sam turned his attention to the nosy German shepherd.

"What's the shepherd's name?" he asked. The first thing the local shelter did with new animals was name them.

"Rocky," the attendant informed him.

"Oh, like the fighter in the movie," he remembered commenting with a grin.

The attendant had laughed and said, "No, not quite."

He hadn't seen why that was funny until he allowed the shepherd to climb onto his lap and he began to pet it. That was when he noticed Rocky was female. He still hadn't thought about adopting her until she started crying pathetically again when he tried to walk away. After the third time, Sam decided this had to be some sort of omen.

"I guess this means I should take her home with me," he said to the attendant.

As it turned out, this was the attendant's first pairing of a stray with a potential candidate. Then, because Sam had done so much free work for them, the shelter waived the usual adoption fees.

"And the perfect union was born," Sam murmured now, looking at Rocky as he relived that earlier time. He was sitting on the family room floor, petting Rocky as she made short work of her freshly filled water dish. Or what had been a freshly filled water dish a few minutes ago.

"Okay, young lady. It's one last run in the backyard for you. Do what you need to do and empty yourself out and then it's bedtime for you, Rocky." He looked down at the dog. "Have I made myself clear, young lady?"

Rocky barked in response.

He knew there were those people who maintained that all conversations with pets were one-sided, but no one would ever convince him that Rocky didn't understand what he was saying to her, no matter how firmly they voiced their opinion.

Sam pulled himself up to his feet. "Well, I don't know about you, girl, but I am definitely ready to call it a day and go to bed," he told the dog. "I feel like I've put in at least thirty-six hours straight."

Rocky cocked her head at him, and he could swear she was trying to make sense of what he was telling her.

"I know, I know, I'm exaggerating, but I really feel that way. I didn't even get to stop for lunch today, and if I don't crawl into bed in the next few minutes, my battery is going to totally die, and I'm going to be good for absolutely nothing come morning."

After he let Rocky out one last time and the dog returned, Sam started up the stairs with Rocky lumbering right next to him.

"Yes, yes," Sam murmured as he took the stairs at a far slower pace than his pet did, "you've heard all this before. Well, I'm sorry, but I'm not up to being clever and interesting after being on my feet and on call all these endless hours. Feel free to run away and find another master if you think you can do better."

Sam paused at the top of the stairs to look at her. She remained where she was, looking up at him,

making no indication that she was about to go anywhere.

"No, I didn't think so," he said as he walked into
his bedroom.

Rocky was less than a beat behind him. She raced
him for the bed and sprawled out on it several seconds before he could reach it.

Sam didn't remember crashing onto the mattress.
And he certainly didn't remember closing his eyes.
But he must have, because the world around him
faded away and darkness descended. It was definitely
time to sleep—and he did.

Chapter Three

Sam's eyes flew open.

At first he thought he'd just imagined the noise. Maybe he was having an exceedingly vivid dream that refused to subside and present itself calmly within the scope of his day-to-day world.

There was absolutely nothing calm about the banging noise penetrating his brain and vibrating throughout his body.

What finally convinced him it wasn't a dream was Rocky leaping up from bed and running to the noise at the front door. Sam didn't even bother to pause and stretch. Instead, he was on his feet, heading toward the door to discover who was pounding on it. And, more important, why.

"Now what?" Sam mumbled, trying his best to get the sleep out of his eyes while attempting to get his brain in gear. By the time he did, he had reached the door, right behind his overly anxious German shepherd. "Calm down, Rocky. Burglars aren't going to pound on the door. They try to sneak in."

Rocky didn't behave as if she believed him.

Grabbing the shepherd around the neck, Sam really wished he had left her collar on so he had something to hang on to. He tried to soothe the animal as best he could as he reached for the front door. "Calm down, Rocky, stay calm," he said in a soft singsong.

At first, he opened the front door just a crack. This was an exceedingly safe city and had been so for years, but there was always a first time, he thought. But as soon as Sam opened the door enough to look out, Rocky seemed to calm down. At least to some degree.

It seemed to Sam that his pet was reacting to the young woman standing on the other side of his threshold, a very attractive, worried-looking young woman.

It was the middle of the night and fairly dark, so it took Sam several moments to realize that there was blood on the front of the woman's shirt.

Sam came to instantly, immediately concerned. "Are you hurt?" he asked. He opened his front door wide, issuing a silent invitation to her to come into the house.

The young blonde shook her head.

Rocky, Sam noticed, had stopped barking altogether. Instead, his ordinarily protective pet was sniffing around the intruder and had obviously made a guess as to where the blood on the woman's clothes had come from.

"It's not my blood," she told the vet she had gotten out of bed. "It's Charlotte's."

Sam peered behind the woman as well as around her. There was no sign of this so-called Charlotte as far as he could see. One hand on the doorknob, he began to close the door, still keeping an eye on both his dog and the noisy visitor who had disturbed his sleep.

"And Charlotte is?" he asked, pinning the woman with an inquiring look.

"My dog that was on the wrong end of a sudden, ugly dispute with a fierce pit bull that must have gotten loose in the neighborhood," she told Sam. "We were taking a late-night walk, and I think that Charlotte was trying to protect me. It all happened so fast, I didn't realize anything was going on until I heard this awful barking and crying coming from Charlotte."

Fearing the worst, Sam asked, "And where's your dog now?"

"I put her in my car and drove over here. That's how I got all this blood on me," the woman told him, waving her hand at the front of her shirt. "I'm sorry to wake you up in the middle of the night like this, but someone I know gave me your name and address and said you were really good with dogs," she explained, adding, "I'm new here, and I had nowhere to go." She flashed an apologetic look at him. He caught himself thinking that he had never had an apology look quite as good before. "I'm very sorry for all this."

"No reason to apologize," Sam told her. First things first, he thought. "You said your dog was in your car?"

The blonde nodded and immediately turned on her heel. She headed back toward a vehicle parked next to the curb. "Yes, she's right out here, Dr. Sterling," the young woman said as she led him to the beige late-model sports car.

A streetlight at the end of the block helped illuminate the area and allowed Sam to see just where he was going. More important, it allowed him to see the sad-looking, mangled creature lying across the Honda's back seat.

The dog attempted to bark at Sam as he approached. It was easy to see that the animal was afraid as well as bleeding.

"What's the dog's name again?" he asked the woman.

"Her name is Charlotte," she answered, opening the right rear door.

The dog was cowering, all but sinking into the back seat.

"Hello, Charlotte. I see you've gotten yourself into a little trouble," Sam said softly, keeping his voice low so as not to frighten the wounded dog. "Why don't you come with me, and I'll see what we can do to get you all cleaned up and to stop that bleeding?"

The miniature collie looked up at Sam with a pitiful expression in her eyes.

"I don't think she can walk," Charlotte's owner told Sam. She wasn't going for pity—she seemed to be genuinely concerned.

Sam regarded the wounded collie with kindness. "I wasn't planning on making Charlotte walk."

With that, Sam leaned into the vehicle, and very carefully and with maximum tenderness, he slowly took the animal out of the car and into his arms, being very careful not to hurt her in any way.

"What can I do?" the dog's owner asked as she shifted from foot to foot.

He glanced in her direction for a moment. "Honestly? Right now, my suggestion is that you try not to get in my way." Despite her diminutive appearance, the dog was rather solidly built. "Did you actually carry this dog and put her into your car?"

"I'm stronger than I look," she told him.

Sam was far from being a weakling, but he felt he had to move very carefully not to drop or jostle the dog in his arms. "You'd have to be," he told her.

"You know how sometimes you hear stories about a parent tapping into a wave of almost superhuman strength that allows them to do things people wouldn't think they could normally do?" she asked.

He was vaguely aware of that sort of thing happening sometimes. "Yes."

"Well, this was one of those times. Charlotte was injured and bleeding, and I just couldn't leave her like that."

Sam could definitely understand that. "You had no one to ask to help you?"

"I'm relatively new here," she repeated. "I don't know anyone in the area very well, and I wasn't about to impose."

"And yet you came pounding on my door," he pointed out, slowly making his way back to his home with the woman's injured pet.

"Extenuating circumstances," she said. "I wouldn't have normally done that."

Sam nodded. He could feel the dog breathing very hard as he held the animal against his chest. "I see your point."

"Is your shepherd in danger of running off?" she asked, looking at Rocky. The dog was dancing from foot to foot in front of them.

"Rocky knows better than that," he told her. "I made sure she was trained well before I allowed her to have this much freedom."

Charlotte's owner appeared uncertain as her eyes shifted toward the shepherd. "Far be it from me to argue with you," she told him. She held her breath as she followed her injured pet into Sam's clinic. "I can't tell you how my heart stopped when I saw that dog charging at Charlotte with those awful teeth bared. I threw dirt into his face to distract him, but it didn't even faze him. For a minute, I was afraid that the dog was going to rip Charlotte limb from limb. That's why I have all this blood on me."

Sam began to shoulder open his door. The woman quickly stepped up and pushed it open for them. "Thanks." He looked her over for a second. "Is any of that blood yours?"

"Honestly?" she asked. "I really don't know. It might be. Things happened so fast, and I managed to get the pit bull away from Charlotte by throwing a bunch of rocks at it, but the pit bull did try to bite me a couple of times. There's no scarier sound than hearing those sharp teeth clamping down next to you."

"When I finish with Charlotte, let me take a look at your arms and all the places you might be bleeding," he told her, nodding at her exposed skin.

"Okay, but Charlotte first," the pet owner insisted.

"That's what I just said," he told her, leading the way farther into the animal clinic. Sam indicated the exam table on one side of the room. "I'm going to put her down here. I think she will feel better if she sees you standing beside her."

"I won't get in your way?" the woman asked, concerned.

"I think you know enough not to do that," Sam told Charlotte's owner. He looked down at his pet. "Rocky, go wait in your play area."

As the woman watched in fascination, Rocky trotted off into a back room. Sam turned his attention to his patient. "Okay, pretty girl, let's see what that big bad pit bull did to you."

The wounded animal cried as Sam very carefully examined the gashes and tears along her skin.

"I won't hurt you, girl," he said, talking to Charlotte softly. "I promise to be as careful as I possibly can." He looked up at the dog's owner. It occurred to him that he didn't know her name, but getting acquainted could wait until later. This was more important. "I'm afraid that I'm going to have to put Charlotte under."

She looked at him with concern. "Do you have to?"

"I'm afraid that she isn't going to let me do what I have to do to her if she's awake," Sam told her. "Charlotte is not going to sit still for a scalpel or a needle piercing her skin when I go to sew her up. The noises that she'll make are guaranteed to break your heart. There is no way that I can do what I have to do when Charlotte is carrying on and crying during the process."

Charlotte's owner nodded, and then she shrugged. "Okay, Doctor, do what you have to do."

"I will," he answered. "And if you will please sit out in the lobby, I can get started."

"If you don't mind, Doctor, I'd rather stay here with you in case you need anything," the woman said, "or if you need any assistance."

"That won't be necessary," he told her. "I don't have an assistant when I operate."

"Maybe you should." She knew she was speaking out of turn, but Charlotte was very precious to her, and she had the impression that the vet was tired when she had roused him out of bed. She was amazed that he had managed to throw some clothes on before he opened his door. "I do have some training when it comes to this sort of surgery. I just prefer someone else taking the lead if it turns out to be complicated," she told him. "The second you feel that I'm getting in the way, just say the word, and I will back off, I promise." She looked at him intently, as if willing him to give a positive answer. "Okay?"

He was ready to turn her down flat. But the truth of it was that he felt that he really did need help in this situation. And although these were actually pretty dire conditions, this would most likely be the best way to test the woman's mettle.

"Okay," he told her, then nodded toward the sink in the corner. "Wash up."

She smiled hugely, then took in a deep breath and went to comply.

"By the way," Sam called after her, thinking he was going to need to be able to call her something as they got to work, "what's your name?"

"I didn't tell you?" she asked. In all the excitement, she must have forgotten, she thought.

"No, you didn't."

"It's Gina."

He nodded. "Nice to meet you, Gina. Let's get to work."

"Yes, Doctor."

He caught himself thinking that had a nice ring to it.

Chapter Four

Sam realized almost immediately that there was more damage done to the miniature collie than was noticeable at first glance. But now that he had Charlotte on the operating table with all the lights shining on the wounded animal, Sam could see that the rampaging pit bull had done a great deal more damage to his victim than he had thought at first.

He had sedated his patient, but even so, he still approached her very cautiously. If Charlotte was even partially conscious, he didn't want to risk frightening her.

"Would you happen to know who this pit bull belonged to?" he asked his unofficial assistant. Gina was right by his side, and she appeared to be nervously observing him as well as her pet.

"A neighbor, I think," Gina answered. She looked at him, clearly worried that something was off. "Why are you asking?"

"A dog that does this much damage to another living creature without being provoked is clearly dangerous. That dog shouldn't be walking around without being restrained," Sam said in all sincerity. "Your dog didn't do anything to provoke the pit bull, did she?"

"No!" Gina denied with feeling. "All Charlotte did was look up at the pit bull, nothing more. I doubt if he really even had time to register her presence. He just came charging around the corner, barking and growling and clearly ready to turn her into a doggie version of fast food." Gina looked down at her pet on the operating table. Her heart was clearly hurting for her poor dog. "I was barely able to get the animal to run off before Charlotte became a pincushion."

Gina was sorely tempted to run her hand along her pet's fur, desperately wanting to comfort the miniature collie. But even though the dog had been sedated, she was afraid that the contact might rouse Charlotte, and then anything the veterinarian was attempting to accomplish would be summarily destroyed or, at the very least, put on hold.

"It's all right," Sam told her. "You can touch her."

Gina looked up at him in surprise. "Do you practice mind reading, too?"

He laughed softly. "No need for mind reading. Remember, I have a pet dog, too. It's not so hard to guess what you're thinking. I would be thinking the same thing if all this was new to me, and I wasn't a veterinarian."

Gina gazed down at her sedated collie. She shivered a little. "When I think of what might have happened..." Her voice faded away. Tears gathered in her eyes.

"You can't dwell on what might have been," Sam said. "You need to focus on the fact that you managed to save your pet, and you ran that aggressive dog off before he could rip Charlotte into tiny pieces." It was time for him to get to work. "All right, are you sure you're up to being in the same room with your pet while I operate?" he asked Gina. "I won't think any less of you if you decide you'd rather take refuge in the waiting area."

But Gina was adamant as she shook her head. "No, I will be fine. I want to be able to help."

"All right, you can stay. After you wash your hands, put on a pair of surgical gloves. You'll find the gloves on that shelf," he directed, nodding his head toward a cabinet against the wall.

Gina followed his instructions, going over toward the sink and washing her hands. Once they were washed, she dried them, then slipped on a pair of surgical gloves.

Sam saw a hint of a frown on her lips. "Is something wrong?"

"Well, they're a little large," she told the veterinarian.

"I wasn't really planning on having an assistant, even though I was turning that idea over in my mind," Sam admitted. "That's why I didn't have a lot of sizes available."

"Hey, I'm not complaining," she said. "You just asked, and I believe in always being honest."

He smiled at her. "Well, that's a really good trait to have."

At that moment, Sam's own dog was whining and circled around the room. Up to this point, Rocky had been behaving so well, Sam had almost forgotten about her. But even so, he knew that he couldn't risk having the German shepherd in the room while he operated on another animal. Rocky might make a sudden move that could really throw everything off.

"Okay, Rocky, my girl," Sam said. "It's time for you to go and stand guard at the door to the clinic."

Rocky obligingly trotted off to the clinic's front door and assumed a guard position.

Gina's mouth all but dropped open. "She understood you," she cried in surprise.

"Dogs understand more than we give them credit for. It just takes a great deal of practice," Sam told Gina with an easy smile.

Gina laughed under her breath and shook her head in amazement. "You know, I'm beginning to think that you're right."

"Of course I'm right. I'm the veterinarian," he pointed out with a grin. "Do you doubt me?"

Gina began to feel hopeful. She was glad she had come to Sam's clinic, even if it was an ungodly hour. "Heaven forbid."

"Good answer," he said. Then, looking at her, he asked, "Are you ready?"

Gina pulled her shoulders back. "I'm ready." She

looked grateful that he hadn't read her the riot act for waking him up in the middle of the night. But her actions were warranted. And he was just doing what a dedicated veterinarian should. Gina came over to the table and stood next to him. "All right, tell me what to do and I'll do it."

"It's simple," he told her. "Just be there to keep her calm and make sure she doesn't suddenly wake up and attempt to bolt off the operating table."

Her eyes widened. "Has that ever happened to you?"

"No, not yet," he answered. "But that doesn't mean that there can't be a first time. How long have you had her?" he asked as he prepared to operate.

Gina didn't even have to pause to think. "I've had Charlotte since she was a puppy. Three years," she specified.

Sam nodded. "So she'll definitely respond to the sound of your voice when she wakes up."

Gina took a deep breath and nodded, never taking her eyes off her pet. She appeared to have braced herself. "Okay, let's do this."

As he began the surgery, Sam expected to hear Gina moan, or at the very least, give some indication that the procedure disturbed her. But to Sam's surprise, his "assistant" remained completely stoic, silently observing as he methodically repaired the damage that the pit bull had done to what appeared to be an exceedingly mild-mannered, easygoing pet.

"How are you doing?" Sam felt compelled to ask

his impromptu assistant when he was partially through the procedure. He noted that Gina had never taken her eyes off her pet while he operated.

"I'm fine," she answered, watching the collie's face. And then, as if she felt compelled to ask, "Is it going to be much longer?"

"Why? Do you want to take a break?" He was about to tell her she should go sit down and rest.

But Gina surprised him by answering, "No, I'm just afraid that Charlotte might suddenly wake up and realize what is going on."

Sam shook his head. "Trust me, she has enough anesthesia in her to keep her out for a long while. She's not in any danger of suddenly waking up."

"Then I'm fine," she assured him. "I just wish she could feel me petting her."

Sam smiled at the woman's concern. "Somehow, she feels it."

"You sound awfully sure of yourself," Gina whispered, as if she could use a little more reinforcement.

"I am," he told her. But he could sense that she wanted more reassurance. As he carefully stitched up the dog, he added, "It's a gut feeling. It's something you learn after a while from working with pets. Trust me."

"I do," she told him in all sincerity.

He spared her a quick look before turning his eyes back to his work. But although he had hardly known Gina for more than just a few minutes, Sam believed she meant what she said. He flashed her a smile. "It won't be too much longer," he promised her.

"Take as long as you need," she told him. "I'm not going anywhere and neither is Charlotte."

Sam laughed. "I kind of figured that part out."

Gina kept her eyes glued to every movement he made.

Sam tried his best to finish up without rushing through the procedure. That wasn't his way, but then, neither was having an assistant at his side. Not that he hadn't thought about it more than once, but it had been just a pipe dream more than anything else.

This wasn't bad, he caught himself thinking.

Sam carefully coached himself through what he was doing. Finally, the last stitch was placed, and he cut the thread. "Done," he announced to Gina.

"You're really finished?" Gina asked him.

"I'm finished," Sam confirmed. "You can stand down."

"I don't need to stand down," she told him, but even as she said it, her legs felt almost watery. "But would you mind if I sat down?"

Sam gestured toward a stool in the corner. "Please do."

She all but collapsed onto it, releasing a huge breath.

"Tired?" Sam asked her, somewhat concerned. She was obviously emotionally invested in her pet's surgery and had been out super late walking her dog.

Gina was about to deny it, then decided there was no point. She wasn't trying to project a superhuman image. Besides, now that the surgery was over, she was suddenly exhausted. "You have no idea," she told him.

Sam grinned at the pretty young woman. He could sense just what she had to be experiencing. He had been there himself a number of times with his own pet. "Oh, yes, I do," he assured her.

Chapter Five

"I don't think it's a good idea for you to be driving home at this hour and in this sleepy condition—wherever home might be," Sam qualified.

He had taken down Gina's contact information, but she wasn't surprised he hadn't committed it to memory. He'd been completely caught up in her miniature collie's condition. "I have a spare bedroom where you can sack out," he told her. "Or, if you would prefer, you can catch a nap on one of my sofas. Whatever your preference is will be just fine with me."

But Gina shook her head. "I couldn't do that," she protested. She didn't like imposing on the veterinarian any more than she already had.

"Why can't you?"

"It just wouldn't be right," Gina insisted, feeling somewhat uncomfortable.

Sam shook his head as if completely lost. "According to whom?"

"Well, for one thing, I don't even know you," Gina pointed out.

It clearly took effort for Sam not to laugh. "I'm the man you got out of bed in the middle of the night in order to save your miniature collie—and I did," he concluded. "What more do you need to know?"

Gina frowned. "When you say it like that, I guess what I said does sound a little silly," she admitted.

Sam smiled and nodded as if satisfied. "All right, then we're in agreement."

"I didn't say that," Gina objected. He was putting words into her mouth, she thought.

"Why don't you take a cue from your pet and just sleep?" Sam suggested. "Trust me, you are going to need your strength when Charlotte wakes up."

Gina had a feeling that the veterinarian knew exactly what he was talking about. She decided to stop fighting him. "Is your sofa out of the way, Dr. Sterling?" she asked.

Sam glanced at his watch. "It's six thirty in the morning. The way I see it, *everything* is out of the way at this hour." He beckoned for the collie's owner to follow him. "The sofa is over here." Something seemed to suddenly occur to him. "Is there anyone you want to call to let them know you and Charlotte are here and safe?" he asked.

The fact that he thought of asking struck her as exceedingly thoughtful. Gina shook her head. "No, nobody local. Besides, I don't intend to sleep very long—if, very honestly, at all," she added.

Sam seemed to bite his tongue. "Sleep as long as

you need to. There is no hurry on my end." He produced a blanket and a pillow for her and set them on the sofa. "Here you go."

She almost told him she didn't need either, but she had to admit that this was all rather nice of him, and the early hour still felt rather chilly. So, taking the pillow and blanket, she told him, "Thank you." Making herself comfortable, Gina spread out the blanket and then curled up beneath it, tucking the pillow under her head. "I won't be long," she repeated.

Sam flashed her a quick smile. "Don't worry—I don't charge by the hour," he assured her.

"I just thought you'd want to know that I would be clearing out soon," she said.

"Duly noted. But I honestly wasn't worried," Sam added as he walked out of the room.

Despite the fact that he'd left the overhead lights on, Gina felt her eyelids grow heavy and found herself struggling to keep them open.

Gina couldn't say when she had closed her eyes; she just knew that she must have. Eyes flying open, she sat up, roused into wakefulness by the tempting scent of toast, eggs and bacon. Her stomach practically growled in response, and she could feel her mouth watering. She couldn't remember having had that response to food in a long time. She really didn't think she was that hungry, but obviously, she was wrong.

It took her a few moments to orient herself, unaccustomed to falling asleep in unfamiliar places. She looked around for Charlotte before she remembered that her miniature collie would still be asleep in the cage that the veterinarian had carefully placed her in.

Blinking the sleep out of her eyes, and not knowing her way around, Gina followed her nose to the source of the tempting smell. She found Dr. Sterling standing by a stove, cooking. He lifted a frying pan off the stovetop and divided the pan's contents between two plates, then placed the pan back on a cool burner.

"You can cook?" Gina asked, stunned.

She had startled him, but he managed not to miss a beat as he turned around to look at her. "Certainly looks that way," he responded. "Why do you sound so surprised?"

She shrugged and walked into the room. "I just thought that being a veterinarian was enough of an accomplishment," she told him. "Being able to cook seems like overkill, in my estimation."

"Are you telling me you don't think that guys can cook?" he asked as he picked up the plates and brought them over to the small kitchen table. "I didn't think you would be guilty of stereotyping," he said.

"It's not that," she protested, then realized that she *was* guilty of that. "Well, maybe it is. Most of the guys I know literally cannot boil water."

"Well, if my brothers and I were guilty of being

unable to boil water, we would have probably wound up starving to death," Sam told her. He took a bottle of ketchup out of the refrigerator and placed it on the table between their plates. "My father worked really hard to build up his company so he could provide for us," he told her.

Gina caught her lip between her teeth but knew it would be impolite to ask the obvious question.

"My mother died when I was a kid," he said, volunteering the information. "There were five of us kids in the family, all boys. I was the oldest. My father hired a live-in nanny to watch over us, but just to play it safe, he also wanted all of us to know how to cook in case the nanny didn't turn out. He didn't want to have a bunch of helpless boys on his hands," Sam clarified.

Gina smiled at him. "Your father sounds like he was a very wise man."

"He was. Still is," Sam added with pride.

She felt herself turning red. "I guess I'm not wording this right. I didn't mean to imply that he was no longer among the living."

"I know. I just wanted to make things clear," Sam said. "I didn't mean to embarrass you. I guess that's the disadvantage of growing up without a mother, not knowing how to behave around women. Although I have to say that Randi did try her best."

"Randi?" Gina questioned, a little bit confused.

"The nanny that my dad hired to raise us after our mother died," Sam explained.

"Is Randi still around?" Gina asked, guessing that the nanny was the one who had taught the brothers the basic elements of how to cook.

Sam grinned fondly. "Oh, she's very much around. I don't think we could get her to run off if we wanted to—not that we would want to. She used to come by every Sunday to check in on us, but she hasn't been over for a while."

"Why every Sunday?" she asked, thinking that sounded rather unusual.

"Sundays are when we gather at my dad's house," he explained. "He's still living in the same house where we all grew up. I really don't think Dad can bring himself to get rid of it. As he likes to say, that was where he was happiest and where he built up all his precious memories." A fond smile curved the veterinarian's lips. "I suppose the same thing goes for the rest of us," he told her. "We all have our own places at this point, but the house where my father lives will always be thought of as 'home' to us."

Sam looked up at her and laughed at whatever expression must have been on her face. "I guess you got more of an answer than you bargained for. Sorry if I overwhelmed you. I don't usually talk this much."

"I'm not overwhelmed," she told him. "If anything, I'm flattered you shared all of this with me. It sounds as if you have an extremely nice family."

"I guess you could say that," Sam agreed with a warm smile. "Although there were times when all I really wanted to do was just string them all up, or at the very least, strangle them."

She gave him a disbelieving look. "You don't really mean that."

"Oh, yeah, I do," he contradicted. "Don't forget, I was the oldest one, which meant that at times I had to watch them. That cut into any free time I had."

Why would he have had to watch them? she wondered. "But you said you had a live-in nanny who was there to watch over you."

He laughed, remembering. "Randi was never a pushover. She was kind, but she was strict, and she had rules she wanted us to follow. And since I was the oldest, I was in charge of the others. It was my job to make sure that they were all well-behaved."

"I never thought of it that way," she admitted.

"Well, in your defense, most people don't," Sam told her. "They think that having five brothers in a family is all fun and games, like an episode from some sitcom." He laughed to himself. "Actually, it's really far from that at times. I have to admit that if any of us were threatened, we were immediately there for one another. But if it was a different sort of situation, you know, something internal, we were there at each other's throats. At least when we were kids."

"And now?" Gina asked him, curious.

"We're so busy with our separate careers," he told her honestly, "we don't have time."

"But you do get together every Sunday," she said, just to stay clear.

He nodded. "It's more for our father than for us," he explained. "And it's also to pay homage to our mother—which in its own way is also for our father. Our mother loved Sunday dinners."

"You sound like you're a very close family," she told him enviously.

He smiled at her. "Well, looking back at it now, I guess that you are right. Although I have to admit that there were times we would wind up squabbling with one another over dinner. But between my dad and Randi, they managed to get us to all behave."

Just then, her collie whined. Sam was on his feet instantly. "Sounds like Charlotte is awake," he said, heading for the clinic where the miniature collie was recovering in a cage.

Gina was right behind him.

Chapter Six

Charlotte was standing in her cage, her sad little face pressed against the bars. The moment Gina came into the room, the miniature collie began to whine and cry pathetically, as if her mistress had come to break her out of jail and erase all the pain.

Seeing her like that, Gina's heart almost broke. She dropped to her knees and reached into the cage as far as she could. Charlotte curled into her hand so she could be petted.

Gina glanced up at the veterinarian. She knew the protocol when it came to dealing with pets after they'd had surgery, but if Sam had any special idiosyncrasies when it came to that, she wanted to make sure she took them into account. She didn't want to break any of the veterinarian's rules. Sam had done her a huge favor, taking care of her dog as well as allowing her to crash on his sofa. Making her breakfast was just a bonus on top of that. She definitely wouldn't want to insult him by stepping on his toes.

"It is all right for me to pet Charlotte, isn't it?" Gina asked. She worded it so that she sounded hopeful rather than just assuming she was in the right. "I'm not breaking any of the rules, am I?"

"As long as you don't pet Charlotte too hard—but I think you already know that, right?" Sam asked with a wide smile.

"Yes. I'd like to take the poor thing into my arms and just squeeze her as hard as I can, but don't worry— I'm not about to do that," she said quickly.

Sam nodded, no doubt familiar with that urge when it came to recuperating pets. "The time you can do that safely will come," he promised her. "Just remind yourself that all this restraint is for Charlotte's own good, and she'll be up and on her feet soon enough. You just have to allow her to heal first, and she'll be better than new."

"I know. I've just never been the patient type when it comes to waiting for something I had my heart set on. I was always good about waiting when it came to something someone else needed." Gina took a deep breath. "That being said, when can I take Charlotte home?"

Sam laughed softly. He knew he would have been disappointed if she hadn't asked that. "Probably later on today. It all depends on how quickly Charlotte re- covers and bounces back." He added, "I can give you a call, and you can come by later and pick Charlotte up if you like."

But that approach didn't really sit well with Gina, and she shook her head. "If you don't mind, I'd like to hang around here until I can take my little girl home with me."

"Why? Don't trust me?" he asked with a smile.

"Oh, it's not that," Gina said, quickly shooting down that accusation. "I'd just like to be around in case you might need me for something." Thinking, she added, "If you have any chores or anything you'd like taken care of, just let me know, and I'll do it."

Sam looked at her as if caught off guard by her suggestion. But he seemed to give it some honest thought, then asked, "Do you really mean that?"

"Yes," she said with feeling. "I wouldn't have said it if I didn't. The one thing you should know about me is that I never say things I don't mean. Ever."

And if she was going to remain here, waiting for Charlotte to be well enough so she could take her home, Gina decided she might as well be useful. As a matter of fact, she could think of it as an audition. She really did want to be the man's assistant, at the least in a part-time capacity. Besides, she had never done well sitting still. Immobility made her feel antsy, although she was not about to tell Sam that.

"You're not even tempted to stretch the truth just a little?" he asked.

Gina shook her head. "Not even a little bit," she told him. "If a person lies once, they're inclined to lie again and again. The second and third times are far easier than the first. It becomes a trap that's hard to get out of, and I'd rather not slide into it to begin with."

Sam studied her for a moment, and then he smiled. "Were you ever a Girl Scout when you were growing up?"

"As a matter of fact, I was," she said, surprised. "My cousin Alice wanted to be a Girl Scout, but she was shy and didn't want to join alone. My mother prevailed upon my better instincts, and I wound up joining with Alice." She smiled, remembering. "I had a great time with her."

"I knew it," he declared. "You have that Girl Scout aura about you."

She wasn't sure exactly how to take that. Was the man making fun of her, or was he just paying her an offhand compliment? But either way, he had gotten out of bed in the middle of the night and operated on Charlotte without complaint, so she could cut him some slack. Actually, she could cut him a lot of slack.

"Well, now that I think of it, there are several things you could do for me if you're actually serious about wanting to do something while you're here," Sam told her, watching her face carefully.

"Great," Gina responded in all seriousness. "Like what?" She hoped she hadn't opened herself up to doing something she might wind up regretting.

"This probably is going to sound a little archaic to someone as tech-savvy as you undoubtedly are, but I need to have my patient files organized according to name and procedure. Since I'm the only one holding down the fort ever since I opened up this 'fort,' things have kind of gotten away from me over the years."

He paused, as if expecting Gina to laugh at him. When she didn't, he continued, "If you don't think of me as being too lax, I'll gather the files together for you so you can help me catch up."

"The only thing you need to do is give me your paper files, show me where your computer is and then just get out of my way," she told him. "I'll take care of the rest. And whatever I don't manage to get to today, I promise I'll come back tomorrow and finish the job then."

He looked about to agree, but then something seemed to occur to him. "Don't you have a job you have to go to?" Sam asked.

"I'm afraid that right now I'm in between jobs," Gina told him. "I do have just enough put aside—I think—to pay you for Charlotte's surgery. If it turns out that I don't, I can make arrangements to pay you off over time—with interest." She had no intention of taking advantage of him. "I'm not planning on skipping out on what I owe you," she told him in all seriousness.

Sam laughed. "I wasn't really worried about you not paying the bill," he said. "Getting back to my original request, do you think you can do it? Can you organize those files I mentioned?"

"No problem. I can do it in my sleep," she told him, adding, "with my eyes closed."

"Well, if I had my preferences, I'd rather that you were awake and your eyes were open," Sam told her.

Gina did her best not to grin as she shook her head. "Picky, picky, picky. I guess I can meet your conditions," she told him with a laugh. "Okay, just give me those paper files of your patients, tell me how you want the end result to look and then just let me get to it."

Sam marveled at how simple she made it all sound. He had to admit that he liked her approach.

"With pleasure," Sam told her sincerely. "And I'll look in on our patient—in between the others that will be arriving. By the way, there's a coffeepot brewing in the front office, if you're interested. And there's some creamer in a small refrigerator, if you need it."

Gina took her coffee black when she wanted to stay awake, but she nodded. "Duly noted." She glanced down at Charlotte. "Mama's going to be working in the other room, sweetie. I'll check in on you from time to time to make sure you're doing all right," she told the miniature collie, leaning in and running her hand over her head.

Gina caught Sam looking at her. He seemed amused, she thought. "What?" she asked. "Why are you grinning like that?"

"Do you always talk to your dog like that?" Sam asked.

She didn't quite follow him. "Like what?"

"Like Charlotte was your child and could understand what you were saying to her," Sam answered.

She didn't understand the confusion. "Of course she can understand. I believe all animals can understand what we say to them. Don't you?"

On some level, Sam had always believed that, but most of the people he dealt with, including pet owners, didn't buy into that, at least not wholeheartedly.

Sam smiled at her. "Really?"

"Of course really," Gina answered.

"Glad to hear that," he said. He glanced at his watch. "My first patient is coming in at eight. The pet's owner has to be at work early and wanted to drop off his pet before then." He often did things like that, which was what put him in such demand with his clients.

Gina nodded. "I'll make myself scarce before they come in."

He went to get the stack of files he had compiled but never seemed to get to, then handed them to her. "Why would you want to make yourself scarce?" he asked.

She looked at him, slightly confused. "Don't you want me to? I mean, I'm not exactly working for you."

"No," he agreed, "you don't. But you did mention that you might want to."

She looked at him, not sure if this was going where

she hoped it would. "Yes, I did..." She trailed off, waiting for him to complete his thought.

"If you're still interested in becoming my assistant, why don't we say that this could be a trial run?" he suggested. "If you still want to work for me by the time you finish organizing those files, I'll hire you."

Gina grinned widely at him. "That sounds really good to me." Just then, the doorbell to the clinic rang. "I believe that's your patient showing up early."

"Do you want to get that for me?" he asked. Was he curious to see how she would act?

"Consider it done," she told him. It didn't even occur to Gina to feel nervous, even though she didn't know who was standing on the other side of the door. She was eager to get started working as his assistant.

Chapter Seven

Sean Sterling was about to start talking the moment that the clinic's front door opened. But he suddenly found himself at a loss for words other than "Hello." He gave the young woman who opened the door a long, appreciative look up and down. The curvy, sexy blonde was gorgeous, no two ways about it.

Realizing that he needed to follow up his greeting with something that conveyed that he was capable of reasonable thought, he asked, "Um, is Sam around?" He peered into the clinic.

"Do you mean Dr. Sterling?" the blonde asked.

Sean laughed under his breath. It was difficult to think of his oldest brother in terms of being a doctor of any sort. As far as he was concerned, the veterinarian the woman referred to was just "Sammy," the brother who had taken care of him and Sebastian when their mother was no longer there.

And now, Sean thought, smiling to himself, his extremely dedicated bachelor brother seemed to have found someone for himself. Or at least it looked that way.

But before he allowed himself to jump to any conclusions, Sean decided to explore the young woman's rather unique wording. A person who was romantically involved with someone did not usually refer to that person by their official title.

"Okay, let's go with that," Sean agreed loftily. "Is *Dr.* Sterling around?" Man, it was really difficult getting those words out without laughing, Sean thought, doing his best to keep the corners of his mouth from curving.

"He is, but he's busy right now," the woman told him, running interference for the veterinarian. In her opinion, the man looked a great deal like Sam, but maybe they weren't actually related. "Is there anything that I can help you with?" Maybe he had a pet in his car.

Sean was going to have to take his big brother aside for a talk. This very probably could be an entirely new development that his brother didn't know how to handle. To the best of Sean's recollection, Sam had never had anyone in his life he had ever referred to as a girlfriend, not in any permanent sense. Or even in a fleeting one, Sean thought.

"All right, I have a question for you," Sean said, taking a new approach. "Have you been with Sam long? In a working capacity, I mean."

"Are you asking me how long I've been working as his assistant?" the blonde asked, doing her best to attempt to clear things up. Now that she thought about it, she could see how the man she was talking to might have made that mistake.

Sean nodded. "I guess that's what I'm doing," he said. He found himself utterly fascinated by the woman.

"I'm not his assistant," she informed him.

"Then what are you doing here?" Sean asked, his voice trailing off.

"Being helpful," she answered. "I'm guilty of waking him up in the middle of the night—"

"Oh?" This sounded even better than he had thought. He might have been grinning too hard.

"A pit bull attacked my dog while I was walking her early this morning. Someone had given me Dr. Sterling's name, saying he was an excellent pet surgeon. My poor Charlotte was in a really bad way and bleeding. I'm new here. I didn't know what else to do or where else to go, so I drove over here and knocked on Dr. Sterling's door even though I knew he had to be asleep at that hour. But rather than read me the riot act for waking him up, he immediately got out of bed and agreed to sew up Charlotte."

"That sounds like Sam," Sean agreed, nodding his head. "All heart and ready to jump in and save a pet, no matter if it's night or day."

The woman looked impressed. "You sound as if you know him well."

"As well as one brother can know another," Sean replied.

She nodded her head. "I thought you looked like him."

"Now, I've been nothing but polite to you," Sean told her, pretending to pout. "There's no reason for you to insult me." And then he smiled. "I'm sorry—I didn't catch your name."

"I didn't throw it," she answered innocently.

"No, I guess you didn't," he agreed with a quiet chuckle. And then he asked her point-blank, "What is your name?"

"It's Gina," she told him.

"Gina," he repeated. "I'm Sean. Sean Sterling."

Just then, Sam walked in and headed directly toward Sean. "I thought that was your voice I heard," he said to his youngest brother. "Are you in here harassing my patient's owner?"

"You know me. I'm just getting acquainted," Sean told him.

"Yeah, I'll bet. What are you doing here, really?" Sam pressed, giving him a penetrating look.

"Oddly enough," Sean said, "Dad sent me." He turned his head toward Gina. "We start work early in the construction business."

Sam ignored that and instead asked, "And just why did Dad send you?"

"He just wanted to see how you were doing. Said something about not having heard from you in a while. This is the distinct disadvantage of working with your father," Sean told Gina. "I hadn't thought about that complication."

Sam glanced at Gina and explained, "My dad."

"He means 'our' dad," Sean interjected.

Sam rolled his eyes. "*Our* dad," he corrected, "started his own company out here years ago."

"What does your father do?" Gina asked attentively.

"He's in construction. As a matter of fact, he built this development," Sam said as an aside, then continued, "Sean eventually horned his way into the company and refused to take no for an answer no matter how hard our dad tried to talk him out of it."

Sean raised his chin. "Our dad knew a good thing when he saw it."

"Which brings us to today," Sam said conclusively, "and what you're doing here." He gave his youngest brother a look.

"I already told you," Sean insisted. "Dad wanted me to check in on you because he said that he hadn't heard from you."

Sam frowned. "The man saw me at dinner last Sunday."

"I mean besides that," Sean said pointedly, "and you know it. Sunday dinner doesn't mean anything— unless you miss it."

Sam laughed, shaking his head. "Does that man have any idea how many fathers don't see their sons for weeks at a time? Months? Sometimes even years?"

"He knows," Sean agreed, "but that's not how our

father raised us. Nor would he deign to put up with it," he added matter-of-factly.

The expression on Sam's face was less than happy. Gina must have noticed. "You don't know how lucky you are," she told Sam. "A lot of people don't have family in their lives, or if they do, they don't know where they are."

"I take it that you belong to that group," Sean guessed.

"My parents are both dead," she told them, though it seemed to still hurt. "I have a sister, but she doesn't stay in touch except when she needs money. Then I get a letter. Once I answer it and send her some money, that's it for communication for a long time. Unless she needs more money." And then she smiled as she looked at her pet. "That's why I guess I'm so attached to Charlotte here." Gina nodded toward the dog in the cage. "She doesn't ask for anything except to be petted and loved."

Sean chuckled, smiling at Gina. "My kind of dog."

Sam frowned at him. "Down, boy," he ordered.

Sean pulled his shoulders back and pretended to salute. "Yes, sir. Well, now that I see you're in one piece and have a perfectly logical reason for not getting in touch with Dad, I will get out of your hair. But call him," he urged. "First chance you get. It'll make Dad happy, and it'll keep him from complaining." Sean grinned. "I guess he's going to need to get another hobby."

"The man's in construction," Gina said. "How much more of a hobby does your father need?"

Sean laughed under his breath. "You'd be surprised."

"You said there were five of you?" Gina asked.

"That's right," Sam answered. "Five brothers, separated by a year to a year and a half."

She paused as if trying to imagine what that was like. "Your father's a very lucky man," she told the two brothers enviously.

Sam fixed her with a look as if intrigued. "You want to tell him that?"

"Now, there's an idea," Sean said, turning it over in his mind.

"What is?" Sam asked, evidently not following Sean's trail of thought.

"Why don't you invite Gina to dinner this Sunday?" Sean asked Sam, nodding at her.

Gina blinked, no doubt completely lost. "Excuse me?" she asked, certain that she had misunderstood what Sam's brother had just said. How had he gotten from point A to point B like that without even blinking?

"My brother seems to be tongue-tied," Sean said. "How would you like to come to dinner this Sunday? I'm sure my father would welcome a pretty face at the table. Heaven knows the rest of us would."

"You're getting ahead of yourself, Sean," Sam told him.

"That's because you can't seem to get ahead at all," Sean said, looking at his brother pointedly.

Gina, meanwhile, was apparently still deciding just what her answer to the invitation was going to be.

Chapter Eight

"Um, Sam, could I have a word with you?" Sean asked, nodding toward the clinic's door.

Sam looked at his brother, somewhat bewildered. "Sure," he answered and waited for Sean to continue. After all, his baby brother had never had a problem talking before. Of all of them, Sean was probably the most vocal, never keeping his thoughts to himself if he felt like voicing them out loud. It was no wonder that Sean was the one who was finally able to talk their father into hiring him, even when Sanford Sterling had been dead set against bringing any of his sons into a business that the man felt was beneath them. That was not the reason, he had claimed, that he had sent them all off to college.

But Sean had other thoughts on the matter and had made them known. The rest of the family always maintained that Sean could talk the wings off an angel in flight if he set his mind to it.

Sean glanced toward the woman standing with them in the clinic, his implication clear. Still, he stressed, "Alone."

To the best of Sam's knowledge, Sean was never shy about any topic, but for the sake of moving this along, he shrugged. "Sure." To Gina, Sam added, "If you'll excuse us, I'll be right back."

"No problem," Gina told him and moved back to organizing the patient files. "I'll be right here," she promised, already sounding preoccupied.

As if satisfied that he had his brother's attention, Sean walked into an adjacent room, then turned to face Sam. "Is she working for you?" Sean asked.

Sam was caught off guard. That was a strange question for Sean to ask. "No." But he paused when he saw the skeptical look come over Sean's face. He supposed that his youngest brother had seen what Gina was doing and figured she had to be working for the clinic. "It's complicated," Sam amended.

"I've got time. *Un*complicate things for me," Sean encouraged him.

Sam sighed. He wasn't going to find any peace until he spelled it all out for Sean. Clearly. "I operated on her miniature collie first thing this morning and told her to come back later today to pick up her pet. But Gina wanted to hang around to watch over her dog. She told me that while she hung around, she wanted to be useful. To her, that means actually *doing* something. She asked me if there was anything I needed to have taken care of. Since I don't have an assistant," Sam said, deliberately avoiding Sean's eyes, "I've let my files pile up. Gina volunteered to put them in order while she waited until she could take her dog home."

"In lieu of payment?" Sean guessed.

"No," Sam answered with feeling. "She didn't even try to barter. She said she definitely intends to pay me for her collie's surgery. She said that she just hated sitting around, doing nothing."

"Sam," Sean said, duly impressed, "you need to snatch this woman up—for more reasons than one." He pinned Sam with a look. "Didn't you tell me—more than once, I might add—that you were thinking about hiring an assistant?"

"Yes, but I wasn't talking about right this minute," Sam maintained.

Sean rolled his eyes. "If not now, then when? Just before you die?"

Sam frowned, annoyed. "No. I just don't like being rushed."

Sean made a face, letting Sam know he wasn't buying any of this. "Sam, you've been talking about getting an assistant for five years now. Trust me, it's way past the 'rushing' point. Hire her," he stressed. "You know I'm right."

"What I know is that you're a giant pain in the neck," Sam told his brother.

"That's beside the point," Sean said dismissively. "But if I wasn't, you'd never do anything. Someone needs to light a fire under you to get you moving for your own good, big brother," he pointed out. "Now hire the woman. You can always fire her later on if you feel things aren't working out."

Sam's frown deepened even more. "Easy for you to say."

Sean gave him an innocent look. "You want me to hire her for you? Then, like I said, if it doesn't work out, I can always fire her for you. You won't have to do a thing except grunt," Sean said brightly. "Does that suit you?"

"I can do my own hiring and firing, thank you," Sam told him. What a giant pain Sean was. "And my own grunting, too."

"Good," Sean said with finality. "Then stop talking about it and dragging your feet and just do it." He placed an encouraging hand on Sam's shoulder, as if silently urging him to take the proper steps. He went on, "When I was growing up, I always looked up to you. Don't give me a reason to change my mind now, Sammy."

Sam closed his eyes. In his heart, he knew Sean was right. He just didn't like being bullied into things. "All right, all right, all right," Sam declared, coming very close to losing his temper.

"So you'll hire her?" Sean asked, keeping his eyes all but glued on Sam's face.

"Yes," Sam almost snapped. "I'll hire her if it gets you to back off and shut up."

Rather than say anything else, Sean pantomimed sealing and locking his lips.

For his trouble, Sam hit Sean in the shoulder with the flat of his hand. "I didn't mean for you to go utterly quiet."

Sean merely smiled widely in response.

"You can talk, Sean. I don't want you falling to the ground, gasping for air," Sam told him. Seeing that he wasn't really making any impression on his brother, Sam said, "Let's go back into the other room. I don't want Gina to think we just deserted her and left her high and dry."

Sean, meanwhile, smiled at his brother's words. This did sound promising. Whether he realized it or not, Sam had just indicated that he cared what the woman thought. While Sam was never outright impolite, he never acted as if he actually cared what a woman thought of his behavior. What his brother had just said gave him a measure of hope.

"By all means," Sean said, turning on his heel to go back to the main room of the clinic, "let's get back to the woman before she decides that we've deserted her and just leaves."

But Sam knew Gina was not about to go anywhere. "She wouldn't leave without Charlotte, and she's not taking the dog until I give her the go-ahead to do so," he emphasized. He was very sure about that.

Sean didn't bother hiding his grin. "How does it feel being king of your own little empire, Sammy?"

Sam didn't answer other than to wave his hand dismissively at his youngest brother. As he made his way back into the clinic, closely followed by Sean, he dreaded inviting her to dinner in front of Sean, but if he didn't say anything, Sean would beat him to it. He really didn't want this turning into any sort of verbal competition. If Gina did agree to attend Sunday dinner, he wanted her coming as his guest, not Sean's.

In his opinion, Gina had looked really hungry to attend a family event. He just felt it was something he could do for her. Never mind that she had dragged him out of a dead sleep early this morning. He'd untangle the details of his reasoning later on.

"Gina," Sam said as he walked into the clinic.

Lost in paperwork, Gina looked up belatedly. "Yes?" she questioned hopefully. No doubt she was wondering if Charlotte had recovered and if she could take her beloved miniature collie home.

"Are you free this Sunday at three o'clock?" Sam asked her. For the first time in his life, he felt as if he was tripping over his own tongue.

She blinked as if confused by his question. "Excuse me, Dr. Sterling?"

"What my somewhat socially awkward big brother is trying to find out is if you are free this Sunday to come over to the house for Sunday dinner," Sean said.

Sam silently upbraided his brother in his mind. He didn't need Sean speaking for him. "You understand that there's no pressure for you to attend," he told Gina, uttering the words through clenched teeth as he gave Sean a dirty look.

"I'm confused," Gina told him. "Are you asking me to come, or is this your veiled way of telling me you *don't* want me to come?"

"My brother has never been suave. Smart," Sean told her with feeling, "but not suave. He's inviting you to dinner. With all of us," he emphasized.

"How many are there in 'all of us'?" Gina asked curiously.

"Five, plus our dad," Sean told her.

"And you all show up?" she asked, clearly surprised.

"Absolutely. Under penalty of death," Sean answered with a grin.

"Who else shows up to Sunday dinner?" she asked, glancing from one brother to the other. She looked as if she had been invited to something from a fairy tale.

Sam had a feeling he knew what she was asking about. "Well, since the days of our mother, you would be the first woman to get invited—other than our nanny, back in the day."

"Really?" Gina asked. Was she flattered or ready to go running off to hide in the nearest closet? "Is that a rule that your dad put in force, or just something that kind of evolved?"

"It's just the way things turned out," Sam told her, doing his best to keep the whole thing low-key.

"Then why am I being invited?" Gina asked.

"Because—" Sam shot his brother a look that had *keep quiet* written all over it "—our dad thought it might be time for a change. He said he intended to start slowly, have us take turns inviting someone over. I'm not sure if he was thinking of us or himself when it came to getting our feet wet. But since you said that you don't have any family living here, or much of one anywhere really, I'm sure if our dad met you, he'd be the first one to extend an invitation to Sunday dinner," Sam said. He paused to take a breath.

"So, how about it?" Sean jumped in. "Are you interested in coming?"

Sam felt he needed to throw her a lifeline. "Unless you're already busy or don't feel like facing six men."

"Six?" she repeated. "I thought you said there were five of you."

"Our dad is a man, too—at least, he likes to think of himself as one," Sean told her.

"Sorry. Of course he is. I meant no disrespect," she told the brothers.

"So you'll come?" Sean asked.

"By the way, whether you do or not, I'd like to hire you as my assistant," Sam told her. "This looks like a very good job," he commented, looking at the way she had organized the files thus far. He hated to admit it, but Sean was right. He did need to hire someone to help him out when it came to his practice.

"Exactly what I was thinking," Gina said. Then, as if to clarify her response, she added, "Yes to the job and yes to Sunday dinner, as well—as long as you tell me where it's at. I'm not all that great when it comes to finding my way around. I'm still somewhat new in Aurora. So, will you tell me how to get to your father's house for dinner?"

Sean grinned at the woman he considered to be his brother's new assistant. "With pleasure." Dad, Sean thought to himself, would be very happy about this turn of events. He could just feel it in his bones. He couldn't wait until his father met this gorgeous woman.

Chapter Nine

"I know my brother can be persuasive," Sam told Gina. "He's got that knack."

Some time had passed before he allowed himself to broach the subject of whatever Sean had attempted to do by talking Gina into attending Sunday dinner. Sam had already seen three patients since Sean had left the clinic.

In that time, Sam had observed Gina working, and he was rather surprised at how good she was at her new job. Her soothing manner managed to calm both the pets and their owners. One elderly woman in particular, Alice Haywood, was overly attached to her aging Lhasa Apso, whose fur was falling out in tufts. In order to comfort the woman, Gina had offered to brew some tea, then looked to Sam as if to make sure that there was some available for her to deliver.

"I have some in the kitchen cupboard," Sam re-called after a little thought.

Gina nodded. "I'll be right back," she promised the dog's "mother" and left the room.

"I don't remember seeing her before, Dr. Sterling," Alice said to Sam.

"That's because she's new," he told her.

"I thought as much," Alice said triumphantly. "Well, she seems like a lovely young lady. Mr. Gibbs took to her right away, and Mr. Gibbs is never wrong. Just how long has she been working for you?"

Sam was not in the habit of baring his soul to the owners of his patients. "Not long," he answered evasively. He kept the fact that today was Gina's first day to himself, thinking it might spoil the impression that Gina had made.

Alice nodded her head as she took in the information. "She seems like a really lovely girl, and I daresay an excellent assistant. People like that just don't come along every day, you know," the older woman told him knowingly.

Sam inclined his head. He was not about to argue the point. "No, I guess that they don't."

Gina chose that moment to return, carrying a steaming cup of tea. "I took a chance that you liked cream and sugar in your tea."

Alice smiled at Sam. "And she appears to have excellent instincts as well," she told him. Her eyes crinkled as she took the cup of hot tea from Gina. "Thank you, my dear." She looked at Sam again. "I would definitely hang on to her if I were you, Dr. Sterling. What do you say, Mr. Gibbs?" she asked her pet, fixing him with a penetrating look.

The Lhasa Apso barked emphatically at his mistress. It sounded as if he was really answering her.

Sam looked at Gina to see if she would laugh. She merely smiled warmly at the woman and her dog.

It struck Gina that there seemed to be an endless parade of pets and owners marching through the clinic that morning and afternoon. She had just a little time to visit with Charlotte between Sam's patients, and then it was back to work for her shortly thereafter.

"You really are busy," she commented to Sam after she had escorted yet another owner and their pet out of the clinic. "Why didn't you look into getting an assistant before now?" she asked, curious.

He shrugged. "I just didn't have time to interview prospective candidates until now."

"Between you and me," Gina said, "you didn't exactly have any time to conduct those interviews now, either. I just kind of happened."

Sam sighed, then laughed shortly. "You do have an infuriating way of being right."

Gina smiled. "Yes, I know. My father used to accuse me of being guilty of doing that. He was right—some of the time," she amended with a quick wink.

He had a feeling that she was telling him that he suffered in the comparison to her father. He didn't want to do anything to chase her away, so he voiced a nebulous promise. "I'll work on it."

"You don't have to do that. You being right—

when that happens—doesn't bother me," she told him honestly.

At the moment, there was a knock on the outer door, and she went over to open it. Gina found herself greeting a rather bewildered-looking man holding a leash with an iguana on the end of it. She felt as confused as he seemed to be, staring at her.

"Did I make a mistake?" the man asked, glancing around the clinic. "Has there been a change, or does Dr. Sterling still work here?"

"Dr. Sterling definitely still works here," Gina said as she looked down at his iguana. "I'm his assistant, Gina. Do you have an appointment, sir?" She would have remembered seeing the notation *iguana* on the appointment sheet.

"Don't call me *sir*," the man told her. "My name is Jake. Jake Anderson. And this," he said, smiling down at the iguana, "is Hoppy. Hoppy and I don't need an appointment. Dr. Sam said we can come in anytime we need to, and he'd make the time to see us."

Drawn by the sound of voices, Sam made his way to the front of the clinic. He smiled the moment he saw who was there.

"It's all right, Gina," he told her. "Jake was my very first walk-in when I first started up my practice. In honor of that, I told him he and Hoppy could always come in whenever Jake felt that Hoppy needed to be looked at." Sam took the older man's hand and shook it heartily. "How have you been, Jake?"

Jake cast an appreciative eye in Gina's direction. "Obviously not as good as you, Doc," he answered. And then he continued, "I think Hoppy ate something that didn't quite agree with him. Since he's an iguana, my thinking is that's not all that easy to do. But I guess it can be done."

Sam took hold of the leash, leading the iguana into the exam room. "Come with me, Hoppy. Let's see if we can't make you all better." He glanced at Gina over his shoulder. "Gina, when my next patient shows up, tell them I'll be with them as soon as I can. I'm going to finish Hoppy's examination first."

She nodded, no doubt thinking that Sam had a number of very strange patients in his practice. "Consider it done, Doctor," she said.

"Cute little thing," Jake said, looking over his shoulder at Gina as he followed Sam into the exam room. "You get her from an agency?"

"Not exactly," Sam answered.

"Then where did she come from?" the man asked, curious.

Sam was pressed for time as it was and didn't want to waste any more of it by telling Jake how he and Gina had gotten together. "It's rather a long story, Jake," Sam answered evasively.

"Some other time, then," Jake said with a nod of

his head. There was humor in his brown eyes. "When you're less busy."

Sam smiled, glad that the man wasn't attempting to argue with him. "Deal."

"Looks like she's working out well for you," Jake went on. "Does she have previous experience?"

Sam didn't answer yes or no. What he did say was "Instinct goes a long way" and left it at that as he got back to his examination of the man's longtime pet.

Things were safer that way, he had discovered.

While Sam was examining the iguana, Gina took the time to visit with her miniature collie. She fed Charlotte a little of the dog food she had discovered that was stored in the clinic for any overnight patients.

But then she heard someone ringing for the vet's attention.

Like several of the other pet owners throughout the day, this one appeared to be very bewildered by her presence. However, this one was quickly pleased to discover that the veterinarian had *finally* hired an assistant.

"I'm Marianne Johnston. My Jo-jo needs to get his shots," the woman announced, nodding at an antsy cocker spaniel. "Can I leave him with you for that while I run my errands?"

Gina had no idea what Sam's rules were when it came to leaving pets on the premises without their owners. They were going to need to go over a lot of points, she decided. This position was far more complicated than she had first thought.

"If you don't mind waiting, Ms. Johnston, let me check with Dr. Sterling. He hasn't had time to review his various rules with me. He said something about tackling them as they came up. So if you could wait right here, I'd really appreciate it," Gina told her, not giving Marianne an opening to turn her down.

As Gina slipped out of the clinic, she heard Marianne saying, "Sure, go right ahead," tacking on an "I guess" to herself.

Gina knocked on the door of the exam room that Sam had disappeared in, then walked right in. She saw the surprised look on his face, but she quickly pushed ahead. "I'm sorry to bother you, but there's a Ms. Johnston in the waiting room asking if she could leave her cocker spaniel here to get her shots while Ms. Johnston does her shopping."

To say that Sam looked nonplussed by the question was putting it mildly, but he seemed to recover well enough. "Sure, as long as she doesn't take too long. Put the cocker spaniel in the other open exam room," he instructed.

"Very good, Doctor," Gina responded and slipped out of the room.

Back in the waiting room, she told Mrs. Johnston, "Dr. Sterling said he's all right with you going to run your errands as long as you promise not to take too long. He has a very busy day ahead of him and he doesn't want Jo-jo to feel deserted or stranded."

Sam, of course, hadn't said any of this, but Gina felt she could be forgiven for winging it in this fashion. The cocker spaniel's owner would be motivated to run her errands quickly and be back at a decent time so she could pick up her pet and pay for services rendered.

"Come on, Jo-jo. Let's get you settled in while you wait for Dr. Sam," Gina told the dog, taking the leash so she could take him into the secondary exam room.

She didn't have long to wait. Gina heard the door to the other exam room closing. She quickly walked back into the lobby. "I'll take it from here, Doctor," she told Sam. "I can do the paperwork and get Hoppy here all taken care of and signed out."

Again, Sam looked surprised and then somewhat relieved a moment later. "Thank you."

"That goes for me, too," Jake told Gina, adding his thanks. Then, before Sam went to the second exam room, Jake said with a chuckle, "You should have done this years ago, Doc." He looked at Gina. "Okay, what do I owe you? What are the damages?"

Gina flipped through the paperwork that Sam had left. It was not easy to read, she thought as she squinted at it. They would need to have a talk about his penmanship as well. His notes appeared to have been made by chicken feet dipped in ink. She checked the numbers there twice before she could finally tell Jake what he owed for his iguana's visit. She expected him to put up a fuss.

Instead, he asked, "You're sure? That's all?"

Gina released the breath that she had been holding, more than a little relieved. "That's what Dr. Sterling said to charge for today's service."

Jake fairly beamed as he took out his checkbook. He kept grinning from ear to ear as he wrote out the check.

Chapter Ten

Sam had to admit that part of him hadn't expected to see Gina coming into the clinic the following morning. The salary he had offered her as his assistant was not exactly a king's ransom. In addition, the work appeared to be nonstop, and as far as he could see, Gina was working harder than he felt someone of her obvious intelligence usually did.

When he opened the clinic door for her, Sam was also surprised to see that she had brought her miniature collie with her.

The moment he unlocked the door and Gina walked in, she was talking, all but snowing him with conversation.

"I know we didn't discuss this when we talked about the job yesterday, but I don't have anywhere to leave Charlotte, and I didn't want her to be alone all day, especially right now. I noticed that there are spaces at the clinic that could easily accommodate a large dog, much less one Charlotte's size. Until I can come up with someplace to leave her while I am at work, would you mind if I brought her to the clinic with me?" Gina asked. "I would be willing to pay a boarding fee for her."

Sam bent down and ran his hands over the miniature collie's fur, saying hello to the dog. Rocky was directly behind him, dancing from foot to foot and appearing very happy to see her friend again.

"Charlotte seems like a very sweet-natured dog, and I have no problem with you bringing her to work." He petted the collie again. "Bring her with you as much as you like. It's not as if she's a vicious animal," he pointed out. "Having her here might even put some of the pet owners at ease, which would be a big plus, as far as I'm concerned."

And then he was even more straightforward with her. "To be honest, I wasn't all that certain you would be coming back today."

She looked at him, evidently somewhat confused. "Why would you think that?"

"Well, yesterday was a rather rough day, and I can't promise that every day won't be like that—or even worse," Sam told her.

"That's all right," Gina answered, waving away his concern. "I don't mind working with animals. I like it." She smiled, clearly thinking about yesterday. "Even the iguana was kind of cute."

Sam couldn't help but laugh. "You're probably the first person in history to refer to an iguana as being 'cute.'" To say that he was relieved she had decided to stay was putting the matter mildly.

"Beauty is in the eye of the beholder," Gina responded.

"I guess it must be." He glanced at his watch. It was almost time for his first appointment. "Are you ready for today's onslaught?"

Gina inclined her head. "Bring it. Just let me get Charlotte sequestered in that pet run."

"No hurry," he told her, adding, "Take your time."

But Gina returned rather quickly, glancing around the lobby. "Is Rocky in your living quarters?" she asked.

Sam nodded. "You're very observant."

"I do my best. I find that things go more smoothly when there are fewer surprises," she told him. Just then, there was a knock on the door. "And so the day begins," Gina declared.

Before she could go to open the clinic's front door, Sam asked, "How's my patient doing? Charlotte," he clarified when she looked at him blankly.

Gina smiled happily. "Charlotte has a little ways to go, but she is practically good as new."

He was glad to hear the positive report, but he did want to check it out for himself eventually. "When I get a little downtime in between patients, I'd like to reexamine Charlotte to make sure that she's healing properly."

"She is. There's no infection, and the stitches are doing just what they should," she informed him proudly. "I don't foresee any problems coming up. But of course,

I would love to have you weigh in if you get the chance. After all, you *are* the doctor."

Sam saw no reason to doubt Gina's take on the subject. This was her miniature collie, and he could see how attached she was to the animal. It would give her insight into the collie's progress. "And you appear to have the makings of an excellent assistant."

For his assessment of her abilities, Sam received a wide smile. What surprised him was his reaction to it.

He found himself completely drawn in by that smile of hers, so much so that he was totally warmed. He was secretly glad Sean had talked him into inviting Gina to attend Sunday dinner. If nothing else, it was a way to show her that he was grateful to her for all her hard work. And who knew where this would eventually lead, he mused as he watched her go to the front door.

When Gina opened it, she came eye to eye with a young woman carrying a birdcage with a cockatiel inside of it. The snow-white bird's head was all but spinning around as it took in its surroundings.

If the young woman was surprised to see that the doctor had someone working for him, she didn't show it. Her complexion was ashen as she walked in. Like her pet bird, her head was almost spinning as she looked around, searching for the veterinarian.

"Is Dr. Sam in?" the young woman asked.

"I'm right here, Dolores," Sam called as he walked

to the front of the clinic. He didn't remember her calling or leaving a message asking if she could come in,
nor had he seen a notation from Gina regarding the
cockatiel. "What seems to be the problem?"

The frazzled woman appeared to be almost in
tears. "I think that Heather swallowed something
she shouldn't have, Dr. Sterling."

"What makes you say that? Is something missing?" he asked. Picking up the bird's cage, he took
a closer look at it from all angles. A tiny chain hung
from the bird's small collar, but he didn't bother with
it. Sam took a closer look at the cockatiel, making
certain that there was a healthy space between them.

"No, I don't think that there's anything missing,
at least nothing that I can see, but she's making all
these strange noises, like she's swallowed something
that's bothering her, and she won't eat, which isn't
like her," Dolores told him.

"Well, let's have a look at you, shall we, Heather?"
Sam suggested, leading the way to one of the examination rooms.

Gina noticed that the cockatiel's owner followed
closely behind Sam, a hopeful expression on her face.
Gina felt sorry for the young woman.

She was about to ask the veterinarian if he needed
anything, but just then, she heard the bell over the
clinic's front door go off again. It looked like it would
be another nonstop day, Gina thought.

Sam Sterling did not need an assistant, she decided. What he really needed was a partner, someone who could pitch in and take on half the work. But it wasn't her place to suggest that. At least, not yet. But maybe, after she was further entrenched in the day-to-day dealings at the clinic, she could safely broach the subject.

She didn't foresee a warm reception to her suggestion at first, but maybe after Sam got used to the idea of having a partner, he might decide that there was some merit to it.

Gina decided to put the idea on the back burner for the time being and resurrect it when the proper time came.

If anything, today was even more fast-paced than yesterday. Gina only had a few minutes at a time to visit with Charlotte. The rest of the day, she went over billing statements, organized files and, of course, admitted patients and their owners to the clinic. She made sure that she took down the owners' statements, detailing the circumstances that had brought them and their pet to see Dr. Sterling.

Sam did send out for lunch, but finding the time to eat it was another matter entirely. Both he and Gina ate their lunches in small increments.

The hours at the clinic were from 7:00 a.m. until 7:00 p.m., although Sam told her he wasn't a stickler for ending his day exactly on time. But today, when he finished examining the last batch of patients, Sam seemed to have something on his mind other than seeing another patient.

"Would you be able to stay after hours?" he asked her as the last pet and their owner walked out of the clinic.

"Do you have something you need organized?" Gina asked, saying the first thing that came to her mind.

"Not exactly," Sam answered evasively.

When he stated it that way, she wasn't sure what to think. "Then what, 'exactly'?" Gina asked.

"How are you when it comes to doing inventory?" Sam asked.

Of course there were things he needed to have on hand to do his work properly. "You tell me what you want me to note down, and I'll be on the lookout for it," she volunteered.

Sam looked at her, bemused. "Don't you have any plans for tonight?" he asked, curious.

Gina shrugged. Since moving out here a little more than six months ago, she still had not built up much of a network of friends. Quite honestly, she felt that it was just her and her miniature collie. She was beyond grateful to Sam for saving Charlotte. Actually, she had been thinking about going to work for a veterinarian or at an animal clinic, so this whole situation could not have turned out better for her if she had planned it. So it went without saying that she was more than happy to help Sam out with anything he might need in order to run his clinic.

"Nothing that can't be bent or worked around," she told him freely.

"I guess that makes me a very lucky employer," he told her.

"I guess that it does," Gina agreed. "At any rate, working for you has me more than willing to move things around. As far as I'm concerned, this job comes first—before anything else."

She had clearly impressed him. "Not many of you people left."

"I wouldn't know. I haven't exactly taken inventory. I just know how I feel about working with animals and about working with you as a veterinarian since you devote your time to working with animals. So, whatever you need, Dr. Sterling," she told him, "consider it done." The bell rang at the front door. "However, at the moment, I think that you have another patient who needs your attention," she informed him.

"I do believe you're right. Let me get that one," Sam said, then added with a smile, "For old times' sake."

She raised her hands as if in cheerful surrender. "By all means. I won't stand in your way. Seeing you might just reassure your patient's owner." She followed up with a broad wink.

Sam laughed under his breath, then went to answer the door while Gina busied herself with the work she had left out on her desk.

But while she worked, she waited for the veterinarian to call her over. She was ready to drop everything if and when he needed her when it came to working with the animals.

Chapter Eleven

By the time Friday rolled around, Gina found that she had gotten into a comfortable routine when it came to her work as a veterinarian's assistant.

She knew her way around the clinic and knew how much time Sam needed when it came to treating dogs, cats or birds, be they parrots, canaries or cockatiels. And there was the occasional hamster and, of course, the iguana. Without disturbing the clinic's supplies, she managed to arrange them so she could get her hands on them quickly should Sam have need of them. After a while, Gina felt that she had arranged everything.

Something else she had noticed over the last few days, with Rocky roaming around the area before the clinic was open and after it was closed, was that the German shepherd lost a great deal of fur. Evidence of that loss was everywhere to be seen, yet Rocky did not appear to be missing fur anywhere in particular on her body.

So on Friday, Gina, having been given her own key to the clinic, arrived early. She'd brought a cordless vacuum cleaner with her and moved around the clinic, cleaning up the tufts of fur that had gotten embedded in the floorboards. She definitely had no patience when it came to messy spaces, Gina thought, working as quickly as she could.

She was so preoccupied with getting the German shepherd's fur cleaned up, she didn't even hear Sam coming into the clinic. So when he came up behind her and asked "What are you doing?" it took a lot for her not to jump and emit a high-pitched scream of surprise. What she did do was swing around and come very close to hitting the veterinarian with her vacuum cleaner.

"You shouldn't sneak up on someone like that," Gina told him sharply, doing her best to breathe normally so that he wouldn't realize just how much he had thrown her off. She pressed her hand against her chest to keep her pounding heart from leaping out.

"I didn't realize I was sneaking," Sam told her. "But you still haven't answered me. What are you doing?"

Gina looked at him incredulously. "I would have thought that would be self-evident," she answered. "I'm vacuuming up the fur that seems to have fallen off your dog as she runs around the clinic, as well as the ground level of your private quarters. The fur is so light that it's hard to notice when it's falling at first. But if you sweep it up, you can see that Rocky seems to lose a ton of it—all the time," she told him with a wave of her hand. "To be honest, I'm surprised that you don't have a bald dog by now. From all indications, Rocky has lost enough fur to build you another dog this week alone."

"Well, she has lost a great deal of fur," Sam agreed. "But it's not up to you to clean up after my pet. I certainly don't expect you to do that."

"I understand that, but the truth of it is, I really don't like working in a messy area. I've never been able to think clearly under those conditions." Gina smiled at him. "Just accept it as a bonus for hiring me on as your assistant."

"Well, if I can't talk you out of it—because I really doubt that I can—I'm going to have to compensate you for the time and effort you spend cleaning up Rocky's fur," Sam told her.

Gina's smile widened. "Well, we can certainly discuss that," she told him amicably. She glanced at her watch. "But that's all I can do for now. Your first patient should be arriving soon."

Just then, the doorbell to the clinic rang.

Gina grinned as she retired the vacuum cleaner, setting it behind a closet door. "Here's your first patient, right on cue," she declared.

"Let me get that," Sam offered, turning to walk through the clinic to the front door.

"Hell no. You're the doctor, I'm the assistant. It's up to me to assist," she said, striding past him.

She opened the clinic's door to a well-dressed

woman holding a cat in a pet carrier with one hand and what looked to be her four-year-old daughter's hand with the other. Gina immediately went to take the pet carrier from the woman. The cat didn't appear to be very happy about the transfer and made a loud hissing sound.

"You must be Mrs. Mullins, and this must be Fluffy," Gina said, looking at the cat in the pet carrier. And then she turned to look at the little girl, who appeared to be attempting to hide behind her mother. "And who is this very pretty little helper with you?" Gina asked, smiling down at the little girl.

The little girl's expression changed. She raised her head proudly, her curly blond hair swinging back and forth around her face. "My name is Shelly," she announced.

"Well, it's very nice to meet you, Shelly," Gina told the child. "Why don't you and your mommy come with me, and we'll all take Fluffy here into the exam room so that Dr. Sam can take a look at her and see what he needs to do to make her all better? Would you like that?"

Shelly's head bobbed up and down enthusiastically, and she said solemnly, "That would be very nice, won't it, Mommy? To have Fluffy all better."

"It would be very nice," her mother answered with genuine feeling. She looked slightly tired. Taking care of Fluffy and her daughter was obviously taking a lot out of the woman.

Gina brought mother, daughter and cat to the first exam room. "Let me put the pet carrier on the examination table, and then I'll go tell Dr. Sam that you're all here," she told Mrs. Mullins. She was about to leave the room when the little girl caught her hand. Rather than pull her hand away, Gina looked down at her quizzically.

"Are you new here?" Shelly asked.

"Not as new as I was," Gina answered with a smile.

The answer did not satisfy the little girl. "Does that mean that you're going to go on working here?"

"Well, that's all up to Dr. Sam, but I would certainly like to," Gina answered.

Shelly nodded her head solemnly, then smiled as if deciding she had taken a shine to her. "I'll tell Dr. Sam to keep you," she told Gina.

Gina took that as serious input. "Thank you, Shelly. I'm sure Dr. Sam would definitely appreciate your opinion on the subject," she told her. Out of the corner of her eye, Gina saw that Mrs. Mullins was smiling broadly at her.

She opened the door to tell Sam that his patient's family was waiting to talk to him—and almost walked directly into him.

Gina flushed. "Sorry," she apologized. "I guess that was just a little too much enthusiasm."

Sam had caught hold of her shoulders to keep them from colliding. Despite that, he told her, "There's nothing wrong with enthusiasm. Enthusiasm keeps the job fresh and you interested in it."

Gina cleared her throat, embarrassed at the near collision. "That's always been my feeling," she told him. As the doorbell sounded again, she said to Sam, "That's my signal. I'll leave you to Fluffy and her family."

Just as Gina slipped out of the room, Shelly stuck her head out, apparently looking for her. Gina paused. "Can I help you?" she asked the little girl.

Shelly's head bobbed up and down. "Dr. Sam said you had a pet dog. Can I see him?"

"It's a her," Gina corrected. "And of course you can." Charlotte was very good with people. Especially children. Gina decided that the patient in the clinic could wait a few minutes. "As long as it's all right with your mother," she said.

"She said it was okay," Shelly told her proudly. The little girl shyly tucked her hand into Gina's.

A warm feeling slipped over Gina. Someday, she thought, she wanted to have a little girl—or boy— of her own. One who was as animated as this little person was, Gina thought fondly. But that day was undoubtedly still very far away.

"Charlotte's right in here," she told Shelly, leading her into the room.

Shelly appeared both fascinated and a little hesitant, but the latter lasted only long enough for Gina to bring her fully into the room.

"Can I pet her?" Shelly asked, wide-eyed and eager.

Gina took hold of Charlotte's collar, making sure that she wouldn't rear up unexpectedly. "Charlotte," she said by way of an introduction, "this is Shelly. I expect you to be on your very best behavior," she told the miniature collie. Bringing the dog closer to the little girl while holding tightly to her collar, she said, "Say hi to Shelly, Charlotte."

Shelly reached up, clearly wanting to pet the collie. "Is it all right?" she asked.

"Charlotte is a little overeager, but she really likes to be petted," Gina told the little girl.

Shelly ran her hand along the dog's fur, slowly at first, then with enthusiasm. The smile on her face was almost blinding. "She's as soft as my kitty," she declared happily as she continued petting Charlotte.

"Yes, she is. Okay, Charlotte," Gina told her pet. "Shelly needs to go back to her mommy now, and I have to get back to work." She looked at the little girl. "Say goodbye to Charlotte, Shelly."

"Goodbye, Charlotte," Shelly declared obediently, petting the miniature collie one last time. Then she slid her hand into Gina's again, indicating that she was ready to return to her mother and her cat waiting for her in the examination room.

"Shelly wanted to come back to see how her pet is doing," Gina told Mrs. Mullins and Sam as she opened the door so Shelly could walk into the room.

Just then, Gina heard the doorbell ring again. "They're

playing my song," she told Shelly with a smile. "I'm going to have to talk to whoever is waiting to see Dr. Sam." Then she slipped out of the room, closing the door behind her.

There was nothing remarkable about the next patient and owner who arrived, or the patient and owner who arrived after that.

The ensuing parade of patients kept Gina on her toes for the next few hours, although she did find the time to pause and wave goodbye to Shelly as the little girl left with her mother and cat. But that was only because Gina had to write up the bill for the visit and collect the money for the cat's exam plus the medication that Sam had prescribed.

Just as in the previous days, although Sam ordered lunch for them both, they had to work through that time period until there was a break in the rush of animals who came into the clinic. They finally had an opportunity to eat almost three hours later.

"I have to tell you," Sam said as they sat down to eat, "all the clients who came in today were even more impressed with you than the ones from previous days. Mrs. Mullins wanted to know why I hadn't hired you sooner."

"Did you tell her that you didn't know me sooner?" Gina asked with a laugh.

"I don't think she's the kind who accepts any excuses," Sam told her.

Just then, the doorbell rang. Sam and Gina sighed loudly in unison.

"I guess it's back to work," Gina declared, getting to her feet and heading toward the front door.

Chapter Twelve

When she learned that Sam put in hours at the clinic on Saturdays, Gina had to admit that she was not surprised. A little overwhelmed, perhaps, but when she thought about it, she had to admit that it seemed par for the course.

"You didn't sign on for six days a week," he pointed out when she surprised him by coming into the clinic on Saturday. She had driven by on a hunch that he might be working, just to discover that she was right.

"Not outright, no," she agreed. "But since you're working Saturdays, then I am, too. At the very least, I should be working with you at the clinic on Saturdays in the beginning. If I wear out," she threw in, cocking her head to look at him a bit more closely, "we'll renegotiate. How's that?"

Sam couldn't help laughing at the idea that this woman was actually opting for more work. Part of him was convinced that he had to be dreaming this. He looked at her and shrugged. "I'm not about to turn you down, if that's what you're waiting for, although

I have a difficult time believing that you really *want* to work six days a week."

"Why?" she asked incredulously. "*You* work six days a week."

"This is my business, and working these hours is what I choose to do to make a go of that business," Sam pointed out.

Gina smiled up at him, utterly composed. "Well, since you put it that way, so do I."

Sam took a breath. For now, he would leave things the way they were. He could revisit this topic later, and he was sure that by then, she would have changed her mind about working Saturdays. Right now, there was something else he needed to talk to her about.

"At the risk of alienating you," he began, watching her face carefully, "are you still willing to have Sunday dinner at my father's house tomorrow?"

She wasn't sure how to take his question. Had he changed his mind about bringing her? Only one way to find out, she thought. She had to ask him outright. "Are you trying to get out of it?" Gina asked.

"No, I am *not*. As a matter of fact, nothing is further from the truth," Sam told her. "I called my father last night to broach the idea that I was bringing someone—"

She immediately jumped to what she assumed was his father's reaction. "And was he upset?" she asked. This was, after all, a family tradition, and she was definitely not family. It wouldn't be a stretch to guess that the family patriarch wouldn't want a stranger at his table. Her attendance had been Sam's brother's idea.

"Upset?" Sam asked incredulously. His eyes narrowed as he stared at her. Was she joking? "My father was overjoyed to hear the news. I can tell you that he said something about being thrilled to have a new person with fresh dialogue sitting at his table."

Gina regarded him dubiously. He had to be pulling her leg. "Oh, I sincerely doubt your father was overjoyed to hear that your new assistant was coming to Sunday dinner."

"Well, you can judge that for yourself when you come tomorrow," he told her. "I've got your address," he said, thinking of the tax forms she'd filled out when he took her on as his assistant. "I'll be by to pick you up at 2:30, if that's okay with you. Dinner starts at three o'clock—give or take a few minutes."

But Gina shook her head. "You don't have to do that, Dr. Sterling," she told him formally. "Just give me your father's address and I can drive to his house myself."

It was Sam's turn to shake his head. "Oh, no, I was instructed by my father to bring you, at least to your first Sunday dinner, so that's what I intend to do. Bring you," he emphasized. He lowered his head to confide, "Between you and me, I think my father is worried that you'll change your mind about coming and decide not to show up at the last minute. So, at least this first time, I will escort you to my father's house. The house, in case you're interested, where all five of us grew up."

She nodded, hiding the smile that rose to her lips. "Yes, I believe you did mention that."

"I did, didn't I?" he realized. For a moment, he looked embarrassed. "Sorry, this is all rather new to me."

She wasn't sure just what he was referring to. "What, talking to a woman? I've seen you talking to women, Dr. Sterling."

He was referring to bringing someone over to Sunday dinner, but first he wanted to clear up her confusion. "What you've seen, Gina, is me talking to my patients' owners," he pointed out. "And there are no patients here at the moment. So in the interest of not being awkward, you can call me Sam. I think we would both feel more comfortable if you did that."

"You're the boss," she told him. And then she rolled it over in her mind. "You're right. Calling you Sam does roll more easily off my tongue than Dr. Sterling, but ultimately, it's your call."

And then she heard the doorbell ring. The first one of the day, she thought. Gina pulled her shoulders back as she turned toward the front door. "Sounds like they're playing our song, Dr. Sterling," she told him with a wink.

He caught himself reacting to her wink. It took him a second to pull back mentally and focus again.

"I guess you'd better go and answer that. I'll be in Exam Room One." He turned on his heel.

He was only partially aware of the smile on his lips. Who would have known six days ago when he woke up to that pounding on his door that his life would wind up changing so much? Certainly not him, Sam thought. And right now, it felt as if his life was constantly transforming. For the last six days, ever since he'd opened his door to that distraught-looking young woman, he hadn't known what to expect, or more to the point, exactly just what to brace himself for.

Walking past a window as he prepared to see his first patient of the day, Sam caught a glimpse of his reflection. Damn, but he was actually grinning. He couldn't remember the last time he had grinned, or even the last time he had actually wanted to.

He blew out a breath as he waited for the exam room door to open. Gina had certainly turned things around and set everything on its ear. Sunday, he decided, was shaping up to be one hell of a day.

The exam room door opened, and Sam cleared his mind to focus on his first patient of the day.

She couldn't get her heart to stop pounding, Gina realized. Thinking back, she honestly couldn't remember the last time she had gone out on a date. Not that this was actually considered a date, she reminded herself.

All right, if it's not a date, what would you call it? Gina asked herself the following morning.

Well, you could call it Sunday afternoon, she told herself.

"You're making too much out of it," she said out loud. "This is just a simple dinner at your boss's house. It's just his way of saying thank you. No big deal."

Just because her last employer was a clod bent on working the people at his company to death, it didn't mean Sam was like that, because he certainly wasn't. Unlike her old boss, Sam's first thought was not about how much money he could collect; it was about how much he could help his patients. Money came last, and despite the economy, his fees didn't reflect high prices. The first thing that had struck her, other than the fact that the man had a great smile and was very good-looking in a dark, brooding way, was that he was hardworking and conscientious.

The unexpected thought that Sam was good-looking caught Gina by surprise. How had that managed to sneak in?

She supposed she was so grateful to Sam for taking care of Charlotte and sewing up all of her wounds that she had just kind of naturally become attracted to the man.

You're making too much out of this, she told herself, annoyed that she couldn't control her thoughts. *This is what happens when you haven't dated since Noah collected two of everything to herd onto his ark.*

Blowing out a breath, Gina looked herself over in the mirror that hung in her small bedroom. Maybe she should have put on the red dress, she thought. It was a little more flattering. The blue dress looked too subdued. But the red was too loud.

Gina looked over at her cell phone. Maybe she should call Sam and tell him something had come up and she wouldn't be able to make it to dinner.

"You're going to have to back up your story. You told Sam that you didn't know anyone who lived here and your sister lived somewhere else. You don't have a viable excuse—unless you just suddenly up and quit," she mocked herself. "C'mon. Since when did you become such a coward?"

She had painted herself right into a corner.

"You don't run from things, remember? So what is your problem?" she challenged. And then it suddenly hit her. The reason she was being so skittish was that she was actually attracted to the man.

"Okay," she told herself. "Picture Sam as being ugly."

Gina frowned. That wasn't the answer. She wasn't the type to be attracted to just looks. She decided to change her approach.

"Picture him like being straight out of a horror movie. A being with an ugly soul," she told her reflection in the hanging mirror.

Gina blew out a breath and shook her head. "It's official. For whatever reason, you have just gone off the deep end. Maybe you should hand in your resignation so that you don't take Sam down with you."

The woman in the mirror looked back at her skeptically. Gina sighed. "Yeah, yeah, I'm just babbling," she said to her reflection. "This is what happens when you don't get out often enough—or at all."

But that still didn't manage to calm her nerves. She needed a different solution.

Gina glanced at her car keys. Maybe there was still enough time for her to get away before Sam arrived. Yes, it was cowardly, but she'd sort all that out later. She grabbed her keys, her purse and slipped on her shoes. She made it all the way to the front door— and that was when the doorbell rang.

There was no back door, Gina thought as a feeling of being trapped washed over her, engulfing her. She supposed she could stay very still and pretend that she wasn't in, but if the man had eyes, he would see her car parked right out front.

Bracing herself, Gina blew out another breath. How bad could it be? She looked back at Charlotte. "Say a prayer for Mommy," she instructed.

The moment she opened the door, Sam's neutral expression melted away into an appreciative smile. "Wow," he told her. "You really look great."

The compliment threw her. "Thank you," she murmured, picking up her purse.

Sam glanced around the room. What was he looking for?

"Where's Charlotte?" he asked her.

She thought that was a strange thing to ask. "I guess in the bedroom. Why?"

Sam smiled at her. "Because she's coming with us."

Gina looked at him, stunned. This man was really full of surprises. "She is?"

"Of course she is. You don't want to leave her alone, do you?" he asked. Almost as if he wanted Gina to feel as comfortable as possible and he knew having her pet with her would accomplish just that.

And right then and there, with those very simple words, Sam Sterling completely won over his heretofore very nervous veterinarian assistant.

"I'll go get Charlotte's leash and be right back," she told him happily.

"I'll be right here," Sam called after her.

Chapter Thirteen

"Are you sure about this?" Gina asked. Sam was driving both her and her miniature collie to his father's house, and she was still struggling with doubts about the wisdom of doing this. What if his father decided for some reason he didn't like her? Would that put her job in jeopardy?

"Sure about what?" Sam asked, sparing Gina a quick glance. "You're going to have to be a little more specific."

She took a deep breath. "Don't you think that springing someone new on your father for what is normally a traditional Sunday dinner is already a bit much for him? Throwing a strange dog into the mix might push this visit right over the top, wouldn't it?" She glanced at her dog in the back seat. "I mean, Charlotte is normally a very gentle dog, but I can't guarantee how she might react to a room full of men she's never met before. She might feel hemmed in."

Sam laughed. It had only been a week, but she knew he had already built up a good relationship with the miniature collie. "I'm sure Charlotte will react just fine. I got my love of animals—especially dogs—from my father. And my mother," he added deliberately. "You don't need to worry. It'll be fine." He smiled at her reassuringly. "I give you my word."

Gina turned around in her seat. She was fairly certain that Sam had installed the special seat belt in the back for his own German shepherd. Right now, Charlotte was putting the seat belt to use and seemed quite comfortable. "I feel bad that you have to leave Rocky at home."

"Trust me, she gets spoiled enough. And just so you know, I don't always bring Rocky to Sunday dinner. My dad requires that his sons turn up, but having their pets there is optional."

"Pets," Gina repeated. "Do all your brothers have dogs?" It hadn't even occurred to her to ask before.

"Just two of them, Sebastian and Scott," Sam told her. "And in case you're wondering, I passed the word along to my brothers that my guest would be bringing her miniature collie with her, so in the interest of tranquility, I suggested that they leave their dogs home."

"That must have gone over like a lead balloon," Gina commented dryly.

"Like I said, the dogs don't always come. And actually, they were a lot more interested in the fact that I was bringing someone to Sunday dinner," he told her. "I explained that you were my new assistant and that you were relatively new in Aurora, so I was bringing you to dinner as a way of saying thank you for all your help."

"Then this really is a first, you bringing some-one to dinner?" Gina asked. Part of her had thought that he was exaggerating that fact just to get her to agree. Another part of her felt a little disappointed that this didn't mean anything more than a thank-you. "Nobody else ever showed up at your table? Nobody new?" she asked incredulously. She was starting to feel even more nervous about the whole thing.

"Thinking back, I have to say no, nobody new ever turned up for Sunday dinner." And then he paused as if remembering something. "Nobody new other than Randi, our nanny slash housekeeper, I mean. Randi used to attend Sunday dinners with us for years. She's part of the family, and she also really isn't. After we all graduated from college, Randi moved into her own place not far away. She still turns up at Sunday dinners on occasion, and I have to admit, things al-ways tend to go a lot more smoothly when she does." Sam smiled fondly. "Randi always knows how to move the conversation along when it suddenly stops."

"Will she be there?" Gina asked hopefully.

"Not this Sunday," Sam responded matter-of-factly. "If you decided you want to do this again, I'm sure she'll put in an appearance somewhere along the line."

"If?" she questioned. That didn't sound very prom-ising, she thought. Was he expecting her to be turned off after tonight?

"Well, no one is going to hold a gun to your head," he told her. "Just wanted you to know that coming back was an option—and to show you how grateful I am that this little venture turned out to be positive." He pulled up in front of a two-story house that was far from new but kept up impressively well. "I didn't know what I was missing until you turned up."

Was he flattering her, or was she making too much out of his comment? She honestly didn't know, but she didn't want to allow herself to get carried away. Finding out that she'd misunderstood would be awkwardly painful.

Belatedly, she realized they had stopped moving. She took in the house for the first time. "Are we here?" she asked Sam.

"Yes," he answered with an amused grin, "we're here." It hit him that he was smiling a lot more. That had to be because of Gina, he thought. And, he concluded, it felt good.

Getting out of the car, he circled around to the passenger side. He opened Gina's door for her, but rather than give her his arm to guide her out, he stepped to the rear and unbuckled the dog's seat belt. He took great care to make sure he was holding on to Charlotte's leash so she didn't bolt unexpectedly. This was a new location for the dog, and he didn't want her getting frightened and running off. After all, she didn't know the area—yet.

Gina was impressed with the care Sam was showing her dog. Yes, he was a veterinarian, but that didn't mean he had to treat her miniature collie as if she was special.

"I can take her leash," Gina told him.

"That's all right. I'll hang on to her for now. You did point out that this will all be new to her, so I don't want Charlotte getting skittish. It shouldn't take her long to get used to the surrounding area as well as to my family."

Gina held up both of her hands. "You know best."

"Much as I would like to bask in that heady sentiment, I really don't. I just happen to know this situation," Sam told her. Keeping a hold on Charlotte's leash, he led the way to the front door, where he surprised Gina by handing her a key ring. "Why don't you open the door? I want to be able to keep my hands free," he explained.

Gina looked at him, taken aback. "Don't you think I should just ring the doorbell, seeing as how I've never been here before? If your dad sees me first, he might think I'm a burglar."

"With a key?" Sam questioned, clearly amused. He was focused on trying to keep Charlotte calm. This was, after all, someplace new for the miniature collie, and she was reacting to the confusing potpourri of different smells.

Gina shrugged at the skepticism in his voice. "There are burglars who manage to get keys to a house," she protested.

"Do me a favor—if and when you happen to meet Randi, don't mention that," Sam responded. "The woman has a vivid imagination, and she has a tendency to worry too much."

Gina nodded. "Understood. And you, young lady," she said, bending down and addressing her antsy pet, "make sure you stay on your best behavior. Okay?"

Charlotte cocked her head, acting as if she was absorbing every word her mistress was saying to her.

With that, and against her better judgment, Gina inserted the key into the lock and pushed open the door. Sam was still holding on to Charlotte's leash, but with the door open, the miniature collie's excitement intensified. Sam still managed to keep her in check, although Gina knew it wasn't as easy as one would think, given the dog's size.

"We're here, Dad," Sam called out.

One minute later, an older, slightly more distinguished version of Sam walked into the modest entrance hall. His full head of hair was iron gray rather than Sam's midnight black. The man's face, given his age and vocation, was amazingly unlined.

"So I see." Bright blue eyes crinkled as Sanford Sterling bent down and petted the eager dog.

Charlotte was fighting to get on her hind legs in order to lick Sam's father's face.

"Hello, girl. Aren't you pretty?" Sanford noted appreciatively. He petted the dog's head with gentle enthusiasm, then raised his eyes to look at the young woman standing beside his son. "And you must be Gina," he said warmly by way of greeting.

"I must be," Gina affirmed, smiling back at him. She had been prepared to be intimidated. Instead, she found herself charmed. She put out her hand at the same time that Sam's father did. "It's very nice to meet you, Mr. Sterling."

Sanford smiled, and Gina felt that she had a glimpse of what Sam would look like in the future. "It's terrific to meet you, Miss..."

"Please, call me Gina," she requested. Having her boss's father refer to her in such a formal way just didn't seem right.

Sanford inclined his head. "Gina," he repeated. It was obvious that he welcomed abandoning formality. "Tell me, how did you talk my stubborn son into hiring you as his assistant?" Before she could frame an answer, he went on with feeling, "You have no idea how long I have been after him to do that. Practically from the day he began his veterinary practice."

Sam clapped a genial hand on his father's shoulder. "Why don't we save that for the table, Dad, so Gina doesn't have to repeat herself half a dozen times to fill in Simon, Scott, Sean and Sebastian?"

It suddenly occurred to Gina that, except for the brother who'd turned up at his clinic that first emotion-filled day, she still wasn't sure she knew all of them. "Are those your brothers' names?" she asked.

His father looked at Sam, feigning disappointment.

"You didn't tell her your brothers' names? Talk about throwing someone in the middle of the pool without their water wings. Come," Sanford urged Gina, escorting his new guest into the oversize living room.

Seated on the sofa, in the midst of conversation, were four young men who eerily resembled one another. Gina recognized one of them: Sean, the one she had met that first day when she decided to help Sam with his files. As she recalled, he was the youngest of the Sterling brothers. It was Sean who had invited her to attend their Sunday dinner. Who knew? If not for him, she might have not come after all and perhaps not even been motivated to work for Sam. One thing had certainly led to another. She owed Sam's youngest brother a lot, she thought.

Sean rose to his feet ahead of his other brothers. "So, you decided to come after all," he said, sounding pleased. "Glad to see that my big brother had the good sense to hire you and bring you here to the old homestead. Sam has a tendency to resist suggestions that make sense most of the time," Sean told her. "Maybe while you put his files in order, you can teach him how to be less uptight."

"I think Charlotte is working on that last part," she answered.

"Charlotte?" another brother asked, confused. "Who's Charlotte?"

"This lovely lady right here," their father said, bringing the miniature collie into the living room.

"Ah, it figures," the brother said, nodding his head at the animal.

"Well, boys—and girl," the senior Sterling said, his eyes sweeping over the people gathered in his living room. "What do you say we all file into the dining room, where we can carry on this conversation over a healthy serving of mashed potatoes, mixed vegetables and baked spareribs?"

"That sounds wonderful," Gina told him.

Sanford's sons said nothing. They were too busy making their way into the dining room. All except for Sam, who remained beside her. "Careful they don't trample you," he warned. "Hot meals have a way of doing that to them."

Gina nodded. "Duly noted."

Chapter Fourteen

Gina had assumed that conversation at the dinner table would be slow moving and at times possibly even nonexistent. After all, she was a stranger to most of the men in Sam's family, and in her experience, men weren't always quick to warm up to strangers.

Much to her relief, less than ten minutes into her visit she discovered that this was not the case. She found to her delight that she was greatly entertained by the conversation taking place all around her. Moreover, the Sterling men were going out of their way to pull her into it. She was charmed that they all seemed to be in competition for her attention. She gave it to all of them.

This was not the experience that Sam had painted for her to expect. There was no downtime, no awkward breaks in the chatter. If anything, Sam turned out to be the quiet one. His father and younger brothers were definitely more talkative.

And the food, Gina discovered, was incredibly delicious.

"This is wonderful," she told Sam's father after she

had sampled everything. The menu had completely whetted her appetite, and each forkful just kept getting better. "Did you have this catered from a restaurant?"

Sanford exchanged looks with Sean, sitting to his right. "Did I have this catered from a restaurant?" he repeated and then laughed. "I'm sorry. I didn't mean to laugh at your question," he quickly apologized. "But in all honesty it did strike me as funny. Let me explain. In honor of my late wife, I taught all my sons how to cook and bake," he told her. "Getting our sons to be self-sufficient was extremely important to her. And preparing meals also taught them the value of a dollar. As you know, making your own meals costs a great deal less than having ready-made meals brought to you. So the boys take turns making Sunday dinner," the man informed Gina proudly.

"Which one of you made this dinner?" she asked, scanning the faces of the five young men at the table.

Simon, the divorce lawyer, raised his hand. "That would be me."

"These have to be the best spareribs I've ever had," Gina told him with enthusiasm. "You should be very proud of yourself."

Simon shrugged off her compliment as if embarrassed by it. "Pride has nothing to do with it. It's a matter of practicality."

"Practicality?" Gina questioned, slightly confused. She could think of a lot of words that might be applicable to this family meal, but *practicality* was not one of them.

"What Simon is saying," Sean said patiently, "is that he doesn't want to starve to death, so for him cooking is a simple matter of practical survival. It seems that being a divorce lawyer has completely soured him on the notion that love is a lasting emotion. So knowing how to get around in the kitchen is extremely necessary."

"He's not serious, is he?" Gina questioned, turning toward Sam. The lawyer's philosophy sounded like a terrible way to approach life.

"Oh, Simon is most definitely serious," Sean told her, following his remark with a broad wink that only served to confuse Gina even further.

"Better to be safe than sorry and stripped of all my worldly possessions," Simon told her. "You have no idea what I've managed to witness in my profession. I have seen dewy-eyed women who swore undying love go on to all but eviscerate the same men they pledged their troth to. Those women try their best to separate the men from their money."

"Other than that, Simon is a happy-go-lucky kind of guy," Sam told her, then laughed.

Gina looked at Sam, not sure if he was putting her on. "I'll take your word for it," she said, thinking that was a safe enough response.

"Hey, don't let Simon dampen your spirits," said Sebastian. He was the next-to-youngest brother and, in everyone's opinion, the brilliant one in the family. Sebastian had completed bachelor's and master's degrees in Shakespearean literature before the age of twenty and had then gone on to become a professor at that same local university while putting up with his brothers' endless teasing. "We've learned to put up with his sour take on things."

"Speak for yourself, pretty boy," Simon said to Sebastian. "I'm not sour—I just happen to see things clearly."

"Yeah, right. Clear as mud," Scott scoffed. "If everyone shared your cheerful take on things, civilization as we know it would die off in less than a generation." He made a dour face at his brother.

"Don't mind them," Sam said, bending his head and whispering in Gina's ear. "Like I said, we don't have guests over for Sunday dinner. It took me a few minutes to figure out what these numbskulls are doing, but they're all clearly showing off for you."

"Oh, I really doubt that," Gina said, waving away his take on the situation. "But if that's actually the case, I have to tell you I'm flattered." She flashed a wide, warm smile as she looked around at all the handsome faces surrounding her. To a man, beginning with Sanford, the Sterling men were all extremely good-looking.

"Hey, big brother, tell us. Where did you find this lovely lady?" Scott asked, nodding at Gina.

"Yeah, and why haven't we ever met her before? Where have you been hiding her?" Sebastian asked.

"Hey, if you were Sam, would you want to bring her here to this crowded man-fest?" Sean asked, looking around the table.

"To answer your question, I 'found' Gina when she came pounding on my door in the middle of the night on Sunday or early Monday morning, take your pick," Sam informed his brothers.

Scott rolled his eyes. "Now he has gorgeous women pounding on his door. Boy, some guys have all the luck."

"It's not what you think," Gina said, noticing the smiles on their faces as they looked from her to Sam. "My miniature collie was attacked by a pit bull while I was walking her. That vicious animal did a terrible number on her. Someone had given me your brother's name and number and said he was an extremely good veterinarian who could practically work miracles."

"Well, I can't deny that Sam is that," Simon agreed, begrudgingly nodding his head.

"Hey, I've got a question," Sean said, raising his hand.

Gina turned in his direction. "And that is?"

"How did you get that pit bull to let go of your dog?" he asked. "From everything Sam has ever told us, pit bulls don't just calmly walk away. Once they sink their teeth into another animal, they won't just let go."

Gina smiled. "They do if you pelt them with a lot of rocks. I was lucky there was a park nearby with a rock garden. I just kept throwing rocks at that dog until he finally ran away. And then I wrapped Charlotte up in a blanket, carried her to my car and brought her straight to the clinic. I was just lucky that your brother lived behind the clinic." She glanced gratefully at Sam. "I don't know what I would have done if he didn't."

"There's a twenty-four-hour animal hospital located a couple of miles from the middle of the city," Sanford volunteered. "You could have taken your collie there."

"I'm relatively new in this city. I didn't know about the hospital," Gina answered. "And at the time, I was really desperate. Charlotte was bleeding a great deal, and I couldn't get her to stop. I have to admit that I was really scared."

"Well, you couldn't have found a better veterinarian to take care of your pet than Sam," Sanford told her with pride.

"Yeah. Much as I hate to admit it, Dad's right." Sean added his voice to his father's.

"A compliment? From you?" Sam asked, pretending to be amazed. "Either I'm dying or you are."

Sean gave him a look that was clearly supposed to put Sam in his place. "And this is why I don't give you compliments, big brother."

"Boys, you're supposed to be on your best behavior around our guest," Sanford chided, suppressing a smile.

"Uh-oh, Dad means business. He's using his stern voice to get us to act politely." Sean winked at Gina. "I guess this means we'd better behave."

Sanford looked at Gina. "This is why we don't have guests over at our house. I always worry that a few minutes of this and anyone would go running out of the house, hands over their ears and screaming." He chuckled. "I must say, you've lasted a great deal longer than I thought you would when Sam told me he was going to be bringing you to dinner."

Gina smiled. She didn't need to pretend. She was really having a good time and didn't mind showing it. "You know, this is just as I would have imagined Sunday dinner being like with a family. It makes me regret that I didn't have a bunch of brothers or sisters myself," she said honestly.

"Are you an only child?" Sebastian asked her curiously.

Gina didn't bother hiding her sadness. "I have a sister," she admitted, "but for all that's worth, I might as well be an only child."

"Huh. I wish I was an only child," Simon declared wistfully.

Before his brothers could agree with him, Gina quickly said, "No, you don't. You guys have a good thing going. There's nothing like family to make you feel loved and a part of something." She glanced around the table, pinning them down with a look. "Both in good times and in bad."

"If you don't mind my asking, how would you know?" Simon asked innocently. "I mean, seeing that for all intents and purposes, you feel like an only child."

Gina smiled at him. "I guess I just have a great imagination."

Sean looked toward his father. "Can we keep her, Dad?" he asked in a singsong voice. "I promise to feed her and walk her and take really good care of her. Please, Dad?"

Sanford laughed, shaking his head, as if pleased with the cheerful atmosphere. "I think you need to take that up with Sam—and with Gina, of course."

"Sam is a spoilsport," Sean complained with a dramatic sigh. "How about it, Gina? Are you willing to stay with us? You won't regret it. You won't even have to work."

"I like to work," Gina pointed out.

"You're being creepy, little brother," Sam told Sean.

"But truthful," Sean countered with a large grin.

Simon laughed dismissively. "Don't pay any attention to Sean, Gina. He fancies himself a Romeo."

"He's nothing like Romeo," Sebastian said, speaking up. "If any of you had ever read *Romeo and Juliet*, you would know that."

Sam turned toward Gina. "Had enough?" he asked.

He seemed to be trying to read her to see if his brothers were irritating her. "I can take you home if you have."

"Oh, but she'll miss dessert if she goes," Simon piped up.

Gina grinned. "Can't have that. Besides, I want to help do the dishes. Sam told me that your dishwasher is broken," she said to Sanford.

Sanford smiled his approval of the young woman whom his friend Maizie had recruited at his request. "You're a guest. No menial labor for a guest."

"How about for a family member?" she asked, looking at Sam's father and wondering what he would say.

Sanford nodded, a big grin on his lips. "Sam, I do like this young woman. If nothing else," he went on, making eye contact with Gina, "I want you to keep her permanently employed at your clinic. If you recall, I gave you the start-up money to open it, so I do have some say in how it's run."

Sam raised his hands. "Fine with me, but ultimately, it's up to Gina."

Six sets of eyes turned to look at Gina, waiting for an answer.

Chapter Fifteen

Gina took her time answering. "Well, it does sound good to me, but why don't we just take this one day at a time and see where this goes?" she suggested honestly. She couldn't gauge how they all felt by their expressions, and she didn't want to come on too strong. She felt she might ruin what could possibly be forming. "You might change your minds about this, and I wouldn't want you to feel as if you had painted yourselves into a corner."

Sanford stroked his chin. "Pretty, smart and cautious." The smile he flashed Gina was close to blinding. "You know, you kind of remind me of the boys' mother."

It was hard for her not to beam at the man. Sam had told her how his father felt about the woman he had married. "That has to be the nicest thing anyone has ever said to me, Mr. Sterling," she told him softly.

"Sanford," Sam's father reminded her. "Call me Sanford."

But Gina shook her head. "Warm as this makes

me feel, this doesn't call for being on a first-name basis with you, sir. At least," she qualified, "not yet. Maybe somewhere down the line."

Sanford nodded, accepting her decision. "As you wish, my dear. Whatever makes you feel comfortable. But right now, washing dishes will be put on hold." His smile was bright, charming. "There will be servings of ice cream all around. Simon, if you would do the honors," he urged the son who was responsible for dinner that Sunday.

Gina frowned slightly. "I don't do well just sitting and waiting to be served," she began, wanting to at least take over serving dessert to the others.

To her surprise, Sam's father told her to "deal with it, my dear." His words were accompanied by a warm smile.

"You heard the man," Sam told her. "Sit."

Gina sighed and threw up her hands. This didn't make her happy, but she was not about to fight Sam and his father at every turn. "Sitting," she responded to both of the men.

"I do like a person who knows when to adjust to the situation." And then Sanford turned toward Simon. "That's your cue, son."

Rising, Simon went to the kitchen and returned with a half-gallon container of mint chip ice cream. Deftly, he scooped ice cream and distributed the bowls to his father, his brothers and Gina. Everyone had seconds.

* * *

It wasn't until hours later that Gina, Charlotte and Sam were finally back in Sam's car and on their way to the condo Gina was renting.

Sam glanced over at his assistant as they pulled away from the house where he and his brothers had grown up. She hadn't said much to him after telling his father and brothers how much she'd enjoyed meeting them.

"So how are you doing?" he asked.

"Just fine," she told him, then turned to look at Sam. "Why? Did you think I was going to disintegrate?"

"The thought did cross my mind," Sam confessed. "Five doses of Sterling men, then throw in our dad, and it all might be a little hard to take."

"I don't see why," she said. "From the way you talked, I was expecting to feel like I'd been dropped on an anthill after being dipped in honey. Instead, everyone was more entertaining and kind than the last person. Either you *really* exaggerated, or you all cast one hell of a spell over me." She grinned at him. "I'm kind of leaning toward explanation number one." And then she turned in her seat to look at the dog behind her. "How about you, Charlotte? Do you think that Dr. Sam exaggerated what his family was like to us?"

As if in agreement, the miniature collie barked.

Gina laughed. Turning back around, she told Sam,

"Charlotte said she didn't think you exaggerated. But then, we know my dog has been very partial to you ever since the day you sewed her up and saved her life. My guess is that Charlotte is going to be your faithful, extremely grateful shadow for the rest of your life—maybe even longer."

Sam smiled in response. "In all seriousness, that's why I got into this business. Animals are incredibly grateful and loyal. More so than a lot of people, in my opinion."

She was quiet for a moment. "That sounds to me as if you've had some bad experiences," Gina guessed.

"No, but Simon told me some stories about the clients he was dealing with that made me glad I haven't had time to garner any experiences of my own," Sam told her, stopping at a red light.

"That sounds like it could be very lonely," she said.

"No," he denied. He didn't have time to get lonely. "Just extremely busy. But that's the price I paid to start up my veterinary practice," he said philosophically. And happily, he thought, the pace hadn't let up yet.

"Well, I, for one, am glad you did," she told him with feeling.

"So," Sam said, deciding to change the subject, "what did you think of my family? You don't look worse for the wear, but for all I know, you could just be a really great actress."

Gina shook her head. "No acting. I honestly had a really great time. Your father and your brothers were all extremely funny, charming and very welcoming. I didn't expect to," she confessed, "but I had a really great time."

"Do you think," Sam began, broaching the subject slowly, "you would be willing to do this again?"

"Very willing," she said with what sounded like genuine sincerity. "I like seeing what actual family life could be like instead of just imagining it."

"Spoiler alert," Sam said, inclining his head toward her. "My dad and brothers behaved better than usual. There are times when they just sit at the table, communing with their dinners and counting the minutes before they can beat a hasty retreat."

Gina didn't seem fazed by this glimpse into his family's life. "That just means they're human. I wasn't expecting to meet a bunch of plaster saints."

"That's good," he responded. "Because if there's one thing they're not, it's saintly." He slanted a look in her direction. "So you really had a decent time? Because if you actually didn't, I want to apologize now."

"Yes, I really did have a decent time. *More* than decent," she emphasized. "There's absolutely nothing to apologize for. I enjoyed getting a glimpse into the world that made you you."

"So then you'll be in tomorrow?" he asked, glancing at her profile.

"Of course I'll be in tomorrow," she answered. "Where else would I be?" Then she added, "I consider myself one of the lucky ones."

Sam pulled up in front of her condo and turned off his car engine. "Come again?" he asked. Had he missed something? To his thinking, he was the lucky one.

"I'm getting paid to do what I always wanted to do. Work with animals," she clarified. "We have that in common."

"I guess we do." He had forgotten that she had told him that.

"I've got one more question for you," Gina said, unbuckling her seat belt but staying in her seat.

Sam wasn't aware that she had asked an initial question, but he went with it. "Go ahead."

"Do you cook as well as Simon does?" she asked curiously.

Genuinely tickled, Sam laughed. "At the risk of sounding immodest, better."

Gina seemed to roll that over in her head, then smiled. "That sounds promising."

"I'll make you something to eat sometime this week," Sam promised, not wanting her to think he was just bragging. He knew what he was capable of. He'd been the one who took care of his brothers when his mother became too ill to cook.

Gina waved at his offer. "Oh, you don't have to do

that just because I'm curious. You work hard enough as it is. I'll just take your word for it."

But Sam wasn't about to be put off that easily. "We'll get back to this," he promised, knowing how this debate would turn out if he kept going. "In the meantime, thanks for coming and putting up with everything. I'm serious."

"And thank you for a great time," she reciprocated. "I'm serious, too. Now, Charlotte and I need to beat a hasty retreat so you can go home and get some rest. You're going to need it. You've got a jam-packed schedule tomorrow," she told him.

Just as Sam turned his head toward her to tell her that the pleasure had been all his, Gina leaned in, saying, "Thank you."

She probably meant to brush her lips against his cheek. But because he had turned his head, their lips pressed against each other.

The contact generated a wave of electricity that was hard to describe. Or ignore. It zipped through Sam with speed, an incredible, unmatched power that was both startling and immensely seductive.

For a long moment, he felt like he had lost the ability to breathe like a normal person. Everything within him was tingling, as if a black-and-white world had suddenly been bathed in warm, magnificent rainbow colors.

He was kissing Gina.

Suddenly and unexpectedly.

This was definitely not what Sam had intended. He should be apologizing to her, not slipping his arms around her and pulling her to him. Why wasn't he drawing away and creating space between them?

In a minute, Sam told himself. *I'll do it in a minute. Just one minute longer, and then I'll pull back and apologize to her. After all, I didn't plan this. It just happened by accident. A very fortuitous accident.*

Summoning more strength than he would have thought necessary, he finally dropped his hands from her body. "I'm sorry. I didn't mean for that to happen," he told her, embarrassed.

"You didn't?" she asked.

He couldn't tell from her tone if she was being on the level, but his best bet was to go with sincerity. After all, she couldn't fault him for that. At least, he hoped not.

"No," he emphasized. "It was an accident, one of those flukes that happen sometimes. You turned your head just as I turned mine, and our lips somehow managed to make contact. I am really sorry if I offended you," he went on with feeling.

"You didn't," Gina told him. "Surprised me, yes, but offended me? No, you didn't do that. After all, you just said it was an accident. And I believe you." She paused for a moment, then asked him, "It was, wasn't it?"

Sam nodded his head a little too vigorously. "Yes."

But he was disappointed that she seemed to prefer that explanation over the fact that the kiss had stirred a tidal wave of incredible, heated feelings.

Chapter Sixteen

Gina and Charlotte stood on the doorstep of her condo, watching as Sam pulled away. Gina took in a deep breath, trying very hard to still her wildly beating pulse.

He would probably never know how close she had come to inviting him in for a drink. Gina had nothing on the premises that could be thought of as hard liquor, but there were definitely things in her cabinet that could give both of them more than just a pleasant buzz. Or at least her, she thought.

And if that happened, she would more than likely wind up dropping her defenses. Heaven knew that, right now, she was desperately trying everything in her power to keep those defenses raised and in place.

Just thinking about it had her heart fluttering. She had to admit that she had never felt this way about a man before. This was definitely a first. But Gina really liked her job, and she felt that the fastest way for her to lose it would be to invite Sam in and act on what she was feeling.

She didn't flatter herself that what she was experiencing right now was anything near mutual. She was going to have to keep a tight rein on her emotions and tread very, very carefully, Gina told herself.

Turning on her heel, she unlocked her door. Gina closed and locked it decisively behind her.

Sam kept his assistant and her pet in his rearview mirror for as long as he could. *That was close*, he thought.

But the odd thing was, he didn't know which outcome he was rooting for. Did he want to keep things businesslike between them or go with the intense feelings he was experiencing?

Okay, Sam did know what he was rooting for, but that could very well mean he might lose an incredibly gifted and able assistant. Every day that went by only served to show him how much he had gained by having Gina helping him in the clinic. Sam really didn't want to go back to steering through the choppy waters by himself if he could possibly avoid it.

Parking his car at the curb, Sam walked into his living quarters through the entrance to the clinic and called out, "I'm home, Rocky."

The German shepherd came barreling out of the room where she had been staying to greet him and all but knocked him down in her happiness to see him. Steadying himself, Sam laughed as he ran his hands along Rocky's fur.

"Are you glad to see me or is it the smell of the

spareribs that has you reacting this way?" he asked his pet.

Rocky was now all but inhaling the bag his father had packed up for him. He'd sent one of his other sons home with a serving of spareribs for his pets, too.

Sam shook his head as he watched Rocky. "You know, you'd get more out of it if you tried eating a little slower and actually *tasting* the meat," he chided the German shepherd.

But Rocky went through the spareribs like a house on fire.

"Okay, have it your way. Me, I'm going to bed," he told her.

Pausing only long enough to refill her bowl with water, Sam went up to his room. He had to force himself to put one foot in front of the other and strip off his shirt and his shoes for bed. He came close to just falling on top of his mattress fully clothed and completely devoid of energy. He hadn't realized he was this exhausted until the allure of sleep pulled him in.

It took him less than five minutes to fall into a deep, dreamless sleep.

The following week was practically a repeat of the previous one. Different pets came in to be treated, but by and large there was nothing new or earth-shattering on the agenda.

Not until Gina took an emergency phone call from

a woman who asked, "What sort of pets does Dr. Sterling treat?"

"The usual ones," Gina answered. "Dogs, cats, an assortment of birds." She thought for a moment, thinking of the parade of pets that had been brought into the office in the last couple of weeks. "Also lizards and hamsters."

"Anything else?" the woman asked, sounding a little uncertain.

"It might be simpler if you tell me what animal you're thinking of bringing in," Gina told her.

The caller took in a deep breath before she finally said, "My horse isn't doing well."

Gina was caught off guard. "Your horse?" she repeated, stunned. She had to admit that this was a pet she hadn't been expecting. "I'm going to have to check with Dr. Sterling about that. I'm new here, and so far, I haven't seen any horses on the schedule." Gina congratulated herself for getting those words out without stumbling. "Can you hold on for a moment?"

The woman sounded rather beside herself as she answered, "Yes, I'll hold on."

This wasn't a joke, Gina decided. Putting the woman on hold, Gina went to knock lightly on the door to the secondary exam room. Then she opened the door cautiously and peeked in.

Sam raised his eyes from the poodle he was examining, a silent query.

"I have a rather distraught woman on the phone asking if you examine horses," Gina told him.

"In an emergency, if she can't get an equine veterinarian to come by and examine it, I can do it," Sam told her. "Get all the details you can and tell her we can come by last thing today." He paused, as if realizing he was taking something for granted. "You are available, right?"

Gina smiled as she nodded her head. "Yes, I'm available," she assured him. Then, so that he didn't misunderstand her meaning, she added, "To accompany you to the ranch." Withdrawing from the room, she closed the door behind her.

Finished with the clinic's scheduled patients for the day, they had driven to an old ranch on the edge of town. Sam had easily diagnosed the stallion and applied a relatively simple solution, bringing a relieved smile from the horse's owner, Molly Sanders.

"Flicka was a gift from my father. My father passed away last fall, and the horse is my last connection to him," Molly confessed. "I'd like to keep Flicka alive as long as I possibly can."

"Well, from everything I can see, once we get this infection under control, Flicka gives every indication of being able to live a long, healthy life," Sam told her. Other than his current problem, Flicka was an impressive piece of horseflesh.

An hour later, Sam and Gina left Molly fairly beaming as they drove away from the ranch and headed back to Aurora.

Gina had offered to drive them back to the clinic, thinking that Sam must be fairly tired. But when she suggested it, he turned her down.

"This is still a fairly unknown area to you, and the darkness here isn't your friend. It's easy to get lost, so I'll drive us back to the clinic—but thanks for the offer," Sam added.

Knowing it was useless to argue, Gina leaned back against her seat. "Dogs, cats, birds, reptiles, hamsters and now horses. You certainly are versatile," Gina commented. "Are there any animals you don't know how to treat?" She could hear the admiration echoing in her own voice.

"I sincerely hope not." And then he smiled at her before looking back at the road. "Maybe a dinosaur."

"Not a problem. Those aren't around anymore except in the movies," Gina reminded him.

"Well then, I guess the answer to your question is a resounding no," Sam told her with a wide grin.

Gina laughed softly. "Brilliant, capable and modest, too," she teased. "Is there no end to your attributes, Doctor?"

His eyes met hers, then went back to watching the road. "I don't know. I guess that remains to be seen," he told her with an easy smile that even in the darkness shot straight into her nervous system, making it quiver.

Twenty minutes later, Sam pulled up in front of the clinic. "You put in a really long day today," he said. It sounded like a compliment.

"So did you," Gina pointed out.

"I should. I'm the vet and this is my clinic," he said.

"That doesn't mean you need to do this by yourself. I'm here to help any way I can," she reminded him.

Instead of arguing, he just shook his head as if in wonder. "I don't know how I ever managed to run this place without you."

"Now you're just flattering me," she said.

"No," he denied, looking at her. "I am just telling you the truth."

Gina raised a quizzical eyebrow, her mouth curving in amusement. She didn't believe the man for a moment. She couldn't allow herself to. "Really?" she challenged.

"Really," Sam told her without even a hint of wavering.

Gina began to open the car door. "Let me go collect Charlotte, and we'll be out of your hair as quickly as possible."

But Sam rounded the hood of his vehicle to help her out—not that she needed it.

Gina smiled up at him. "You don't need to go out of your way like that, Doctor. I am perfectly capable of getting out of the car all on my own."

"I know that," he said. "This is just my way of saying thank you for all your help."

"You're paying me for doing that," Gina reminded him.

"There's help, and then there's help," he said, changing his tone between the two words. "And after what I've been through in getting my clinic on its feet, I've learned not to take a single thing for granted."

Gina nodded seriously. "I don't, either." But even still, right now, she found herself responding to the way Sam was treating her. His treatment could change eventually, or possibly abruptly, but so far, it hadn't and gave no indication that it would anytime soon. If anything, it only seemed to be getting better.

This was what she got for leading a solitary life, Gina told herself. If she had gotten involved with men on any regular basis, she wouldn't be melting like this at any display of kindness.

No, she corrected herself. It wasn't that she had been living a solitary life. She just hadn't lit up inside before when someone paid attention to her. Up until now, she hadn't had time for it. It wasn't until Sam that Gina began to feel as if she was actually lighting up inside.

Over and over again, she thought with a smile that she managed to hide—or at least she thought she did.

"Okay, let's show Charlotte that you're here to take her home," Sam said, unlocking the clinic's door.

The moment he did, they could hear the miniature collie's agitated barking.

"Looks like someone knows that her mom's here to pick her up," Sam commented with a grin.

"There are those canine instincts again," Gina marveled as she made her way to the room where Charlotte was playing with Rocky.

When Gina and Sam walked in, all furry activity stopped abruptly as two pairs of eyes turned toward the humans. Charlotte instantly barked a happy greeting at her mistress, leaping up excitedly and dancing around on her hind legs.

Delighted, both Gina and Sam began to laugh wholeheartedly.

Chapter Seventeen

It just kept getting better and better.

With each day that passed, Gina felt she had definitely made the right decision to help Sam with his clinic. Without being conceited, she felt that she was the right person for this job.

Actually, at this point it wasn't just a job. Gina felt as if working in Sam's shadow was more of a vocation, a calling. It was what she had always been meant to do. Up until now, she had held down jobs merely to keep body and soul together so she could eat and pay rent. If even one of those jobs had been remotely satisfying, she wouldn't have constantly been busy looking for the next job.

Since she had begun working at the clinic, she was no longer looking. She had found her rightful place in the scheme of things.

And that was also applicable, in no small way, not just to what she was doing, but how she felt about what she was doing. That went for the animals she was working with as well as the veterinarian she was working beside. He never asked anything of her that he didn't ask of himself; that went for the hours she put in as well.

Gina had to constantly remind herself not to get too carried away. She knew that she very easily could with no effort—in less than the blink of an eye, she thought, her mouth curving.

"Something funny?" Sam asked as he paused at her desk on his way into the second exam room. A husky and his master were waiting to see him. These days, Sam was able to work his way through an afternoon's patients at less than an exhausting pace.

"No," Gina replied innocently.

Sam's eyes narrowed. "You're grinning."

She maintained her innocent expression and shrugged. "I'm just happy, I guess."

Sam didn't tell Gina he was happy to hear her response, but he really didn't need to get a confirmation from her about how she felt.

Four Sundays had gone by, and he had invited her to four Sunday dinners, and she had shown up to all of them. It had gotten to the point that not only did he look forward to the relaxed atmosphere at these dinners, but he realized that his father and brothers looked forward to seeing Gina—which was a great feeling.

Sam hung back for a moment longer before going to Room Two. "Does that mean that you'll be coming to Sunday dinner again? I'm asking," he explained quickly, "because my dad asked me if you would be there."

"Your dad's a very sweet man," Gina said with enthusiasm. "You know, I don't understand why he never got married again."

"The torch that my dad's carrying for my mom is just too heavy and too bright for him to consider someone else. I don't think anyone would ever be able to get him to move past it," Sam said.

She smiled at him. "You know, that really sounds like a challenge."

Sam read between the lines and immediately tried to veto what she must be thinking. "Oh, no, please don't try to play matchmaker where my father's concerned." From the way Gina's smile widened, he knew he had guessed correctly.

"Why not?" she asked innocently. "Don't you want to see your father happy?"

"Of course I want to see him happy. What I don't want to see is my old man handing my head to me. Look, we'll talk about this later," he told her. "I've got a patient to see in Room Two right now, but I'll get back to this after hours if you want to talk further."

Gina inclined her head. "Oh, absolutely."

She didn't get to talk to Sam again until the clinic's front door was finally locked for the day.

"Isn't your family tired of seeing me at the dinner table with them?" she asked him. When he raised his eyebrows, she explained, "I really don't want to wear out my welcome."

"You're kidding, right?" he asked. "You've made Sunday dinners something for the rest of us to look forward to."

Gina shook her head. "You don't have to lie to spare my feelings."

He looked at her, clearly surprised. "I'm not lying. And those aren't just my sentiments. I'm telling you what my father and brothers have expressed. It seems like you've cast quite a spell over all of them—no easy feat, I don't mind telling you."

She wasn't sure how he actually meant that, or even *if* he meant that. "That wasn't my intention, Sam."

"Maybe not," he allowed, "but it still happened. And it's not a bad thing. This is one of those rare times that my whole family seems to be in complete agreement."

"Okay, now you're just pulling my leg," Gina told him.

"No, I'm not." *Although the prospect of that is definitely not off-putting*, he couldn't help thinking, his eyes skimming along the outline of her body. He found his appetite growing to greater proportions and unbelievable heights. For just a second, their eyes met and locked.

Gina felt a warm surge traveling through her, touching every single part of her body. It was happening again, she thought. She could feel desire growing, taking possession of her. She needed to be on her way, or she was going to wind up just melting right here on the spot.

"I think it's time for me to take Charlotte home," she told him.

Sam knew he should step out of Gina's way, even encourage her to take her pet and be on her way. But the words telling her to go refused to leave his lips.

And then he thought of something.

"Tell you what. Why don't I make you and Charlotte dinner?" Sam suggested, bending to pet the miniature collie's head.

Gina didn't think that was a very good idea, but she didn't want to tell him that. She went with logic instead. "Well, for one thing, you have to be tired. You put in as long a day as I did."

"Actually, cooking relaxes me," he told her.

She waved her hand, not believing him. "How is that possible? Cooking always makes me feel uptight."

Sam shrugged. "Different strokes for different folks, I guess. So, about dinner. Are you game?"

Gina nodded. "I'm game, but I'm also going to feel pretty guilty, putting you out like this."

"You're not putting me out," he insisted. "I wouldn't have suggested it otherwise." He thought for a moment. "Would you feel better if you assisted me in this venture?" he asked, a smile curving his mouth.

"Yes, I would," she answered.

"Okay, consider yourself my assistant in this as well," Sam told her. "It's like extending our work relationship to another level." His smile widened. "Does that work for you?"

Well, she certainly couldn't just walk out on him now, Gina thought. So she nodded her head and said, "Yes, it does."

"I'm glad." Sam grinned again. "I've never cooked with an assistant before." His eyes met hers. "This should be an interesting experience."

Interesting wasn't the word she would have used, but Gina supposed that in a pinch it would do. "Just tell me what you want me to do, and I'll do it," she told him.

From the expression on his face, she realized how that sounded.

Clearing her throat, Gina said in a deeper voice, "You know what I mean."

Sam nodded. "Sadly," he told her, "I know exactly what you mean. Okay, let's get to work." He led the way to his kitchen.

The refrigerator appeared to be totally stocked. Gina remembered how it had looked just the other morning when he invited her to have some orange juice.

"Do you have elves?" she asked him whimsically, gesturing at the fridge.

Sam laughed. "No, but I do have a brother who

knows how to shop and fill a refrigerator. And he owes me a favor."

"Well, in some circles, that's even better than elves," she joked.

"There were times growing up when I would have rather had the elves," he told her seriously. Sam opened the refrigerator door wide. "Okay," he said, waving a hand, "what's your pleasure?"

Gina shrugged. It really made no difference to her. "I'm fairly easy to please. You pick."

He decided to try to learn a few things about her tastes. "How do you feel about pork chops?"

That was easy. She had liked those ever since she was a little girl. "I like them breaded and fried," she answered.

"I do, too." He glanced over at Rocky and Charlotte, who appeared very interested in what was going on. "And I guarantee that the dogs will be happy to eat the leftovers."

Gina looked at him. "What makes you think there're going to be leftovers?" she asked innocently. "I think you know by now that I'm not one of those people who just nibble delicately."

"Is there a reason for that? Other than good cooking, I mean," he asked.

"Food was hard to come by when I was growing up. At the risk of sounding as if I stuff myself, I learned to appreciate every morsel that finds its way to my plate," she said. "I thought you might have picked up on that these last few weeks."

"I just thought you were trying not to insult my brothers' cooking," he confessed.

"Well, there's that, too," Gina allowed with a smile. "But if that were the case, I would have just nibbled the way you anticipated. But at your father's table, there has never been any need to pretend. So far, your brothers are excellent cooks. When is it going to be your turn?" she asked.

"As a matter of fact, my turn is this Sunday," he told her.

"Fantastic," she exclaimed. She pretended to be calm as she asked, "Am I allowed to help you this Sunday, or does this have to be a solo venture?"

"Well, my brothers didn't have anyone working with them, but then, they don't have anyone in their lives who *can* cook," he emphasized.

She nodded and stepped up to work beside him, doing her best not to get in his way at the same time. "So I can consider this a rehearsal for Sunday," she told him, reaching for the potatoes he put out for her to peel and dice.

"Only if you want to—you're not required to help," he insisted. "You can just be a guest and enjoy yourself. No one will think any less of you."

"Maybe not, but I will," she told him. "I told you that first Sunday, I don't like being a sponge."

"Then I guess it's settled," Sam concluded. "You'll be my assistant there, too."

Gina smiled at him. "Happy to comply, Doctor."

Chapter Eighteen

Much to Sam's surprise and pleasure, he and Gina worked as well together in the kitchen as they did in the clinic. Once he told her what he was planning to prepare, Gina seemed to instinctively anticipate his every move in the kitchen, just as she had begun to do at the clinic. Dinner was ready in record time, and they were both rather pleased with the end result.

"I'll do the dishes," Gina announced once they had finished eating.

"The dishwasher will do the dishes," Sam told her pointedly.

"You had it fixed?" she asked, surprised. He had mentioned the other day that the dishwasher was broken.

"*I* fixed it," he corrected her. Sam prided himself on being able to repair a number of things that would cause the average person to call in a repair person.

Gina looked rather impressed. "I guess you're pretty handy."

Sam smiled. "I'd like to think so."

"Still," Gina said, "I feel that the dishes are cleaner

if I'm the one washing them instead of a machine."
She turned her back to him to run hot, sudsy water
in the sink.

"You really don't have to do that," Sam told her,
coming up behind her and attempting to take a dish
out of her hands. "Sit back for once. You already have
enough to do."

Gina refused to let go. "Oh, and you don't?"

"I already told you, the clinic is my practice and
my responsibility," Sam reminded her.

"Maybe I want to start up my own practice," she
challenged, turning around to face him.

The problem was that she turned in what amounted
to be the circle of his arms, her mouth incredibly
close to his. The warmth of his breath traveling over
her face startled her. Her lips were all but brushing
against his.

Her heart leaped as she remembered the first time
they had been in this situation. When she had moved
to kiss his cheek and wound up kissing his mouth
instead. Since that time, she had found herself longing for a repeat performance. A longer, more sensual
repeat performance.

And then suddenly, it was happening.

Sam framed her face with his hands and brought
his mouth down to hers. This wasn't just a light meeting of their lips only to pull back. This time Gina
could feel the passion hiding just beneath the surface. Passion that spoke to something within her, and

though she knew she should pull away, she really, really didn't want to.

So she didn't.

Instead, her arms went around his neck, and she closed the gap between them, drawing Sam in. Before she really even knew what was happening, she felt her body pressed achingly close to his. She had absolutely no desire for any sort of separation between them. Her pulse throbbed, racing madly throughout her entire body.

"This shouldn't be happening," Sam told her. But there was no conviction in his voice.

"I know," she answered, but did nothing to create even the smallest amount of space between them.

He drew his head back just for a moment, his eyes searching hers. He must have found the answer he needed because he brought his mouth back down to hers with even more passion.

Sam picked her up in his arms and carried her to the one bedroom downstairs. Pushing the door open with his shoulder, he set her down so her feet touched the floor. Then he drew back again to look at her as well as to give her an option. This was all new and he didn't want to push ahead and presume anything.

"If this is going too fast for you or if you want to stop, all you need to do is just say so," he said.

"And you'll stop? Just like that?" she questioned, surprised.

"Well, it wouldn't be 'just like that,'" Sam told her.

"But I definitely don't want to do anything that you don't want to do or that makes you uncomfortable. This won't have a prayer of working if it's just one-sided."

"A prayer of *working*," she echoed, emphasizing all the word implied. "Does that mean you want to do this beyond tonight?"

The look he gave her could have easily melted an entire mountain of snow. "Hell yes," he told her in no uncertain terms.

That was all she wanted to hear. Yes, she knew that men lied to women in intimate situations. She also knew that the reverse could be true. This time, when Gina brought her lips to his, she held nothing back, lighting a bonfire within her that heretofore had no equal.

Breathing hard, Sam drew back one last time. "Is that a yes?" he asked.

Frustration all but echoed in Gina's voice. "If I have to answer that—" she began.

Gina didn't get a chance to finish. Or to even breathe normally. The rest of what she was about to say was submerged in a whirlwind of passion that captured them both.

They fell onto the bed, bodies entwined with one another as each rained kisses on the other's face and any skin they were able to access.

Gina dragged Sam's shirt off his shoulders and arms, her fingers skimming along his bare skin, her lips passionately anointing the areas being exposed.

Sam returned the favor, mimicking her movements and fanning the bonfire within her. Bit by bit, clothing disappeared, until they were both dressed only in the other's warm gaze and hot touch.

The little voice in her head that had initially shouted "Stop!" slowly faded to a soft whisper and then nothingness. It was replaced by a yearning that threatened to finally consume her. Her body curled up and around his, continuing to build the fire within her.

So this was what it was like, Sam thought, what he had heard people talking about and praising for years. Until now, he had just shrugged his shoulders, telling himself that if this wild, elusive thing called love was meant to happen, it *would* happen, and he left it at that. He certainly hadn't thought it could grow to these extremes.

Not until Gina had come his way. Suddenly things began happening inside of him. His attention was being drawn away from the events of his day-to-day life and from his time-consuming, nonstop practice. Now there was something beyond that, Sam realized, and that thought did not leave him feeling unhappy.

Gina twisted and turned, eager for Sam's touch. Each pass of his hand generated more and more heat along her skin and inside of her, her hunger growing ravenous.

Suddenly, Sam moved so that his body was directly over hers, heat emanating from him. He linked his hands with hers, and as their eyes met and held, he coaxed her legs apart with his knee and then entered her, moving his hips with an ever-growing urgency as their bodies finally became one.

The explosion finally came, the euphoria of it nearly consuming them as it traveled urgently through their entire bodies. They clung to one another, absorbing the fierce shudder that vibrated through them until it finally settled down, leaving a warm feeling behind.

Sam raised his head to look at her. "Wow." Kissing her forehead softly, he repeated, "Wow."

Gina was having a great deal of difficulty stilling her pounding pulse. Finally, she was able to ask, "So this is over?"

Cocking his head, Sam asked, "Come again?"

"You just kissed my forehead like a big brother, so I just wanted to know if that's your way of saying that this is now over." She was only a little serious, but there was indeed a part of her that was afraid that was what it meant.

"No, it's my way of saying that you exhausted me beyond all comprehension and this is all I have the energy to do," Sam told her. "I'm just waiting for my energy to come back, and then we can pick up where we left off."

She laughed softly. "You're going to have a very long wait. You really drained me, too."

"At least that feeling is mutual," he said. "I guess that means we're well suited for one another." Sam smiled. "I'm also guessing that I'm not supposed to say that."

She eyed him quizzically. "Why not?"

"Well, it takes the mystery out of things," he told her.

"I wasn't aware that mystery was called for in this case," Gina said innocently.

"According to authorities on these matters, mystery is what helps propel things along between two lovers," Sam told her.

"Do you really believe that?" she asked.

Sam shook his head. "Just telling you the popular theory. I don't believe in playing games. But then, and this might not be a good thing to admit, either," he allowed, "I've never really had a steady girlfriend. I never learned all the games that need to be played in a relationship."

Gina moved so that her body curled into his again. "I was always too busy holding body and soul together to get involved in all those so-called games." She raised herself on her elbow to look at him. "For the record, I don't believe in playing games, either."

Sam pulled her down to him, fanning the flames between them to new heights again. He grinned at her. "I just believe in going with the truth."

"Very alluring and sexy. Me, too." Gina sealed her lips to his, starting their erotic dance all over again.

Chapter Nineteen

They made love three times that night. Which accounted for the extremely happy glow Gina felt within her the following morning.

Even so, as the days went by, Gina knew she shouldn't attach too much attention to what she was experiencing or even become the slightest bit used to it. She had heard too many stories about people feeling undying love, only for it to do just that: die, leaving people utterly bereft and extremely empty inside, like everything had just been ripped out.

She didn't want to go through that in any way and was completely determined not to. She attempted to construct an impenetrable wall around herself in order to remain invulnerable from anything to do with Sam. She was already responding way too much, way too strongly to the man's charms.

And he really *was* charming.

Gina slanted a glance in Sam's direction in the clinic one morning. It was definitely not easy to stay strong. They had made love a number of times, both before and after they had spent a traditional Sunday dinner with Sam's family. He made her heart smile with so very little effort.

Going over the paperwork from his latest patient, Gina struggled not to stare at Sam as he spoke to the owner. It was certainly hard not to give in when every thought in her head revolved around the veterinarian.

Such as this Pekingese, aptly named Furball, who had come in with a pronounced limp. A limp that she seemed to have acquired with no sign of outward injury.

"But there *has* to be a reason," Mrs. Martin insisted, looking as if she was close to bursting into tears.

Sam took a breath. He would have thought that the reason was self-evident. "Oh, I'm afraid there is."

Pulling her shoulders back, Mrs. Martin braced herself with a frown. "I don't like the way that sounds, Dr. Sterling."

"I'm afraid that to rectify this particular situation, it's going to take a lot of discipline on your part, Mrs. Martin," Sam told her.

The woman pulled her shoulders back even farther, looking every inch a soldier ready to go into battle for a beloved cause. "Tell me," she urged. "I can handle it."

Sam had his doubts about that being even remotely true. This whole situation could have been avoided if Mrs. Martin had exhibited the slightest bit of self-control and not grossly overfed her Pekingese at every turn.

"Furball is limping like that," he told her, "because she is way too heavy. You're a pushover, and you've fed her too much. She looks up at you with those great big, sad brown eyes, begging for treats, and you give in and toss food at her just to placate her." Sam didn't mean to criticize, but he had to tell her the way he saw things.

"But Furball looks so terribly pathetic when she's hungry," Mrs. Martin said, looking concerned that she was to blame for her beloved pet's weight. Perhaps she thought her explanation was good enough to absolve her of blame.

"You have to understand that Furball is a very bright dog. She has learned how to use looking pathetic to get what she wants," Sam told Mrs. Martin.

The dog's owner appeared stricken.

Gina turned away from her desk. The expression on Mrs. Martin's face tore at her heart. The woman looked extremely guilty. "Mrs. Martin, if Furball was your child instead of your pet, would you allow her to overeat like that because she stuck out her lower lip and pouted at you?" Gina asked in a kindly voice. She was sympathetic for what the woman had to be going through.

"No, of course not," Mrs. Martin answered with pronounced feeling.

"Then should you allow your dog to do that sort of thing?" Gina asked logically.

Mrs. Martin opened her mouth defensively, then

closed it again, clearly stumped. "No, of course not," she finally answered.

"And why is that?" Gina asked, aware that Sam was watching her. When Mrs. Martin didn't say anything, Gina said, "It's because you love Furball, right? Do you love her any less than if she were your child?" Gina knew from Mrs. Martin's file that, for all intents and purposes, she regarded Furball as her child.

"No, of course not," the woman protested adamantly.

"Well, you're going to have to remain very strong when she turns those big, sad eyes to look at you," Gina told her. "Think about the good you are doing by staying so strong."

She glanced toward Sam to see if she had overstepped. His approving smile and the way he nodded at her let her release the breath she had been holding. She hadn't made a mistake. Not only that, but Sam didn't resent her butting into his practice. She was just trying to make the woman realize what Sam was attempting to convey about her pet.

"I am going to write a prescription for something you can give Furball that will fill her up so she doesn't feel hungry," Sam said to Mrs. Martin. "If Furball feels full, she's not going to haunt your every step, trying to get you to give her treats. They're pretty straightforward when it comes to their appetites. This is all going to take a little while," Sam predicted, "but she will lose the weight and stop limping when she loses that extra weight."

Mrs. Martin had tears in her eyes as she looked down at her pet. "Really?"

Sam nodded. "Really," he told the woman with compassion.

She drew Furball onto her lap, although it obviously was not easy for the woman, and hugged the dog to her. "I don't know how to thank you, Dr. Sterling," she told Sam and then looked at Gina as well, including her in her gratitude.

"Just stick to your promise and don't overfeed Furball," Sam advised. "And that will be thanks enough for us."

Mrs. Martin nodded. "Oh, I won't overfeed her," she promised. "I've definitely learned my lesson."

"Remember," Sam told her, "what you perceive as kindness is actually harming the poor thing. Overeating puts a strain on Furball's heart, and you don't want to be responsible for doing that, do you?"

"No, of course not," Mrs. Martin cried with more than a little feeling.

"Glad to hear that. Gina, print up a copy of that special diet plan for Mrs. Martin to use when she's feeding Furball," Sam said.

"Right away, Dr. Sterling," Gina told him, going over to the filing cabinet. She retrieved the diet plan that Sam had asked her for and took it over to the copy machine. After quickly running off the pages,

Gina placed them in a folder and handed it to Mrs. Martin. "There you go," Gina announced.

Mrs. Martin glanced at the two pages, absorbing the information.

"If you have any questions," Sam said, "please don't hesitate to call me. And here," he said, writing on his prescription pad and tearing off a page, "is that prescription I mentioned. There's a phone number where you can reach me 24/7."

"And if I call it, you'll answer?" Mrs. Martin asked skeptically.

Sam smiled at the woman, petting Furball's head gently. "Yes, that's the deal."

Gina could almost read the woman's mind. "Dr. Sterling is quite serious. The first time I met him was when I brought my own dog to him. Charlotte had been attacked by a pit bull, and Dr. Sterling was kind enough to sew her up."

Mrs. Martin looked stunned. "Is this true?" she asked Sam.

He nodded. "Oh, it's true, all right. What Gina neglected to tell you is that this all took place at three o'clock in the morning."

"You really are one of the good ones, Dr. Sterling," Mrs. Martin told him.

Gina smiled. "He really is. Instead of reading me the riot act that I hadn't been careful with Charlotte when I realized there was a pit bull in the street, he took care of my dog and then later hired me as his assistant," she told Mrs. Martin proudly. "I guaran-tee that you will never find a better animal doctor for your pet."

"I am beginning to realize that," Mrs. Martin agreed. "I plan on telling all my friends. I belong to an exclusive club with a great many animal owners in its ranks. Once I finish singing your praises, you're going to have more business than you can possibly handle, Dr. Sterling."

"The doctor is already at maximum capacity," Gina said to the woman.

"Then I guess I'm lucky he was able to shoehorn me in," Mrs. Martin said with a gleeful smile. "And I intend to tell all my friends about him so he can pick and choose his clientele."

Gina glanced at Sam. She knew he was loyal to his original patients. She just hoped he wouldn't wear himself out. She knew firsthand that he had trouble turning people away.

"You know," Gina said once Mrs. Martin and Fur-ball had left the clinic, "you might be forced to take on a partner."

"We can handle the extra business," he told her.

"We?" she questioned. "I'm not a veterinarian."

"No, but you're my assistant—and what you don't know, I can certainly train you so that you do," Sam predicted.

That sounded really promising, Gina couldn't help thinking.

Chapter Twenty

Gina found herself looking forward to Sundays a great deal. Sam, his four brothers and his father might not actually be her family, but she was beginning to think of them in that light. If she were given the option of selecting a family from scratch, the Sterlings were definitely the ones she would choose every time.

Except for Sam, she thought.

The feelings she was experiencing for the veterinarian were definitely not platonic. It might be rather premature for her to say, or even think, but she was beginning to believe that she was falling in love with the man.

She had never felt anything even close to this sort of emotion before, just as she had never felt remotely close to being part of a large family before Sam's father and brothers came into her life. This was all completely new to her, but exceedingly welcome.

Gina liked the warm feeling she experienced when she and Sam walked into his father's house and were greeted by his family. She had to admit that growing up she had felt almost like an inconvenience to her mother, like someone who'd gotten in the way of her mother doing something else with her time and her money.

But from the very first moment she met the Sterlings, she had felt welcomed by them.

"Hello, Sam, Gina," his father called out when they walked in. He paused, looking at Gina with an exceptionally bright smile. "You're looking particularly lovely today, my dear."

Sam arched an eyebrow at his father. "Dad, behave yourself," he warned.

"Gina knows I don't mean anything by it, don't you, Gina?" Sanford asked. "I'm assuming you told her that your mother was the only woman for me ever." He glanced between them. "I am really hoping that you two have the good fortune to experience something like that yourselves. Take it from me— there is no better feeling than loving someone as intensely as your mother and I loved one another."

Sanford turned toward the rest of his sons, who were already seated around the dinner table. "That goes for the rest of you as well."

"We know, Dad. Believe me, we know," Sebastian told his father with more than a little feeling.

"I didn't mean to insinuate that you don't," Sanford said. Then, jerking his thumb at Simon, he told Gina, "Simon was in charge of preparing the family dinner today. So, what did you decide to grace us with today?" he asked his son.

"Why don't you wait until I put it on the table for you?" Simon suggested.

"Ah, a surprise," Gina guessed, smiling at the solemn man.

Sean rolled his eyes. "That's what we're all afraid of," he confided to her in a stage whisper accompanied by a broad wink.

Gina felt it was up to her to come to Simon's defense, even if she hadn't sampled what the man was prepared to serve. "That wasn't very nice, Sean."

"Hey," Sean protested. "Simon's my brother. There's no law that says I have to be nice to him," he said to the woman whom he and the rest of his brothers thought of not just as Sam's assistant, but as Sam's girlfriend as well.

"Boys, boys, boys, settle down," Sanford told his sons sternly. "We have company. Remember to behave yourselves, please."

Gina looked a little disappointed. "I would think that by now you wouldn't think of me as company."

"She's right, Dad," Sam said. "Gina's not company anymore. She's morphed into family."

Sanford's face lit up. "Is there something you want to tell us, Sam?" he asked, his voice trailing off hopefully.

Sam shrugged. "Just that she's been here so much, she should think of this as her second home."

Gina silently told her pulse to go back to beating normally. There was no reason for it to speed up to

double time. Yes, she and Sam had made love, glorious love, a number of times now, but that kind of
thing happened between a man and a woman who
clicked. It didn't necessarily mean anything serious
or permanent.

It certainly didn't necessarily mean what she wanted
it to mean.

With effort, Gina pulled her lips back into a smile,
although she had to admit that she was forcing herself to appear happy in front of Sam and the others.
She wanted Sam to believe that she didn't need this
to be anything more than a passing, pleasant experience. She couldn't wait for dinner to be on the table
so that they could get to the business of eating.

When it was finally served, it turned out to be a
tasty rendition of Hungarian goulash. She looked at
Simon with unabashed surprise. "This is very good,"
she told him.

"You sound as if you didn't expect it to be," Simon
observed somewhat defensively.

"You're a divorce lawyer," she pointed out. "Most
lawyers go out to eat a lot. They don't bother preparing things for themselves."

"They do if they're my sons," Sanford told her
proudly. "Eating out can get really expensive. This
way they understand how to save their money for the
important things. Being frugal is the very first lesson I taught each one of my sons. That's something
they're not about to forget and can put to good use."

"And that is a very valuable lesson," Gina agreed.

Sanford smiled at her, feeling extremely satisfied with himself for being instrumental in arranging for Gina and Sam to initially get together. He glanced at Sam and said, "Looks like your assistant gets me."

Gina beamed at the family patriarch. "Thank you. I consider that to be a compliment, coming from you, Mr. Sterling. And yes, I do."

"Bright and polite. What more can a man ask for?" Sanford asked Sam.

Gina grinned. "A lot of things, more than likely, but that would be a good start for a relationship."

Sanford winked at her as if they were sharing a secret. "It would indeed. But please, call me Sanford, not Mr. Sterling," he said, repeating the request he had made the first time they met. He put his hand on top of hers, as if about to share a secret. "My wife would have really liked you," he told her.

He turned toward Sam. Sam had been old enough when Shirley passed to form an opinion about what her reaction would be now to someone like Gina. "What do you think, Sam? Think your mother would have liked Gina?"

Sam inclined his head. "You know, she would have. I think you're right about that, Dad."

"Thank you, Mr. Sterling," Gina said, nodding at Sam's father. "I am exceedingly flattered by your comment."

Sanford slanted a glance toward his oldest son.

Sam looked rather pleased with what Gina had said. He really, *really* wanted to tell Sam that he was the one responsible for Gina being in his life, that he had found Gina and was behind her coming to Sam's clinic. He hadn't been instrumental in having her pet injured, of course, but he was behind her knowing about Sam's services. Sanford had also had a friend of his plant Sam's name and qualifications in Gina's head while she was trying to find a job to her liking. Luckily, she had known about Sam when her dog needed it the most. Funny how things turned out, Sanford thought.

But he knew that he could never say anything. For one thing, because this was working out so well, he wanted to have Maizie suggest another suitable young lady for one of his other sons. He intended to "plant" the appropriate son's name with the appropriate young lady that she provided him. Next up, Sanford thought, would be Simon. His divorce-lawyer son really needed a push in the right direction. Simon had become jaded to the subject of marriage, thanks to what he did for a living.

Once Sam and Gina were all wrapped up, Sanford intended to turn to Maizie again for help finding a match. He would hope that lightning could strike twice.

Out of the corner of his eye, Sanford saw Gina rising from the table. "Are you going somewhere, my dear?" he asked her, curious.

"I thought I'd take care of the dishes," she told him.

She felt good about being instrumental in taking care of cleanup.

"Regardless, Gina, you are to remain seated. Scott, you can take care of the dishes." He saw that his third son was about to protest, but he interrupted him. "Consider it a dry run for next Sunday."

"Dad, I've been doing this forever. I don't need a dry run," Scott protested.

"When you walk through that door, Scott, I would appreciate it if you left that argumentative side of you outside," his father told him seriously.

"Well, that went well," Gina said as she and Sam drove away from the house where he had grown up several hours later.

"If you mean that my father seems pretty taken with you, I totally agree," Sam told her. "Don't forget, until you appeared at our table, the only female who ever took a seat at our dinner table was Randi—and once we were grown, she stopped making regular appearances at Sunday dinner."

"From everything you tell me about her, Randi sounds like a pretty terrific person. Will I ever get to meet her?" Gina asked.

Sam glanced at her, a thoughtful expression on his face. "Would you want to?"

"Oh, very much," she told him enthusiastically. "After all, she helped raise you and your brothers, didn't she?"

Randi had done a great deal more than just raise them, Sam thought. The woman helped forge their paths through childhood and into adulthood. "Yes, she did," Sam told her.

"Well, she sounds like a pretty amazing lady to me," Gina said.

Sam smiled, remembering certain things from his own childhood. "Oh, she really is."

"Then I would really love to meet her," Gina told him.

"Okay, I'll run it by Dad," Sam told her.

Gina settled back in her seat. "You do that."

There was no missing her smile, Sam thought, feeling its effects and definitely enjoying it.

Chapter Twenty-One

After conducting extensive interviews with an aching heart, Sanford had chosen Randi Wayne to be his housekeeper and his sons' nanny because of her maternal and loving nature. While he was not looking for a replacement for his wife, he was searching for someone who could care for his sons and help them through this extremely difficult time.

He didn't come right out and tell Randi that. He wanted to see how she would work out before making her think that he was awarding her the position because of the way she came across.

Randi turned out to be far better than he had even thought she was going to be. And the woman only kept getting better and better with each passing month. To Sanford's relief and delight, he found that Randi actually did seem to love the boys. She went more than the extra mile when it came to them. She devoted herself to the boys, and it was obvious that they loved her for it. Sanford really didn't know what he would have done if he hadn't had her there, picking up his slack, looking over their homework as they got older and doing the hundred and one things that growing boys needed to be done.

Between missing Shirley and working long hours to keep his construction company going and earn a comfortable living for his five boys, Sanford was hardly around. There were times when Randi had to keep her employer in line, subtly of course, in order to avoid any hard feelings between Sanford and his sons.

It wasn't easy, but the kindhearted woman found a way to manage it all. She had always been extremely tactful, and she really did genuinely love her young charges through all the stages of their childhood, up to and including young manhood. Randi made certain that all five of the Sterling brothers were raised with a loving eye monitoring their progress.

Because of the circumstances that they were raised in, Randi made sure that she was always there for the young brothers. She tended to think of all the Sterling men as part of her own extended family, even Sanford, although she would never say anything to the man to make him think that she cared about him— although, in actuality, Randi really did.

So when she heard Sam on the other end of the phone line, Randi was nothing if not extremely surprised.

"Is anything wrong?" she asked, immediately trying to imagine what it might be.

All five of the Sterlings were grown young men now and always very busy with their careers. The last time she had heard from any of them was a few months ago. She knew for a fact that Sunday dinners were still very much a part of their lives, but she never assumed she was invited to attend unless an invitation was actually extended.

"No, nothing's wrong, Randi. I just thought I'd invite you to Sunday dinner this week," Sam told her.

To say she was surprised was putting it mildly. "That's very sweet of you, Sam," Randi told him. "Is there any particular reason why you're inviting me?"

"Maybe I just miss seeing you," Sam answered evasively.

Randi read between the lines. "Uh-huh. Now tell me the real reason you're inviting me to Sunday dinner."

She heard her former charge sigh deeply on the other end. "Well, if you need a reason," Sam told her, as if throwing up his hands in surrender, "I have a new assistant at the clinic."

"You mean you have an assistant at the clinic. If this person was a 'new' assistant, that means you would have had a previous assistant, and we both know that you've never had one before," she said knowingly.

"You really are a stickler for precision, aren't you, Randi?" Sam asked with a laugh.

"That's the only way to be accurate," Randi maintained. "That way, people won't have to wonder if you're being truthful or not."

Sam chuckled. "Ah, same old Randi."

"Hey, watch that 'old' stuff, son," the woman chided.

"And while you're at it, stop dancing around the subject. Be honest with me. Why are you inviting me over for Sunday dinner to meet your assistant? What makes him so special?"

She really hoped her former young charge wasn't attempting to match her up with someone. There was only one person who had won her heart, and she wasn't about to say anything about that. That would be the fastest way to get herself permanently banished from Sanford's table, and that was something she had no desire to do.

"Well, for one thing, he's a she," Sam told Randi, almost laughing.

Randi suppressed a cry of glee. "You're kidding," she exclaimed.

"No, I'm not," Sam told her. "She's a very nice person, and she wants to meet the woman who helped raise my brothers and me."

This was just getting better and better, Randi thought. "You told her about me?"

"The subject came up of who helped raise me after my mother died," Sam told her. "I wanted Gina to appreciate what a really wonderful person you are."

"Gina," Randi repeated. "Is she as pretty as her name?"

There was no point playing coy, Sam thought. If she came to Sunday dinner, Randi would be able to judge Gina's appearance for herself. "She is. So, will you come?"

Randi laughed under her breath. "You would have to tie me up and toss me into a closet to keep me from coming, boy," she said.

Sam laughed softly at the idea. "Nope, not planning on doing that."

"Good. Because being with you boys taught me a few things about how to get out of tight spots," Randi informed the young man she'd had the pleasure of watching grow into a vibrant adult.

"All right, I consider myself forewarned. So, should I tell Dad that you're going to be there this Sunday?" Sam asked.

"Absolutely," she told him with enthusiasm. "Shall I bring dessert?"

"No need," Sam told her. "Just having you there fulfills the requirement for something sweet."

Randi chuckled. "This Gina has certainly managed to change you."

"How so?" he asked.

"I don't remember you talking like that the last time we all got together. Is dinner the same time as always?" she asked, just in case things had changed.

"Same time," Sam assured her.

"I'll be there with bells on," she promised him.

"I'll let the others know that you're coming," Sam told her. "They'll all be happy to hear you'll be there for Sunday dinner. We've all missed you, Randi."

"And I've missed you. All of you," Randi said with emphasis. "See you Sunday."

* * *

Sam lost no time calling his father to let him know that Randi would be coming to dinner, along with Gina. He had planned to leave a message but was surprised to hear the line being picked up.

"Guess who's coming to dinner this Sunday, Dad," Sam said, getting over his surprise. His father hardly *ever* answered the phone.

"Tell me or don't tell me. I really don't have any time for games today, Sam," Sanford said, stopping short of being curt.

Sam took that to be his cue. "Randi is coming."

Like Randi, Sanford must have thought that her coming by had to mean that there was something wrong. "Anything wrong, Sam?"

"No, nothing's wrong. We just haven't seen her at the dinner table for a while. So I asked her to come by." Sam paused, then added, "Gina said she wanted to meet her, and I thought Sunday dinner would be the best setting."

"Gina *asked* to meet Randi?" Sanford asked, surprised.

"It was her idea," Sam told him. And then, just in case his father had some objection, he asked, "It is okay, isn't it?"

Sanford was glad there was no way Sam could see him; he was grinning so hard over the news, Sam would have known something was up. "Absolutely," Sanford assured his son. "I'd be curious to hear what

Gina has to say about the woman who devoted so much of her life to bringing you boys up right."

He heard Sam laughing to himself. "You, too, huh, Dad?"

"Well, this is the first young woman you've ever invited to the house for Sunday dinner—or anything else," his father pointed out. "That does make a difference, Sam."

"Don't make a big deal out of it, Dad," Sam told him uncomfortably.

"Not me," Sanford said innocently, as he hung up. "I'm not making a big deal out of anything."

And now, Sanford thought, the young woman had expressed an interest in meeting the nanny who'd helped raise all five of his sons. That spoke volumes. Gina was apparently becoming more entrenched in their day-to-day lives. This was a very good thing, and he intended to encourage that as subtly as he could, Sanford promised himself.

He glanced heavenward. "I really do miss you, Shirley. I think you would wholeheartedly approve of Gina," he said softly, his eyes misting over. "These last few years have really been a lonely struggle without you. Thank you for sending Randi my way to help out with the boys. I know that was your doing. There could be no other explanation for it. I know you've been right here beside me, guiding my every step when it comes to the boys, and I really do appreciate that," he whispered.

"Who are you talking to, Dad?" Sean asked, coming into the trailer that served as a mobile office on their current job site.

Sanford gave his youngest son a look meant to silence him.

Sean nodded as if the answer to his question suddenly occurred to him. "Oh."

"What do you mean, 'oh'?" Sanford asked, becoming defensive.

Sean smiled at him. "I realized you were talking to Mom."

"What would you know about it?" Sanford asked.

"You have a habit of talking to Mom when you have something on your mind," Sean said, and then he smiled. "I do pay attention, Dad."

"All right. Now try paying attention to the job," Sanford said, pointing toward the door.

"I do, Dad. Trust me, I do. I wouldn't want to incur your wrath by dropping the ball."

Sanford looked at him, perplexed. "Incur my wrath? Where do you get this stuff?"

Sean merely smiled. "I already told you, Dad. I pay attention to what's going on."

Sanford shook his head and murmured a few choice words under his breath as he went to walk around the worksite.

Chapter Twenty-Two

Sam noticed that Gina was acting somewhat nervous as they drove to his father's house the following Sunday afternoon. At first, he thought maybe he was imagining it. After all, she had taken on the position of being his assistant at the clinic without any difficulty whatsoever. Doing new things just seemed to come naturally for her. And she was the one who had asked him to arrange for her to meet Randi. Why, then, did she suddenly seem so nervous about this meeting? Had he missed something?

Rather than wait for Gina to say anything, he decided to come right out and ask her. "This might just be my imagination, but are you all right?"

She looked at him like she had her hand caught in a cookie jar. "Why do you ask?"

"You seem to be acting rather nervous," he told her.

Gina let out a long breath. She was being ridiculous, and she knew it, but she just couldn't help it. She really wanted this to go well. "Do you have any advice about what to say or not say when I meet your former nanny?" she asked him.

Coming to a stoplight, Sam glanced in Gina's direction. The question she asked didn't sound like her. "Are you nervous about meeting Randi?" he asked in disbelief.

"No," Gina denied a little too quickly. Then, in the next breath, she amended, "Yes," only to arrive at her ultimate reply, "Maybe."

That didn't make any sense to Sam. He was accustomed to Gina being bold and just forging ahead. Why was she waffling this way? This just wasn't like her. His assistant was an extremely strong person.

"For heaven's sake, why?" Sam asked. "You were the one who asked to meet her."

"I know, I know." Embarrassed, Gina shrugged. "You told me that Randi was and still is a very important person in your life. I just thought I should meet the woman who played such an instrumental part in raising you and your brothers."

"Well, she did," he agreed. "But that doesn't seem to be a reason for you to be so nervous about meeting her."

Before Gina could think twice about it, the answer came out: "Because I really want her to like me."

He glanced at Gina, not quite believing what he was hearing. Was this confident young woman afraid that his former nanny wouldn't like her? Why? "Don't worry," Sam assured the woman whom he had up until now thought of as the personification of confidence. "I guarantee that Randi will like you."

"You don't know that," Gina contended.

"Of course I do," Sam countered with feeling. "I know Randi. She is a sweet, loving woman who has great intuition about things that matter. That's why Dad picked her to be the one who helped raise us." He grew quiet for a moment. Then Sam confided, "I suspect that Randi reminded him a lot of my mother."

Gina was still concerned about the way this first meeting between her and Randi would go. "But what if she *doesn't* like me?"

Sam sincerely doubted there was any danger of that, but saying that most likely wouldn't reassure the woman he found himself falling in love with. So he went with the most logical response to her concerns.

"I could see how that might bother you, but in the grand scheme of things, that really doesn't matter," he said firmly. "Look, my father likes you, my brothers like you, and what matters most of all here, *I* like you. Is that good enough for you?" he asked, looking in her direction again.

Gina couldn't believe they had gotten so serious so quickly, but they had. This wasn't just some hypothetical conversation they were having, she thought. It seemed to her like it was a dead serious one. Some things, of course, were still left unspoken, but she had a feeling they would come to the surface eventually. At least, she could cross her fingers and sincerely hope so.

She gave Sam a fleeting smile. "Of course."

Sam slanted a quick look at her. "I'm not sure I believe you. But for now, I'll pretend that I do."

"Well, I'll take whatever I can get," she answered. "And as for why this is important to me, I always do better if I feel like I'm in a friendly situation where I'm not the object of angry looks."

Sam pulled his vehicle alongside one of his brothers' cars. It looked to him as if everyone was already there. He needed to learn how to arrive earlier, he thought, instead of being the last one in the door.

"Looks like we get to make a grand entrance," he told Gina, turning off the engine.

Now that they were finally here, she could feel her nerves going into double time. Gina frowned slightly, looking at the other vehicles in front of the two-storied house. "Not exactly what I was hoping for," she admitted.

"Well," he told her, "we can turn around and go back to the clinic." Sam looked at her face, trying to gauge what she was thinking.

Gina stared at him as if he had just lost his mind. "No, we can't," she protested. As nervous as she was, she wanted to meet this woman. It was a hurdle that would only grow higher the more she put it off.

"Sure we can," he countered. "We can do anything we want to."

Gina looked at him as if he was just paying lip service to an uncomfortable situation. "No, we can't," she repeated. "I asked you to invite your nanny to Sunday dinner so I could finally get to meet her."

But he was ready to slip out if that made her feel better. He just wanted her to know that he was in her corner. "I won't say anything if you don't," Sam told her.

Her brow furrowed. "You're serious," she said in surprise.

Sam's eyes lightly washed over her. She felt as if they were caressing her. He drew closer to her until they were only inches apart. "Very," he whispered.

The word seemed to ripple along her skin, warming her to the point that she felt she needed to fan herself. "I'll accept that," she told him, attempting to regulate her pulse.

"Sure you want to go in?" Sam asked.

He was not making this easy for her, she thought. "I am utterly sure that I want to go in," Gina answered, squaring her shoulders.

Sam presented his arm to her. "Then let's do this."

"Happily," she answered. Her heart slammed against her rib cage as Sam opened the front door and ushered her in front of him.

"So what is she like?" Randi was asking Sanford. "Is she a nice person?"

Instead of answering himself, he looked toward his sons. "You guys want to take that one?" he asked.

As the youngest, Sean felt it was up to him to answer. "You are going to really love her, Randi. She
actually talked Sam into making her his assistant at
the clinic, and you know how long he held off doing
that. She puts in long hours helping him take care
of the animals, and when there are no patients, she's
busy digitizing all the files."

Meanwhile, Sam was leaning his head in toward
Gina so she could hear what he was telling her as
they came into the house. "Breathe, Gina, breathe,"
he whispered to her. Her face was slightly flushed.
Up until now, he'd had no idea that meeting Randi
meant so much to her. He felt touched and concerned
at the same time.

"I am breathing," Gina protested as she watched
six pairs of eyes turn in her direction.

His father and brothers were, as usual, all here
ahead of Sam. And there was one rather attractive-
looking woman seated at the center of the table, smiling at them as they entered. This had to be Randi,
the woman who'd helped raise all five of the Sterling brothers. Gina held her breath as her eyes met
the woman's.

At that moment, Randi got up and came toward
her, hands held out to the first young woman who
had ever come to their table. The man she had spent
these last twenty years working for had told her all
about how his oldest son had taken to this young
woman. According to Sanford, Gina had made an

"unexpected" appearance at the clinic in the middle of the night with her injured dog, and Sam, being the dedicated veterinarian that he was, had immediately brought the miniature collie into his clinic and sewn up her wounds. In apparent gratitude, the young woman had volunteered her services and offered to work for Sam, organizing his files or whatever else needed doing to get the clinic running smoothly.

Randi found herself liking the young woman immediately. Her eyes crinkled as she took Gina's hands in hers. "Hello. I've heard very good things about you," she said.

"And I you," Gina responded, relieved at the display of friendship. "Sam told me all about how you helped raise him and his brothers. And how much you helped him study for his exams when he decided to become a veterinarian."

Genuine warmth emanated from the former nanny, creating an exceedingly good feeling within Gina. The brothers might have been deprived of their mother during their formative years, and that was an awful thing, but it seemed to Gina that this woman had done whatever she could to help make up for the tragic loss. The fact that all five brothers had gone on to college and done well in their chosen fields was a testament to how much Randi had cared for them, even when they had all gone on to earn different degrees in different fields.

Randi waved her hand, dismissing the praise. "Sam was a self-starter. Actually, all the boys were," she told Gina. "I did what I could to help set them on the right path, but they did most of the work." She smiled, remembering those years. "It was quite an education for me as well." She looked around the table, getting down to business. "Who made dinner today?"

Scott raised his hand. "That would be me, Randi. But I didn't do the dessert."

Randi looked as if she was about to head over to the kitchen counter immediately. "I can whip up a batch of chocolate chip cookies, provided I can find all the ingredients." She had enjoyed baking for years.

"No need, Randi," Sam told her. "Gina wanted to make a batch of her killer cookies to show you her gratitude for coming to Sunday dinner so she could meet you."

"Her gratitude?" Randi echoed in disbelief. "I have been waiting for an invitation to meet this young woman. If I hadn't received one soon, I would have forgotten about being polite and happily crashed this little Sunday tradition of yours." She looked at the faces around the table, her face softening. "I have really missed you boys—and now I will have someone new to miss the next time you all forget to invite me on a regular basis."

Gina flashed a smile at the older woman. "I'll be sure to remind them," she told Randi.

Sam smiled to himself. The two most important women in his life were bonding—and he, for one, was absolutely thrilled about it.

Chapter Twenty-Three

"I like her," Randi told Sam.

Sam nodded, pleased to hear his former nanny's assessment of the woman who had effortlessly captured his heart. Dinner was over, and Randi and Sam were cleaning up the kitchen at Randi's insistence because she wanted to have a word with him. "I'll be sure to tell her, Randi. I know that Gina will be very pleased," he assured the woman he regarded so highly.

"Never mind me, Sam," Randi told him. "Whether or not I like her is beside the point. That girl needs to hear those words coming from you—that *you* like her," she emphasized.

"Oh, I think she already knows that," he said casually.

"Because you told her?" Randi asked, watching Sam's face to get some sort of confirmation on the matter.

"I don't have to," Sam insisted. "Gina's pretty good like that. She just intuits things."

Randi sighed as she rolled her eyes. "Oh, Samuel, Samuel, Samuel, I raised you better than that. Some things you just cannot take for granted, no matter how much easier it is to go that route. Women need to *hear* those comforting words, boy. As do men," Randi added pointedly. "This is not just a one-way street. You're a smart guy. I would have expected you to know that."

Sam shrugged as he continued to wash dishes. "I've been a little busy running the clinic."

"Which, according to my sources, Gina has been helping you with," Randi said.

His mouth curved. "It looks like you're more caught up with my life than I am," Sam said.

"I make a point of keeping up on the lives of the people I care about," Randi told him.

"Who's your source?" he asked her point-blank.

Randi laughed as she set aside the last dish she had dried. "Oh, no, that stays with me, Samuel," she said. "Am I right? You haven't told that young woman how you feel? I can see it, right there in your eyes."

"Well, if it's right there in my eyes, then I don't have to say anything, do I?" he asked, amused.

"You know better than that," Randi told him. "Those particular words are always nice to hear. C'mon, boy," she urged. "I never thought of you as being a coward."

The accusation took him aback. "I am not a coward," he protested.

"Then what's stopping you from telling that girl what you just admitted to me?" she asked.

"What if she doesn't feel the same way?" he asked.

He would have hated to bare his soul and then just be pushed away.

"Oh, come on, boy," Randi said, waving away his fears. "That young woman definitely feels the same way about you as you do about her."

Gina chose that moment to come into the kitchen and quickly looked from Sam to Randi. "Are you two still washing dishes?" she asked, surprised. "Even if you were doing them in slow motion, you should have been finished by now."

Randi chuckled. "Like I said, Samuel, this young woman is very likable." As she made her way around her former charge, she whispered in his ear, "It took you long enough, but when you finally got around to picking someone, you certainly made the right choice." She patted his arm in approval.

Turning toward Gina, Randi said, "It's been a pleasure, dear, and one I hope will be repeated. Very happy to meet you."

Gina waited until the woman left the room and then looked toward Sam. "What was that all about?"

"That was Randi giving you her seal of approval," Sam explained.

"She's too sweet to do anything short of that," Gina commented. "Your dad picked a really nice woman to take care of you guys."

"There is no arguing with that," he agreed. He hung up the towel Randi had been using. "Well, the kitchen's all cleaned up. What do you think of us hitting the road and going back home?" he asked. "I'd say that right about now, Rocky and Charlotte are really beginning to miss us."

Gina nodded. "You're probably right. Heaven knows that I certainly miss them. I can be ready to leave in a few minutes. Just let me make the rounds and say my goodbyes."

"I really appreciate that," he said suddenly. "As do my brothers and my dad," Sam threw in, just in case the woman who had won his heart hadn't realized that.

The smile she gave him was positively blinding.

"Someone famous once said *always leave them wanting more*," Gina told him brightly. "So this might be a good time to go."

Randi was just about to go home herself, but she paused long enough to give Gina a warm, heartfelt hug in parting. "Lovely finally meeting you, my dear. I hope this is the beginning of a long, wonderful tradition," Randi told her with enthusiasm. Releasing her, Randi added, "Soon," making it sound like a promise.

Gina glanced toward Sam's father. "I certainly hope so," she replied, looking from Sanford back to Randi. Her meaning was extremely clear.

For a moment, Randi remained standing beside the man she had worked for all these long years. She eyed Sanford. "That is one very lovely young girl," she told him with feeling.

"Careful, Randi," Sanford warned. "Your age is

showing. Sam's new assistant isn't a girl. She's a young woman."

Randi laughed softly to herself. "Since when did you get to be such an expert on proper terms?"

"I pay attention," Sanford told her with a touch of indignation.

Randi's smile only grew wider. "If you say so, Mr. Sterling."

"Why? Don't you think I pay attention?" he asked her.

Randi feigned surprise, placing her hand on her chest. "Me? Of course I think you pay attention. I never said anything to the contrary, Mr. Sterling." It was hard to keep her smile from completely taking over.

Sanford gave her a knowing look. "Uh-huh. You would be more convincing if you weren't grinning so hard, Randi."

Randi winked at the man she still thought of in fond terms. "I'll work on it, Mr. Sterling."

"You know, I think it might be high time for you to refer to me as Sanford, or at least stop referring to me as Mr. Sterling," Sanford told her.

"I'd be happy to comply." She glanced toward the front door.

Without a family of her own, and after all the years she spent raising them, Randi had a real tendency to think of the Sterling boys as her own sons. In truth, the five young men represented the family she had never been blessed with in real life. Her eyes swept lovingly over the ones who hadn't left yet for their own homes this evening: Sean, Scott and, of course, Sam.

She placed her hand on Sam's shoulder the way she used to when he was a little boy. It had been her way of holding him to something he had said.

"Until next week, then?" she asked him, searching his face for confirmation.

Sam smiled and nodded. "Until next week, Randi." He made the words sound more like a promise than just a throwaway remark.

Gina leaned in and echoed, "Until next week."

She could take it for granted that she herself would be invited back to sit at the large family dinner table. It felt nice, she thought, to feel as if she belonged to something after all these years of *not* belonging to anything. This had been a long time in coming, but she had finally achieved that dream, and her insides felt as if they were doing cartwheels and cheering all the way.

Inspired, Gina squeezed both Randi's and Sanford's hands and then leaned in to brush a kiss on each of their cheeks.

The only time she had ever felt happier was after she made love with Sam. But this, Gina thought, was an extremely close second.

Chapter Twenty-Four

They had put in another grueling day at the clinic. This was on top of several days just like it when they worked practically from dawn to dusk. Of course, that was broken up with making love, sometimes late in the evening, sometimes in the wee hours of the morning. Looking forward to those moments was what kept them going.

They took turns staying at each other's homes, although for the most part, they stayed at Sam's because of its proximity to the clinic. That and the fact that they both wanted to be near the animals kept at the clinic overnight.

Through it all, neither Sam nor Gina could remember ever being happier.

"So, things seem to be going pretty well between you and Gina," Simon noted one Sunday, taking his older brother aside after dinner.

Sam had been clearing up dinner with Gina, but she had temporarily stepped away from the kitchen. Simon had seen it as his opportunity to talk to Sam alone.

Sam braced himself, thinking that he was about to get a lecture from the divorce lawyer about getting into something that could have dire consequences. He tried to keep his response civil. "No offense, Simon, but I'm just not in the mood for a lawyer lecture right now."

Simon's eyebrows drew together in a dark line over the bridge of his nose. "Who said anything about giving you a lecture?"

"Isn't that why you waited until I was alone to talk to me?" Sam asked.

"You have a very suspicious mind, big brother." Simon laughed shortly. "I might have said that I'm soured on the subject of marriage, but I wasn't looking to set an example for the rest of you—especially when you seem to have found the only woman who has a heart of gold and shares your love of animals."

Sam looked at his brother, curious. "What makes you think Gina has a heart of gold?"

Simon laughed, waving his hand at Sam. "Hey, I have eyes. I get paid for having sound judgment and observing things."

Where was this leading? Sam wondered. "And?"

"And Gina seems like a terrific person who came into your life even though the rest of us could definitely have used that sunshine that she's spreading."

"And I can't?" Sam questioned.

"I never said that," Simon pointed out. "I just wanted you to know exactly what you have here." Then, in case there was any question on Sam's part, Simon made his position crystal clear. "Gina is a very rare, special young woman, and if you don't get your act together and ask her to marry you, I predict that you're running the very real risk of losing her."

Sam's attention was riveted on Simon now. "Why? What have you heard?"

"Nothing specific. I just have great intuition," Simon casually declared.

Sam couldn't believe what he was hearing, especially not from Simon. "So you're advising me to propose to her?"

Simon didn't answer immediately. Instead, he asked, "Do you love her?"

Sam thought on the matter before finally saying, "Yes."

"Then what the hell are you waiting for?" Simon asked.

Sam shook his head in wonder. "You know, I never thought I'd be hearing this coming from you."

"Yeah, well, I never thought I'd be the one saying it, either." Simon's lips pulled back in a smile. "But I am. I think that our brothers are all half in love with her as well, so if I were you, I'd snap her up before one of the others decides to sweep her off her feet while you're dawdling around."

Out of the corner of his eye, Sam saw movement near the doorway. He instinctively knew it was Gina, so he was smiling broadly by the time he turned toward her. "Have you been there long?"

"Long enough," she answered, her eyes smiling at Sam.

Simon pulled back his shoulders. "I guess this is my cue to leave," the lawyer announced. He paused for a moment. "If you find that you ever want to move on from this guy, I've got files that need to be reorganized. You know where to find me," he told Gina, then left the kitchen.

"I guess you made a really good impression on my brothers," Sam said, replaying in his head what Simon had told him. "But then, I would have expected nothing less—from you and from them."

Gina looked at him uncertainly. "Are you trying to get rid of me?"

How had she managed to get that out of what he'd just said? "Are you serious?" he asked in disbelief.

"Well…" Her voice trailed off as she shrugged.

"There's no way I'm trying to get rid of you," he assured her. "As a matter of fact, I'm trying to find a way to ask you the most important question of my life."

And possibly of my life as well, Gina thought. Out loud, she told him, "I'm listening."

He took a deep breath, feeling like the air had gotten stuck in his throat. He had never had trouble verbalizing his thoughts before, but right now, they were all jumbled in his head.

She couldn't put up with watching him suffer through

this—which was why, before Sam could put words to his thoughts, she told him, "Yes."

"Yes?" he asked, slightly confused. Was she saying what he thought she was, or was that just wishful thinking on his part?

Gina smiled widely and repeated her answer. "Yes."

Afraid of getting carried away, he wanted to be sure that they were both clear about this. "Just what are you saying yes to?" he asked.

"I am saying yes to the phrase that is apparently stuck in your throat," Gina said. And then she took a deep breath, plunging in feetfirst, praying she hadn't just made a really huge mistake. "You are asking me to marry you, right?"

The look of total relief on Sam's face was impossible to miss. "Yes," he told her, "I am asking you to marry me."

"Then for heaven's sake, do it," Gina urged him. "Say the words." Then, if there was any confusion as to what she was telling him, she said, "Ask me to marry you."

Every woman deserved to hear those words, he thought, if that was what she wanted. So, taking a deep breath, Sam plunged in.

"Gina, will you make me the happiest man on the face of the earth and say yes? Say that you will marry me?" he asked his assistant, making it official. And then he added, "Bearing in mind that if you turn me down, you will not just be breaking my heart, but the hearts of all my brothers as well as my father's and the woman who raised me."

Gina laughed, shaking her head. "No pressure there."

"Nope," he agreed. "None." His eyes crinkled as he looked at her, impatient to hear the words. "Well?"

Gina look in a long breath, her eyes meeting his.

"Hey," Sean called out, coming into the kitchen. "You guys washing the dishes or forging new ones?" He looked from Sam to Gina, his eyebrows raised quizzically.

Sam frowned at him. "You know, your timing couldn't have been worse."

It took Sean a couple of moments to untangle that. Then suddenly light dawned on his face. "Oh, I'm sorry. I can leave." He turned on his heel, ready to make his way out of the room again.

"No need," Gina quickly assured him. "We're almost finished cleaning up here."

Sean looked a little uncertain, glancing from his brother to the first woman besides their nanny to be invited to Sunday dinner. "Is that all I interrupted?" he asked suspiciously.

Sam slanted a look at Gina. Maybe she wanted to take this time as a reprieve. Maybe she really didn't want him asking her to marry him. He had been so focused on making her his wife that he hadn't thought the idea might not appeal to her to the same degree it did him.

Things felt as if they were stuck in a holding pattern, and he desperately wanted to get them moving again. "Gina, could I talk to you?" he asked her.

She glanced toward Sean. "You don't want to be rude to your brother."

Sam laughed. "Sean has a skin that's tough as a rhino's," he told her. "He wouldn't know rude if he tripped over it."

"See what I have to put up with?" Sean asked Gina. "I'd be very careful if I were you. You're hooking your star to a man who is as kindly as a splinter."

Sam's eyebrows drew together. "She doesn't need to hear that from you."

"Well, she needs to hear it from someone," Sean pointed out.

Both brothers turned almost in unison toward Gina, who laughed.

"Something funny?" Sam asked.

"You guys are. I never had a close family," she said for the umpteenth time. "And I am really enjoying the way you all play off one another."

Sam breathed a sigh of relief. He had allowed his fears to temporarily paralyze him and keep him from moving on. Maybe because he wanted her so badly that he was fearful of losing her.

Sam made up his mind right then and there.

He needed to subtly feel her out in order to make sure that Gina was up to this, that all her talk about sharing things with a family was something she truly wanted. Once he was sure of that, then he would proceed with a proposal next Sunday in front of everyone. If anything would make her feel part of the family, it would be that.

The moment he made his decision, he knew it was the way to go.

Chapter Twenty-Five

Sam had never felt this nervous before. Not even when he took his exam to get certified for his veterinarian license. He had been very confident about that, he recalled. But the stakes were higher now, and he wasn't confident any longer. He felt a little like a trapeze artist about to take a flying leap without a net beneath him.

Sam had a feeling that Gina wouldn't exactly take kindly to the description, but butterflies were practically dive-bombing all throughout his stomach. He could honestly say his stomach felt tied up in proverbial knots.

Hell, this wasn't like him. He had treated animals that could by no stretch of the imagination be called friendly.

What if she turned him down? Wouldn't this be easier for him to do if he were more confident of her mindset? He rubbed his damp hands against his jeans to no avail.

It would have been wiser if he did this in private, without an audience.

Wiser, maybe, but definitely more cowardly. Since this was the first proposal to happen within their family since his parents, he knew it had to be special. He had to put his best foot forward. And that involved asking Gina to marry him in front of everyone at the Sunday dinner table.

Of course, he was hoping that she would say yes. Hoping, but since he was a realist, he wasn't counting on it—at least, not 100 percent. He vacillated over that outcome. When she was in his arms, and they were in bed, he felt confident that she would say yes. But once they were in the clinic, going about the life that they were so dedicated to, his confidence was not quite as strong about the answer that awaited him.

He just needed to ask, to pop the question and roll with the answer. All he could do was pray she would take pity on him and say yes.

Why wouldn't she say yes? Their relationship wasn't all in his head, he silently argued with himself as they drove to his father's house the following Sunday. He didn't have that good of an imagination.

Gina turned toward him. A question had been nagging at her for the last week, and she finally decided to put it into words. "Are you all right?" she asked Sam.

"Yes," he answered. His curiosity got the better of him. "Why do you ask?"

Sam was the first man she had given her heart to.

Her heart as well as her body, she thought ruefully, and she had no idea what to expect. Was he growing leery or withdrawing from her? Maybe this was what the end looked like, she thought, and she was just too naive to realize it. Their working relationship would be an added complication. Maybe Sam didn't want to say anything because he was afraid she would quit the clinic. Never mind that this was her ideal job. What she was experiencing with Sam just raised that to new heights.

She felt as if she had just built a house of cards and a windstorm was on its way.

She realized that Sam was waiting for her to tell him why she had asked if there was anything wrong.

"Well, for the last few days, you've been tossing and turning in bed instead of sleeping," she pointed out. "That usually happens when a person has something on their mind." She pressed her lips together. "I'm not trying to pry. But if there's something wrong, I just want to help."

You can, he thought. *You can say yes.* But Sam knew that was a dangerous way to go if he didn't immediately elaborate. Instead, he told her, "I appreciate that," and hoped that would satisfy her for the time being.

But it didn't.

"I didn't say that so you would appreciate it. I meant what I said. I want to help you," she insisted.

"In order to do that, you have to tell me what's bothering you."

Sitting up straight in the driver's seat and keeping his face forward, Sam kept his expression from registering anything, afraid she could read something in it. He shrugged and went with the ever-popular "It's complicated."

"I assumed that. If it wasn't complicated, you would have said something about it already," she told him. "Either that, or you would have just handled it yourself."

He sighed. Part of him wanted to blurt out the proposal right here and now. But he had already run this by his father, and his family was expecting him to propose to Gina in front of all of them. He definitely didn't want to disappoint them or come off like a coward in front of all his younger brothers.

Sam blew out a breath. "It's nothing for you to worry about."

Gina felt an overwhelming sadness wash over her. He was blocking her out. And here she had believed that they were a team. *Looks like I was wrong*, Gina thought. Maybe she wasn't as integral a part of his team as she had thought.

"All right," she declared gamely, going along with him. "If you don't want to share, you don't want to share. Either way, we need to get ready to open up the clinic. Your first patient is coming in at seven."

Well, that hadn't gone well, Sam thought. He couldn't wait until this was completely behind him—provided he heard the answer he was hoping to hear. Watching this play out in front of him in slow motion was all but killing him.

When Sam and Gina walked into the Sterling house several hours later, Sanford immediately gravitated to his oldest son. One look at Sam's face told him that the secret was still a secret.

"You look like you've seen a ghost, son," Sanford commented.

"Yeah, I've seen more color in a bottle of milk," Sean told his brother. "You feeling okay?"

"That's what I asked him," Gina told them.

"I take it he wasn't exactly forthcoming," Simon guessed.

"The dogs at the clinic are more talkative," Gina said. "We checked on them just before we came here."

Randi chuckled as she came in from the kitchen, drying her hands. "So he has you talking to the animals, too. Knew it would just be a matter of time before he indoctrinated you. In my opinion, you two are very suited for one another."

Then she seemed to notice the way Sam and his father looked at her. "What? Am I wrong?" she asked.

Sanford shook his head. "No, just sometimes, Randi, you talk a little too much."

Randi laughed, shaking her head. "That's to make

up for the fact that you guys don't talk at all. Think of me as a counterbalance to all your tight-lipped behavior."

Gina turned toward Sam, her eyebrows drawing together. "Why are they talking in code like that?" she asked.

He had his doubts that anyone was fooling Gina. She was exceptionally bright and able to catch on to any situation rather quickly. Still, he felt it was time to be completely honest with her. "Because they've never been part of a real live proposal before."

Gina looked at Sam, her heart slamming against her chest. Telling herself to be calm and not jump to any conclusions, she said, "Oh? Then I suggest you get on with it."

Sam squared his shoulders, ready to plunge right into this. Apparently, Gina knew more about what was going on than he gave her credit for. It figured. He had spent more time worrying about the way this would come off than he had actually spent wording the proposal.

His hand felt clammy as he reached into his pocket. The ring box was beginning to feel rather heavy, and for a moment, he had some difficulty pulling the small black velvet box out of the recesses of his pants. Pulling hard, he managed to extract it from where it was wedged.

Sam felt as if his insides were actually trembling. At the last moment, he remembered the form he needed to hit and dropped down to one knee. He pushed open the small box, and the diamond ring caught the light, sending a rainbow twinkling and dancing around for the entire audience looking on.

All around him, his brothers were smiling and poking one another. Sam drew in a long breath, then began to tell her what was in his heart.

"Gina, my whole world changed when you came into it. And now I can't imagine life without you there or without you in the clinic," he confessed. What he was saying might not be as romantic as it could have been, but he was telling her what he felt. "Will you make me the happiest of men and say that you'll be my wife?"

Gina stared at him. Everything felt incredibly numb inside of her. "You're serious?" she finally asked, her mouth so dry that her lips were all but sticking together.

"I've never been more serious in my life," Sam told the woman he had first met banging on his door in the middle of the night.

"Oh, come on. Put the poor guy out of his misery already," Sebastian urged.

"Hey, I don't believe in the sacred institution, and even I'm thinking that you were made for one another," Simon told the couple, smiling from Sam to Gina.

Gina dropped to her knees right in front of Sam, putting out her hand so that he could slip the ring onto the proper finger. Trying to keep from trembling, she held her breath, waiting.

Sanford couldn't begin to say how happy he was watching this unfold in front of him. He had picked this woman as the right one for his son, and he was glorying in what he had set in motion. But he kept his enthusiasm to himself, waiting for Sam to make it official.

"Give him an answer, dear," Randi prompted Gina. "Put the sweet boy out of his misery."

"What if her answer just pushes him further into his misery?" Sebastian asked.

Gina waved her hand at the men about to become her brothers-in-law. "No offense, guys, but I don't need a Greek chorus behind either one of us telling us what to say."

"That's right, dear. This is all up to you," Randi said. "Give him his answer, because I am dying to hug you."

Gina's smile all but took over her entire face. "Gladly." Still on her knees, she looked at the man who had brought such changes into her life. "Yes, Sam."

"Yes, what?" Sam asked, wanting it all to be perfectly clear, not just to her, but to the rest of his family as well.

"Yes, I will marry you," Gina told him.

The rest of her words were drowned out by the cheers of congratulations that erupted in the room.

Dinner, at least for the time being, was all but forgotten.

Sanford went and retrieved the bottle of champagne he had been saving in anticipation just for this day.

One down, Sanford thought, *four to go*.

* * * * *

Her Fake Boyfriend
Heatherly Bell

MILLS & BOON

Bestselling author **Heatherly Bell** was born in Tuscaloosa, Alabama, but lost her accent by the time she was two. After leaving Alabama, Heatherly lived with her family in Puerto Rico and Maryland before being transplanted kicking and screaming to the California Bay Area. She now loves it here, she swears. Except the traffic.

Visit the Author Profile page
at millsandboon.com.au for more titles.

Dear Reader,

Welcome back to the bucolic gulf coastal town of Charming, Texas. I love it here!

We first met Finn Sheridan and Michelle LaCroix in *Once Upon a Charming Bookshop*. You've heard of opposites attract, and in this case Michelle is a family law attorney and Finn is a divorced man who didn't enjoy the process. It may seem they have a fundamentally different view of the world, but Finn and Michelle are actually two people who are very much alike. While Michelle is a sharp attorney on the path to partner, Finn has slowed his roll after his dedication to a sport won him Olympic gold.

Both are overachievers at heart who believe in hard work and sacrifice. When they're thrown together in a fake relationship that will benefit them both, plenty of fun and shenanigans ensue. Oh yes, also, they fall in love. For real. In the process of getting to know each other and falling in love, both learn love isn't something you achieve. It's something that happens to the luckiest of people who open their hearts and minds wide enough to allow love inside.

I love to hear from you. Contact me at heatherly@heatherlybell.com.

Heatherly Bell

DEDICATION

This dedication is for my Michelle. I still think of you.

Chapter One

"Hey, isn't that your *girlfriend*?" Noah Cavill said.

Finn Sheridan looked up from scrubbing the floor of their catamaran. He saw Abby a few feet away down the dock in a clinch with an unfamiliar man.

"Yep, that's Abby."

He recognized the tight jeans, the long blonde hair. She was definitely his type. Beautiful, carefree and fun. Never worked *too* hard but just enough to be responsible. She knew how to unwind and relax. And she'd been exactly what he'd needed at the time.

"Hey, I'm sorry." Noah threw aside the rag he'd been using to polish the guardrail. "If I caught Twyla with some other guy like that, I'd have to kill the dude."

Finn chuckled. "I should have clarified. Abby's my *ex-girlfriend*. And she can do whatever she likes. I'm not going to *kill* anyone."

"Wait. What? Since when is she your ex-girlfriend? Just last week you two were at the house with me and Twyla, watching the game. You looked…happy."

"I was happy. It was a good game." Finn shrugged.

"I'm not talking about the game! I mean you and Abby. Weren't you into her? She seemed to really be vibing with you."

"Yeah, she was great. She is great."

"Then I don't understand." Noah froze as if he'd just re-membered he left the oven on or had another thought that disturbed him. "You're kidding me."

"When I'm kidding you, you'll know." Finn straightened, sliding his hands down his board shorts.

Life as part owner of Nacho Boat might sound glamor-ous to some, but the truth was far from it. Sure, he got to be on the water every day, but he also had to clear and clean the deck after taking a group of men fishing for marlin. Still, the work was exactly what he'd wanted and came at a good time when Noah suggested that Finn invest in the business alongside him. A few months ago, he'd bought Nacho Boat Adventures from the previous owner and al-ready had plans to expand. Like Finn, his oldest friend Noah was no stranger to boating.

For Finn, investing in the business with his family's help was a nice change from constantly being in competition with someone else. He'd already experienced the peak at the Olympics and had the gold medal to prove it. Well, in theory he had the gold.

He still missed having the medal with him some days and the memories of the life of a competitive athlete that came with it.

Point being, now he only competed with himself and that's the way he liked it.

"Okay, so you and Abby are finished. Please don't tell me you're still having these two-week-long relationships and moving on," Noah said.

"Okay, I won't tell you. And it's not two weeks. Not that I've been keeping track."

"That's okay, Twyla and I do it for you."

"Don't. It's not true." But Finn counted quietly in his head.

"It is." Noah sat on the bench and started to name the

women Finn had recently dated on one hand. "Since you started dating again, every two weeks, almost like you set an alarm. Next!"

Hell, maybe it only took him that long to figure out whether he wanted to spend more time with a woman. He was fast and efficient in more than one way, apparently.

Finn faced Noah. Behind him, the beautiful Gulf Coast sunset was beginning to crest in hints of red, purple and gold. The salt air filled his lungs and brought about faint memories of over a decade of training and racing. Sailing.

"Maybe I can figure out whether a relationship is going to work out sooner than most people do. That's all. I didn't realize it was exactly two weeks but whatever."

"And how can you figure this out in only two weeks' time? You haven't even met her family in that short a span."

"Experience."

Finn didn't want to ruin Noah's day, but a divorce taught a man a lot about who would and who wouldn't make the distance. If it wasn't going to happen, why waste his time?

"Okay, I get it. Your divorce was a romance killer. You two wound up hating each other. But what was wrong with *Abby*?"

"Nothing. She's just not right for me. We're not right for each other."

"Huh."

Noah seemed to mull this over as if he couldn't figure out if Finn was a genius savant in terms of relationships, or if he was simply commitment phobic after a bad divorce, as he'd often been accused. But he wasn't, and also it wasn't just a *bad* divorce. His divorce had been like *The War of the Roses*. Like World War III. Until he'd finally given up and let Cheryl take everything she wanted. By then all he'd really wanted was out.

He'd lost something that meant a lot to him in the process: a gold medal and a relationship he'd thought might last forever. Love, gone. Friendship lost too.

"Look, we can't all fall in love with our best friend."

Sure, Finn wanted what Noah and Twyla had. The assurance that no matter what happened between two people, they'd never *hurt* each other on purpose. Noah and Twyla loved each other far too much for that, with a love that went deeper than physical attraction and magnetic chemistry.

But they had that, too, damn overachievers.

"I think the divorce is still playing hockey puck with your brain."

Finn didn't want to believe that, because it meant Cheryl had taken far more from him than a medal he'd earned due to years of practice and commitment. It meant she'd taken his peace of mind and the chance of any future happiness with it.

"Look, I obviously know it's tough for me to consider anything long term with a woman. I can admit that. But I'm not hurting anyone. All of the women I date want temporary, too. And that works for me right now."

"Okay," Noah said with a sigh. "As long as no one is getting hurt."

"Wow." A lightbulb went off in Finn's head. "Don't tell me you're worried about *Michelle*."

"I'm sorry, but I still feel guilty. I didn't mean to hurt her, and she moved here from Austin because of me."

"You didn't ask her to move here."

"No, of course not. I was trying to break up with her."

"Guess she didn't get the memo."

Were she not Noah's recent ex, Finn might like to get in line to enjoy two weeks or however long of Michelle La-Croix. She was beautiful, smart and funny with long legs and an amazing figure. But she wasn't dating anyone, because clearly, she was still not over Noah. Nothing less attractive to a man than someone still pining over her ex.

"She got fired from her job!" Noah was still going on, trying desperately to expunge his guilt.

The problem was, Noah had always been in love with Twyla but until recently, he'd had no idea she felt the same. Once he did, well, that was all she wrote. No other woman stood a chance.

"Not your fault. Plus, she landed on her feet. She's found a new home over at Pierce & Pierce."

"Twyla calls that place P&P, after Pride & Prejudice. Says it sort of redeems the whole divorce attorney thing."

The same law firm his ex-wife had hired to fleece Finn of everything he owned but his underwear. The little shark Arthur, Jr., had been Cheryl's attorney. Finn's attorney was a nice woman who thought they should mediate and try to part as "friends."

She was a dreamer, in other words.

And that was the other, much bigger problem with Michelle LaCroix. She was a family law attorney.

One of the best.

Michelle LaCroix stood from her desk and stretched. With a sedentary job like hers, she had to remind herself to get up every twenty minutes or risk heart disease. Sitting was the new smoking, after all. She'd never smoked a day in her life and if she died of coronary heart disease, she was going to be very pissed.

Closing her laptop, she strolled to look out the window of her office. In the distance to her right, the lighthouse appeared in the fading rays of the sunset. To her left were the bright lights of the Charming, Texas, boardwalk twinkling like matching stars. Across the street was Once Upon a Book, the bookshop her former nemesis, Twyla Thompson, owned and managed.

Even if Michelle was unhappy that she'd had to start over after working for years to make partner at her law firm in Austin, she had to admit Charming was the perfect place to do it.

The town was well named—a picture-postcard place situated along the Gulf Coast of Mexico. When she'd arrived here six months ago, Michelle had driven along the curvy coastline in her rental, taking in the views. Her exboyfriend Noah's hometown was everything she'd expected from a bucolic coastal town with a converted lighthouse, piers, docks, and sea jetties. She'd found a temporary rental in a row of private and secluded cottages along the beach, owned and managed by some retired rodeo cowboy who loved to surf.

Foolishly, Michelle had actually come here for another chance with Noah. She'd had no idea he'd been in love with his best friend for over a decade. To be fair, even Twyla had been unaware. Still, it was neither Noah nor Twyla's fault Michelle had been fired from her old law firm. The entire reason had been professional jealousy, the kind a woman in her field met with far too often.

Gus O'Connor, former friend and associate, had taken it upon himself to forward a private email meant to be only between the two of them. She'd complained about a senior partner, and he'd forwarded that personal email to everyone in the firm. That's how her former law office staff learned Michelle believed Richard Styles walked as if he had a stick up his butt.

Stupid, stupid, stupid. She knew better than anyone how dangerous and exposing email could be. But she'd been off her game, heartbroken over the breakup with Noah. She'd then made the colossal mistake of venting with a colleague who often made his own jokes at Richard's expense—though he'd been clever enough not to put anything in print. But no one cared to hear that, because while she was in Charming on the first vacation she'd had in years, the shit hit the fan. Texas was an at-will work state, and Richard didn't need a reason to let her go. He used the fact she'd taken too much time off, and promptly fired her.

She'd landed on her feet as she always did. Agile. Like a cat. Arthur Pierce Sr. adored her and had hired Michelle on the spot.

"You're just what this firm needs. A breath of fresh air."

A *woman,* in other words. The firm hadn't grown much over the years and now consisted only of a father and his son, Arthur Jr., hence the highly *original* name of Pierce and Pierce. Snort. Arthur Sr. was nearing retirement, and Junior was a real piece of work. Every morning he'd grin at her lasciviously as he walked by her office on the way to the better corner one.

"Already here?" He'd chuckle all the way, knowing he'd never have to work hard a day in his life because of dear old dad.

But Michelle told herself that Junior was good for her. He reminded her to never let her guard down again. She worked harder because of him and was highly motivated. Right now, this was a good thing because she vowed to make partner one way or the other. If nothing else the name needed some originality, and LaCroix was a fine name.

And would it be good to make partner here in Charming? Yes, yes, it would. Noah and Twyla would finally stop feeling so damn guilty. She'd send news of the promotion to everyone at her former Thomas and Styles law firm in Austin and tell them all to eat her dust. Especially Gus. She'd have the last laugh. Success was always the best revenge.

"Are you still here?" Arthur Sr. stood in the frame of her door, glancing at his watch. "It's seven o'clock. Stop trying to impress me! I already can't love you more than I do, or my wife will get jealous. Go home to your boyfriend and take the poor man out to dinner. You rarely see him."

Oh, yeah. That. Arthur had implied that were she to ever make partner, he'd need to be assured she had deep ties in Charming. He had to know that with a family law firm he'd built from the ground up, he could trust that she wasn't going to go back to Austin. In a weak and rather stupid moment of which she'd had far too many lately, Michelle told him she had a boyfriend. She also told him they were getting quite serious.

She'd pictured Noah, of course, but hadn't given him a name. Good thing because Noah was no longer a possibility. He was, in fact, quite engaged. As in to be married to someone else *engaged*. So, she kept calling her imaginary guy "my bae" and "my boo," even if she wanted to throw up every time she said it.

"As a matter of fact, we're going out to dinner tonight." She started to shove papers in her briefcase. "I better get going or I'll be late. Thanks for reminding me."

Work-life balance was important to Arthur. With a son like Junior, at least he'd never had to worry that his own son would work too hard.

"I'd like to finally meet him," Arthur said. "Lynn and I want to have you both over for dinner."

"Oh, sure. I'll tell him. Let's talk about it and arrange a date."

She'd been stalling for weeks, and she could stall a bit longer. Eventually, she'd find someone to date, even if it was casually, and she'd introduce that man to Arthur. No one had to know their relationship was new.

Arthur left before she did, and Michelle brought up the rear not long after, shutting off the copy machine, coffee-maker, and lights before locking the doors. A burger from the Salty Dog Bar & Grill sounded good tonight, which she would eat alone in her little beach shack while listening to the waves. And watching her true crime shows. She got in her sedan, called in her order for pickup, and drove the short distance from downtown to the row of restaurants on the boardwalk.

Twyla wasn't a social butterfly, so Michelle rarely ran into her and Noah here. The one time she had run into them a couple of weeks ago, Twyla had waved her over. She was trying to be friends. Trying *too* hard. Michelle wound up pretending there was a work emergency. Someone who wanted a divorce, like, immediately. They bought it somehow.

Tonight, the place was slammed, filled with couples. Glancing at her watch, Michelle realized it was actually already Thursday. Damn. The weekend again. After tomorrow, she'd have no work for two days. Last week, Arthur had sent an email to the three other people in the office: no more working on the weekends. Their clients would survive their divorces without them. They were attorneys, not counselors. Except the truth was in many ways they were both.

"Believe me," Arthur had once said to Michelle, "I made the mistake of working too much and losing sight of what's truly important. Now I'm on my third marriage and I've learned a few things. Family time is crucial to a successful life."

Michelle had nodded at Arthur's wisdom while simultaneously making the decision she could just as easily work at home on the weekends. She'd been bringing files home ever since. Her work was consuming, passionate, and she loved it that way. Nothing was more dramatic than two people who'd decided to end a marriage. On her client list now, she had a poor man whose trophy wife had cheated on him repeatedly and had the nerve to fight the prenup due to her own "pain and suffering."

She'd married a seventy-five-year-old man, after all, so how could she be blamed for getting her needs met elsewhere? She'd actually tried that defense, and her lawyer should be disbarred for allowing it. That case would wrap up soon, and the woman would get her settlement and not another cent. Zip. Zero. Nada. Michelle was a good attorney, thank you very much.

As her bad luck would have it, Noah and Twyla were here tonight. She spied them holding hands and sitting on the same side of a four-person booth. They hadn't seen her, and she hoped she might be able to get out of there before they did. She took her spot in the long pickup line and averted her eyes from anyone else she might know.

But just then she heard the sound of a booming voice she recognized.

"Michelle!"

Holy legal briefs, it was Arthur Sr., sitting at a nearby booth with his lovely wife.

Chapter Two

Swallowing the pebble of anxiety in her throat, Michelle nodded, smiled and waved.

Just here to pick up an order, she mouthed.

But Arthur wasn't having it.

He waved her over. "What good timing. I finally get to meet this fella of yours. Where is he?"

"He's not here, change of plans." Michelle glanced wildly at the take-out line hoping her meal would be ready soon and she could make a quick getaway. The trick to not being caught in a lie was to avoid hard-hitting questions. There was a little truth in every lie as long as no one dug too deep.

"Change of plans? Don't tell me he stood you up!" Arthur said.

"Oh, honey." His wife, Lynn, reached to pat Michelle's arm. "I'm so sorry."

In all honesty, this wasn't the first time she'd had to make excuses for her fake boyfriend. Twice before, he'd had the stomach flu. She'd made sick excuses for him so often that even Arthur was beginning to worry about this imaginary man's health. He'd suggested dietary supplements and the name of a holistic doctor in nearby Houston.

She waved dismissively. "No, no. I'm going to take him dinner. That's our change of plans. Staying in, you know. So romantic."

"Here you go, Michelle." The waiter handed her a take-out bag. "One hamburger, extra onions, curly fries, and a chocolate milkshake. Thank you for your order and please come again."

Michelle lost count of how many times she'd been in here and no one had *ever* walked her order *over* to her. This is what she got for being a regular and supporting their business.

"Um, thanks."

Arthur frowned. "You're eating without him? Don't tell me he's sick again."

Unfortunately, she occasionally ordered takeout from the Salty Dog when she worked through lunch, and Arthur recognized her standard order.

"No, I...turns out he's already eaten dinner."

Lord, she was normally faster on her feet than this. Like the time in the middle of a trial when she'd had to pivot because her client's husband was an idiot and had revealed undisclosed overseas accounts while under oath.

Great. Now Noah and Twyla had seen her and were waving hello. She waved back, not wanting to be rude.

"Honestly, I'm beginning to wonder if this man *exists*. What's his name again? All you ever call him is Boo," Arthur said, voice dripping with suspicion.

"How silly, Arthur," Lynn said on a laugh. "Who would lie about having a boyfriend?"

Yes, who indeed. Maybe someone who would do anything to impress her new boss. Squeezed from all sides, she was like a rabbit caught in a trap about to gnaw his own paw off.

Okay, so she'd exhausted this ruse. What to do, what to do. Admit she'd lied? Fake a terrible breakup? Then what?

"Um..."

And just then in walked possibly the most undependable man in town. Possibly the universe. Surely at least Texas.

Finn Sheridan.

He always gave her dark and sultry looks, but being Noah's best friend, he'd probably heard too much about her. Not that she'd ever date *him*. He was too close to the situation she'd just left. She wanted a new beginning. But for now, Finn could work. What she needed from him was just temporary, and she'd heard he was a temporary kind of guy anyway. This was right up his alley. Throw in a few perks and he just might go along.

Finn started to make his way to Noah and Twyla's table, which meant he had to pass her. And in what could only best be described as an out of body experience, Michelle called out to him, "Finn!"

Finn blinked.

"There you are, Boo!" Michelle ran over and threw her arms around him.

Finn seemed to freeze in place, his arms remaining where they'd been at his sides. "Huh?"

"Please," she hissed in his ear. "Go along with this and I'll make it worth your while."

"Go along with *what*?"

"Long story, I'll explain later. For now, pretend you're my boyfriend."

Hands on her waist, he set her back a step, eyes narrowed. "Have you been drinking?"

"No. I wish! Listen, there's someone here I need to impress."

"With *me*?" He quirked a brow.

"Well, you'll do."

He scowled. "I'm not interested in pretending. I know

you're a lawyer and this is your life, but the rest of us don't lie to people daily. Excuse me."

He tried to step aside, but she grabbed him by the lapels of his navy peacoat and planted a kiss on him. Nothing too crazy as she wasn't big on PDA, especially when she actually *knew* people were watching. Arthur hadn't taken his eyes off them since she'd run over to Finn. Still, his lack of resistance surprised her. So did the buzz through her body. Finn was not a terrible kisser, as it turned out. And dear Lord he smelled good.

When she broke the kiss, Finn was staring at her through the dark rimmed hipster glasses he always wore. Funny, she hadn't noticed his mossy green eyes before this moment. The look he gave her said simultaneously that he thought she should be committed to the nearest mental hospital and also the idea made him a little sad.

Well, she could work with that.

"Please." She clung to his lapels and shook them. "How would you like your bar tab paid for the next year? All you have to do is pretend you're my boyfriend tonight."

"That's it?" He eyed her suspiciously. "You're not going to show me what's behind door number two later, revealing my untimely certain death?"

"What are you even *talking* about?"

"I know how you lawyers like to mislead people."

"Never. I fight for *my* clients." She took a deep breath. "There's no catch. I mean, c'mon! How hard is this going to be for you? And you get free beer for a year."

At last, Finn seemed to consider it. He scratched his chin and tipped his head. Then he waved at someone with a tight smile and a curt nod. When Michelle turned, she saw it was Noah and Twyla, smiling hugely.

Because they no longer had to feel guilty about loving each other.

"Well, *they* sure look happy," Michelle said, turning back to Finn. "What do you say? Two birds, one stone?"

"He does feel mighty guilty about you."

"As he should."

Finn scowled. "What am I saying? You're fine. *He's* going to be fine."

"Given time."

"Guilt never killed anyone. I should know."

"Maybe not but it puts unnecessary stress on the circulatory system. Too much stress can decrease longevity and affect relationships. Therefore, pretending to be my boyfriend will help Noah and Twyla's relationship. If you care about them, if you care about Noah's heart health, you will do this."

"Nice guilt trip."

Finn shook his head as if he thought he too might also be a little unhinged, but he held out his hand to shake.

"Never call me *Boo* again and we have a deal. Maybe I'm crazy but just for tonight, and tonight only, I'll give in to your manipulation. I'll be your fake boyfriend. For one year's beer tab."

Finn was caught between wanting to ease Noah's conscience and the desire to turn away because none of this was his business. Familiar territory. In his experience, getting involved too deeply in any situation spelled trouble. But one night of make believe for a year's worth of his bar tab? Even he couldn't walk away from that deal. He was still trying to rebuild after the divorce and investing in Nacho Boat hadn't exactly left him flush with cash.

So, while he had a feeling he might live to regret this,

he allowed Michelle to tug him toward the booth where a familiar-looking older white-haired man sat with a middle-aged woman.

"Arthur, meet my boyfriend, Finn Sheridan. Finn, this is Arthur Pierce, my boss."

Ah, yes. Her boss. No wonder he recognized the man. Okay, so tonight would be a little like surgery without general anesthesia. Like being stabbed in the chest repeatedly with an ice pick. Two lawyers, one dinner. Michelle owed him. *Big time.* The bar tab might not be enough, but he'd start there. Maybe he'd insist that she make it ten years and not one.

"Well, hello! We finally meet. I was beginning to think you were a figment of Michelle's imagination." The man stood to offer Finn his hand. "This is my wife, Lynn. You look so…familiar."

That's because your bloodthirsty son was my ex-wife's attorney.

The man didn't seem to register the recognition, but then again, they hadn't run into each other during any proceedings. Finn had forgiven Arthur Sr. for having a ruthless man for a son. Once, near the end of their settlement, Finn had walked by the office to find the senior Pierce in the midst of a tense conversation with his son. Lots of finger jabbing toward the conference room where they'd all four been meeting.

Finn had the impression he did not approve of the way Junior had handled any of it. And his attorney had confided in Finn that she wished they would have dealt with Senior instead, who'd had a change of attitude after a massive heart attack last year. Like her, he believed couples who'd once loved each other should part as friends.

"Honey." Lynn put her hand on Arthur's arm. "He's the Olympian. Sailing, was it?"

"Noah and I own Nacho Boat now, but yes, that's right."

"Oh yes! *That's* why you look so familiar."

"That must be why." No need to remind the man he was the idiot who'd lost everything in the divorce.

"Please join us. This is perfect. Lynn and I have wanted you both over for dinner for ages."

"Well, I already ordered." Michelle held up her bag.

"Without me, pookie bear?"

"Remember, you said you're trying that new diet."

"Which diet would that be, my angel?"

"The...the one where you don't eat any fried foods?"

Finn motioned for Michelle to take a seat and he did the same. "That sounds like some other Finn Sheridan. One that exists in an alternate universe."

"You're thin so that's certainly not an issue," Arthur went on as if he hadn't heard him. "But giving up fried food might help with those digestive issues. Michelle, did you get him those supplements I recommended?"

"Um, yes," she said but wouldn't look at him.

Finn wanted to hurt Michelle and it hadn't even been five minutes. Under the table, he lightly pinched her elbow and she jumped.

"What can I say? She always looks out for me."

"Arthur had the worst case of diverticulitis until he started with supplements," his wife said. "Think about it."

"I will," Finn said through a clenched jaw. "In fact, I'll start taking those tonight."

"Well, even if you're not eating with us, at least let's have a cocktail together. Mine is a mocktail, but feel free to order the real thing." Arthur tapped his chest. "My cardiologist says alcohol is toxic to my heart. And I intend to be around a long while."

"That's a good thing," Michelle said, "because I plan to work for Pierce & Pierce for a long time to come. In fact, I can't wait to do more for the firm. I was just telling Finn how I—"

Arthur held up both palms. "Let's not talk about work. We don't want to exclude our partners."

"Thank you, sweetheart," Lynn said. "If I hear talk of one more deposition or brief, I'll have to commit hari-kari."

"I'm sorry," Michelle said. "I just came from the office, and it tends to take me a while to switch tracks."

Lynn waved her hand dismissively. "How did you two meet?"

Finn smiled, crossed his arms, and leaned into Michelle. "I'll let pookie bear take this one."

"Remember, Arthur? I told you…we met through Noah. We wound up spending so much time together, and then we just hit it off." Michelle scratched her temple.

"Tell me about your boat charter business," Arthur said. "I assume you do rentals? Fishing expeditions and that kind of thing?"

"Absolutely." Finn went on to explain their business model. "We rent equipment and we've mostly done fishing charters lately but we're growing fast."

He explained their plans to have a small fleet eventually. There would be company parties, more expeditions, surfing, diving, and sailing lessons. Noah was thinking big.

"Having an Olympian's name attached must be a boon for business," Arthur said. "You know, our firm is small, but I've always wanted to sponsor a team-building event. Something where we all have to spend time together, get to know each other outside of the office. You know?"

"Arthur, that sounds wonderful," Lynn said. "And invite the domestic partners along, too. We can all participate."

"Oh, wow. That sounds great," Michelle said, elbowing Finn in the gut. "But they're just not quite ready for something like that."

"When could you be ready? Because I would pay whatever it takes. Employee morale has been at an all-time low. Other than Michelle, I don't like what I see at the office. Too much stress. Not enough fun and cooperation. And *she* works far too hard." Arthur pointed to Michelle. "Work-life balance is important, right, sweetheart?" Arthur turned adoringly to his wife.

So, Arthur would pay *whatever it takes*. God knew he had the money. Word was he was the second wealthiest man in town, second only to the mayor's husband.

Noah would be thrilled with the new business. So would Finn. He had to think like a businessman. Plus, the whole idea seemed to panic Michelle, an added bonus.

"Sir, the way I look at it, I'll do whatever it takes to make this happen." He put his arm gently around Michelle's shoulder and winked. "Why don't the two of us start by taking the boat out this weekend? We can talk more about a team-building event then. I want pookie bear to have a great working environment. That could only mean good things for me *after* business hours."

"Fantastic!" Arthur clapped his hands. "Let's book it."

"Consider it booked."

Chapter Three

Michelle stood with Finn outside the Salty Dog, her arm stiff around his waist, waving at Arthur and Lynn as they drove away. The moment the headlights of their luxury sedan turned in the other direction, Michelle hopped away from Finn like he was toxic waste. This was *so* unacceptable. Outrage pulsed through her veins. She'd had plans to work at home all weekend and not go on a stupid boat ride with Finn. What a nightmare.

"What was *that* about? I asked for one night from you, and now we have to go out with him on Sunday!"

"Hey." He held up both palms. "That boss of yours is loaded. And Noah and I could use the business."

"You're bloodthirsty. A year's worth of your tab wasn't *enough*?"

"Not nearly. You didn't mention I'd have to eat dinner with *two* divorce attorneys. Cruel and unusual punishment."

"Oh, c'mon! Arthur is a sweet man."

"Yeah." Finn snorted. "A sweet man who knows far too much about my nonexistent digestive issues."

Her cheeks burned. "I'm sorry, but I needed a bunch of excuses as to why he could never meet my boyfriend. After a while I gave up on 'he's busy' and had to go for illness."

Finn scowled. "Explain why you need a fake boyfriend."

"Oh, you wouldn't understand."

"Try me."

"Well, for one thing, Noah feels guilty and sorry for me, and I'm so very sick of that." She crossed her arms, daring him to contradict her.

"That still doesn't explain why you lied to your boss."

"That part of it you wouldn't understand because you're a man. Living in a man's world."

"Let me get out my violin. You don't strike me as the kind of woman who lets any man hold her back."

"I'm not, but this is a small town. And Arthur…well, he's hopelessly old-fashioned. He thinks he's done well to hire a woman and bring some balance to the firm." She held up air quotes. "But the truth is, he thought I was a flight risk. I had to convince him I had a boyfriend so he'd think I have a reason to stay."

"What does it matter whether he thinks you're going to stay or go? You get paid the same either way, right?"

"No, actually, because if he thinks I'm committed to this town, he'll make me a partner and change the name from a patriarchal one of father and son. Pierce and LaCroix has a nice sound to it."

"Ah. Now I see your evil plan."

"It could have stopped tonight. Just one night was all I asked."

The corner of his mouth curled up. "Look, *you* don't have to show up this weekend. Make up one of your stomach excuses. I'll show up to take care of this and make friends with your boss. Don't worry, I'll be sure to talk you up."

"Somehow, I don't trust you."

"You probably shouldn't." He shrugged.

"Fine, if we're going to spend the day together, we should probably get to know each other a bit better. Come by the office tomorrow afternoon and we'll go over a few details."

"Hell no. I'm not going to step into that den of sharks."

Michelle rolled her eyes. "Shows how much you know. Get your insults straight. It's den of *thieves*, and a *shiver* of sharks."

"Either way."

"Fine, come by my house."

She gave him the address, they set a time, then parted ways, Finn saluting her.

"See ya, sweet cheeks."

"Don't *call* me that," Michelle hissed, but he didn't seem to hear her.

Either that, or he didn't care. He'd already been stopped on the way to his car, talking with some beautiful woman Michelle didn't recognize.

"You had to pick the town's womanizer for your fake boyfriend," Michelle muttered as she fumbled with the key fob and started her sedan. "Not smart, Michelle. Not. Smart."

She might have graduated summa cum laude from Texas A&M, but Michelle had never read the authoritative textbook on men. She'd read everything she could find on relationships, but nothing seemed to work for her. Were she blindfolded and told to walk into a room of men and pick one, Michelle would instinctively turn straight toward the unavailable one. This was her special skill. Finn was indeed gorgeous with wavy golden hair that curled around his neck and was constantly windswept. His deep green eyes were striking…but they were also mocking and never seemed to miss a thing. And apparently he was an Olympian.

How had she not known that before tonight? But it wasn't as if Noah had told her everything about his life and friends here in Charming. If so, she might have saved herself a little trouble. She'd met him outside the law firm in Austin when a frazzled ex-husband had pulled the fire alarm to get out of his deposition. The fire crew showed up, Noah suited up in his turn-out gear looking like a calendar model. She could tell when she'd first met him, a long way from his hometown, that he was a bit out of sorts. A little lost. Possibly a bit lonely. Homesick. She'd noticed the pining in his gaze but hadn't realized he missed his best friend, Twyla, back home. Truthfully, Michelle wasn't even certain *he* had realized what was wrong. *Men.*

Noah was a good man, and he hadn't purposefully strung her along. He'd never been all in with her, and looking back she could see it now. Then, after a nearly devastating accident changed his outlook, Noah had pulled away even further. Too busy with her overwhelming workload to notice, it was weeks before she realized they'd grown apart. Noah decided to come home for Christmas and hadn't invited Michelle along. She got the message. His half-hearted apology told her the rest. They'd been a mistake. He was moving on.

And she should, too. It was true she had plenty of opportunities to date, but a part of her still wanted to cling to the old ways. Bury herself in her work. This time she had a good excuse. She had to make up for lost time and all the years of dedication she'd wasted at Thomas & Styles. Because investing time and energy into dating never felt very rewarding when every attempt at a relationship fell apart. Michelle could be good at a lot of things, but romance wasn't one of them. She should just give up on finding someone permanent and go for more of these temporary hookups like Finn did. If it was good enough for a man, it was good enough for Michelle.

Her best friend, Talia, continually reminded her that she was in a field that may have made her a bit jaded about love and romance. Talia wasn't entirely wrong. On the one hand, Michelle didn't want to be alone her entire life, but on the other, statistics showed that she only had a 50 percent chance of landing in a long-term marriage, anyway. Long term in her business was more than five years. Sometimes it was better to accept the inevitable and get used to being alone. And she'd been ready to do that except for Arthur Sr.'s archaic tendencies. Bless his heart.

But once she made partner, she'd change a few things around Pierce & Pierce besides the name. She'd drag them kicking and screaming into the new millennium. An era in which a professional woman did not have to be in a relationship with a man in order to be considered trustworthy. But, at least for now, she had herself a fake boyfriend. When it came to Finn, she understood what she was getting. He was no mystery. Finn Sheridan was a player. She saw his kind coming without the need for binoculars, thank you. This made him the least likely man to ever break her heart.

When Michelle stepped inside her cozy little cottage on the shore, she realized two things in rapid succession: first, she had to straighten up if she was going to have company. Not everyone would appreciate ye old legal brief décor. Attorneys were among the last of a dying breed who still clung to paper. Everything was digitized, but judges still loved their printouts. Michelle did too and had reams of paper strewn all over her house in key places. The couch and end table where she did her weekend light reading. The kitchen table where she made notes on arguments while she ate. Bed, where nothing but sleep was going on anyway.

Second, the place was too sterile. She'd decorated lightly because this was only a beach rental so no need to get too comfortable. In a few more weeks, she'd start looking for a more permanent house to rent. She had light blue curtains in the kitchen and splashes of color everywhere because she'd read that was good for mental health. Also, maybe she should get a dog. Or a cat. A cat would be less trouble, Michelle guessed, but still provide adequate company. Then again, she didn't want to become a cat lady. That sounded...bad.

She picked up her phone and texted Talia:

I need a pet. I'll have company then.

Talia: That would be cruel to the dog. He'd die of loneliness.

Michelle: What about a cat?

Talia: How about coming home so you have your best friend around every day?

Michelle: Can't. I've got Arthur on the ropes. I'm indispensable to him. He adores me. I'll make partner any day now.

Okay, so maybe Michelle was indulging in a little well-meaning hyperbole. But Talia would spread the word and that was the point. The sooner the idiots at Thomas & Styles regretted their decision to get rid of her, the better.

Michelle: So...dog or cat?

Talia: Tarantula? You just keep him in a box. People will be afraid of you. And I hear sometimes you can pet them.

Michelle: Absolutely not.

Talia: How about a snake? Another box, low maintenance. Plus, kind of cool.

The very idea made Michelle want to gag. She could already hear all the lawyer jokes Finn would come up with.

"Great pet, Michelle. Are you two related?"

Michelle: Stop giving me weird suggestions!

Talia: Hey, keep Austin weird.

She followed this with a thumbs-up emoticon, followed by longhorns, followed by a musical treble, followed by a lone star. Yeah, Michelle got it. Austin was better than any other city in Texas. The world according to Talia. But she hadn't been to Charming yet, which came by its name honestly. Michelle loved the people here, even Twyla, which said something. Arthur was a sweetie, just a little old-fashioned and stuck in his ways. But she'd fix that.

Michelle got busy taking out the kitchen trash filled with the week's take-out containers, straightening her legal briefs, then taking down all her silk bras and panties from where she air dried them in key spots all over the house. Perks of being single. While she deeply resented even caring what Finn thought of her, a streak of pride ran deep through Michelle LaCroix. Always had.

It mattered what people thought of her.

She didn't understand carefree attitudes like those of Finn Sheridan for whom life was one big party.

Finn had just gotten off the phone after giving Noah the good news about Arthur's business when he opened the door to the home he shared with his younger brother, Declan, and found a poker game in full swing.

Declan tipped back on the two legs of the kitchen chair he was seated in. "Want me to deal you in?"

Finn stopped in his tracks and pointed. "*He's* not twenty-one."

He hadn't been bothered when he'd noticed the beer in Declan's hand. But Tee, one of their staff at Nacho Boat Adventures and a good kid, was definitely not of age.

"I'm not drinking." Tee held up his free hand. "Boss-man."

At least it was better than some of the other names Tee had come up with to call him and Noah, like "Nacho man." Finn hated being called the boss, but ever since he'd become part-owner, Noah insisted he not be the only one to feel one hundred years old. So, yes, Finn was someone's boss now. Yikes. It was one thing to feel responsible for Declan, but it was another thing to feel that way for anyone else. He'd already tried the "responsible for someone else" gig once. Tried the whole picket fence dream and came away with a stick.

His entire career and Olympic dreams had involved competing only with himself and having few people to answer to. Now someone, an entire staff of someones, had to answer to him.

Too bad Declan would never be one of them.

One cursory glance and Finn noted the load of dishes in the sink. His younger brother was a slob. Finn was trying to expect more out of him, but the guilt he felt over his brother still dogged him. Maybe if not for Finn and their family's relentless focus on him in their pursuit of Olympic gold and financial backing, Declan would have found his own way. Instead, he'd had to move to areas where Finn could have access to the best teachers. The best mentors. It meant several months across the country in the four years he'd been in high school. It was why they'd moved to Charming in the first place. Declan had put off his own interest in a pro baseball career because their father decided Finn's prospects were better.

The worst thing about this was how much Declan never seemed to care. Not an ounce of resentment from Declan, who was the human equivalent of a golden retriever. Good-looking, carefree, and happy. Friendly. He'd taken Finn in without any questions when he'd lost everything in the divorce. Which didn't make any of this easier. But the six-foot-plus man-child was going to have to grow up. He'd had a series of dead-end jobs after leaving the minor leagues a few years ago. For now, he worked at the Salty Dog as a bartender, which meant his life was one big party.

Around the poker table, Finn also recognized some of the short order cooks and a waiter from the Salty Dog Bar & Grill, along with the only woman here. Declan's current girlfriend, Casey. She hung all over him as per usual. It seemed another thing Declan could not do was hang on to a woman in a long-term relationship. It had been this way since his high school days.

A disturbing thought hit Finn front and center.

Was he turning into his brother via proximity? No. Oh hell, no. There was only room for one Sheridan brother to be a ladies' man. That had never been Finn. He'd always been a one-woman man in long-term relationships. Prior to his marriage, his shortest one had been two years.

But he had to admit that until Noah mentioned the two-week length of his relationships, Finn hadn't actually noticed. Once he did, the thought sobered him. This was exactly who he *didn't* want to become: a player who didn't take relationships seriously. He also refused to be a cliché; the bitter divorced man unable to commit again. Somehow, he'd become that man without even noticing it happen. He should get back into a serious relationship before he grew too set in his ways to be good to anyone. It would be a good example to Declan, too. Maybe when he saw Finn happy and settled, he'd see that it could be done.

The timing was unfortunate. Now he'd been pulled into this ridiculous scenario with Michelle, which had instability and chaos written all over it in bold letters the size of the "Hollywood" sign. But damn, when she'd kissed him… yeah. All coherent thought had gone on hiatus.

So, this was going to be fun. A weekend pretending to be her boyfriend. This would be the last time Finn would have a short-term relationship for Noah and Twyla to tease him about. After this, he'd try to get serious again.

One of the cooks pulled out a chair with his foot. "Have a seat. Your brother is on a losing streak."

Declan threw his cards down. "I'm having a bad night, that's all. It happens."

Even losing couldn't bum Declan out.

Finn took a seat, eyeing Tee. "We're not betting money here, are we?"

"No, because that would be wrong." Declan flashed a grin. "I'm not corrupting minors."

"Hey! I'm eighteen, dude," Tee said with his trademark wannabe swagger.

"Where's Abby?" Casey reached to playfully ruffle Finn's hair.

"Oh, yeah." Declan shuffled the deck of cards. "What's up with Abby?"

"We're not dating anymore." Finn pushed Casey's hand out of his hair.

"Wow, that was quick." Casey laughed, tossing her dark hair back. "I'll bet you broke her heart."

"She probably broke *his* heart," Tee piped in.

"Nobody's heart was broken." Finn accepted the cards

Declan dealt him. "I saw her out tonight with someone else. She's fine."

"Geez, it was two weeks." Casey splayed her cards out in her hands.

"Why does everyone know that?" Finn barked.

"I had no idea," Declan said, putting his palms up.

Maybe this was a good moment to set the stage for this farce with Michelle. After all, it was clear everyone had come to expect this out of him, right or wrong. They thought he had a two-week timeline for his relationships. He had no clue exactly how long he and Michelle would have to indulge Arthur, but certainly as long as it took to organize the team-building event. That would be at least two weeks, give or take. He'd discussed it earlier with Noah.

"Anyway," Finn said. "I'm taking Michelle out this weekend on the boat."

"Michelle?" Tee sat up straighter. "You mean *Michelle* Michelle?"

"Yeah, that one. Noah's ex." Finn smirked.

"She hired y'all?" Declan said, throwing in a chip.

Around the table the sounds of chips being joined together pinged and rattled.

"Her boss did. Michelle's coming because…well. Because I asked her out on a date."

Declan lowered the cards he'd been studying. "And she said yes?"

"Don't sound so surprised," Finn said.

"Hoo-boy." Tee whistled, along with the cooks on either side of him. "You lucky dog."

"Please don't break her little ol' heart," Casey said. "She's already been through a big enough heartache with Noah."

Yeah, Finn knew all about it. He wasn't interested in being second to anyone but least of all Noah, who was one of the nicest guys anyone ever had the pleasure of meeting. No way Finn could compete with that. Nor did he want to and that was the point. He was still only in competition with himself.

"I wouldn't dream of it." Finn studied the hand he'd been dealt. A lousy one. He laid his stack down. "I'm out."

So, he'd hang in there for a couple of weeks with Michelle. Whatever it would take.

He'd honor his agreement with her, then move on. Tab paid for a year. Break up. No one would be surprised.

But after this, he'd get serious about meeting someone special. Possibly settling down again. He'd be thirty-three this year. The first doomed marriage didn't have to be the measuring stick by which he'd judge all his serious relationships. That one had been a fluke. A mistake.

He'd been too caught up in winning, and she'd been too caught up in being with a winner.

Chapter Four

Most people loved Fridays because it was the last day of the work week. Michelle appreciated Fridays, too, but for different reasons. It was her last chance to enjoy the work week. She got in even earlier than normal, and stayed later, because for the next two days she couldn't have court appearances or depositions. Not quite as dedicated as Michelle, judges, court reporters, and clerks wanted weekends off. After Arthur's imposed "no weekends" rule, she couldn't even sneak into the office any longer.

It was not unusual for Michelle to skip lunch on Friday. She milked the day and had often been the attorney to step in for others on a last-minute appearance in court. Nothing gave her more pleasure than strolling down the austere hallways of law. There, rules were enforced that assigned order into a mixed-up world. To Michelle, little was more important than the letter of the law. Without it, they'd have anarchy. Without family law, wives or husbands might have to leave a bad marriage with little to nothing to their name. Not on Michelle's watch.

And it helped that the city hall building in Charming was almost obscenely beautiful. A grand staircase was the focal point as one walked through the double glass doors. The inside was decorated in white and gold, and the vaulted ceiling gave the sensation of being inside a cathedral. There were Roman-style pillars and balconies, and skylights that allowed bright rays of sunshine to spill in.

Family and civil court were located on the first floor. Justices of the peace and the clerks were on the second floor and near the mayor's office, at the top of a winding grand staircase worthy of the one at the castle in *Beauty and the Beast*. The floor and banisters were marble. Crown molding decorated the walls. It was so beautiful that a city hall wedding could never be a plain and boring affair. In fact, there was a waiting list to get married there.

Charming believed in preserving its history, and the building had been there since the town was founded. It had survived *two* hurricanes.

If Michelle could, she'd live at city hall.

She arrived at the office and found that as usual, she'd beat everyone there, so she unlocked the doors she'd locked the night before, flipped on light switches and the Xerox machine, and started the coffee.

"Good morning," said Rachel Harmon, their clerk/paralegal/receptionist when she waltzed in an hour later. "Thank God it's Friday!"

She said this every Friday.

"Right," Michelle muttered. "And good morning to you."

The world required another saying for people who loved to work, like maybe Oh no, it's Friday. Or Thank God it's Monday, TGIM. Had a nice ring to it.

"You doing anything fun this weekend?" Rachel crossed her arms and leaned into the doorframe of Michelle's office.

Usually, Michelle had to make something up, like: "My boyfriend and I are going to the movies," or, far closer to the truth, "We're staying in."

This time, she got to say, "We're going boating on Sunday."

"Oh, fun!" Rachel practically levitated with joy. "It's supposed to be sunny with zero chance of rain."

That meant it would be hotter than a jalapeno on the Gulf, so she'd have to dress accordingly. No pantsuits, in other words. Plenty of sunscreen. A hat.

"Um…" Michelle set her pen down beside her legal pad where she'd been making notes on last week's deposition transcript. "And what are *you* doing this weekend?"

Rachel was an awfully kind girl and Michelle hadn't been friendly enough. Given the way her last office friendship had resulted in a betrayal, she'd kept to herself since being hired. One might even say she'd been a bit cold. Distant. No one could blame her for feeling protective about workplace alliances, but Michelle figured as long as she didn't indulge in any office gossip, she should be safe.

Adorably surprised at being asked, Rachel stepped all the way into the office.

"Oh my gosh, we're going to the music festival in Austin! I'm so excited. There's a group of us going, and we'll make a weekend out of it and check out the whole city. I've always wanted to go. I can't wait."

Talia would probably be there, too. Her boyfriend was the lead singer for Five Inch Nails. Or Nine Inch Nails? Either way.

"You'll love Austin."

"Oh, that's right!" Rachel pointed. "You're *from* Austin. Arthur grabbed you up from that firm when you came down here on vacation to…uh…when you…"

Rachel bit her lower lip and averted her gaze. Here it came again.

The sorrow and the pity.

No wonder she'd invented a fake boyfriend.

"You can say his name. It won't kill me. Noah and I are friends. It's all good." Michelle waved a hand dismissively.

"Really? That's good. Because I know about bad breakups."

"It wasn't a bad breakup." Michelle forced a smile and picked up her pen. "We just grew apart."

When he moved to Charming to reconnect with the woman he'd always secretly loved.

"At least you have a new boyfriend now. You guys are always together. What's his name? You never said."

This was the awkward part of conversations. *Details.* She'd avoided talking to Rachel for more than one reason.

"Finn. Finn Sheridan." Michelle made curly cues with her pen on the side of her notepad.

"Oh." Rachel seemed to lose her enthusiasm.

"Why? What's wrong?"

"Finn is the guy you're serious with?"

Michelle rolled the pen between her two hands. "Yes, why do you ask?"

Rachel blinked. Then blinked again. She was probably privately counting all of Finn's many conquests, and hell, maybe Rachel was even one of them. Awkward.

"I thought he and Abby were going out."

Yikes. Yes, this *was* a small town.

"Not anymore."

"Well, okay then. As long as you know about her."

"Oh, yes. Sure."

Okay, so her fake boyfriend dated a lot. It wasn't like Michelle hadn't noticed. There might have been a better choice for a fake boyfriend, perhaps someone who was more dependable. But hey, she had to work with what she had.

"Anyway, I finally agreed to go on the boat with Finn.

He's been bugging me. Such an enthusiast. A former Olympian, did you know that? Arthur and his wife are going, too."

"Oh, fun." But it wasn't said like the first "fun."

The door opened and Rachel rushed back to her spot near the front.

"Good morning! How can I help you?" she said in her usual cheery voice.

Probably someone for Arthur Jr. who was late as usual. Arthur Sr. was taking Fridays off for the foreseeable future, post–heart attack scare. Michelle unfortunately didn't have any appointments today, so she bent her head and went back to her deposition notes.

Only seconds later, Rachel was back in the doorframe. "Michelle? We, um, we have a walk-in."

Behind her stood a diminutive woman Michelle had already met. To all who knew her personally, she was a powerhouse. Part of the powerhouse couple of Tippy and Teddy. Tippy Goodwill.

The mayor of Charming.

Michelle rushed to stand up and meet her halfway. Holding out her hand, she greeted the mayor. "How are you? Is there something I can do for you?"

"I want a divorce. As fast as possible."

Michelle inched the box of tissues closer to Tippy. One of the few items they could never run out of in a family law firm were tissue boxes. The mayor didn't look on the verge of tears; in fact, she appeared to be her usual fierce self, but one could never be too safe.

"Ted is in El Paso for some business deal, or so he tells me! But I know it's to meet another woman. I've seen all the signs. He lost weight, joined a gym, and started lifting weights. Last week he had a pedicure! Does he think I'm stupid? A woman knows when her man is trying to impress someone else."

Michelle ignored that. She'd heard a lot worse. "And does he have any idea you'll be filing today?"

"Actually, I'm afraid he's going to file while he's in El Paso. That's where he's from, you know. Originally. Before we moved down here right after we were married."

"If he files in El Paso, all court proceedings will have to be held there."

"That's what I heard, which is why I'm here. I'm going to beat him to it. There's no way I'm going to *El Paso* to get a *divorce*!"

"You could always wait a bit, let the emotions settle. Talk to him?"

This was the part of being a divorce attorney Michelle detested. She was not a marriage counselor and had a difficult time coming up with the kinds of platitudes that, in her opinion, had little place in the dissolving of a marriage. Her real skill was in the courtroom, if it came to that, which too often it did not. She could file papers today and start the wheels in motion. Great way to end a Friday. Maybe by Monday they'd have made up. Stranger things had happened.

"We've been married for forty years. If this could be resolved by talking, we would have done so." She crossed her legs. "No. This is it. I've thought about it, and I want a divorce."

"We can file the paperwork today, but—"

"Yes, good, and I'll start working on everything else. We'll have to sell the lighthouse we renovated. Oh, poor Cole and Valerie. They'll have to move, and they just had a baby. And dividing up the properties will be a nightmare. We have dozens of rental homes. IRAs and funds up the wazoo. We bought stock in Apple early on."

Holy legal briefs. These two were gazillionaires. Arthur was going to make her partner and hug her the moment he found out how much money they'd make from this divorce. The billable hours could be astronomical. They usually were in a divorce where so many assets had to be divided.

In the next second, Michelle mentally slapped herself. She didn't do this for the money. She did this out of love for the law, but she was keenly aware that most law firms viewed success through the lens of money and billable hours. Making Arthur a small fortune was how she'd make partner—and then Thomas & Styles would rue the day.

"Excuse me." Junior popped his head in Michelle's doorway. "Was that our esteemed mayor I saw walking in just ahead of me?"

Damn it all, she'd forgotten to close the door in her haste to help Tippy.

Tippy turned. "Hello, Arthur."

"Artie, please. Arthur is my father." He approached, faux concern lining his eyes and pinching his lips. "I hope this is just a courtesy visit?"

"No, it's business." Tippy straightened. "I'm hopeful your law firm can get me a quick divorce."

"Well...*fast* is going to be difficult," Michelle said.

She refused to lie to her clients. Given the amount of assets Tippy had just described, either her husband was going to walk away without a cent or their divorce could be a long, drawn-out and contentious one. Wealthy people always had the most expensive divorces, second only to those with minor children.

"We can do fast, of course," Junior said and hooked a

thumb toward the hallway. "Care to come into my office so we can talk about it?"

Michelle held back the gasp and the sting of anger that made her want to throat punch Junior.

Instead, she stood. "We were talking about the situation."

Junior gave her the smoldering look he tried on women, which would never in a million years work on Michelle.

"You're new here, Michelle. I'd be happy to take this case." He turned to Tippy. "I'm a partner here, as you know."

"Yes, I *know*," Tippy said. "Your daddy started the firm. He and I have known each other ages."

"Pierce and Pierce," Junior said, not catching Tippy's condescending tone.

But Michelle had, and she liked Tippy even more. She had Junior dialed. But then again this was a small town, and she was its mayor.

"I was hopeful your daddy would take my case, but he isn't quite the man he used to be, is he? Not after the heart attack, bless his heart."

"Oh, he's good, but just not taking any new cases. He hands everything off to me." Junior cleared his throat and tugged at his tie. "His partner."

"Isn't that sweet," Tippy said, turning back to Michelle. "Daddy and *son*. That would have warmed the cockles of my heart back when I had a heart. I'm out for blood, Artie. And I want a woman to be my attorney."

Junior sucked in some air and behind Tippy's back slid Michelle a contemptuous look. She could almost feel the dagger sliding into her back.

"Of course. Well…if that's what you want. Michelle, please take good care of our mayor. She's a valued client around here." He slowly shut the door.

"I'm afraid I've given you a little trouble, haven't I? You know he won't be happy about this," Tippy said. "He's always had it too easy, that one. You can do this for me, can't you? I want Ted to grovel and *beg* me to stop fighting him. He's going to go to his knees. That's what I want."

Yikes!

"I promise you that I'm going to be the best advocate you've ever had. I go all in for my clients, and I'll tell you a secret. Arthur doesn't want us to work on the weekends, but I still do. I just work at home now." Michelle powered up her printer. "There's little that matters to me so much as the law and justice. You have a few forms to sign, and we'll get this going for you right away."

"Ted is going to be so sorry he ever met me. Like you, I've worked hard all my life in a man's world, and I don't mind telling you: I want a lot more than *half* of everything. I've earned it."

Michelle clasped her hands together and set them on her desk. "I will fight for you."

This had turned out to be a wonderful Friday.

Chapter Five

The next morning Finn fully expected questions from Noah about the previous night, but at first, he wasn't sure how much he should tell him. This deception was Michelle's, and Finn simply the putz getting paid to participate. So to speak. He'd spent the past few minutes explaining to Noah that he and Michelle weren't actually a thing. Therefore, Noah's guilt wasn't actually going to be relieved, as Michelle had suggested. Finn wasn't going to lie to his best friend.

"She needed a little help with her boss," Finn further clarified.

He and Noah were prepping the catamaran for a short trip around the bay with a group who'd rented the boat for a sunset cruise.

"But how were *you* able to help her?"

"It's stupid. You won't like it."

"Believe me, I saw you two together, and if anything, I'm happy for you. Michelle is beautiful and wicked smart. Maybe it will work out with you."

"I'm telling you, it's not what you think. She just needs me to—"

"Look." Noah held up his hands. "You don't need to tell me any more."

Finn laugh-snorted. "I'm supposed to pretend I'm her boyfriend. It was just going to be for one night."

"You agreed to that? *Why?*"

That was the question of the day, because as much as he wanted to believe it was, the bar tab wasn't the reason he'd agreed. Still, it worked well enough as an excuse to share with Noah.

"She's paying my beer tab for a year." Finn smiled, remembering how for a moment he thought he might have actually had a streak of good luck for a change. He was Irish American, but the luck had never materialized. Everything he'd ever had was obtained through hard work, sacrifice and dedication.

But last night, his tab. Then the kiss. Whoa, the kiss. Who knew someone that tensely wound and uptight could kiss him with such heat he nearly forgot where he was? After that explosive kiss he'd pulled back and for one moment he saw her again like he had for the first time. Before he'd known *who* she was.

On that day, he'd done a double take at the blonde walking toward him on the boardwalk, thinking he heard a choir playing in the background and saw fireworks going off in his eyes. Dayum.

Then she'd walked right past him and straight to Noah.

Michelle, formerly Noah's girl. The magnetic pull he'd felt toward her in that first moment screeched to a halt and gasped one last dying breath. Anyway, last night the buzz of the kiss had quickly been ruined when he'd been forced to discuss his nonexistent digestive issues while he sat and had dinner with two attorneys. At that point, even the kiss hadn't been enough to alleviate the evening. She'd have had to make out with him to call it even.

"Maybe it would have ended there, but Arthur Pierce was interested in what we're doing here. We talked. I opened my big mouth and now we're taking the boat out this Sunday."

"I for one am grateful for your big mouth. That rock sitting on Twyla's ring finger set me back a bit."

"He also talked about team-building events for office morale, that kind of thing."

They were prepared when their guests eventually arrived en masse, ten women all wearing colorful leis around their necks. One by one they made their way on board. A tall and slender brunette wore a pink sash across her that boldly proclaimed, "I'm the bride."

"What's this?" Finn said, observing their dresses, which seemed far too elegant for a casual boat tour.

"I don't know." Noah squinted. "Maybe the bachelorette party?"

Finn noted two of the women in the group were hauling a full-length mirror on board and walked over to help. He had to admit, his curiosity was piqued.

"Thank you," the woman named Mimi said. "Just right over here so she can face the sun as it sets over the horizon."

Finn helped place it starboard. This was to be a sunset cruise around Galveston Bay. Always a romantic couples time, but there was no reason why a bunch of girlfriends couldn't enjoy it.

"Do you want to see the reflection of the sunset in the mirror?" Noah asked, joining them.

Mimi laughed. "It's for the vows."

The bride joined them, wearing her long and flowing off-white dress. "Didn't anyone tell you? This is a wedding. I even have a ring."

"She's marrying herself," said Mimi.

Finn had officially heard it all. He was literally speechless.

Noah wasn't. He brilliantly said, "Oh. Um…"

"Haven't you heard of sologamy?" The bride placed a hand on her heart. "I'm choosing myself."

"She just had a bad breakup with the father of her child," one of the other women half-whispered in Finn's ear. "It's time to choose the only one she can depend on. Herself."

Well, hot damn, that was a good point.

Finn had always hoped to get married again. Someday. He'd liked being married, just didn't love being married to the wrong woman.

After they'd pushed off and pointed the catamaran westward, Finn and Noah stood nearby and watched quietly. Reverently. With her best friends and sister in attendance, the bride recited her vows in the mirror as the sun crested in a splash of red and orange streaks. She said she would never again romanticize a partnership above her own self-worth.

It was, in a word, beautiful.

But also sad.

Finn had been surprised to learn that Michelle was still staying in the vacation beachside cottages within walking distance of the boardwalk. He figured by now she would have rented a house in town to further prove her intentions to plant roots in Charming.

There were only a few things Finn did know about Michelle LaCroix, other than the obvious:

1. She wore pantsuits exclusively
2. She worked all week, weekends, and holidays
3. She wore her hair in a ponytail so tight her eyes squinted
4. Her favorite book was *Rebecca* (according to Twyla), but she didn't have much time to read anything besides legal briefs (also according to Twyla)
5. She was a bit self-absorbed at times (according to Noah, and Finn took this with a grain of salt)

When Michelle opened the door, she still wore her ever-present workweek pantsuit, leading Finn to believe she lived in it. He'd been hoping to at least catch a glimpse of those legs. Her hair, at least, was down around her shoulders. Her eyes were nicely almond shaped and a shade of hazel that looked almost golden in the ambient light.

She also wasn't wearing her heels, which made her several inches shorter, and he'd be lying not to admit he enjoyed towering over her.

"You're not the pizza guy."

"No, sorry. Am I late?" He glanced at his nautical watch. "I was at a wedding a few minutes ago and lost track of time."

"You were at a *wedding*? Just now?"

"Yeah, on the boat." He put up his palms. "And don't ask because you wouldn't believe me if I told you."

She waved him inside. "Okay, let's get down to business."

Yeah, she was all about business, and his naughty thoughts wandered to whether she would also like to issue orders in the bedroom. He shoved them off deck and metaphorically watched them drown. No time for foolishness.

"A pizza is coming so we can share it if you like bacon and chicken."

"Thanks. I was under the impression dinner would be included." He plopped down on the sofa.

She rolled her eyes and dug in the side pocket of her briefcase. "I've prepared a short biography about my life. Everything you need to know should be in here."

"Is that right?" He flipped through the stapled three-page-long document and whistled. "Well, well. Summa cum laude from Texas A&M. Congratulations to me. I love a smart woman. But everything isn't in here."

"What's missing?"

"Favorite color."

"That's not important." She crossed her arms.

"Sure is. Favorite color tells a lot about a person."

"Like what?"

"Whether you're a happy person or an angry one." Finn was just making this up as he went along. It was fun to argue with her.

"I disagree, and it does not tell you a thing. That's faulty logic. You assume a favorite color can't change daily. What if I like blue one day and yellow the next?"

"C'mon! Everybody has a *favorite* color. Don't be obtuse about this."

"I don't have one, actually, because I disagree with your theory."

"Well, you better pick one, quick, because you're half a person without it." He shook his head.

"What's *your* favorite color?" She snapped her fingers. "Quick!"

She was trying to catch him in an inconsistency and damn if he'd let her even if his favorite color also changed weekly. "Easy. It's blue."

"Okay, that was fast."

"It isn't a lie. Go ahead, *pick* one."

"Fine, I like bright colors like hot pink. Sometimes yellow and orange, depending on my mood. Are you happy?"

"Ecstatic."

He flipped through the pages. She'd denoted her birthday, astrological sign, place of birth, parents' names, best friend, former boyfriends, schools she'd attended. Vacations she'd taken, the food she preferred (pizza). Nothing juicy or saucy like what positions in the *Kama Sutra* she preferred.

He almost fell asleep reading.

"This is woefully incomplete." He set it down. "What's your favorite breakfast?"

"That's important?"

"Possibly *the* most important thing. If we're sleeping together, and we would be if this were real, then I'd know whether you like eggs for breakfast. And *how* you like them."

"Oh." She swallowed. "Then I…like my eggs scrambled."

A moment passed between them in which he imagined how she would look wearing nothing but his T-shirt.

"Good to know."

"And how do you like your eggs?"

"Please. I don't eat breakfast."

Once the pizza arrived, Michelle got a reprieve from all the highly personal questions. For a few minutes, it had felt like an interrogation. Like playing Whac-A-Mole, in which as soon as she knocked one out, another one reappeared. In five minutes, Finn learned more about her than Noah had in six months of dating.

They ate quietly from paper plates, Finn as always appearing so at ease and self-assured in his own body. He had turned out to be far more of a challenge to her than she would have guessed. She didn't know many people who liked to argue as much as she did, other than her colleagues. It was, in a word, refreshing. He didn't seem put off by an opinionated woman. Noah used to check out, his eyes glazing over whenever she'd argue with him, as did pretty much every boyfriend she'd ever had.

"I have to know a few things about you, too." She wiped the corner of her mouth with a napkin. "You don't eat breakfast, and you like bacon and chicken pizza, apparently. You're a gold medalist and divorced. Born and raised in Charming, right?"

"Wrong."

"No?" This surprised her. He and Noah had met in high school, so she knew he'd been here for a while, at least.

"Olympian dreams led us here. A coach lived along the Gulf Coast and offered to work with me. So, my family dragged my brother and me along just so I could have my chance at the gold." He took another slice of pizza.

That's right. He had a brother, Declan. She'd seen him around. Hard not to notice him since he bartended at the Salty Dog, was a huge flirt, and one of the most attractive men she'd ever laid eyes on. He and Finn almost looked like twins, but Finn was slightly taller.

"How long were you married? In case it comes up."

Of course, she was also curious.

Finn had been married once, which meant he'd fallen in love enough to make a lifelong commitment. As a divorce lawyer, she wasn't one of those people who looked at divorce as a colossal failure. Divorce was simply inevitable in her view, or at the very least representative of a common miscalculation. There were two kinds of love: temporary and permanent. And couples didn't know which they were until they were in the thick of it. That was why, in her opinion, marriage was the greatest risk any couple would ever take.

Finn quirked a brow. "You should just ask Arthur Jr. He knows all about my marriage."

"Why?"

Michelle narrowed her eyes and then it occurred to her that—dear God, had the firm represented Finn's ex-wife in the divorce? It would make sense why he didn't want to come to the office and relive that difficult period of his life.

"He was my ex-wife's attorney."

Michelle dropped her slice of pizza. "Are you serious?"

"He's good, too. When all was said and done, I came away with nothing more than my clothes and my truck."

Michelle's felt a peculiar churning in her stomach. "*And* your gold medal, right?"

Finn shook his head and smirked. "Nope."

"Oh my God, Finn."

Arthur Jr. wasn't that great of an attorney. What this meant to Michelle was that Finn must have had a terrible attorney.

"Whatever. My father should really be the one to have it. He was the one who invested his life savings in me."

"*You* should have it. I know how dedicated an athlete has to be to reach that point. I'm glued to the Winter Olympics every year."

"Figure skating?" He smirked.

Again, he'd nailed her. "Yes."

"In answer to your question, Cheryl and I were married four very long years."

A short-term marriage, in which a couple usually didn't have many finances and investments comingled. But God knew four years could be an eternity to two people who were miserable.

"No children?" She didn't think so but best to ask.

"Thankfully, no."

"Property?"

"Yes. She has it now."

"Finn…" She lowered her voice. "You had a really bad attorney. I'm sorry."

"Or Junior is a great attorney."

"He's not. I assume this went to trial?"

"You'd assume wrong. I laid down and played dead. Too tired to fight anymore. By that time, I just wanted…out."

"You don't strike me as the kind of person who gives up easily. Olympic medalist and all."

"Well, you have to *care* enough to fight for something."

He was right, of course. There were only a handful of men she'd seen walk away from a marriage with almost nothing to their name. And some were incredibly decent men who viewed the divorce as their own personal failure.

"What else are you doing this weekend, fake girlfriend?"

It was like he could read her mind. Had she been stealing glances at her briefcase, revealing that she was dying to do some work on Tippy's divorce?

"I have a new case."

"Damn, which sucker is getting railroaded now?"

She crossed her arms. "No one. This will be a fair and amicable divorce if I have anything to do with it. It just might be...lengthy."

"They usually are. I don't think there *is* a thing called a quickie divorce. Do I know the formerly happy couple?"

He'd hear about this sooner or later, since Charming was a small town.

"It's our mayor and her husband."

Finn's eyebrows rose. "You're kidding. Those two have been married forever. I thought they were happy."

"No one knows what goes on behind closed doors." Michelle shrugged.

Finn scowled. "Ted is a nice man. I hate to see this happen to him."

"I'm not a marriage counselor, *Finn*. I am a family law attorney and I provide a service. This is what Tippy wants."

Did she sound a bit defensive? That was probably true. But she had no gender bias at all and had represented plenty of men in the past. If Finn had been *her* client, he wouldn't have lost that medal, that was for damn sure. That was a hill she would have died on.

"On that happy note, I better go. I think I've got my degree in the University of Michelle LaCroix." Finn stood, closed his eyes and pinched the bridge of his nose. "I'll see you Sunday, sweet cheeks."

"Don't call me sweet…" But the rest of the words died on her tongue.

At this point, he could call her anything he wanted.

Chapter Six

Finn wasn't shocked to see Arthur and his wife were the first to arrive at the docks early on Sunday morning, but he was a little surprised they were both dressed like models for a *Yacht Life* photo shoot. Arthur wore a Panama hat with sunglasses, boat shoes, white trousers, and a navy blazer. His wife wore a blue-and-white ankle-length dress with a white scarf tied under her chin and owl-shaped sunglasses, Jackie Kennedy style.

"Welcome aboard."

Finn wore his usual *Nacho Boat Adventures* staff outfit of a cap, long-sleeved T-shirt, and board shorts. Somehow, he now felt underdressed.

Arthur shook Finn's hand. "Son, I'm sorry I didn't remember that we represented your ex-wife in the divorce. Those were the days, before my heart attack, when I was a bit more cutthroat. No hard feelings?"

"None."

Anyway, Finn recalled a kinder and gentler Arthur—in comparison, at least. It was Junior Finn he had a real problem with. At one time, Finn had wanted to push his face through a plate glass window. Junior excelled in the combative divorce, while Finn had wanted something less contentious. He thought Cheryl wanted that too, but she'd let Junior take the lead.

"I wasn't planning on throwing you overboard or anything. That would be unprofessional."

Arthur chuckled, a bit nervously. Finn led the couple to
their seats and went about final preparations, noting that
Michelle was cutting it close. Maybe she hoped he'd leave
without her.

He wouldn't. Not a chance in hell. Oh, he'd noticed her
staring longingly at her briefcase yesterday like she couldn't
wait to dive in the moment he left. But for today, work
could wait.

The least she could do was join him in this farce.

Finn whipped out his phone and texted:

Don't get any bright ideas. We don't leave port without
you.

"Won't Michelle be joining us?" Arthur's wife asked a
moment later.

"Well," Finn said. "She spent most of yesterday running
to the bathroom but seemed fine this morning."

"Oh, my goodness," she said. "You must get her to try
the supplements, too."

"I will." Finn smiled. That's what she got for being late.
Stomach problems. "Definitely."

"Here she is now," Arthur called out.

Finn heard the sound of a car door slamming and looked
in that direction to see…legs. He nearly swallowed his
tongue. Michelle wore casual shorts and a tank top. Oh
damn, those legs. Better than he could have imagined. Bare.
Long and curvy. He held out his hand to help her aboard
and she put one sandaled foot out, displaying pink-painted
toenails. Bright pink. So, she hadn't been lying or making something up on the spot. Note to self: she likes pink.

Once she had one foot safely on board, Finn yanked her the rest of the way into his arms. She made a strangled sound as she reached out, arms clinging to him for dear life. Or just not to fall into the drink.

"Hello, my angel," he said loudly then lowered to kiss the top of her head and give her a hint they were being watched. "They're already here. And you're almost late."

"I'm sorry. I—I couldn't decide what to wear." The insecurity flashing in her eyes pulled something tight in his chest. "Is this okay?"

He lowered his gaze, lingering a moment on the soft tanned flesh below her neck. "Perfect. Hope you don't mind joining Jackie Kennedy and her date Mr. Onassis. There's plenty of seating."

"Michelle!" Arthur waved her over.

"Go ahead, I'll get us going." He let Michelle go, but not before lightly slapping her behind.

She turned to give him a death glare. "Do that again and you'll lose an arm."

He chuckled. Zero sense of humor on her today. Still, he enjoyed watching her perky butt walk away from him. Enjoyed it so much he probably stared a bit too long.

For the next few minutes, Finn did his thing, navigating and steering the boat farther out of the bay. They had the wind with them, the sunshine bright in the sky without a cloud in sight. No big swells, the ocean calm enough to make for a smooth ride. Finn was, figuratively and literally, in his wheelhouse.

Beyond him, Arthur, Lynn, and Michelle chatted amiably. Years ago, in another life, Finn had hung out with people of wealth and influence. They'd all been interested in a success story like his. Taking photos with that year's Olympian earned them points with their elite friends. They were clearly winners, who associated with the best of the best.

Finn had hated every minute of it but did it for his father.

Arthur pointed to the lighthouse now in the distance and Michelle nodded. The lighthouse belonged to the Goodwills, Tippy and Ted. A retired Navy man, Ted had it renovated years ago, even repurposing a ship's winding staircase. The portholes were kept as windows. They'd even kept the telescope. Finn had been inside, a couple of years ago at the mayor's reelection party.

They'd rented the home out for years, and Finn guessed that would be among the many assets they'd divide up. It was disconcerting to know that even forty-year marriages sometimes ended in divorce. Finn had always been under the impression when a marriage lasted that long it was rock solid. Either that, or the couple excelled at putting on a good front. And there was probably no person better suited than someone in public office to put on a good presentation for public consumption.

After a few minutes, he chose a good spot to anchor out, then went below deck to find the ice chest he'd brought along this morning. Noah had agreed impressions were important for people like the Pierces. Were it Junior, Finn would have given him a good push off deck and left him to his own devices. But he understood how someone with the power, wealth and influence of Arthur Pierce Sr. could help Nacho Boat. Finn was not above using his own influence and so-called status to help Noah.

He joined the happy couple and Michelle. "A little something from the captain."

"Oh!" Lynn's hand went to her neck. "Champagne."

"That's very decent of you," Arthur said.

Finn uncorked the bottle, the popping sound making Michelle jump.

"Don't worry, pookie bear. Does this remind you of that time the cork hit you in the forehead? Quite by accident, I assure you."

Both Arthur and Lynn found that hilarious.

"You poor thing," Lynn said. "I've always been terrified that would happen to me."

"I forgot about that." Michelle narrowed her eyes at him. "Thank you for not hitting my head this time."

"My pleasure." Finn filled their glasses.

"A toast!" Arthur held up his flute. "To this beautiful day and weather and to our captain."

"To love," Lynn said, glancing first at Arthur, then Michelle and Finn.

"To success," Finn said.

"Hear, hear," Arthur said.

They all turned expectantly to Michelle as she raised her flute.

"To satisfying work."

Judging by the expressions on the stunned faces surrounding her, Michelle shouldn't have toasted work. Finn quirked an eyebrow. Arthur shook his head and Lynn made an audible gasp. But given that Arthur was Michelle's boss, who'd *hired* her, then wanted her to guarantee to him that she'd stay, she didn't have much else on her mind. Other than her career, which, let's face it, was her life.

There was nothing left *to toast*, because admiring the way Finn wore a pair of board shorts didn't seem appropriate. Or the way he seemed self-assured and fully in charge of the ship's controls. He was back there behind the wheel, steering and doing...*mechanical* things. Sexy things involving torque, engines and horsepower. She'd always been attracted to men who worked with their hands.

"Dear, try again." Lynn patted Michelle's shoulder.

"She can do better." Arthur elbowed Finn.

Now Finn put his arm around her and drew her close to his tall, rock-hard body. "I believe in you, angel."

"Um, okay, I'd like to make a toast to…" Michelle began. "To…"

To Finn's deep mossy green eyes.

To those sexy glasses he rocks.

To his golden and wavy windswept hair.

To his incredibly kissable lips.

To his muscular legs and his…um, big…feet.

To his abs-solutely wonderful abs.

"Here's a toast to long, deep kisses that go on for days and make your knees weak," she said, looking at Finn.

She hoped her expression said: *Are you happy now?*

"Oh, my," said Lynn and fanned herself.

"I'll drink to that!" said Arthur.

"So will I," Finn said, clinking with her flute.

They all drank. Thankfully past that awkward moment, they gathered at the front of the boat. Michelle faced the wide and deep bay. Blue water and skies as far as the eye could see, but she could no longer see land and the idea made her slightly…terrified. Solid land was that lovely place where she could run and walk, and there was less chance something would jump out and grab her.

"How far out are we?"

"Three nautical miles," Finn said. "Random fact: this is the legal distance for scattering ashes at sea."

"Do you guys provide that service?" Michelle said.

"Nah."

"This is absolutely gorgeous," Lynn said, taking her phone out for a photo op. "Arthur, we should get a boat."

"Oh no, darling," Arthur chuckled. "They say there are only two good days in the life of a boat owner: the day you buy it and the day you sell it."

Michelle and Finn laughed while Lynn pulled a sour face.

"Do you have many parties here?" Lynn turned to Finn.

"We offer a sunset cruise. In fact, we just had one yesterday," Finn said. "A woman married herself. She had all her friends and some of her family with her."

"How utterly sad," Lynn said. "She probably needs some sort of counseling, poor thing."

"I wonder what a psychiatrist would have to say about that," Arthur muttered.

"Nothing good, I imagine," Michelle said.

"I thought it was kind of beautiful," Finn said wistfully, surprising Michelle.

Maybe that was the way she'd go someday. She was probably the only person she'd ever really be able to count on to always be there. If she ever married, she had to assume it would end in divorce. The only question was whether it would be a short- or long-term marriage. Both had their appeal, their advantages, and disadvantages. She was definitely getting a prenup.

"It's what modern life has come to because of people like me and Michelle," Arthur said sadly. "People have lost all hope in the institution of marriage."

Lynn rubbed his shoulder. "Oh, Arthur, stop being so hard on yourself. You didn't *cause* their divorces, after all."

"We simply provide a service once a couple has already decided they can no longer make the marriage work," Michelle said.

"That's right," Lynn said. "Listen to Michelle."

Michelle had wanted to bring up Tippy's divorce and beat Junior to the punch. But surely, he'd already complained to his father about how Michelle had swooped in and taken "his" client.

"But maybe I could have done more to help, to discourage my clients. Moving forward, I'd like our firm to take a less-contentious approach to a couple's divorce. Work harder to push them toward mediation and out of the trial system," Arthur said. "We made a name for ourselves by going to trial and winning, but it's time to roll it back."

"I would certainly agree with that." It was the first time Finn had spoken in several minutes.

"On a happier note," Lynn said, quite obviously redirecting since Arthur appeared ready to weep, "may we have a tour of your boat? Below deck, perhaps? I'd love to see where everything happens."

"Absolutely. This way." Arm extended, Finn indicated for Lynn to go ahead of him.

This was Michelle's chance, so she reached for Arthur's arm to still him. "Arthur, may I speak to you for a moment?"

"Of course." He waved to let his wife know to go ahead without him. "Be with you in a moment, sweetheart."

"No work talk." Lynn pointed as she sashayed away, Finn following her.

"I'm sorry, but this is work talk," Michelle said.

"I had a feeling." Arthur sighed and placed a hand on her shoulder. "You remind me of a younger me, the female version. I don't fault you for your ambition. I only want you to avoid the pain I've been through. You're like a daughter to me."

The words slammed into her heart with a jolt. Michelle thought she understood pride. But until that moment, pride had been a drop of rain. By contrast, this moment washed over her like an ocean's wave. The only other man she'd ever heard utter those words to her was her father. He was French, spoke in somewhat broken English, and called her "Michelle ma belle" or "my Michelle."

You don't need to be perfect, ma belle. I will love you anyway.

Of course your mother and I are proud you've earned superior grades. But it isn't what you do that makes us love you, it's who you are.

I'm so proud of you, ma belle.

Which is why it had been particularly painful when he'd left them. It wasn't because of anything she'd done wrong, her mother had assured her. Her father missed home too much and understood Michelle's mother would never agree to move to France.

It was the one refrain she'd heard plenty of times since she'd become a family law attorney.

It isn't anything you've done wrong, Timmy or Robby or Jessica. Your parents just can't live together anymore.

What a crock.

No matter what anyone else told them, kids always made it about them. If you don't want the children to think it's all about them, don't get a divorce.

Or don't have children in the first place.

But of course, it wasn't that simple. Never.

Her father left Michelle not because of what she'd done, but because of who she was. She wasn't worth staying for. She wasn't worth fighting over.

Now, hearing Arthur say he considered her like a daughter made all those feelings of raw hope return. She'd waited a long time for a man she admired to say, "I'm so proud of you." But Arthur hadn't quite said that, had he? He'd just said she reminded him of his younger self. A self he'd abandoned for a reason. Still, she refused to let ambition be a dirty word. Arthur was a man, so he wouldn't understand how hard she'd had to fight.

"I wanted to let you know that Tippy Goodwill dropped in on Friday. She wants a—"

"I know." Arthur shook his head slowly. "Artie told me."

Of course he had. Michelle imagined he hadn't hesitated to tell Daddy how mean the new colleague had been for not lying down and playing possum so *he* could have the client.

"I do realize it would be more in keeping with the status quo for a partner to represent her. It wasn't anything underhanded on my part. She just walked in and no one else was in the office that early other than me. She didn't ask for anyone in particular. But Artie—" she almost choked on the word, but Arthur had asked her to call his son by the childish nickname to distinguish between them "—came in and was surprised to see her there. I got the distinct feeling he thought since you wouldn't represent her, he would."

Arthur nodded. "I heard everything. Don't let him bother you. Tippy and Ted are two of my oldest friends. If my firm has to represent one of them, I'd rather someone other than a Pierce handle the case."

"And is Artie okay with this?"

"He isn't. But you let me worry about that."

"Thank you. I won't disappoint you."

"I know you won't. Just please, as a favor to me, let's try to keep it civil between these two. Encourage them in every way to be fair to each other. There was love there for many decades. I would like them to remember it."

"Of course." Michelle bit her lower lip and tried to smile. "I'll do everything I can to make it happen."

But keeping things fair was going to be difficult.

Chapter Seven

"**W**hat a *wonderful* morning!" Lynn said when Finn pulled into the dock a few hours later. "Thank you, Captain."

"We'll need to do this again soon." Arthur held his hand out to his wife to help her. "What about the team-building day? When can we arrange for that to happen?"

Finn eyed Michelle, waiting for her cue. Naturally, he loved the idea because of the business, but maybe he'd already pushed her too hard with this outing.

"Team building?" Michelle said.

She was obviously playing dumb. Finn put his arm around her. "Don't you remember, my angel, the night I finally met Arthur?"

"Oh, right. But I don't really think we need to—"

"Michelle, you can't let Tippy's divorce case derail you from spending time with this wonderful man." Lynn shook a finger. "I thought the idea of a team party sounded fantastic and a good way for you to balance work with your love life."

"But we can do the team building anywhere," Michelle protested, shrinking a bit under his touch. "We don't need to do it on a boat."

Finn pulled her closer, sandwiching her between his arms to the point that she couldn't move. "Everything is better on a boat. Haven't you seen the commercial? You're *happier* on a boat. You laugh more. Once you board the boat, you'll already feel friendly, which will establish a baseline of trust from that point forward. I think it's a great idea."

Michelle gave him a look similar to the one she'd given after her toast, after which all *he'd* been able to think about was long, deep kisses that lasted for days.

Her lips, eyes and entire body said: *look what you're making me do!*

"I'll talk to our scheduler, and get you on the calendar," Finn said before Michelle could come up with another argument or Arthur could change his mind.

They could do an all-day event, bring on food and beverages, charge them their highest rate. It would mean seeing Junior again, but Finn could take it. This time they'd meet on his turf. And if there came an opportunity to shove him off portside when no one was looking, well…

"That sounds amazing," Michelle said without an ounce of sincerity. "There's nothing I'd rather do than encourage us all to trust in each other more. If a boat makes it easier, so be it. I guess I could use some more vitamin D!"

"Then we're in agreement!" Lynn glowed. "Oh, Michelle, I'm having a little gathering at the house Friday night, and I'd love to have you and Finn over."

"Remember, we've been wanting to have you two over for weeks," Arthur said.

"Oh, darn." Michelle grabbed Finn's forearm, her fingernails digging into his flesh. "We have that…thing. Remember?"

For a professional liar, Michelle didn't think fast on her feet. And Finn refused to help her. "What thing?"

"You'd forget your head if it wasn't screwed on, boo."

She reached to tousle his hair. "It's that…thing that *you* know… Noah invited us, I believe?"

"Oh *that* thing." Finn lowered her hand, holding it tightly at her side. "That's nothing. I'll cancel it."

"Fantastic!" Arthur waved, leading his wife down the gangplank. "See you then."

To her credit, Michelle stood trapped in his arms without so much as a body twitch until the Pierces drove off, which took several minutes. His hand rested low on her back, and she was so close he could feel each inhalation she took. That meant he couldn't miss the fact that the breaths were coming faster and shorter. She sounded like a train winding up to climb a steep hill.

Finally, she looked up at him, her amber eyes filled with such fierceness that even he stepped back.

"What are you *doing*?"

"Helping you."

"Helping *me*? Face it, you're helping yourself. You want to charge the firm more money to take the boat out. And you're trying to be all buddy-buddy with Arthur. Don't think that I can't see what you're doing."

"What I'm doing? You mean besides *helping* you?"

"You've already helped me. And I repaid you." She waved her finger between them. "This was an even exchange. One fake boyfriend for one night in exchange for a year's beer tab. Now you're adding all kinds of extra stuff in that wasn't part of our plan."

"If it makes you feel any better, you can forget about my tab."

"What? No! That was our deal."

"You *want* to take care of my tab?"

"I want you to stop…stop…"

"Distracting you?"

She blinked, but he could tell that he'd hit a nerve. Maybe she didn't appreciate Finn redirecting her from the work that consumed her. No one understood passion that took over a life more than he did. For him, it had been the sport of sailing for much of his adult life. Nothing about that had been balanced. An athlete had to give it their all, never leave anything on the table. That sacrifice cost more than the average person sitting on the sidelines realized. But other than the physical aspect, the dedication and strength it took wasn't all that different from a CEO or lawyer sitting behind a desk or computer monitor. Winning and the pursuit of winning, in any form, was all-consuming.

She two-finger pointed to her eyes and then to his. "You *can't* distract me. I'm all about focus. Attention to detail."

"Uh-huh. I would bet that Arthur is less impressed by what you do than by who you are."

Her jaw gaped, and then she squinted, clearing her throat. "What did you say?"

"You heard me."

"I did. And who I am is a kickass attorney." She crossed her arms, then rubbed one elbow. "Arthur knows I can do what needs to be done."

"Right. Got it. When it comes to your new client, just don't lose sight of the fact you're dealing with two people who presumably did love each other once."

"Are you letting your opinion of your buddy Ted color your judgment?"

He didn't appreciate the accusation. "I'm suggesting there might be two sides to everything and you're only representing one."

"That's the way it has to be. Otherwise, it's a conflict of interest."

"I get the feeling you dive in deep and forget who you are for a while when you're working on a case."

"You don't know me, *Finn*."

"I think I do because I used to be the same way. Focused. Hard driving. Ambitious."

"I understand. And I'm guessing that's how you lost your wife."

Ouch. Leave it to Michelle to give it to him straight, zero subtlety involved. She was right, of course, though that didn't make it any easier to hear.

"But first, I lost myself."

He shrugged, thinking he might have been married *because of* his lack of focus on anything other than the sport, and not the other way around. Had he been paying attention, he would have seen he and Cheryl weren't right for each other from the very beginning. She'd loved the limelight, parties, all the adulation and fame by association. Finn had always enjoyed time alone. He liked small towns and preferred gatherings with close friends.

In the end they'd stayed together out of habit and not because of a passionate kind of love.

"I'm not married or in a significant relationship other than this fake one with you. I have nothing to lose," Michelle said.

The words hung between them, and they disturbed Finn. She was probably thinking about Noah, and how she'd already lost him. Why bother doing anything other than throwing herself into her work?

"Isn't there anything else you care about? All I'm suggesting is that you don't let your career be everything. You're not exactly like I was, working toward an event that happens every four years, but sooner or later you'll have to slow down. Make sure you have people who care about you in your life. Not just people who care what a great attorney you are."

"Are you saying...you really are *worried* about me?"

"Don't sound so surprised. This has nothing to do with Noah and Twyla. I understand ambition and I recognize it in you."

"Then if anything, you should admire me."

"Who says I don't?" He reached to touch a flyaway hair.

He shouldn't touch her now. There was no reason. But he couldn't seem to help himself. It was like his fingers, his hands, had already learned her geography. She had a breathtaking kind of face that he'd noticed the moment he laid eyes on her. He'd been dumbstruck in that moment, keeping a healthy distance between them. He appreciated her beauty the same way he admired a gorgeous sunset from afar, or a solar eclipse while wearing the special shades.

Protection and separation.

But right now, just a step away from her, he saw something else entirely. Something new.

It wasn't just her obvious physical attributes. There'd been plenty of pretty women in his life. But Michelle radiated a glow that pulled him to her like a magnet. He felt unexplainably close to her, like he'd known her for years. It didn't make any sense, but he couldn't clear it from his head and the sensation hung between them, like the other shoe waiting to drop.

"I...just so you know, I won't *let* you distract me." She stared at his lips.

Distracting her would be an enjoyable use of his time, and he'd be up for it in a second. He studied her lips, questioning his next moves, but not wanting to argue with himself either. Not right now. He would fight this or regret it later. But right now, he wanted to kiss Michelle and do it with intention. And without an audience.

Just one step closer, and he reached for her, sinking his fingers into her hair, which, my God, was softer and silkier than he'd imagined. She didn't protest, didn't move back an inch, and when he lowered his head and pressed his lips to hers, her hands clutched his waist. This was very different from their first kiss in the bar when she'd grabbed him by the lapels and hauled him down. It was a somewhat shocking moment then, and now? Oddly, this one felt natural. Easy. He went deeper with the kiss when he heard a soft moan escape from her. She was definitely enjoying this, maybe almost half as much as him.

Finn heard someone's throat clear and was torn from the moment. Michelle stepped back so quickly she almost lost her footing.

"Easy," Finn said as he steadied her.

"Oh, um, hey, boss," Tee, junior captain in training, said. "Sorry to interrupt y'all."

"You're not interrupting," Michelle said, as if those words were going to take away the fact they'd been making out for the past few minutes.

"What's up?" Finn asked, moving toward Tee.

"Another inquiry about sailing lessons." He nudged his chin toward the woman standing behind him.

Finn held up a palm. "Be right with you."

A great deal of interest in sailing lessons had been unleashed once everyone heard Finn had become part owner of Nacho Boat. But no one seemed to have noticed they didn't have a sailboat. Yet. Granted, Finn would be happy to give lessons, but he'd prefer to mentor younger people who were taking the sport seriously. So far, there had been a few women who dropped by or called and asked if lessons were available yet.

"Hmm," Michelle said quietly. "Isn't *she* pretty."

"Jealous?"

She tipped her chin. "Jealousy is an unproductive emotion. If someone doesn't want to be with you, that's their choice. Better to know sooner rather than later."

"That's very enlightened of you."

It could be a lie, of course. But it could also be the view from an extremely detached person who'd never really lost someone she deeply cared about. In that case, poor Noah.

"I guess I'll see you on Friday." She tucked her hair behind her ears.

"Yes, you will. I wouldn't miss it."

He gave her a hand and helped her off the boat, where he watched one of the best butts he'd ever laid eyes on once again walk away from him.

He went inside the small Nacho Boat hut house near their dock to explain to Josie Tunelo that they would add sailing lessons as soon as their fleet grew. He chatted with her for a few minutes and then spent the rest of the day helping Tee with some inventory, checking the engine on the new addition to their fleet, wiping down their paddle boards and helping Noah set up for their next charter. Though Finn loved little more than being on the water, he'd be the first to admit that co-owner of Nacho Boat was one of the least glamorous jobs he'd ever had.

At the end of their day, Noah headed home to Twyla and Finn headed to the Salty Dog. Declan was working tonight, and Finn may as well get started on that free tab he had going. And there was his brother behind the bar, flirting and serving up drinks.

"Hey, look who's here," Declan said, immediately setting a cold beer and napkin in front of an empty stool. "It's my favorite brother."

"I'm your only brother." Finn took a seat.

"Heard about your tab. Michelle arranged it with the boss. You've got to tell me what in the world you did to earn that."

"Wouldn't you like to know." Finn grinned.

He felt too guilty now about the running tab. He'd need to put a stop to that.

"Hey, what's wrong with Teddy?" A regular sitting two stools from Finn hooked his thumb toward the back. "He's never in here alone."

Finn turned and there at the farthest booth in the back of the restaurant section was Ted Goodwill.

He looked every bit like a man who'd just been given bad news and Finn could guess what it was.

Chapter Eight

"Maybe he and his wife had a big fight," Declan said.

"But they *never* fight," the other man said.

"That could be the problem." Declan crossed his arms and leaned his back against the counter. "Arguments are great. Get it all out in the open and deal with it. Hash it out. Then, all that make-up sex. Nothing like it."

Finn snorted. "Okay, Dr. Sheridan. Do you charge by the hour?"

Ever since taking on this bartending gig, Declan fancied himself an amateur psychologist too.

Taking his beer with him, Finn excused himself and made his way to the back booth of the restaurant. There Ted sat alone, nursing a tumbler of an amber-hued liquid strongly resembling Scotch. If Finn knew Ted, it was Malt Scotch and the best brand they carried.

"Hey, Ted."

Ted glanced up. He looked like he'd shoved his hands through the little tuffs he had left of his hair so many times they were sticking out to the sides making him look a little like Bozo the clown.

Poor sucker.

"Oh, hey there, Finn. How are you, son? How's business at Nacho Boat?"

Just like Ted to change the subject and take the attention off himself. He was always so damn friendly.

"Good. But how are *you*? Everyone's a little worried. You don't look so happy."

Ted waved a hand dismissively. "Ah, I'll be fine. I just got hit with a zinger today. Imagine! Sunday, the day of rest. I thought I'd come home and surprise my wife by taking her out to dinner. You know the new Thai restaurant on the other end of town that just opened? I've been wanting to support the place and put my money where my mouth is."

"Couldn't get reservations?"

Finn had to play along. He wasn't going to tell Ted that he'd known about the divorce before he did. A man could only take so much humiliation.

"Ha! I wish." He took a swallow and set his glass down. "You might as well hear about this because it will be all over town tomorrow. My wife has hired the services of Pierce & Pierce."

"She wants a divorce?" Finn tried to throw a little surprise in his voice but probably failed.

"Forty years of marriage, three grown children, five grandchildren and *now* she wants to give up."

"Well, what do you want?"

Ted blinked, as though it hadn't occurred to him anyone would ask. "It doesn't matter. Tippy gets what she wants. It's always been this way."

"Maybe it's time for that to change."

"What do you mean?"

"I mean, don't make it easy for her."

"None of this will be easy. That woman is my life." Ted sat up straighter, running fingers through the sides of his hair again. This time he smoothed the hair down. "She thinks I've been with another woman."

Finn quirked a brow. "Have you?"

"Now, does that sound like me?" He laid a hand on his chest. "I flirt a lot, sure. But nothing more than that. It doesn't matter one way or another because she's convinced of it."

"Sounds like she's just upset. Maybe this will all go away."

"Not if Artie Junior has anything to do with it. At his birthday party when he was thirteen, I failed to buy him the correct video game. Spoiled brat. He's going to enjoy dragging me through countless depositions and paperwork up the wazoo."

"Maybe you haven't heard yet, but Michelle LaCroix is going to represent Tippy."

"Oh, hell, is that permanent? I thought maybe she was simply doing the initial filing." Ted closed his eyes and pinched the bridge of his nose. "I'm done for. Michelle has a reputation that comes all the way from Austin. She's a shrewd woman. I admire that, but I never want her on my bad side."

"Look, Ted. I've been where you are. If you don't fight, you're going to wind up with nothing. Don't let these attorneys take everything you two have built away."

Finn didn't know about this side of divorce. Being married for four years as opposed to forty were two different worlds. In Finn's case, he'd been the one to file after having been separated for six months. Cheryl, who'd already moved in with some other dude, had claimed to have been blindsided. It wasn't true, of course, but it made better copy when she'd hired Pierce & Pierce.

"I want to talk about this, but that's going to be tough when she changed the locks and won't take my calls. I ask you: How do you prove a negative? She claims I'm having an affair because I lost a few pounds and joined the gym.

But I have high blood pressure and she was always bugging me to get healthier!"

Poor Ted. This was all far worse than Finn imagined. It would be easier if the man *was* cheating and didn't love his wife anymore. Then all Finn had to do was advise him on getting an attorney who was just as fierce of a competitor as Michelle would be. But if Ted was going to lose the wife he loved, at the very least he should keep some of the wealth they'd both accumulated over the decades. It was too late for Finn, who now wished he'd fought harder for what he'd earned on his own, but it wasn't too late for Ted.

"You know what, Ted? I'm divorced, too, and I regret every day that I didn't fight harder to keep what was mine."

"I hadn't thought of it that way. I'm used to giving Tippy everything she wants. If she wants a divorce, I'll give that to her, too."

Well, good grief. The man was far too nice for his own good. Reminded him of someone else he used to know.

Him.

"Take it from me. Don't roll over and be the nice guy. Go get yourself a damn good attorney. And fight."

There was at least one person besides Arthur at the firm who seemed excited about a team-building day.

Rachel was ecstatic about spending a day on the water and getting paid to do it and didn't seem to care she'd have to spend it with her coworkers. Arthur had assigned her to do the research on the tasks.

"I can't wait for this! It's going to be *such* fun. Maybe we'll do that one exercise where you have to fall back into your partner's arms."

"You couldn't pay me enough money to do that one.

Artie would drop me in a New York minute and Arthur isn't strong enough to catch me."

"Well, I wouldn't drop you!"

"I know you wouldn't." Michelle smiled. "I trust you."

"But the thing is, you need to do the exercise with someone you *don't* trust. So they can prove to you they're worth trusting."

"Uh-huh."

At this point, she wasn't even sure she'd trust *Finn* to catch her, though he wouldn't be part of their team-building exercises anyway. Still, she pictured letting her body go, Finn catching her, wrapping those admittedly proven strong arms around her. Keeping her in place, not letting her go. The same way he'd done a few days ago on the boat. And those kisses. Well, she wouldn't mind at all reliving those.

"What are you thinking about?" Rachel asked now.

Michelle snapped out of it. "What do you mean?"

"You were staring off into space with a little smile. Are you thinking of a 'get to know you' game? I read about one that sounds kind of fun. It's called 'human knot.' Each person is holding another's left hand in a circle. Then you have to work together to untie the knot without letting go."

"Hmm, sounds fun."

That was a lie. Truthfully, Michelle didn't like games of any kind and seemed to lack the DNA required to enjoy them. She hated trivia, charades, Clue, Twister, Monopoly (the game that never ended) and anything that didn't involve arguing.

The phone rang and Rachel went back to her desk.

Michelle bent her head and got back to work. The case of *Goodwill vs. Goodwill* had just begun, and she wanted to stay on top of everything. At least Artie had been civil with Michelle earlier this week, not even mentioning the case, which she found refreshing. Maybe he would come around after all.

"Michelle, you've got a call," Rachel said. "Henry Hall from Hall and Associates."

"Did he say what it's regarding?" Michelle didn't know a Henry Hall.

Just then, Artie strolled by her office, chuckling. "Better take it."

Great. Michelle picked up the phone. "This is Michelle LaCroix."

"Henry Hall here, Hall & Associates in Houston. Sending over representation today via facsimile and emergency filing. We're representing Theodore Goodwill in Goodwill v. Goodwill."

She didn't understand why Artie had been chuckling a moment ago. As if Michelle couldn't hold her own in a highly contested divorce. She'd assumed she'd have a fight on her hands.

"I look forward to working with you."

"Do you?" He chuckled. "I should warn you that I don't lose."

And if only Michelle had a nickel for every man who'd ever said that to her. "Well, if we do right by our clients, *nobody* has to lose."

She was trying to take Finn's advice to heart. Hours later, that evening, she remembered his words.

I used to be the same way.

Focused. Hard driving. Ambitious.

And of course, he had to have been. She couldn't very well imagine an athlete got to the Olympics any other way. Of all people, Finn had to understand that it was impossible to back down from a goal when you were this close. She didn't know much about Finn Sheridan, but in that moment, she realized they had at least one thing in common. He'd experienced being at the pinnacle of success, and while she had yet to make partner, she was close. She'd been close before, too, but there was still somewhat of an old boys' club in certain circles.

"I should tell you that my client has no intention of selling any of their jointly owned properties," Henry said. "Especially not the lighthouse."

"That's…interesting. What does he have in mind?"

"He's suggesting buying Tippy out. He will be the new owner under a newly named corporation. He's looking into financing now and with all his contacts and proven success record, it shouldn't be difficult."

My, how kind of him to discount all of Tippy's hard work.

"Sounds reasonable, as long as it's fair market value and equitable shares." Michelle tapped her pen on the edge of her desk. "I'll talk to my client."

"And of course, we need to get started on mediation. There's no judge in Charming that will take a case that hasn't been through two attempts at mediation. I have the names of some people we've used in the past with great success. They're mostly in Houston."

"We filed in Charming."

"Yes, but there are no family law mediators in Charming."

What? No retired attorneys or judges offering their services? You couldn't throw a stick in Austin and not hit a retired judge.

"Okay, send me the list." Michelle hung up and walked to the front desk. "Rachel, I'll need everything we have on Houston family law mediators. I'll have some names for you soon."

Artie emerged from his corner office. "Rachel, how are we doing on that case law I asked you to look into?"

"Still working on it, Artie."

Michelle turned to Junior. "Did you happen to refer Ted to his attorney?"

"Nope, I actually did not. But I got a call yesterday. Henry wanted to know why I wasn't representing Tippy. I explained we've got a wunderkind attorney on board and that you'd be taking point on this one."

"Thanks for the vote of confidence." Michelle nodded. "I intend to make a lot of money for this firm, and I figured you'd appreciate that."

"Of course I do."

But as he closed the door to his office, somehow Michelle didn't believe him.

Chapter Nine

The week flew by and before Michelle even realized it, it was Friday again. Friday, a week from when Tippy had walked into the office and announced she wanted a divorce. Since then, Michelle had talked to her twice a day, if not more. Tippy called frequently, because she'd apparently decided not to talk to her husband any longer.

Even if every phone call she made to Michelle cost her money, Tippy called and kept Michelle on the phone with apparently little to no care how she was running up her billable hours. She'd sent over a hefty amount as a retainer for their services, but the way things were going, if she didn't stop calling, she'd plow through that money faster than she should. The divorce had proven to be more contentious than expected because Ted wouldn't agree with just about everything Tipsy wanted. And it appeared he didn't understand the word *compromise*. Neither did her client, for that matter.

There were still depositions to get through, mediation, and hours of pretrial work ahead of Michelle. The Goodwills' finances were a quagmire that they'd have to iron out with the help of experts. Michelle had spent time looking and talking to structured settlement negotiators.

"Michelle, it's the mayor again," Rachel called out. "She sounds upset. Again."

Michelle picked up the pen near the phone and started tapping it against the edge of her desk.

"Hey. Everything okay?"

"Absolutely not!" Tippy shrieked and Michelle had to hold back the phone an inch. "His shyster attorney says Teddy wants to remain the owner of the lighthouse. He'll buy me out."

It was Michelle's understanding he wanted to do the same with all their mutual properties, with the exception of their personal home. But Michelle wasn't going to bring that up right now. Whatever was unpleasant, whatever brought about discord, Michelle kept in the tight fist of her hand.

"Yes, but he will pay fair market value. You could walk away from all this a wealthy woman."

"I already *am* a wealthy woman! But not many people own a *lighthouse*! You want to know who owns a restored lighthouse? Me, that's who!"

"Yes, but—"

"And please don't start with fair market value. How many other lighthouses are available for sale in Charming? None! I was in real estate, Michelle, there are no comps! Besides, I *can't* let him own the lighthouse. I'm the one who found it, negotiated with the previous owner, arranged for the ship restoration. I found the retired ship's staircase!"

"But...you were going to sell it in the divorce anyway."

"Sell and split the profits so neither *one* of us owns it. But he can't have it. That would be incredibly unfair after I did all the work!"

"So, you want someone else to enjoy all your hard work?"

"Exactly, maybe a nice couple like Cole and Valerie, but certainly not my ex-husband!"

But Cole, one of the owners of the Salty Dog Bar & Grill, and Valerie, a schoolteacher, could never afford to buy the lighthouse.

"Would you prefer to buy *him* out, Tippy?" Michelle felt a migraine coming on.

"No."

She didn't want to believe this entire divorce would be held up on a lighthouse neither one of them had ever lived in. But it was, let's face it, the ultimate status symbol. It was the status symbol of status symbols. They went back and forth on this issue, but Tippy's reasoning was circular. It wasn't as if Michelle hadn't run into this kind of dilemma before. A divorce made all couples highly emotional and overwhelmingly unreasonable. Honestly, Tippy wasn't being fair. If Ted offered to buy her out, she shouldn't refuse. Well, she could, but she'd hold this divorce up for possibly months. Years. Over a single piece of community property. So far.

Unless maybe that was what she wanted. A long and contentious divorce in which she'd punish not only Ted but also herself. Michelle had not once, not twice, but *three* times nearly asked Tippy whether she actually *wanted* a divorce. But that wasn't her place. She was simply providing a service and doing the best for her client. She'd venture this was exactly what Henry Hall was doing, too. She'd bet *he* wouldn't suggest couples counseling to Ted, no matter how unreasonable he became.

After receiving their notice of representation, Michelle had done her due diligence. Hall and Associates represented several high-profile clients, including the ex-wife of a former Astros player. Yeah, she got it. They were hot stuff compared to the tiny boutique firm of Pierce & Pierce. But they'd never been up against her.

Michelle glanced at the clock. She'd been on the phone for an hour with Tippy, not the best use of her time. All she'd done was listen to her vent and assure her she was doing everything she could on her behalf, and she would continue to do so.

As if her life depended on it.

Michelle had to wind this call up. "So, I'll talk to Ted's attorney and see if they can be convinced to sell to a third party. Maybe I'll put together some figures of what the lighthouse could be sold for on the open market in a bidding war and that might make Ted think again."

"Oh, Michelle, that's brilliant! Once Teddy sees how much money he *could* have, he can't possibly refuse."

Michelle hung up and glanced at the time. She typed in an hour, then deleted it. She'd bill down to the half hour. Then she stopped short when she realized *Junior* wouldn't reduce out of the kindest of his heart and neither would Mr. Hall. So why the hell should she?

She typed in one hour on her billables, gritting her teeth.

For the first time in weeks, Michelle looked forward to leaving the office. Paperwork and motions had kept her chained to her desk for most of the week and now she had the dinner party at Arthur's. A moment she'd dreaded since she'd lied to Arthur about having a serious relationship. In the beginning, she dreaded coming up with yet another excuse for why she and her fake boyfriend couldn't attend. Now, she feared the idea of showing up with Finn and pretending to be a couple who'd dated for months. She wasn't sure they could pull this off.

But ever since Sunday, Finn, and that kiss, she hadn't tried very hard to come up with a reason, either. She *wanted* to see Finn even if it might be uncomfortable.

She really didn't know why he'd kissed her when Arthur

wasn't there, unless he wanted to prove something to himself. Clearly, Finn was a competitive person by nature, so maybe he was just trying to show off his skills.

He might not like Michelle's profession, but he certainly seemed to like landing on her lips just fine. Whether Finn was truly interested in her or not didn't matter. At long last, this dinner party was an opportunity to really demonstrate to Arthur that she was ready and willing to be part of this community. That she could be social and meet and schmooze on behalf of the firm.

She and Finn had texted during the week and, after some severe arm twisting, he'd eventually agreed that *she* could pick *him* up. After all, this whole thing had been her idea, and Finn really was being a good sport about it. Finn had offered to drive himself and meet her there, but how would that look?

"Like you worked late, and I came from the port?" Finn had said. "We both work late."

"No. First, we'll look like a couple of workaholics with no work-life balance, and it will *look* like we're not actually together."

"Are you telling me you're joined at the hip with your real boyfriends? Because I don't buy that."

"No, I'm not, but this makes sense for several reasons."

She'd launched into a five-point argument, wishing she had time for a PowerPoint, as to why arriving together gave off a better vibe. Eventually Finn agreed with a loud sigh.

Truthfully, she liked to drive her car and remain in control of any situation. This way she would stay as long as she liked, leave when she wanted and not just when her date was ready. He could leave with her or find another way home. This was her modus operandi in a relationship. Control, and she never relinquished an inch. In some ways,

Tippy reminded Michelle of herself. But in most ways, she'd begun to remind Michelle a lot of her own mother. Christina.

Her mother had also refused to compromise. Her job as a programmer could be done remotely from almost anywhere in the world. She *could* have met Michelle's father halfway and agreed to move to France for a few years. They might have had a wonderful experience and later returned to the US. She was sure her father would have come back with them. He'd simply been lonely and homesick for his own country.

Michelle could have been educated abroad and learned another language via full immersion. She would have aced college French instead of having to study all hours of the night. A lot of things might have happened, not the least that she'd still have a father in her life. But they didn't love each other, and the bottom line was compromises were made only when two people were in love and wanted to be together.

Michelle left the office early, leaving Rachel to lock up for a change. At home, she showered, reapplied her makeup, straightened her hair, and stepped into her little black dress. The hem fell just above the knee, not appropriate for court, and she rarely had a chance to wear it. Tonight, she paired the dress with her red strappy heels. Hair? Straightened. Makeup? Flawless. Grabbing her little black purse, Michelle headed to Finn's place, which she already knew he shared with his brother, Declan.

And it was Declan who opened the door when she knocked. She allowed the glint of male appreciation in his eyes to wash over her with a rush of feminine satisfaction. She had no interest in Declan, but it still felt good to have her attractiveness acknowledged. After being cast aside for

Twyla, Michelle had become a little more sensitive about those things than she ever had been in the past. Looks had never been all that important to her because she'd had nothing to do with them. They wouldn't get her good grades or acceptance into law school. Her looks were simply part of her mother's lucky gene pool. Michelle hadn't accomplished her looks, in other words, but it was nice to know men still noticed her.

"Wow… I mean, uh, hey there." He waved her inside. "You're here for Finn, right?"

"Yes, we have a dinner date."

"If you're having second thoughts, I'm the younger, tremendously handsome, and all-around far more capable brother. Bonus, I happen to be available tonight." He splayed his hands wide with a grin that made it obvious he was teasing.

"You're adorable but much too young for me. Go get my date, please." She shooed him away.

But just then Finn appeared behind Declan.

"Here he is," Declan said.

Holy sworn deposition. The man cleaned up well. It occurred to her that she'd never seen Finn wear anything but board shorts, jeans, T-shirts, peacoats and windbreakers. Now, he was dressed in dark slacks and a long-sleeved blue button-up. Brown beard stubble covered his chin and jaw. Michelle swallowed hard.

Nope. I'm not going there.

She did not want to be in the position, after that kiss, to start imagining: *Oh my God, does he actually like me?* This wasn't eighth grade, and she didn't care whether or not Finn liked her. Much. As long as he faked it well, that should be her only real concern.

They said their goodbyes and Finn led her out the door, hand low on her back.

"I can take my truck," Finn said. "There's no need for you to drive me like a chauffeur."

"We already had this discussion."

"Right. And your arguments were sound, counselor."

"Thank you."

He stopped halfway to her sedan. "Should I ride in the back and call you Jeeves?"

"Don't be silly. You'll sit up front with me, talk to me and everything." She unclicked the car doors and Finn rushed to open hers.

She did her best to pretend that didn't impress her, but the first and last man to have opened a door for her was Noah. Not surprisingly, the two were cut from the same gentlemanly alpha male cloth. But she was definitely an alpha female. Hard not to be in her profession.

"Is this going to be a problem?" Michelle said, once Finn had buckled in the front seat.

"Is *what* going to be a problem?"

"That I'm driving us."

"Hey, you won the argument."

"Are you going to get all wounded male sulky and quiet because I insist on driving us?"

"No, Michelle, I didn't sleep through the women's rights movement."

"I would hope not."

He smiled. Finn was a good-looking man but when he smiled it transformed the geography of his face. His smile was easy and slow, a lot like the man. It continually surprised her that he'd been an Olympian. She supposed his new lifestyle might be more relaxing, though she couldn't imagine the stress of owning a business. At the least, he wasn't alone in what he was building now. He and Noah were in it together and they could spread the goals around.

Michelle always felt like she was in competition with herself. *By* herself.

"I don't know who else will be there tonight." Michelle drove in the direction of Arthur's home following the GPS coordinates she'd recently added. "I could have asked but I've had a busy week."

"Is the mayor keeping you on your toes?"

"She calls at least twice a day."

Finn whistled. "You're going to earn your keep."

"I'm sure we both will. Ted hired a prominent law firm in Houston. I have a feeling he's going to be just fine in this divorce."

"Isn't that a good thing?"

"Sure, I mean, I don't want to win if it's too easy." Time to change the subject to more pleasant talk. "So, I don't have any idea if you'll see anyone you know tonight. Sorry about that in advance."

"We can handle anyone. I think we're pretty convincing."

She had begun to think so, too. Finn was making this easy.

"Finn, I know I've been difficult about this arrangement, and it wasn't at all what you'd expected. I wanted to thank you again for helping me out."

"Well, it's not exactly a hardship." There was a slight pause. "You're really rocking that dress."

A sliver of delight rolled through her, but she pushed it aside. It had become a little bit of a mantra: *I don't care what he thinks, I don't care what he thinks.*

"I appreciate you noticing." She cleared her throat, trying to be polite. "And you...you certainly clean up well."

He snorted. "High praise. Did you expect me to smell like salt water and perhaps seaweed?"

No, but she also wasn't prepared for this. He wore a tantalizing cologne, a light scent that only made her want to get closer.

"I just mean, you look—"

"Like I put some effort into this?"

"Well, yes. And I do appreciate it."

"I wouldn't want people to think you're dating a hobo."

"Please, there's no way anyone would confuse you for a hobo even when you're not dressed up."

"A beach bum, then."

"You're not wearing your glasses."

"Wearing contacts tonight. You're welcome."

"Actually, I like your glasses."

She pulled up the circular driveway leading to Arthur's expansive home on the outskirts of Charming.

From the outside, the home looked every bit the showcase it was meant to be. Gabled windows faced the street, with touches of sandstone and brick. The lawns were lush and green.

"Do you want a home like this someday?" Finn said, surveying the castle.

"God, no. Who would clean it? Certainly not me."

He chuckled and together, they walked toward the front door, Finn holding her hand.

"You're making me nervous," Michelle said.

"Me? Why? I should be the scared one. I'm a single fish about to be swallowed up by a school of sharks."

"Shiver. *Shiver* of sharks."

"Are you going to do it, or should I?" He held out his finger poised for the doorbell.

"Go ahead." She nodded.

Michelle half expected a butler to answer the door and ask for their engraved invitations in a posh English accent.

The home exuded that kind of wealth, but it was simply Lynn who opened the door.

"Michelle! Finn! You made it. Please come meet some of our friends." Lynn waved them inside.

Not surprisingly, the home was impeccably decorated. Marble floors, art that looked like it might belong in a museum, vaulted ceilings, and one floor-to-ceiling window overlooking the meadow outside. Arthur was schmoozing with guests, but to Michelle's surprise after introductions, she learned there was not another lawyer in attendance. They met a gallery owner, an angel investor who funded worthy causes like struggling bookstores, Lynn's oldest friend and a retired high school librarian, and George Loren, the head of the Charming Historical Society.

Unfortunately, the high school librarian knew Finn quite well and gushed all over him. She would be the difficult one to convince tonight, if anyone.

"Is this your date, Finn?" Mrs. Drew, the librarian, asked.

"Michelle, meet my favorite teacher," Finn said. "She didn't teach a subject, that's why."

"Oh, Finn. Don't let him fool you, he was my best student. A big reader."

"When I had time."

"When the girls would leave him alone for two minutes, that is." Mrs. Drew laughed.

"He won't confess to being prom king, but I have my suspicions," Michelle said.

"Oh, he was far too shy for that."

"And too busy to campaign for votes," Finn said.

Finn, shy? She was suddenly a lot more worried about conversation with all these strangers tonight, mostly because she didn't know Finn as well as she should. With any luck, they wouldn't appear to be two people who'd just recently met and were out on a date.

Finn sat between Mrs. Drew, and the art gallery owner. Michelle was on the other side of the owner, who seemed to far prefer Finn's conversational skills. She was too far from the angel investor, William something or the other. Instead, she got stuck making very stilted conversation with the head of the Charming Historical Society.

"Charming is a small town filled with heritage. Our citizens don't always appreciate the importance of keeping the integrity of old stately buildings and classic architecture intact. We can't cut corners when it comes to quality. It's like everything in life. The old ways are always the best ways."

And sometimes they're not.

But Michelle bit her tongue, smiling when she had nothing nice to add to the conversation. Meanwhile, two spaces to her right, Finn held court. Charming Finn Sheridan, ladies' man.

"How long have you and Michelle dated?" Michelle overheard Mrs. Drew ask.

Michelle heard Finn field the question easily, smoothly moving from how long they'd been dating to how well they got along.

"Maybe due to her profession, Michelle is great at resolving conflicts," Finn said.

The librarian smiled over at Michelle, a little twinkle in her eye. "How wonderful."

His eyes met Michelle's and he held her gaze for long enough to cause a roar to start in her ears. Something a whole lot like desire curled tight in her stomach and she had to look away first.

"As long as I admit I'm wrong, and she's right, the argument is quickly over." Finn chuckled.

Fortunately, everyone laughed, appreciating the humorous tone in Finn's voice. Even she laughed a little bit. Sure, she'd been accused by exes of always needing to win an argument. She wasn't exactly proud of that.

"You'd rather be right than happy" was a common refrain. How about both? Couldn't she be both right *and* happy? Apparently, not so far. What she needed was a man who could accept not always knowing more than his significant other did. Who could accept not always being the center, authority, and final say on a subject. Noah had been that man—but there had been other issues with him.

The dinner was amazing, a roasted chicken and rice with pine nuts.

It was Mrs. Drew who spoke up first. "Aren't you allergic to pine nuts, Finn?"

"Most nuts," he said. "It's fine. I'll just eat the chicken."

"Arthur, I specifically asked you to check for any food allergies," Lynn said.

"I did," Arthur said and stared across the table at Michelle. "You didn't say anything."

"Well, I… I…" Michelle stammered, thinking this was information she could have used!

"It's my fault." Finn tapped his chest. "I haven't really wanted to mention it, even to Michelle. It just doesn't come up often."

"Well, goodness. This is important information, Finn," Mrs. Drew scolded him. "The people closest to you must know."

"Yes, you're right." He looked over at Michelle. "Sorry, honey. I should have said something earlier."

Honey. Well, that seemed far more sincere than pookie bear or angel. It sounded so…real.

Arthur chuckled. "It's almost like you two don't even know each other."

Well, the only thing to do in response to that was burst out laughing, so Michelle did. Finn was kind enough to follow her lead.

After the amazing dinner Finn couldn't eat, dessert was served. Crème brûlée, a favorite of Michelle's. She wanted to lick the ramekin dry, but she wouldn't. The questioning looks Arthur kept throwing her way were disturbing enough not to want to draw any further attention to herself. Any minute now he'd put her under a bright light and start interrogating her. It might not matter so much, but Michelle had lied and misled Arthur. Perhaps unnecessarily, but either way she'd done it.

Now she wanted to support the fabrication in any way she could.

She thought for certain the jig was up when Arthur asked, "Where are you taking Michelle for her birthday, Finn? Do you have any plans?"

"Arthur!" Lynn chided. "Maybe it's supposed to be a surprise."

"No worries," Finn said with a chuckle. "I want to take her to Telluride for a ski weekend."

"You might want to reconsider that." Arthur narrowed his eyes.

Probably because she'd once joked she had never skied a day in her life, hated the idea, and had no intention of ever strapping wood on her feet and hurling herself down an ice-covered hill.

Chapter Ten

"You've never skied in your *life*?" Finn demanded on the ride home.

He hated not driving and should have insisted. It had thrown him completely off his game.

"Finn, I'm a fourth generation Texan. When would I have learned how to snow ski? Seriously? When?"

Until that moment, he'd had a great time and couldn't recall when he'd laughed this much. Then Michelle didn't know about his *allergy*. Had Mrs. Drew not been there, he would have been able to cover, and no one would have been the wiser. But his nut allergy, which admittedly had lessened in later years, was well-established history at their local high school.

"You should talk. It is vitally important to let everyone in your circle know you have a nut allergy!" She turned to him at a stoplight. "Does Noah know?"

"Of course."

"Oh my God, Finn!" She slapped the steering wheel with gusto.

"Fine, sue me."

They were both incredibly frustrated, because similarly, he imagined, neither one of them enjoyed knowing they'd lost credibility with the Pierces. Until those two moments, he was sure no one questioned the two of them being a couple.

Except the real shame of it all, in his mind, was that they were just playing at this.

Because Michelle was unlike anyone he'd ever met before, and he found himself cursing his bad Irish luck that it hadn't been him to meet her before Noah. She was smart, funny, and shockingly patient when required. He'd overheard George griping to her over certain movements in the country that were tipping the scales in what he saw as a negative way, without once acknowledging that they were tipping in Michelle's direction for a change. Or maybe he was just simply that oblivious. He'd used the old-school excuse of being "from another generation where this sort of thing wasn't a big deal."

Even Finn had cringed. But Michelle continued to smile when Finn thought she probably wanted to throat punch the man. She added her thoughts, always politely stating facts. And for an upwardly mobile attorney, she also didn't seem particularly impressed or intimidated by all the overt wealth displayed. Considering what he'd been through in his marriage, Finn found this more than refreshing.

She sighed. "Glad that's over. That's the most peopling I've done in a long while."

"It's exhausting, isn't it?"

"*What?* You really think so? But you looked so at ease talking to everyone. They all loved you."

"Hey. Fake it till you make it. And any woman who can smile while George mansplains the 'Me Too' movement to her deserves a gold medal of her own."

"I love that you said 'mansplaining.' It took all my strength not to clock him. But you know, mixed company and all that."

"Save your battles for the courtroom."

"Exactly."

She turned onto the coastal road that twisted along toward the heart of Charming. The boardwalk. The renovated lighthouse.

"You really get me."

He did, and this worried him a little bit. For someone who had decided he wanted to move beyond temporary, Michelle was exactly the wrong choice. She'd *chosen* him because this was temporary, and he'd agreed. It wasn't exactly fair for him to change his mind midway. It occurred to him that once, he'd chosen the wrong woman at what had seemed the right time.

Now he had met the right woman at the wrong time.

If not for bad luck, he'd have no luck at all. She was fresh off a breakup that had stunned her, and though she might claim to be moving on, Michelle struck him as someone who, like him, didn't want anyone's pity. If she still felt something for Noah, she would keep it close and quiet. She was a class act, too, and wouldn't want either Noah or Twyla to feel any guiltier than they already did for loving each other.

"Do you have to go straight home?" Finn said now.

"Why?"

"I hope you know that we're really going to have to hang out together if this is going to work at all. We both nearly blew it tonight. And it's cooled down. I want to show you something."

"Really, Finn, if you want to make out, just say so." She smirked.

"Yes, of course I do."

Her cheeks colored a pleasant shade of pink. "Well, at least you're honest."

"But I meant what I said. It wasn't a euphemism." He pointed. "Turn up ahead."

He led her off the winding road, toward a location only known by locals. The lane ended at a lookout point with a slight elevation giving a clear view of Galveston in the distance. In this spot, on a clear night like this one, the stars seemed to shine brighter. Away from the downtown lights of the boardwalk and lighthouse, they didn't have to compete for top billing.

"Beautiful, isn't it?"

She nodded, flipping off her headlights. "Is this where you used to take all the girls?"

"What girls?"

"Please. Don't try to act like you weren't crowned prom king."

He snorted. "Not me. You're thinking of Declan."

"You look just like him. I imagine you both could have been prom kings."

"Nah, I spent more of my time sailing. They don't give out crowns for that."

"Didn't they used to?" She chuckled.

Ah, she was making a reference to the ancient Olympic crowns made from leaves and olive branches.

"You got me there. I guess I was crowned, in a sense. Eventually."

"What was it like, being the best of the best?"

If he wasn't mistaken, there was a tinge of awe in her tone. Most people treated what he'd accomplished with deference, but Michelle wasn't most people.

"In the end it was a quick minute of my life. In the grand scheme of things, the kind of moment you miss if you blink. All the years of work and dedication for one moment of glory. But yeah, it was worth it. I'll never say it wasn't."

"I read that many Olympic athletes go on to have careers that have nothing to do with the sport they excelled in. One is a dentist; another is an Army sergeant. All types of various careers. I didn't find a single lawyer, though."

"You googled Olympic athletes?"

She shrugged. "I felt like I should know you a little better if we were going to fake date."

"I'm flattered."

"What? You didn't stalk *me* on social media? I'm insulted."

"Ah, I've backed off socials. They were giving me a migraine."

He unbuckled, stepped out of the car, then walked around to open her door. She accepted his hand, and they walked a few steps to get a much better view. The waves lapped gently, the Gulf calm tonight. A slight wind whipped her hair and a strand landed on her lips. She pushed it off.

He didn't let go of her hand.

"Why family law?" he asked, and to let her know he wasn't judging, he squeezed her hand.

"It's pretty cliché. I wanted to understand humans better. Here's the thing: I think sometimes divorce is the only option."

"I agree. When the love is gone, you may as well bring the relationship to a legal end. That was how my divorce went. Painful but necessary."

"So, it isn't divorce you hate, but just divorce attorneys?"

"It turns out I don't hate them all." He lowered his gaze and let it linger on her full lips.

They were still lipstick pink, and he wanted to kiss her until he'd stripped all the color away.

"Finn? Do you want to make out?" She met his eyes and smiled, and his heart stopped beating in his chest.

"Yeah."

The sound of his voice was a croak, but hell yeah, he was on board.

Michelle couldn't remember a time when she'd ever been this drawn to a man.

She had to reach back to high school, when she'd had an infatuation with the captain of the football team. She'd been the proverbial smart girl who tutored athletes. But unlike the rom-coms, no athlete ever lowered her glasses, tossed them aside and suddenly saw her as a beauty.

They all had girlfriends, of course, cheerleaders mostly. She'd pictured that moment anyway. In her teenage fantasies, Jake Wyatt would see her in a different light and kiss her. And every time Jake Wyatt, who was a dead ringer for Liam Hemsworth, smiled at her, her mind became this vacuous hole.

And that was how this felt, too. *I'm making out with Finn Sheridan!* Finn, the man who drew long and heated gazes from women everywhere he went. Finn, the sulky quiet type who wasn't so sulky now. The man she thought had never given her a second glance. Somehow he'd noticed her.

The best thing about all this was he'd make the *perfect* rebound guy. When he was ready to move on, she'd be fine with it. When she understood, when a man made his intentions clear, she was fine and dandy. She *could* be fine and dandy...probably.

Alright, so she'd never done this before. She'd never purposely determined that a relationship would have a timeline. A deadline. But that's how her relationships wound up anyway, so what if she went in with very lowered expectations?

They liked each other once they'd stopped arguing. She loved the way he kissed her, like she was oxygen, and he'd run out of it. Like she was ice cream, and he was a sugar addict. His hands were talented, those large and callused palms that roamed everywhere and caused little earthquakes of pleasure from every part of her body.

Back in the car, she drove them as quickly as she could, conversation nonexistent as she wondered if she still had a stash of condoms in her bathroom—and whether they'd expired. But when they reached her house, Michelle got shy at the door, unsure whether this was such a good idea anymore.

"What's wrong?" he said, obviously sensing the mood change as she went inside and began flipping on lights. "Change your mind?"

"No." She whipped around to face him. "Did you?"

"Never." His hand slid from her waist down to her behind. "This is—"

She rose to her tiptoes and covered his mouth. "Let's not talk anymore."

And they didn't, for a long while, kissing like they were going for the gold. It was all going so incredibly well, dare she say silver level about to reach gold, and she jumped when the doorbell rang.

Finn, who had his hand between her thighs, froze. "Expecting anyone?"

"No."

They both stared at the door like maybe if they looked at it long enough the door would turn transparent, causing the person to reveal themselves.

"Michelle?" someone called, sounding just like Tippy in a sing-song voice. "Oh, Michelle?"

"You do house calls, counselor?" Finn quirked a brow.

"Not usually." Michelle stood and smoothed down the skirt of her dress.

"Tell her to go away," Finn said, leaning back and splaying his hands behind his neck. "She's on your time now."

"I can't *do* that. She's a very high-profile client. And she's here. Outside."

"After hours. Are you going to charge her overtime?"

"What's that supposed to mean?"

"Meaning," Finn said, sounding more than a little frustrated, "that you're about to work, I imagine. At eight o'clock in the evening."

"If she has legal questions, I'll answer them. Then send her on her way."

"Take your time," Finn said, standing. "This was probably a mistake anyway."

"Finn," Michelle said under her breath, her desire taking a nosedive. She was disappointed, too.

"Yoo-hoo, Michelle! I see the light is on in there," Tippy called again.

"I'll get out of here so you two can have some privacy." Finn walked to open the door himself. "Hello, Mrs. Mayor. Please come inside. I was just leaving."

"Oh, Finn. I didn't realize I was interrupting anything." She looked from Michelle to Finn and back again.

"You weren't interrupting." He smiled. "We were just talking about the weather."

"It has been horribly hot, hasn't it?"

"Scorching." Finn slid Michelle a look.

It's Texas in the summer, people, Michelle wanted to say. *What did you expect? Snow flurries?*

"Well, I should really get going," Finn said. "I'll call you tomorrow, pookie bear."

Great, he was back to pookie bear, a sure sign he wasn't happy with her.

"Night, night, boo!"

Two could play this game. Before he shut the door, she was pretty sure he growled.

At no point in her career had Michelle ever had a client in her home. But hey, this was Charming, and the *mayor*. She'd also never facilitated the divorce of a public personality. It was all new territory and a little intimidating. In the past she'd had no problem creating boundaries with clients. No, they could not call her on the weekends. She never gave out her personal number. But this was Charming where everyone was so…yeah. Charming.

"Lord, aren't you two so sweet," Tippy said. "Ted and I were the same way, you know? Once upon a time, before he became an idiot."

"Can I get you something to drink?"

"No thank you, dear." She found a place on the couch and patted the place next to it. "I have news. And I hope you won't be too upset."

"Oh, no. What's wrong?"

"I've changed my mind about the lighthouse."

That was the bad news? Michelle could work with this. "You've decided to allow Ted to buy you out. That's wise. You can come out of this sale set for life."

"Oh no, I have no intention of letting Ted buy me out. But in a way he's right. One of us should own it so that our renters can stay there. I don't know what I was thinking. Valerie and Cole have been wonderful, and if I can't live there, I'd like them to stay. Forever, if they'd like to."

"Then if Ted doesn't buy you out…"

"I will buy him out, of course. It was my find."

"I remember." Michelle felt herself lose another brain cell.

"He'll just have to get over himself. At least he should be happy that Cole and Valerie can stay."

"Ted seemed insistent that it should stay in his family, however."

"Well, that's too bad, isn't it?"

"I'll give his lawyer a call first thing on Monday."

"You do that. I honestly wish Ted had gone with that lovely woman in town, Stella Leibowicz. She's a darling woman. I had hoped to have her calming influence for Ted. All she wants is for two spouses to part as friends, which is really all I want."

"Is it?" Michelle quirked a brow.

"As long as I get everything I want."

"Actually, in a good divorce, of which I've seen plenty, compromise is a key ingredient, especially when there's the complexity of a long-term marriage."

"Long term?"

"You and Ted have what we refer to in the business as a long-term marriage. Short term is under five years, and unless there are children involved those separations are quick. Sometimes, couples can consider a bifurcation."

Tippy narrowed her eyes. "A bifurcation."

Michelle brought her hands together and separated them. "To separate, bring apart. This makes it possible, for instance, if one of the spouses needs to get married again quickly for whatever reason."

Tippy made a little sound in the back of her throat that sounded like she was strangling.

"Are you *sure* you don't want some water?"

Tippy shook her head and Michelle continued. "Then afterward, it gives the attorneys and mediators plenty of time to divide up the assets and come to an amicable and official divorce."

"Has Ted mentioned bifurcation?" Tippy said, hand to her throat.

"I haven't actually brought this up with his attorney yet. But I will, if you're interested. It's the only way I can think of getting you the 'quickie' divorce you want."

"I'll...think about it."

A few minutes later, Tippy finally left, a little downtrodden it seemed to Michelle. She couldn't help but think Tippy wanted someone to convince her to drop this divorce but it had sort of taken on a life of its own. And Michelle could not be expected to be the one to talk her out of what would be several months of billable hours and her possible chance at a partnership.

She thought about calling or texting Finn. Would he come back now?

She didn't think so. Hooking up wasn't part of their deal. They'd both just been caught up in the moment after the party. She'd been lost in the heat of his green eyes, his strong hand sliding down her thigh. All his overwhelming handsomeness. He was right. In his own words, it had been a mistake.

So, instead, Michelle curled up in bed with some research on bifurcation.

Chapter Eleven

Michelle hit the beach early the next morning.

The air was muggy and hot, so she ran closer to the waves. Everything was tougher to do in sand, so she could run less of a distance and still accomplish the same workout. Usually, she tried to run in the mornings before the day became a form of Hades on Earth. But she was a Texan born and bred and used to this weather. Tourists called this heat climate change, but in Texas the residents called it summer.

I'm not proud of your accomplishments, I'm proud because of who you are.

Honestly, she'd once assumed those to be the loving words of a father. She'd never seen herself as someone who had to accomplish All The Things in order to be worthy of love. Achieving her goals had always been how she functioned, who she was at her core. It would be nice to have a better balance, sure, but maybe she'd do that *after* she made partner. Mentally, she wrote it as number two on the list she kept going in her head. First on the list was of course making partner at the law firm. Her career and financial security would be set.

1. Make partner
2. Work on achieving proper work-life balance by making friends in town

3. First child before thirty-five (she'd had to move that back from thirty)

4. Husband/partner to grow old with (try not to force it this time)

5. Buy a house big enough for a family of four (two children)

Just ahead, she spied the same woman she'd seen a week ago when she'd been running. Michelle had just passed her by without so much as a wave because she seemed busy. She had a small baby with her and had been talking to a surfer type, who kissed her, then waded back out into the water.

Be approachable. Make friends in Charming. You're going to be here for a while.

It just didn't feel natural to chat when Michelle didn't have an agenda. A point to make. What would be her goal in talking to this woman?

See number two.

Michelle slowed herself to a stop and stuck out her hand. "Hello! I'm Michelle LaCroix, attorney at law."

The pretty brunette blinked. "Oh. Hey there. Maribel Hunter, um, PhD."

"Glad to meet you. Is that your baby?" She pointed to the little tent that seemed to be a little type of housing for the baby from the harsh rays of the sun.

"Yes, this is our son, Julian." She pointed in the distance. "And that's my husband Dean out there on the waves. He's just a glutton for punishment."

"I've seen you here before." Michelle wiped a trickle of sweat rolling down her neck.

"We're visiting for a week. We live near San Antonio right now but like to come down here a few weeks every summer." When the baby made a sound, she went to him and picked him up. "I hope you're enjoying your stay here?"

"I love my beach house. Too bad they're only temporary rentals."

"I know what you mean. When I first stayed here, I wanted to make it my permanent home."

"Okay, well. Good to meet you."

The woman waved.

Michelle took off again, satisfied she'd finally met someone. She'd also done her networking for the morning. One of the many things she'd done when arriving in Charming was join the Chamber of Commerce just in case she got desperate and had to start up her own law firm. But that would have required an influx of cash she did not have. Fortunately, Arthur had hired her, and she rarely had to attend a meeting anymore. But that didn't mean she shouldn't still get out there and meet people.

Her phone buzzed late in the afternoon when she was in the middle of proofreading a legal brief she'd spent most of the day writing.

Yes, she was working on the weekend, but there was nothing good streaming anyway.

The text message was from Finn:

Want to come to the Salty Dog and have a drink with me? Don't tell anyone, but my tab is paid for the year. I plan on living here.

Hopefully, please God, he was joking. While Michelle was doing okay in the finances department—her severance package quite attractive, thank you—she had limitations. At this rate it might have been cheaper to hire an escort.

She sent a rolling eyes emoticon followed by many dollar signs and a fire emoticon.

Actually, she was happy to know he wasn't making a big deal out of the previous night. He wasn't sulking. Being seen with him in public would feed the gossip mill, and this was likely his intention. Smart. If she wanted to grow that monster, she needed to give it fuel. Since he was already spending her money, she might as well take advantage of it.

After changing into shorts and a tank top and driving over, she waltzed into the bar, far more crowded than she'd seen it in the past. Then again, she'd never been here on a Saturday night. The place was slammed, and she almost immediately spied Rachel, with a group of women around her age. When she noticed Michelle, she did a double take before she waved. This was good. Sweet and helpful though she was, Michelle suspected Rachel was a bit of a corporate spy for Arthur Sr. Definitely good that she'd see Michelle and Finn here together and possibly report back to the boss.

They hardly seemed to know each other? Ha! She'd fix that.

Finn was at the bar, his back to her, but when he turned, there was a rather gratifying slow slide of his gaze that went up her body. He walked to meet her halfway and, hand low on her back, led her to an empty stool.

Michelle climbed up. "I forgot you were Irish when I offered this deal."

"Don't worry, I'm not your classic Irishman. For instance, I don't have any of the luck."

"So, that whole Irish good luck thing is just a rumor?"

He snorted. "For me it is. You know the red-bearded guy wearing a green hat they trot out every St. Patty's Day?"

"The green little man they call St. *Patrick*?"

"That's the one. He's sticking up his middle finger at me."

"Oh, c'mon, Finn. That can't be true."

"No lie. I've had to work hard for everything I have. Luck was never a part of it."

"Well, what about the night you happened to waltz in when I needed a fake boyfriend? You got your tab paid for a year. A few seconds earlier or later and it might have been someone else."

"Yeah, that was my luckiest day." His gaze was soft as it slid to her lips and then back up to her eyes. "And don't worry, I'm paying tonight."

"You don't have to. I meant what I said and it's only fair."

"Fair or not, I asked you to come here and I'm not going to let you pay for our drinks."

"I guess tonight can be a draw."

"Michelle?"

She turned at the voice she recognized to see the gay couple she'd helped with an adoption as one of her first cases at Arthur's firm.

"Hey, guys."

Billy came closer and enveloped her in a hug, catching Michelle by surprise. She wasn't used to hugs in her profession. She noticed Finn's brow quirk and the way he angled his body so he might be able to get between them in two seconds flat.

"I'm Finn Sheridan." He stuck out his hand to intercept any more physical affection. "Michelle's boyfriend."

"I'm Billy and this is my husband, Roy."

"Oh, yes," Michelle said, remembering their names now. "How are you two? How's the baby doing?"

"She's…perfect," Billy said dreamily. "It will all be final and official soon."

"She's with the grandparents tonight. Couple's night." Roy hooked an arm around Billy.

They both smiled, their love and adoration clear. A few months ago, they'd been in a desperate situation, trying to finalize an adoption while dealing with the expense of having to hire a family law attorney and running into even more prohibitive fees. When Arthur brought her the case, he hadn't expected that Michelle would make it her pro bono one. Each attorney at P&P was encouraged to pick one case for which they would volunteer their time and fees. It was a common practice at all the firms Michelle had worked. She just hadn't expected it would be her first case, or that she'd get such gratification from the experience. She'd never seen two people happier to become parents.

"If not for Michelle, I don't know if we'd even be parents right now," said Roy. "She waived her fees for us."

"It was nothing. I was happy to help."

After a few more updates on their baby Georgina, now nearly eight months old, they were called to their table.

She went back to the mojito cocktail Finn had ordered for her, taking a sip from the straw. Finn gave her one of his slow and easy smiles, the one that made her think of long and lazy days under a beach umbrella.

She sucked in a breath. *"What?"*

His smile went even wider. "Nothing. I feel like maybe my luck is changing."

Tonight, a few things had been fundamentally established for Finn.

One, Michelle turned heads when she walked into a room. That did not surprise him, but what did shock him was the protectiveness that reared at some of the ogling. Maybe Michelle wore pantsuits most of the time to avoid this kind of reaction. Made sense. It was difficult for women, who sometimes felt they had to dress down to be taken seriously in a man's world. Bull hockey in his opinion but he'd seen it time and again. And it wasn't as if Michelle was flashy. Not at all. She just happened to have an amazing body and long legs that should have their own zip code.

Second, she wasn't the harsh and bitter attorney he'd imagined who lived to cut a man's balls off.

Third, she was capable of unwinding and forgetting about work for a while. She'd proved it last night until Tippy showed up. He may have been a little hasty in leaving.

Earlier today, he'd battled with himself over whether he should suggest they spend a lot more time together making out and more. You know, to make it seem real once they were in public.

But it seemed an angel sat on one shoulder and the devil on the other:

She's a nice girl, much nicer than she wants you to think, the angel said, as he played the harp.

Don't toy with her feelings.

The devil lit a cigarette and coughed: *You're both consenting adults.*

Finally, he'd split the difference and casually tested the waters to see if she might want to see him again. If she wanted to meet him on neutral turf. He was somewhat surprised when she agreed. He also told himself that he was doing this for her, helping with this charade. It would be much easier if that was the end of it.

There was no real reason he couldn't be with Michelle LaCroix, he told himself. No reason at all. Just hang out and see where this went. She didn't have to know his intentions. Telling her how he felt would only scare her off. She'd more recently than him been through a bad breakup, and he remembered all too well what that felt like. The sense of failure. The deep-seated fear that you should stay away from something you were clearly no good at.

"I see you made your choice." Declan set a soft drink in front of Finn. "So, you like my brother."

"He's alright." Michelle gave him a sly wink.

"Yeah, sure, I guess, if you like the silent broody type." Declan wiped the bar.

Finn rolled his eyes. "Don't talk about me. I'm right here."

"Oh, didn't see you there," Declan deadpanned. "You're so quiet."

Michelle leaned forward. "So, Declan. What do you do besides make the best mojito I've had in a while?"

"Fall second to my big brother, apparently." Declan smirked.

Finn told himself that Declan didn't realize how hard those little remarks of his hit him. To Declan, life seemed to be one big joke. For Finn, there was always a sad underlying truth to his comedy routine.

"Aw," Michelle said. "Poor baby."

"Let me get out my violin," Finn muttered.

"No, I'm not kidding." Declan gestured from Finn to Michelle. "This is just one prime example. He was *the* athlete all through high school and beyond, which meant he got all the girls."

"Stop," Finn said, growing more irritated by the second.

"Do tell." Michelle ignored Finn.

"Maybe he got hit in the head one too many times because he forgets he was also an athlete," Finn said. "Varsity team as a freshman."

"That's impressive," Michelle said. "Tell me. Did you get all the Irish luck in the family?"

"Nope. All gone. The Sheridan family lost our luck in a

poker game way back in eighteen seventy-six," Declan said. "Family folklore. I'll have to tell you that story sometime."

Michelle laughed and then gave Finn the side-eye. "You do that, unless I can pry it out of Finn first."

A loud chorus of greetings from the entrance led Finn to turn in that direction, and he saw the mayor walk in. Tippy had always been exemplary with her constituents, greeting and spending time with anyone who wanted to chat a moment. She and the man she was with were stopped several times.

"Who is that with the mayor?" Finn said.

"That's her date," Declan said as if he hadn't just dropped a loaded missile. "They were in here yesterday, too. Just missed Ted, who has dinner here every night. But dang, they won't miss him tonight."

Finn followed the direction of Declan's gaze and there sat Ted alone, hovering over a half-eaten dinner of steak and potatoes. He looked up in time to see Tippy headed toward a table opposite his and his face became so red Finn feared he was having a cardiac event. Then he clutched his chest and Finn went on high alert.

"Hopefully she doesn't want another after-hours consultation."

Unfortunately, she almost immediately saw Michelle and headed in their direction.

Michelle slipped off the stool and met her halfway. Finn was right behind her.

"Michelle!" Tippy threaded her arm through the gentleman's. "This is my friend, Percy. Percy, this is my fabulous attorney. We stopped in to have a late dinner."

"She's off the clock." Finn draped an arm around her shoulder, earning a glare from Michelle.

"I always have time for you, Tippy," Michelle said.

"Aw, my heart, that's so lovely. But no business tonight!"

Tippy clapped her hands, and Finn wondered whether she'd started drinking at home. She looked way too happy for someone going through a contentious divorce. "Hang on to Finn, Michelle. Maybe you can heal him. He got burned badly in his divorce, and that can really change a man."

"Not this man." Finn cleared his throat.

Really, was that what it had come to? Everyone in Charming talked about him behind his back? *Poor Finn. His ex-wife took everything he had.*

Finn was grateful for his brother, who at least always gave him shit no matter what.

"Tippy!"

The booming voice behind them made everyone turn.

Since he'd been old enough to drink at the Salty Dog, Finn had definitely intercepted his share of bar fights. They almost always centered around a woman, except for those times after the NFL playoffs when half of the crowd was particularly giddy about winning, or horrible about losing. But all those fights were between bruiser-type guys who drank too much and loved to communicate their feelings with their fists.

Never between a pair of older men, one of them clearly jealous over his wife's companion and ready to stake his claim.

"Ted." She clung to her date's arm, not noticing Percy had begun to shrink away from her. "Lucky for you, my attorney is here. You may speak to me through her. Michelle?"

"What are you doing? You're a married woman," Ted roared.

"Well, not for long." Tippy sniffed. "And anyway, you should talk!"

"Ms. LaCroix." Ted turned to Michelle. "Please tell my

wife how unseemly it is for her to waltz in on the arm of another man when she is still very married to me!"

"Let's all calm down," Michelle said with the grace of a practiced attorney. "There's no need to make a scene."

"Tell my husband we could get divorced a lot faster if he would agree with me on everything," Tippy said. "I want to buy the lighthouse from you, Teddy. Let me have it. You can be an even wealthier man."

"Never!" Ted yelled. "Tough luck!"

Finn had never seen sweet and friendly Ted this angry. "Ted, relax. Why don't we all go outside."

"Good idea," Declan said. "Get some fresh air."

The two ignored everyone but each other.

Tippy pointed. "*I'm* the one who found the lighthouse and coordinated the renovations."

"So what? I'm the one who provided the funds."

"I'm the one who found the perfect tenants!"

"I'm the one who didn't want to kick them out!"

"Please, let's talk about this outside." Michelle went to Tippy, leading her outside.

Percy seemed to have disappeared, which in Finn's opinion was a very smart move on his part.

Finn followed Ted, who stalked out the front door, head low, hands stuffed in his pockets. This had to be an all-time low for poor Ted. Finn wished he had words of comfort, but he'd never felt as possessive over his ex as Ted seemed to feel for Tippy.

At the entrance and several safe feet away, Tippy and Michelle were deep in discussion. All that could be heard were Tippy's words:

Lighthouse.

Mine!

No way.

"I'm sorry, Finn." Ted dragged a hand through the tufts of his hair again. "That was so undignified of me. I'll talk to Declan next time I'm in. Hell, I better apologize to the owners, too. And poor Debbie was waiting on me. She must be horrified. I never raise my voice in public."

"I'm guessing everyone knows this must be a tough time for you. We've got your back, Ted." Finn clapped his shoulder. "I take it you called that attorney in Houston I referred you to?"

"Yes, and thank you. You were right. It's good to have a fighter in my corner. There's no God-given reason I shouldn't fight Tippy every step of the way. If this divorce is what she wants, I'm going to get what I want, too. I'm tired of being a southern gentleman. Look where that got me! A wife who humiliates me in public. My body isn't even cold." He pointed a finger in Tippy's direction. "And that lighthouse is going to be part of the Goodwill family until the day I die!"

"Right." Finn took a deep breath. "Ted, why don't you head home. I'll take care of your bill."

"Oh, that's not necessary."

"It avoids you going back in there and having to deal with a bunch of questions you don't want to answer."

"Good point." He dug in his wallet and handed Finn a crisp one-hundred-dollar bill. "You want to know the irony? She accused *me* of cheating, for which she has absolutely no proof since, oh let's see, it's not true. And she shows up with *that guy*!"

"Yeah, not a good move on her part."

"I think I'll ask my attorney if can put the screws to her if I accuse her of marital infidelity. Would serve her right, prancing around this way."

"It's worth a try."

Ted held out his hand. "I want to thank you again for referring me to my attorney. When I think of what could have happened otherwise…"

He might have wound up with an attorney like Finn's and later regretted it all.

It was one thing to be a good guy, quite another to be a pushover.

"No problem, Ted. You deserve the best money can buy."

Finn watched the man walk to his Cadillac, get in, and drive off.

Only then did he turn to find Michelle standing right behind him.

Chapter Twelve

"**I**'m sorry, did I hear that right?"

Michelle *had* heard right because there was nothing wrong with her hearing. This question was just a test. A test to see if Finn had the nerve to also *lie* to her. First, conspire behind her back to get Ted one of the best attorneys in Texas, then lie to Michelle about it. And she'd been ready to accuse Junior of finding Ted his attorney, even going against his own interests to screw with her! She should have known. The devil was in her own backyard, and she'd opened the door and let him inside.

Finn quirked a brow. "It's not cool to eavesdrop, pookie bear. What did you overhear?"

Ah-ha! She had him now, on the witness stand, caught in his own deception.

Your honor, I ask for the right to interrogate this man as a hostile witness.

"You referred Ted to his attorney? *You*?"

"I did. Why? Is there something wrong with that?"

"Nothing, except that you could have told me. This makes my life a lot more difficult. And you did it on purpose!"

"What I did was make sure the poor man had someone to represent and protect his interests. It's what you would have done, too. Weren't you the one who told me I'd had a terrible attorney?"

"You *did* have a terrible attorney, and I would have done so much better for you. Just like I intend to do my best for Tippy now."

"That's great, let the other guy do his best. You're not afraid of a little competition, I'm sure."

"Of course I'm not. I just didn't expect it coming from you. This is why it's suddenly so difficult. *This* is why Ted won't give up the lighthouse!"

"Why should he?"

"They're both being unreasonable. There has to be some compromise."

Finn shrugged. "Look, Ted is a happy guy and a good man. The last thing I want is to see him destitute."

"Oh my God, Finn. Just because that happened to you doesn't mean it will happen to Ted. Don't lose any sleep over him!"

"Are you kidding me? He was ready to roll over and let Tippy have whatever she wanted until I talked him out of it."

All the air left her body at once. "You...you *talked* him *out of it*?"

"I provided a little guidance. Input." Finn shrugged. "I guess he thought about what I said and reconsidered."

Michelle's gut burned like a three-alarm fire, and she felt feverish. Clammy. This was her fake boyfriend making her life hell. Arthur wanted them to have a better work-life balance, did he? Finn had suggested she *worked* too hard. How was she supposed to find time to have a relationship when she had to log in overtime to figure out a way to fight this? To figure out a way to win?

Wait. A *relationship*? What was she thinking? This wasn't a relationship. She and Finn were a short flirtation. A hookup. A fake boyfriend. Exactly what she'd ordered off the menu. She'd temporarily deluded herself into believing she might have someone on her side for once. Finn wasn't doing anything unexpected here. He clearly did not have her back nor should she be surprised he didn't.

She was an idiot to think he might actually care, even a little. This thing was nothing more than an arrangement between the two of them. Nothing more than two people seeking a little temporary comfort and pleasure. That glimmer in Finn's eyes earlier tonight, the moment he'd told her his luck might be changing, obviously had nothing to do with her as much as she'd wished it had.

She wanted to be the flash of good luck that would change a man's life for the better. Well, she wanted a lot of things but rarely had time for any of them.

"And you were so sweet earlier."

"I'm still sweet." He stepped closer and memories of their last almost hookup flooded her synapses.

His heated gaze. The tough beard stubble scraping against the sensitive flesh as he kissed down the column of her neck. The strong beat of his heart under the pads of her fingers.

Michelle took a deep breath, her palm splayed against Finn's chest, giving him a little shove. "If you'll excuse me. I now have some damage control to do."

Strutting inside, Michelle found Tippy seated at a table with her male friend.

In her years as a family law attorney, Michelle had learned a great deal about body language. The careful distance Tippy kept from Percy showed that she didn't really know the man. So, this was something new? Or something old, possibly resuscitated. Either way, Michelle had to know and also issue a low-key warning to her client. Because though Texas was a no-fault divorce state, a wronged party who could prove excessive infidelity might have grounds for a more favorable settlement. They couldn't risk it.

"May I have a moment with my client?" Michelle handed Percy her most practiced, I-will-kick-your-ass-with-my-words smile.

Percy couldn't get out of there fast enough. "I'll be right back."

"Take your time." Tippy sighed and rearranged the place setting.

"We need to discuss something." Michelle folded her hands on the table. "Are you having an affair?"

Tippy flinched. "That's none of your business, young lady."

Michelle was used to this pushback from clients who'd been caught doing something wrong. "Even if he was wrong to make a scene, Ted was right about one thing. You are still married. You've just given Ted and his attorney ammunition. If you're having an affair, that could impact the court's opinion of you, which could affect the outcome of a fair and equitable settlement."

"*I'm* not having an affair, he is." Tippy's lips trembled, her eyes watery.

"And Percy?"

"He's…an escort." Tippy spoke in a hushed voice. "Nothing sexual, mind you, but a woman my age…well, who would be interested in dating me aside from my money? I'm lonely and wanted to catch up to Ted's philandering ways. He's way ahead of me."

"Do you have proof?" Michelle strummed her fingers on the table. They might still turn this around. Fidelity went both ways.

"Not actual proof but a wife knows."

Michelle swallowed her pity because she did not have

time for this. "I would advise you not to be seen in public with that man or anyone else until after this is all finalized. Your husband was upset, and emotional people can become vindictive."

As she said the words Michelle realized she wasn't talking about Ted Goodwill. She was talking about her client. She'd actually shown up here tonight to get a reaction from her husband, and she got one.

"I have to ask you," Michelle said, forcing her words to be soft. "Are you sure you want this divorce? Maybe counseling could help."

"No, it's too late. You can't take some things back after they've been said."

Her words were laced with regret, an emotion Michelle understood far too well. She wished she knew what to say to make this better...but it wasn't her job to be a counselor and she didn't have the right words. She didn't have the right training.

"It's my duty to let you know that this might get ugly. As you well know, Ted hired a law firm with a fierce reputation."

"And I hired you because *you* have a reputation." Tippy patted Michelle's arm. "You know what it's like to be tossed aside. To be disregarded as if you're of no consequence."

Super. Michelle wasn't aware everyone in *town* knew her story. She'd tried her best to keep that quiet, not wanting to appear pitiful. But apparently, she hadn't been successful. People still saw her as the woman thrown over for Twyla, the better one. The sweeter one.

"Don't be mad at Finn for telling Ted to hire that attorney, either."

Michelle quirked a brow. "I'm sorry?"

"I heard all about it, dear. I'm the mayor. You don't think

someone gave me a call the moment Ted hired them? Unfortunately, our divorce is going to be a small-town scandal and you're right in the thick of it with me."

"Finn should have told me, that's all."

It wasn't that she didn't want Ted to have a good attorney, but it felt disingenuous for Finn to be involved in any way—especially since he hadn't been upfront with her about it.

"Men have a way of keeping the best parts of themselves closed up tight." Tippy sighed. "If you're lucky, very lucky, they share a piece of themselves with you that they've never shown anyone else."

Maybe subconsciously, Michelle turned, and her gaze automatically tracked straight to Finn like a laser beam. He was leaning forward, engaged in conversation with Declan and another man Michelle didn't recognize.

Something told Michelle she'd be lucky to ever see something real coming out of Finn Sheridan.

On Monday, Finn somehow caught the short end of the stick and wound up with counter duty inside the Nacho Boat Adventures shop. Noah was taking a much-needed break, planning his wedding with Twyla, Tee was studying for a test, and their receptionist wasn't coming in until the afternoon.

The heat of the day pressed down on the A-frame hut and the fan just wasn't cutting it. Already he'd removed his shirt and stood in a pair of board shorts. He wanted to dunk his head in an ice bucket. At least outside he'd get the occasional cool breeze off the coast. But the truth was, his grouchy mood was only partially due to the heat. The rest of it was from…frustration of a different sort.

On Saturday night, he'd gone home alone. Despite the fact he could feel Michelle's gaze boring into his back with the heat of a thousand suns, she had chosen not to rejoin him at the bar. By the time he'd tried looking for her, she'd been gone. Great. Just fine with him. For all he knew, she'd left with Tippy, getting an entire night's worth of billable hours. Yeah, Finn understood. Michelle was driven, ambitious and competitive. And he probably should not have referred Ted to the Attila the Hun of attorneys and inserted himself into this misguided competition. He just couldn't stand to watch Ted miserable, and giving him something to fight for at least gave the man some purpose.

That lighthouse was apparently the one sticking point in their otherwise amicable (cough-cough) divorce. The way Finn looked at it, if they truly wanted out of the marriage, they'd figure it out. Usually the person who most wanted out would cave. Maybe that's how it should be. Sometimes in order to get what you wanted, you had to give something up. It struck him that Ted wasn't the one who wanted a divorce, so Tippy should be the one to give in. Besides, damn it, he liked Cole and Valerie, who regularly hosted parties at the lighthouse to which Finn sometimes got invited. They shouldn't have to move over the whims of a couple who'd decided to make each other miserable.

Twice today, Finn stopped himself from texting Michelle. Her anger was one thing, and he could handle that. What he kept remembering, however, was the shocked and hurt look in her eyes when he'd turned to find her behind him. She'd trusted him, past tense, and he'd ruined that. He'd disappointed her. Why he should care was another mystery, but he did. Michelle had this hold on him he couldn't explain.

Still, the day was going well, and Finn sold a couple of boards and rented out equipment, taking license numbers and pertinent information. Then two punks came in.

At least once every few months, Finn had to deal with someone, usually much younger, challenging him to a race. Sometimes it was all in good fun, with a great deal of admiration thrown in and the assurance that it would be an "honor." Finn always declined, stating he was done with his competition days. But today, a couple of teenagers who tended to hang out at the dock from time to time and make fun of Tee showed up. Dumb and Dumber, Finn called them. Their actual names were Nolan and Billy.

"Weren't you on the back of a cereal box?" Dumb said.

"Who, me?"

"Yeah, that one time. Wheaties. That was you." Dumb nodded, as if this was information Finn wouldn't know and had to be told.

Did you miss that time you were on a cereal box?

Still, the attitude and condescension were obvious. Among some Neanderthals sailing wasn't considered a *real* sport. It wasn't football, hockey, soccer, or even baseball. A whole lot more like golf, in other words. In addition, since it was an Olympic sport, it was regarded as a rich kid's pastime and not to be taken too seriously. As compared to, you know, all those poor and destitute NFL athletes.

Okay, so maybe he was in a bad mood.

"Know what? I think you're right. That was me."

"I knew it!" Dumber smacked the counter. "I bet I could beat you."

"Yeah, he's old now," Dumb said. "What are you, thirty?"

"So, you're saying, because I'm old now and not very good, *now* you can beat me?"

Dumber didn't seem to understand he'd just cut himself down. "Yeah, sure can!"

"Well, sure, maybe you can at this point." Finn chuckled. He highly doubted it.

"Okay. Let's do this thing," Dumb said.

"Right now?" Finn said.

"Nah, I have to go get my gear," Dumber said.

"We've got everything you need." Finn gestured to the wall of equipment behind them. Maybe he could make a sale out of this.

Later he and Noah would laugh about it.

"When do you want to do this?" Dumb said.

Finn should have let it go. Instead, they made a date for the following week. Apparently, Michelle had revitalized Finn's competitive streak.

Chapter Thirteen

Monday mornings meant Arthur Senior was in the office bright and early, just after Michelle. He held a "power-up" meeting in which everyone was to bring an inspirational quote to share with the team. It was always Rachel who had the best ones, of course. Stuff about climbing mountains and crossing rivers, fords, and streams. Snort. She had a very cool Pinterest board pinned with inspirational quotes Arthur didn't know about. Actually, Arthur didn't know about *Pinterest*.

Michelle was prepared as always, thank you. She'd had Rachel privately make her a list that she kept in a file on her desktop as a time-saver. As long as she didn't use the same one Rachel did, it was all good.

"Winning isn't getting ahead of others; it's getting ahead of yourself," Michelle said now. "I thought a lot about this one over the weekend."

"Wonderful!" Arthur slapped his desk once. "I *like* that. We need to think of being in competition with ourselves, just like so many athletes do. Take Finn, for instance."

Oh, she'd rather not. She'd gone home alone Saturday night and heard not a peep from him all day Sunday. Since she was the offended party, *he* should be the one to grovel in this fake relationship.

"Yeah, that works with golf but not in the NFL or NBA. It's all about teamwork for competition. We all win together when one of us wins," Junior said, scoring a direct hit with his proud daddy.

She hoped he'd remember that when she made a name for herself by winning the biggest divorce case to hit Charming in decades. She'd make partner and change the name on the front door. Junior would probably cry and make a federal case out of it.

Of course, Junior's quote was about being the best version of yourself or some such nonsense she knew he didn't actually believe.

They then went over the calendar for the week and as per usual Junior asked if Michelle would please take his Friday afternoon appearance, which would take all of ten minutes of her valuable time. It felt like Junior was getting ahead of himself in trying to take Fridays off like his father. But his insistence on keeping his Friday afternoons free was the main reason Michelle thought Junior might want her to stay an associate forever. He didn't realize she'd happily do it even after she made partner.

"Of course, not a problem. Please leave the file with Rachel and I'll take a look at it."

"Nothing much to the appearance," Junior said.

Translation: even you can do it.

Just when Michelle thought the meeting was over and she could get back to actual *work*, Arthur clapped his hands.

"Alright! Team building! Let's talk."

"Sorry, but this sounds like a terrible idea," Junior said, making a show of glancing at his Rolex for the time. "Do we really have the time for this sort of thing?"

For once, Michelle agreed with him, but she wouldn't give him the satisfaction of saying so aloud.

"We must *make* time for this," Arthur's voice boomed, demonstrating he'd probably make a good judge should he ever be asked. "It's important. This is the first time in many years we've had an associate on board, and it's more important than ever that we act as a cohesive unit."

Junior gave Michelle the side-eye, meaning that of course this was her fault, because she was the associate who existed. Michelle lifted her calendar sheet in his direction and pointed to Friday.

"Rachel, what have you got for me?" Arthur put his fingers together like a steeple.

"Oh, so many great ideas!" Rachel piped up. "They can be done anywhere, even on the boat."

"And why do we have to do this on her *boyfriend's* boat?" Junior interrupted. "Isn't that a conflict of interest?"

Arthur sighed and Michelle imagined it was caused by the woes of having an idiot son.

"It's not, since it was *my* suggestion to rent the boat, not hers. I like the boat idea. And anyway, you could use some sun."

Junior scowled and seemed to take great offense, even if he closely resembled a cross between Casper the Ghost and Ichabod Crane.

That only made Michelle think of Finn and his tawny golden skin. His wind-tousled hair. She might have possibly overreacted the other night. He was only trying to help his good friend. Now he probably wouldn't want to see her again, and she'd have to go back to making up digestive issues for her fake boyfriend. As for the team building, he'd probably play along because of his stupid beer tab—and because renting the boat out to Pierce & Pierce would make his company a lot of money. But the shame of it was she really couldn't ask for any more than what he'd already given her.

Arthur turned to Rachel. "Let's get back to these team-building activities."

Finally, a few minutes later, the meeting concluded, and Junior nearly ran out the door, Rachel right behind him.

"Michelle, wait a second." Arthur stood and closed his office door.

Uh-oh. "Is there a problem?"

"I heard about Saturday night."

She shouldn't be surprised word had traveled. The place had been packed with customers.

"Yes, that was unfortunate. Don't worry, I've talked to her, and I think she understands the situation."

"I *am* worried. You're looking at it like their attorney. But these are two of my oldest and dearest friends. I hate to see them hash it out in public and have it get ugly."

"Well, Arthur, as you know, divorce can be unpleasant, to say the least. No one is ever truly happy about it."

It continually surprised her that one heart attack had rendered an otherwise competent man a little clueless when it came to the business he'd been in for decades. Not to mention the hands-on experience he'd gotten from his own two divorces. Sometimes even she wondered if she should switch legal fields, perhaps to something a bit less stressful. Michelle had once watched a family law attorney actually punch his client's husband and wind up in jail for the night. She'd seen a husband jump across the witness stand to try to throttle the opposing counsel. Most people behaved like reasonable adults, but then there were what Michelle referred to as "the others."

"It's our job to make a miserable situation at least tolerable. Let's remind these two what they loved about each other once upon a time," Arthur said.

Michelle wanted to scream: *that's not my job!*

But instead, she smiled. "Of course. I will do my best."

"And another thing."

"Yes?"

Arthur cleared his throat. "I'm concerned. Now, this isn't any of my business, but as you know I think of you as a daughter. You and Finn...well. He's a nice guy, isn't he?"

"The best."

"And I get that, I do. Former Olympian, easy on the eyes or so my wife tells me. But he...just doesn't seem that into you. Honestly, Michelle, he couldn't even remember you hate skiing! After dating for nearly six months. Something just doesn't seem quite right. He should be far more considerate."

"Oh. Yes, well, that's my fault," Michelle lied. "I lied to him and told him that I do like to ski. Just because, I don't know, I wanted to try."

"Michelle, Michelle." Arthur shook his head. "That was a mistake. Never begin a relationship with a lie. Lies are like mold that slowly grows and takes over, destroying everything in its path."

While that was possibly the worst analogy Michelle had ever heard, it certainly was to the point.

"When you've lost trust, in any relationship, you've lost everything. How do you think he felt when you had to tell him the truth? Pretty bad, I'm guessing."

"Uh-huh. Good point."

She chewed on her lower lip. So, tell Arthur the truth now and risk her job, or double down?

"For instance, if we should ever lose trust between us."

Arthur pointed between them. "Then I'm sure you know we could never work together."

Double down it was.

The rest of the afternoon passed quickly as Michelle reviewed case law, consulted the myriad financial paperwork coming in daily on the Goodwills, and spoke with opposing counsel to get on a mediator's calendar soon. They further discussed what she'd come to think of as *The Lighthouse Fiasco* and came to no feasible compromise. Shock.

Rachel and Junior had already gone for the day when Arthur stopped by her office.

"Say hi to that boyfriend of yours. The dinner party was a huge success. My wife still talks about how graciously Finn behaved with our guests."

Michelle heard the sound of the front door chime and Arthur turned. "Well, never mind, I'll say hi myself! Hello, Finn. Nice to see you at the office. This time under far better circumstances."

Michelle stood and straightened the lapels of her jacket, running her hands down her pant legs so they'd be straight and not rumpled at the knees after sitting for hours.

He was here. She hadn't asked or invited him and yet he was *here* only two days after their disagreement.

Maybe Finn didn't have to grovel. She was going to give him a pass because if she had a good friend who was ever divorced, she'd want him or her to have the best counsel. Finn had simply done what any good friend would, and she should forgive him.

In the doorway, Finn shook Arthur's hand.

"Ah, did you bring Michelle dinner?" Arthur boomed. "Good man. I was about to kick her out of here."

She and Finn met halfway across the room, each reaching for a mutual hug almost seamlessly, him bending to press a kiss against her temple. How about that, they'd done that in the perfect choreography of two people who were actually seeing each other.

"I was about to go," Michelle lied.

"She's lying," Finn said, like a freaking psychic. "What can I say, Arthur? She works too hard. It's my job to remind her there's a whole other world out there."

Words that would have previously antagonized her swept over her like a calm coastal breeze. The deep timbre of Finn's voice spiked through her, triggering thoughts of cozy late-night pit fires by the beach. Pleasure buzzed through her body at the sight of him, and she wished Arthur would hurry up already and leave them alone. He was very much a father figure. Annoying, talkative. Not getting out of the way.

Finally, he did, waving and claiming he wouldn't be in the following day.

"But call if you need me!"

For a moment, she and Finn simply studied each other in the sudden quiet of the room. To her it felt like they were metaphorically circling each other. They didn't actually know each other, and she didn't know how to do this because *this* wasn't supposed to be real. And yet it was. Something authentic had happened the other night, something that was not part of their plan. They'd veered off course and should either get back on the main road or take this detour and see where it led.

Michelle wasn't fond of detours when she couldn't see far enough ahead. This one was thick with the kind of fog she hadn't seen in years. She wanted signs and arrows. Blinking lights. Something.

"Hey." Finn tugged on a single lock of her hair.

It was only then she realized it had fallen loose from her ponytail.

"You entered into the shiver of sharks." She smiled to soften her words.

"Yeah. I was motivated." He tipped her chin. "Truce?"

She nodded. "Let's see. What did you bring me?"

If this was his light form of groveling, she'd take it. She accepted the take-out container from the Salty Dog and opened it. Inside was her favorite meal, the one she'd ordered on the night she'd first kissed Finn. She'd taken that cold meal home and tried to reheat it the next morning, but it just didn't taste the same. Burgers and fries never did.

Michelle would ask how he knew what she liked, but by now she understood that Finn *noticed* things. Possibly everything. This shouldn't surprise her, but now she wondered how much more he'd noticed. Had he picked up on her newfound appreciation for him? Or the invisible thread that seemed to pull taut between them whenever he was in the vicinity? Did he notice the way her cheeks flushed and were a little warmer than normal?

Lord, apparently, she'd developed a crush on Finn Sheridan.

The single most unavailable man.

I'm doing it again.

"I'm sorry that—"

"Look, I'm sorry I—"

They both spoke at once, effectively cutting each other off. Finn chuckled and made a motion with his hands, as if to indicate she should go ahead.

"I'm sorry if I was rude to you the other night," Michelle said. "Tippy really threw me off my game by showing up with that man and then Ted starting a shouting match."

"It would have upset anyone."

"I'm not angry you referred Ted to a good attorney. It was…what I would have done."

"But I should have told you."

Michelle slumped back in her chair. "Look at us being all mature. Maybe Tippy and Ted could learn something from us."

Finn snorted. "They probably could."

Michelle cleared an area on her desk and set napkins out, then ripped open the bag filled with sweet potato fries and the burger.

"Join me."

He grabbed a fry. "Fine, but I shouldn't be encouraging this. Do you eat at your desk a lot?"

"Hmm. What's a lot?"

"Got it. When I have to define it, I know it's too much. But listen, promise me something."

"Yes, I will try to spend less time at work. Stop and smell the roses."

"Not that. Let's promise each other that no matter what happens between Tippy and Ted and, God help us all, 'the lighthouse,'" Finn held up air quotes, "you and I won't let it affect our…"

His voice trailed off and Michelle waited in anticipation to hear how he would define them.

When she didn't fill in the word, he did. "Friendship."

That was as close to a word as any she found entirely appropriate to define whatever "this" was between them. And as it turned out, since arriving in Charming without a job or a boyfriend, Michelle needed more friends.

"I agree one hundred percent."

"But I was thinking," he said, leaning back and clasping his hands behind his neck. "If we're going to sell this relationship, truly sell it, we should probably spend more time with each other and be seen together. In public."

Michelle hid her sigh of disappointment. She'd rather

spend more time in private with him, but that would hardly accomplish their purpose.

She nodded in agreement. "The more people believe us, the more Arthur will. We nearly screwed up, but we can recover."

"I suggest events where there will be large groups of people."

Well, he'd certainly given this a great deal of thought. "Sure. Good plan."

Michelle had no idea where they could go to be seen besides the Salty Dog. She didn't get out much.

"Like the Salty Dog?"

"I was thinking the boardwalk."

"Okay."

Ironically, she hadn't spent much time there, even though it was directly across from the Salty Dog. But the lights were bright enough to make an impressive display she could see even now out her office window.

"Lots of activity there right now. Every summer the Mr. Charming contest starts, and a lot of the boardwalk vendors participate. It can be fun."

"Mr. *Charming*?"

"Besides all the Christmas stuff we do around here, it's our town's biggest event. Cole Kinsella has won two years in a row, but he's bowing out. The winner gets a sizable chunk of cash to invest back into their business."

"Hmm, I can think of a few people who should run for Mr. Charming."

Noah was certainly way too charming for his own good, and then there was Finn...women certainly found him quite "charming," if you wanted to go by the gossip mill.

Michelle ate quietly for a few minutes. "Can I ask you something?"

"Sure," Finn said.

"Is it true you only date women for about two weeks before you break up?"

He scowled. "Who told you that?"

"Well…it was Rachel. She expressed some concern. Not that it matters to me, you understand. It's just…maybe we don't count."

"No, we do count." He leaned forward. "But this is different. Truth is, I actually never put a timeline on anything. It just kind of worked out that way, I guess. Until Noah said something, I didn't even notice."

Finn, not noticing? *Highly unlikely.*

"So, you're okay with this thing between us going on beyond your allotted two weeks?"

He nodded. "Piece of cake."

Of course, it didn't matter to *him* since they were just two people having a good time while pretending to be a real couple. She'd take it.

It could be worse.

Chapter Fourteen

Finn wanted to know everything. Where the bodies were buried, where Michelle liked to shop for food she had to *cook* instead of order. Whether or not she ever actually cooked. What she did for fun.

"Tell me about yourself, counselor. Besides your insatiable appetite for the law."

"We already went over this."

She was probably thinking of the ridiculous document she'd given him with her age, birthplace, and blood type. Boring stuff that neglected to mention she didn't have any interest or desire to ski. Again, information he could have used. Maybe she just wouldn't let him close enough so that he could get to know her. Really know her. But getting to understand Michelle LaCroix was suddenly something he wanted more than he'd once wanted Olympic gold.

"Margarine or butter?"

She blinked. "Are you kidding me?"

"I'm not. According to my mother, this is a vitally important question and usually sparks fierce debate."

"Butter, of course," she deadpanned. "Anyone who says margarine is a heathen."

"Agreed."

"What else?" She grinned now as if she was actually enjoying herself. "That was easy."

"If you could go anywhere in the world, and money was no object, where would you go?" Finn steepled his fingers, trying his best to assume a scholarly position.

"Paris, France."

"You didn't even have to think about it for long."

"What about you?" she said, hiding her eyes from him by pretending to be fascinated with her meal. "Where would you go?"

"Rio de Janeiro."

"Why?"

"I could ask you the same. Why Paris?"

She squinted at him. "But I asked first."

"I was there for the Summer Olympics. Very stressful time, and I never got to do anything but compete. Prepare to compete. Worry about coming in last. Anyway, I hear it's a beautiful place. I'd like to spend downtime there when I could just relax."

"I never thought about that. I've been to plenty of attorney conferences where I spent my entire time in workshops and meetings. New York City, San Francisco, Seattle. I got to see Times Square because that's where the hotel was located but that's about it."

"Why Paris?"

"That's where my father is from, and after the divorce he moved back. I always wanted to visit him there. Besides, Paris is, you know, the city of love." She made a face and stuck out her tongue.

Finn blinked, feeling like he'd found a gold nugget in the middle of the desert. So, she came from a divorced family. Interesting choice of profession.

"Why didn't you ever go?"

"He used to come here to visit me instead."

"Used to? That's a big trip for custody visitation."

"Hmm. Not surprisingly, he only visited once a year. But by the time I was in junior high he had himself a new family, so…"

She let the sentence die out as if it didn't matter. As if it hadn't clearly devastated her having a father who stopped caring. Who loved her some, but not enough. Who didn't want to show her his own birthplace. Take her around to all the special places he'd visited as a child.

"You definitely need to see Paris someday. Soon."

"Sure. I'm sure I will."

She was simply picking at her meal, a bite here or there, and he couldn't help but think he'd ruined her appetite by asking too many personal questions.

"I noticed you left something out of your bio."

She met his eyes. "You mean besides the skiing, and the whole butter versus margarine controversy?"

"Yes, Michelle. Your parents are divorced. Isn't that something your boyfriend would know?"

"That's not important. I'm not the one who's divorced, and I rarely discuss it. Why would I?"

"Seriously? A divorce attorney from a divorced family? How's that not significant to who you are?"

"Um, as a *family law* attorney," she corrected him, "I had a fifty-fifty chance of coming from a broken home. The odds of that are what the odds are for everyone. So yeah, I fell on the wrong side of that fifty percent."

"Is that why you went into family law?"

"It may have been an influence." Having lost interest in her meal, Michelle was now scribbling on a pad.

Finn decided to ask the most pertinent question of all. "Who had the better attorney?"

"Apparently my mother did." She crossed her arms. "She

and I are not close. Two years ago she moved to Florida with her boyfriend. What about *your* parents?"

Finn scratched his temple and fought a smile. "Still together."

"Oh, lucky them."

"Yep. I wish I knew their secret. Still silly in love with each other. They should bottle and sell it."

"They would be billionaires and maybe I'd be out of a job."

She smiled and it was the first unguarded one he'd seen from her tonight. When he'd surprised both her and Arthur, her smile had been uncertain and tight. Like maybe he'd come to start an argument and she didn't want to hash things out in front of her boss.

"The hardest thing I've ever done is tell my parents that my marriage wasn't going to make it. I never gave up on anything in my life until then. My father had been my coach all my life, and I expected him to talk me out of getting a divorce. Instead, he said he'd known all along we weren't right for each other and praised me for hanging in there as long as I did. He told me I deserved to be happy and not simply live in misery for the rest of my life."

"That must have been a relief in a way."

"My parents are two people I've never wanted to disappoint, so yeah. It was...a gift."

"Well, they sound like good people."

"The best."

Michelle had abandoned her scribbling and was now tracing the corner of a paper with the tip of her finger.

"Was it...a lot of pressure to try and have a perfect marriage like your parents do?"

This is where he should lie like a rug and expound on what an inspiration they'd been when he was growing up.

Explain how they were the benchmark to which he measured all other relationships. But that wasn't exactly the truth, was it? Because truthfully, yes, they had been an inspiration. Until he failed. Then their marriage became this impossibly high standard he worried he'd never meet.

It would have been one thing if they weren't happy but simply tolerated each other because of the commitment they'd made. He would have expected that of his father, who was a bit of a drill sergeant when it came to athletics and setting goals to crush them. But he clearly loved his wife, and none of it was for show. Finn lost count of how many times he'd interrupted them slow dancing in the kitchen.

And he wanted that. He wanted his soulmate, someone who would always have his back.

Was there pressure?

Like a tourniquet around his neck.

And if there was ever a second time, Finn would not fail.

"Yeah, you could say that."

Michelle closed the top of the take-out container and stood. It was only then he realized they'd been talking for a couple of hours, as all the businesses downtown shut down for the night, including Twyla's *Once Upon a Book* across the street.

Without words, he went ahead of her and held doors open as she went through the office flicking off lights, turning off the copier and main printer. She locked the office.

"Are you always the last one to leave?"

"Too many times. I sometimes just lose track of time."

"That can be a good sign and usually means you're enjoying something that has all of your attention."

"Or that I have a tendency to hyper-focus on a task."

"Or maybe you've forgotten to have fun."

"No, I haven't!" She stopped halfway to her car. "I can

have fun with the best of them. You should see me when I cut loose and have fun! I'm unbeatable. The last time was a sorority party in my junior year of college. I climbed up on a table and took a dare to twerk. Twerk! And if I'm going to go by the reaction of my friends, I killed it. *Murdered* it."

Finn's lips were quivering in that half-amused way he had. "Easy, counselor."

"Sorry, but that sounded like an insult."

"Not an insult." He paused. "Maybe a...challenge of sorts."

"Oh, Finn. You child, you do not want to challenge *me*."

"No?" He quirked a brow.

"Not unless you want to lose."

"I wouldn't mind losing at this one."

They quietly walked to her car.

"Sorry I kept you late."

"It was a good 'get to know you' session. Better than the first one."

"Yeah, and during the second one there wasn't much talking until Tippy showed up."

She met his gaze and gave him a little smirk. "Sometimes talking is overrated."

"Wow, and spoken from an orator. I'm going to remember *that* as a badge of honor."

"You should." She placed her container in the car, then turned to him. "Goodnight, Finn."

Her eyes were shimmering in the moonlight, and he almost felt his heart changing. He took her hand, kissed it, and spoke through her fingers.

"Goodnight."

This is where she could ask him over, or he could invite himself. But if he wasn't careful, he'd give in to this combustible energy between them. He already realized he wanted a lot more than this fake relationship, this dance they were doing around each other. For now, he needed to let it ride. He had to take it slow. He couldn't make any mistakes.

So, he didn't say another word. Didn't kiss her. Instead, he watched her drive off.

On Wednesday, Finn drove out to his parents' house as he did once a week to check in. After his father, Dan, had retired from his job at the post office, and his mother from her job doing the occasional real estate deal that had helped finance much of Finn's training, they'd moved to a property on the outskirts of Charming. It held the distinction of being the only fixer-upper left in Charming and plenty of elbow grease plus pension dollars were steadily going into the improvements. They were in no hurry, a good thing because it was going to take a few years since his father refused to hire anyone.

"Why spend the money when I can do it myself?"

Every Wednesday his father seemed to tackle sanding a different portion of the back deck that would someday be the showpiece. The house sat on a small hill, and the view from the deck was spectacular. In the distance were the lighthouse and all the sandy beaches of the coastline. His father said better than being near the water was having a good view.

"Finn!" His mother greeted him at the door. "Just in time. He's going to kill himself out there. Yesterday, I caught him on a ladder. A ladder! Please talk some sense into your father before he makes me a widow. I'm far too young to be a widow. Are you staying for dinner?"

"Sure, Ma."

"Good boy. I called Declan, but he has no time for his

mother. All he does is work at that bar pretending he doesn't have a mother who loves to cook for him."

"He's just trying to make a living."

"Well, when you see him tell him he's breaking his mother's heart. That ought to do it." She disappeared into the kitchen, banging pots and pans.

"That's right, pile it on," Finn muttered.

The old Irish guilt. Catholics had nothing on them. Guilt was a way of life for the Sheridans. They might be sixth-generation Irish Americans, but some old habits died hard. Luck they didn't have, but there was guilt enough to spare.

He grabbed two Guinness from the fridge and went to meet his dad. There he was on his hands and knees, wearing Declan's old kneepads from when he'd tried for one season to play roller hockey just for fun. But because he wasn't any good at it, compared to baseball, Dad made him stop. At least the kneepads were still hard at work.

The sander stopped making its grinding sound when his father sensed Finn behind him.

"Ah! You're here."

"Take a break, Dad." Finn offered a cold beer. "Talk to me."

He stood, wiped his brow, and accepted the drink. "I'll take a break when I'm dead. One of my goals is to finish this deck by the end of summer. Your mother might complain but wait till you see her face when this is all complete. We're going to be able to sit here side by side on two Adirondack chairs and just gaze at our view. Would you like to see the Excel spreadsheet? I'm right on track with my goal."

"What's this I hear about you climbing a ladder yesterday?"

"Sweetheart! Really?" he yelled toward the house, throwing his hands up.

"She's worried. Your laparoscopic knee surgery was less than two months ago. The last thing you want is for the knee to give out when you're on the top step."

"She worries too much. I'll show her tonight how little she has to worry about my knees." He winked.

Finn covered his face with his hands. "Please, Dad. That's my mother you're talking about."

Dad chuckled and elbowed him. "You should be glad your old man can still get it on with his wife. I make her a happy woman. Happy wife, happy life."

"I think in some countries this kind of thing is considered child abuse."

"What? It bodes well for you, being able to still be sexually active well into your sixties. You'll be just like your old man. Do you have a problem with that? No, I didn't think so. Just make it a goal. You'll slay it, son."

Goals. To his father, life was a series of goals to be conquered. The key was the goal had to be something within your control. Something measurable and quantifiable. Finn had been the same way for most of his life, and so had Declan before he went his own way. But Finn was taking a sabbatical from goal setting. He was doing life one day at a time, waiting to see what happened. He'd been trying this method for a while now, since his divorce, and he understood the idea disturbed his father. As if everything he'd taught his son had been wasted breath.

But Finn felt great about it because the things he really wanted now were not measurable anyway. How does one quantify true happiness? Satisfaction?

"How's your brother doing?"

Finn knew this question was coming. Because if his father had worried his way through Finn and the divorce, he worried two times as much about Declan. It was a bit late to worry about him in Finn's mind. His parents should have made Declan more of a priority earlier on, but it was tough to tell two people who cared so deeply about their children that they'd made any mistakes at all. The ones they'd made had never been intentional.

"He's doing fine."

Finn was nothing if not loyal to his brother. Comments about Declan's inability to commit to anything, be it woman or career, were not going to be brought up. At least not by him. He'd give his father two more seconds to do it. Two, one...

"Bartending is not the best use of his skills," his father muttered, then took a pull of his beer. "What's this, his third career? Fourth?"

"I'm not counting," Finn said.

It was his third.

"We have to get him back on track."

Finn walked to the edge of the deck, enjoying the sight. It was the kind of view he saw for himself someday. A wife, kids. Kids he would encourage but never push. The fact he saw himself as a husband again someday with children didn't surprise him. What did surprise him is how he saw Michelle at the center of it all. He kept trying to shake the image out of his head, but it wouldn't let go.

"Let's not worry about Declan. He'll find his way. Maybe he's been struggling since he didn't make it to the major leagues but—"

"He lost focus, that's why!"

And money and other resources for the training he should have had early on.

"Right. Well, there's a lot he can still do, like coaching, and he just needs to figure it out for himself. Give him time."

"That's hard for me. There's nothing I hate worse than wasted potential."

Truer words were never spoken. But he didn't have control over his sons' decisions anymore and that killed him. A new sense of empathy for his father washed over Finn because he was beginning to understand what it felt like to desperately wish you'd made a different choice.

Finn clapped his father's shoulder. "Okay, Dad. Let's get to work."

Chapter Fifteen

Michelle didn't know what to think.

With most men, she would know. *Most* men left clues for a woman to find, like loose pieces of a puzzle. Like socks left two inches from the laundry basket. But Finn Sheridan was *not* most men. First, he'd kindly delivered her dinner and next, sent her on her way without even trying for a kiss. She assumed, too, the rather romantic and almost tender kiss of her hand was because they'd been seen in public. A couple of women had been strolling down the street when he'd walked her to her car in full view of anyone who cared to look, the lamppost casting them in its ambient light.

He had obviously approached this mission with the same enthusiasm with which he'd gone for the gold. Finn was a pro and the best fake boyfriend she'd ever had. Deep inside, the competitive spirit was alive and well in him. He might give others the impression he was carefree, but when he set his sights on a goal he did not lose.

There had been radio silence for two days until he'd phoned to invite her to the boardwalk on Saturday afternoon. It would be hot and humid, but Michelle was up for anything. He didn't have to know that she simply wanted to be in his company. She had a built-in reason to want to spend time with him in public so no need to reveal the sad truth of her uncomfortable crush. Given more time, she figured she'd get over the thrill of hanging out with Finn. Probably just about the time this ruse was over.

Finn was not at all what she'd expected. He was a bit salty, like herself, and a bit grumpy too. Sweet didn't come to mind when a person looked at Finn Sheridan. Vocal and antagonistic, yes. And let's not forget sexy. The arm candy alone would do it, but then there was the ever-present beard stubble, the wavy golden hair and green eyes framed by those hipster glasses. And by the way, she'd never seen a guy rock a pair of corrective lenses like Finn.

It seemed these days that every single one of her thoughts ran back to Finn Sheridan in one way or another.

And it made her crazy in a way she hadn't been in years.

That alarming realization made her think that she could cancel their date tonight. These growing feelings for Finn were dangerous, and anyway she had so much work to do. There were briefs to read, as Ted's lawyers were drowning them in paper. It was a tactic, of course, both for billable hours and in hopes they'd wear them down.

But it was a fact even she couldn't argue that if she didn't spend more time outside her cute beach shack, she wouldn't ever meet anyone. Other than Finn, whom she'd already met. And Noah and Twyla. Declan. She'd never gotten around to meeting the couples who rented the other units and seemed to come and go a few days at a time. She was the only long-term renter so far. Ironic. Her, and the surfer guy and his wife, who she still passed every morning on her run.

Michelle was staying in shape for this guy, whomever he was, who might come along someday and sweep her off her feet. At least he wouldn't have much to lift, so it should be easy. It probably wouldn't be Finn. He didn't look like the kind of man to fall second to anyone, and the facts were that even Michelle wasn't 100 percent sure she'd ever put a man before her career.

After her run, she showered and spent most of the morning deciding what to wear. It was tricky because she had to protect herself from the harmful rays of the sun and also not melt. She wanted to look attractive but show only the right amount of flesh. The amount that said, "Hello, world. I'm fun but not sleazy." She slathered on SPF 1000.

Shuffling through far too many combinations of shorts and tank tops, skirts, and gauzy peasant-style blouses, she settled on a simple sundress. A friend had given it to Michelle a year ago for her birthday as a prank and somewhat veiled dare. She hadn't worn it. In a buttery yellow, it was a print with pineapples and was the most whimsical piece of clothing Michelle owned. Or had ever owned. The dress fell to just above her knees and had matching sandals and seemed appropriate for a day outside the courtroom.

She'd noticed Finn's fascination with her hair whenever she wore it down, so she chose to forego the ever-present ponytail. That was mostly for work, anyway. She was going to unwind and prove to Finn and anyone else paying attention that she could work-life balance the crap out of the day. Someone would look at her today and say, "That girl should win an award for having the most fun ever."

Yes, sir, she was going to have so much fun that Finn would ask her to tone it down a bit. Ha!

She was ready for him when he showed up exactly on time, having won the driving argument since he claimed to have a special parking pass for the boardwalk. He stood braced in the doorway when he saw her and made a show of lowering his glasses to peer over the tops of them, his gaze doing a slow slide up and down her body.

But all he said after a slow whistle was, "Yellow."

"With happy pineapples lest you think I'm incapable of being quirky. I can have fun with the best of them."

"Well, your dress certainly says so. I approve, but don't think I didn't catch you giving your briefcase one last longing look."

Damn! "I was just making sure I'd zipped it up before I left."

"Right. You wouldn't want all the papers to slip out, get together and have a party without you."

She smirked but followed him to his car. To her utter shock, it wasn't a truck. Noah drove a truck. She just assumed…but when the handles appeared, Finn opened the door to his electric sedan for her. Electric! It was somewhat encouraging to realize Finn wasn't entirely destitute after his divorce. He might be living with his brother and appreciate help with his tab, but he'd invested in Nacho Boat and drove a nice vehicle. Her worries about his financial situation after the divorce eased. She was always secretly encouraged to discover proof that divorce didn't have to mean utter devastation. People recovered. They moved on despite a big loss and went on to live full lives. Therefore, she wasn't the worst person on earth to facilitate a difficult time in a couple's life.

Yes, okay, so there were times when her profession sucked the marrow right out of her. She loved the law and arguing a particularly difficult point, but the emotional toll divorce took drained her every now and then. She tried to compartmentalize, but the sadness fell on her like a cloak some days. The grief over a person ending a part of their life made navigating some days dark and hollow. She didn't always fully succeed in pulling herself out of that dreary place.

Once they arrived at the boardwalk and parked, Finn held her hand everywhere they went.

"I usually hold hands," he said.

"Yeah, me too." Except Michelle couldn't even remember the last time she'd held hands with anyone.

The gesture was a bit on the sweet side for her, and she always made a joke when a man tried to hold her hand. "What are we, third graders?" She'd shake them off by pretending to need to take something out of her purse or use her phone. Her college boyfriend had called her borderline frigid.

Wonder whether he was still selling used cars.

"I'm still coming for that sailing lesson!" an older gentleman called out.

"We'll be ready for you soon," Finn said.

At least every third person they passed waved to Finn.

They walked along the seawall where on one side families were enjoying a summer day on the coast. On the other end of the boardwalk lay a small amusement park with a roller coaster, and an old-fashioned Ferris wheel. From time to time, families would stroll by, kids sticky with sweat and sugar, holding stuffed bears and balloons.

People were casually strolling past souvenir gift shops, a taffy shop, and restaurants. Many of the vendors were giving out free samples today, such as the taffy shop, where a young woman had entered the Mr./Ms. Charming contest.

The crisp aroma of the Gulf filled the air, along with the tempting smells of kettle corn. Next to movie theater popcorn, kettle corn was Michelle's secret passion. She noticed a sign in the window that proudly proclaimed their participation in Mr./Ms. Charming.

Finn stopped moving beside her and quirked a brow. "Since you stopped walking, I'm guessing you want something?"

She pointed. "They're participating in the Charming contest. I may as well throw my support behind someone. It's the Charming thing to do."

"Good one." Finn went ahead, opening the door for her. "Tanner's a good kid. A little misguided, but he has a good heart."

Inside, the smells intensified to the point she felt as though she'd arrived at Saint Peter's pearly gates. The only people allowed into heaven understood the beauty of the perfect mix of salty and sweet. That was her! She practically danced up to the counter and a moment later the man behind the counter turned.

"Welcome to the Lazy Mazy! How can I—wow." His name tag read "Tanner," but he gaped and must have forgotten his manners or the fact he was supposed to be "charming" because he simply stopped talking.

Michelle glanced down at her dress, which he was eyeing. "I know, they're pineapples, but let's not make a big deal out of it."

He continued to stare.

"I'm thinking of throwing my support behind one of the Mr. Charming candidates and you'll do. I do love me some kettle corn. Do I get a special deal if I vote for you?" Having fun, she batted her eyelashes.

"Please," Finn said. "Take it easy on the charm, Michelle. He's only human."

"You don't have to vote for me. It's twenty percent off today because the contest just started. But I'd love it if you would vote for me. I'm trying to help my boss expand the store."

"So you can make even *more* kettle corn?"

"Right. We pop it in the back in those huge kettles like the display one in front. But one of those suckers broke, and so production is slowed down."

"We can't have that. I'll take a large, and I really hope you win. You have my vote."

Finn, who'd been beside her only a moment ago, was now having a conversation with a pretty woman who had two children with her. While Tanner shoveled corn into a large plastic bag, Michelle turned to watch them. The little girl was adorable, wore glasses and pigtails. The boy looked slightly older but stood protectively near his sister.

He was speaking earnestly to Finn. "As soon as I get old enough, I'm going to go for the Olympic gold just like you did."

"He's such a fan of yours," the woman said. "We still have the old cereal box stashed away somewhere."

"Me, too," said the little girl. "I'm a fan."

"But you're not going to go for the gold?" Finn bent low as if the question was serious and he was entirely invested in her answer.

It reminded Michelle of another man, long ago, who had the gift of making a child feel like the center of the universe. Her father.

"Well," the little girl said, then took a deep breath, "I think I'll let my brother do that first."

The adults chuckled.

"You'll have to work really hard for the gold," Finn said, straightening to his full height. "But I know you can do it. Just pick a sport you really love so you won't mind spending all your free time doing it. Good to see you, Amy."

He waved to their mother then Finn rejoined Michelle at the counter.

"Ex-girlfriend?" Michelle said.

"Amy, Declan's high school girlfriend."

"But not...*his* children?"

Finn chuckled. "Oh, no. Nope, she married someone else. Declan missed out."

Inexplicable jealousy spiked through Michelle's belly. Yes,

the woman was beautiful. But Michelle had no right to be jealous, even if there *was* reason to be. Finn had just looked so natural talking with those two kids and ruffling the boy's hair.

Finally, Tanner brought back her large-size bag. "Oh, hey, Finn."

"Tanner." Finn nodded.

"So...you two are..." Tanner gestured between her and Finn.

"Yep," Finn said, his arm snaked around her waist.

"That's right," Michelle said.

"Are you entering Mr. Charming?" Tanner asked Finn as he accepted Michelle's cash.

"Nah, I'm pretty underqualified."

"Oh, I don't know about that," Michelle said. "You were pretty charming back there with Amy."

"Who, me? I wouldn't know charming if it slapped me in the face."

Tanner cleared his throat. "Even though I'd welcome the competition since Cole finally bowed out, I think it's my turn to win this year."

"Your *turn*?" Finn said.

"I've worked hard for this," Tanner said, apparently dead serious.

"You don't deserve to win because you worked hard," Finn said, a slight tick in his jaw. "You win because you're the best."

"Yeah, well, I'm already the best." Tanner winked at Michelle. "Born that way."

"You know who some real competition for you might be?" Finn said. "Noah."

"That's true. Charming should be his middle name," Michelle muttered.

Tanner went positively still. "I... I think it's too late for anyone else to enter."

"That's too bad," Finn said. "But I'll mention it to him anyway just in case. You could use the competition, right? No fun to win without a challenge."

"Sure, sure."

He still had the smile frozen on his face when Finn held open the door and waved.

"Oh, Finn." Michelle laughed. "You devil. You're not going to tell Noah to enter, and you know it."

Michelle loved this evil side of him. She couldn't see Noah ever doing something this sneaky and sly. He was too sweet.

"The whole entitlement thing bugs me. It's 'my turn' to win. What the hell is that? If winning was really about taking turns, it wouldn't be much of a competition, would it?"

"Spoken by a former gold medalist, I would say that's freakishly accurate."

Finn's shoulders seemed to tighten as she'd noticed they did every time that medal was mentioned. She vowed not to mention it again.

"But also: get off my lawn, kids!" Michelle nudged his elbow, hoping to lighten the mood.

"Geez." He stopped, removed his glasses and wiped them clean. "I guess I do sound like an old man. Got to watch that. I could go from grumpy to curmudgeon in a single second."

Michelle wanted to tell him that would never happen because even if he wasn't classically sweet, Finn *was* kind and generous. He'd demonstrated that several times, in the way he looked out for his friends, in the way he looked out for her. But she didn't say any of those things.

Instead, she said, "Could we stop somewhere so I can eat without making a pig out of myself?"

Chapter Sixteen

Watching Michelle enjoy the kettle corn straight out of the bag, without a care in the world, was quickly erasing the mild unpleasantness of Finn's exchange with Tanner. He didn't want to turn into a curmudgeon, after all. And he was here, right now, enjoying himself more than he had since…since he couldn't even remember when.

Michelle LaCroix was dressed in *yellow.* A yellow dress with pineapples all over it. It was almost like she was trying too hard, and his chest pinched at the thought. She was even ambitious when it came to having fun, and he wondered where that insatiable sense of competition had come from. She was more like him than he'd realized.

Because he had to look no further than himself to find at least one answer as to why someone would work so hard to excel: you did it in order to please and impress someone you'd adored for most of your life. In his case, his father, who'd dedicated so much to Finn and his dreams. In Michelle's case…he didn't know. She no longer seemed particularly close to anyone in her family, rarely talking of her mother, and even less of her father.

"I'm having a great time," she said now. "I think I'm really rocking this whole work-life balance."

"Yeah, you are."

"In college I had more fun, probably. But I've been so focused on making partner for the last few years. There hasn't been room for fun in my life."

"Why is being a partner so important?"

He already knew the answer. Like him, she was driven. It was a goal. Why do the minimum when you can do better? Why not always do your best?

She was quiet for several seconds, kicking her legs. "It was always the plan. And honestly, I was *so* close, and then...well, you know the story."

"Not all of it. Noah said you got fired for taking time off."

She scoffed. "That's the party line."

"But not the truth?"

"The truth is I trusted someone I shouldn't have. A colleague and I used to complain to each other about one of the partners. Usually this wasn't done via email, of course, but I lost my head and replied by email while I was down here. It was a mistake. For some reason, he took it upon himself to forward that email to several other staffers in the firm and from there...it sort of went office-viral. Everyone saw my unsolicited opinion that my boss walked like he had a stick up his butt."

Finn whistled. "Yikes."

"The official reason they asked me to resign was because I'd taken too much time off. Which was a lie, of course, but they didn't really need a reason to get rid of me. And suddenly, my mostly male associates had far less competition than they did before. Coincidence? Probably not."

"Damn, I'm sorry."

"It was so humiliating and my own fault, which made it so much worse. I should have never let my guard down.

I hadn't failed before, not at anything having to do with my career."

"That's tough, I know, but some of us are glad you stayed. You could have moved on. Any law firm in Texas would be lucky to have you. *Arthur* is damn lucky to have you."

"Yes, he is, isn't he?" She smiled, her confidence in her own abilities shining.

She was breathtaking.

His cell buzzed in his pocket and Finn pulled it out. A message from his mother in all caps, read:

WHY WON'T YOU PICK UP YOUR PHONE? I'VE BEEN CALLING YOU NONSTOP FOR THE PAST TEN MINUTES. YOU KNOW I HATE TEXTS. YOUR DAD'S KNEE GAVE OUT AND HE ALMOST FELL OFF THE LADDER. I BLOCKED HIS FALL BUT NOW HE'S COMPLAINING THE WORK WON'T GET DONE IN TIME. IF HE TRIES TO GET BACK ON THE LADDER, I MIGHT HAVE TO KILL HIM. PLEASE COME OVER AND TALK TO HIM. I DON'T WANT TO BE A WIDOW.

His mother was the only person he knew to use periods and zero acronyms in her texts. Now if only she could understand how to lay off the all-caps feature. She said it was so she could see and proofread better and didn't seem to understand that it was seen as shouting.

Finn groaned. "I'm going to have to cut this date short. I'm sorry."

"Why? What's happened?"

"My father nearly fell off a ladder. He's got a bad knee from his years playing football and had a total knee replacement a few weeks ago. But you just can't keep the man down."

"Oh no." Michelle closed up her bag and started gathering up her things. "Let me go with you and see if I can help."

Finn dragged a hand through his hair. He didn't really want Michelle meeting his parents when they were all in the middle of a mini crisis. But she looked so determined, quickly standing, and smoothing down her skirt of pineapples.

"I can't ask that of you. This was supposed to be a fun day. You know, the whole 'show me you can unwind' day."

"Plus, being seen in public."

"Yeah, right, that." He'd almost forgotten his primary goal.

"You've helped me so much, though, and I want to help you, too."

"Are you sure? They can be a handful."

"Who? Ozzie and Harriett? The two lovebirds? I have to see this in action."

"As long as you don't stare at them like they're a science experiment."

"That would be a social experiment, but I promise."

Five minutes later, they were on their way to his parents' house where he'd been only a few days ago.

"Here's what you need to know about my dad. He never met a goal he didn't conquer. Perfect marriage? Done. Two children? Done and done. Help son get the gold? Done. Retire comfortably? Done."

"Well, we should get along."

"Not so much. He tends to make *his* goals other people's goals. And when they bought this house, he sold my mother on retirement and the fact they'd slowly turn it into their dream home."

"That sounds kind of lovely."

"It might be except he can't stop improving the place. It's already pretty perfect. But he still wants a skylight here, mosaic tile there, a new deck even if there's nothing wrong with the old one."

"Ah, poor guy, he sounds bored."

"He's supposed to be enjoying his retirement, not starting a new career in home improvement. You should see him. He has every book they've ever written on the subject, watching the TV show like it's his religion."

"It's good to have hobbies."

"Aren't hobbies supposed to relax you, though?"

"Hmm. You've got a point."

"He claims he's enjoying himself, but I find it difficult to believe. During his recovery after the surgery, he was miserable. He couldn't take his daily walk, couldn't coach basketball at the Y, couldn't work on the house."

"That's interesting. I guess I had really imagined retirement differently, too. I figured you work so hard when you're young it would be time to do nothing."

"Which is tough for some people."

"My mother, for instance, knows how to do it right. She swims and golfs."

"How do you picture your retirement?"

"I have not pictured it, honestly. I thought maybe I'd slow down a bit, maybe put up my shingle to offer mediation services and just work less."

"You'd like to be a judge?"

"Oh God, no. Mediation is different."

"It's a lot like being a judge though, isn't it?"

"Sure, but on a smaller scale. You work with people and get them to *want* to compromise. It's easy to do with the threat of a real judge looming if you don't find a way to agree. Plus, you don't have to wear a robe."

"But the robe is the cool part." He pulled into the driveway that led to his parents' home at the top of a small hill. "Here we are."

"Oh my." Michelle sucked in a breath. "This is beautiful."

"A nice place to live out your golden years."

His mother met them at the door, and she clearly did not expect to see Michelle.

Her eyes widened, and her smile followed. "Finn, I didn't realize you were on a *date*. You should have said something, sweetheart."

"Well, you sounded homicidal." He led Michelle inside and made the introductions.

"It's nice to meet you. Finn and I weren't doing anything special. Just hanging out at the boardwalk," Michelle said, offering her hand to his mother.

Typical of his mother, she pulled Michelle into a hug. "I'm a hugger! And I *love* the dress."

"Thank you. A gift from a friend." She met Finn's gaze. "Finn didn't even notice."

"I did!"

"You didn't say anything."

He tipped back on his heels. "I *said:* yellow. That was me, acknowledging the dress."

"Oh, good grief, Finn. You can do better than that!" his mother said.

"Finn! Where are you, son? She won't let me get up from this chair," his father bellowed from the den.

"Excuse me. Be right back." Finn followed the sounds of his father's voice, finding him in the den as suspected on the wheelchair rental from his post-surgery days.

"Finally. Talk some sense into your mother, would you? If I get out of this chair, she says she'll either divorce or kill me. Neither sounds appealing, but I can't just *sit* here!"

Naturally he made this sound like someone had asked him to commit high crimes.

"Would it really kill you to slow down?"

"Slowing down gets us way off schedule. The house has to be ready for our thirty-sixth wedding anniversary this fall." He pointed to the huge chart he had on the wall with entries for each day.

Finn knew it well. There had been similar charts in his bedroom, and in Declan's from the time they were young boys. Declan rebelled, but Finn accepted and excelled. The differences between the oldest child and youngest were clear from the start.

"I thought retirement wasn't supposed to have a schedule."

"Everything in life has a schedule." His dad rolled himself from behind the desk, using his good leg. "Did I hear a woman's voice?"

"Yeah, that's Michelle, my... I'm sure Mom's giving her the tour." He tried for distraction from questions about Michelle. "Dad, you have a gorgeous place anyone would admire. Why don't you just enjoy it?"

"What makes you think I don't enjoy it? And pretty soon your mother and I will be able to enjoy having a glass of wine while we watch the sunset from our deck. We'll see how she complains then!"

"She has a point. The deck was fine until you decided to strip, sand, and re-varnish. You could be enjoying that glass of wine right now."

"I'd be done by now except for this stupid knee."

It had to be tough for a man like his father, who would never let age in itself slow him down. His body, however, had at least attempted to.

"No one is going to fault you for hiring someone to finish some of these jobs."

"For something I can do myself?" He waved his hand dismissively. "So, about this Michelle. Tell the truth to your dear old dad. Is she a contender?"

Finn rolled his eyes. "*You're* going to love her."

Michelle had just had the grand tour of a house, which in almost every sense of the word belonged in *Architectural Digest* as a jewel of a showpiece. The three large rooms downstairs were filled with beautiful skylights bringing in natural light. There were large bay windows, wood floors that gleamed, and a kitchen large enough for an island that housed modern cabinets in a dark cherry wood. She was in love. Someday, when she had a family, they'd have a house like this one.

"I hope you'll stay for dinner," said Mrs. Sheridan as she placed a bowl of green grapes on the table. "Finn hasn't brought a girl home since—well, since his ex-wife. I'm sorry to bring her up. How awkward of me."

"It's okay. Divorce is very tough on families. It's never just a couple divorcing. They're also separating families, friends, an entire network. It's traumatic."

"You've also been divorced?"

"No, but I'm…a divorce attorney. I see it a lot."

Mrs. Sheridan quirked a brow. "I never liked her. I can say it now. As a mother, I try to always be supportive of my son's choices. But marriage is hard enough. It has to begin with a very special kind of love. Not that there's any such thing as a marriage without issues. I love my husband, but he does drive me crazy. He isn't taking retirement well."

"I've heard."

"He's a Type A personality and I'm not. How we managed almost thirty-six years of marriage is a mystery."

"Love, I'm sure."

"Love does forgive all manner of wrongs."

"How did you two meet?" Michelle always loved hearing of these origin stories.

For a long time, Michelle's parents told her one story of how they'd met (at a library where they were both studying) until her aunt Sally told her the truth: Pier and Christina met at a bar. It certainly wasn't a romantic story, mostly involving her mother's lust for men with heavy French accents. Not surprisingly, their rather tenuous connection didn't last.

"That's a very funny story. I actually dated his brother first." After pouring from a pitcher of iced tea, Mrs. Sheridan made a motion for Michelle to sit at the table. "We weren't a good match, it turned out. He broke my heart, the cad. But guess who consoled me?"

"His brother?"

"The *older* brother I never thought would give me a second look! Oh, he was so handsome. He played varsity ball, and all the girls were after him. But...he picked me." She went hand to heart. "Imagine! Me. Lorna Murphy. I was younger and not nearly as sophisticated or cool. But I guess he had a thing for nerdy girls who wore glasses."

"Wrong," said a deep voice from behind them. "I had a thing for the prettiest girl at Sandoval High School."

The man with a voice reminiscent of Finn's rolled himself on a wheelchair into the kitchen.

"Oh, Dan." Lorna rose and met him halfway, cupping his jaw adoringly. For a moment, it seemed no one else was even in the room as they gazed tenderly at each other.

Dan Sheridan looked like what Finn might in about thirty years. Handsome and distinguished, with an air about him that commanded a room. His golden hair was shot through with silver strands, and he had the same mossy green eyes.

Finn cleared his throat. "Okay, you two. Don't forget your son is here."

"It's nice to meet you, Michelle," Mr. Sheridan said, parking himself at the table.

"They're staying for dinner," Mrs. Sheridan announced.

"No, folks. Listen. Michelle has to—" Finn said.

"I'd love to stay for dinner."

Finn quirked a brow as if to say that he'd been trying to give her an excuse and she'd just sabotaged him.

"I mean, if that's okay with Finn."

"Of course it's okay," Mrs. Sheridan said, elbowing Michelle. "He wouldn't deny me the chance to have some female companionship for a change."

"Fine by me." Finn smiled, a gentle tug of his lips.

And as it turned out, Finn's mother was an amazing cook judging by the succulent roasted ham and potatoes she served. She brought out a caramelized apple cake she'd made the day before and all four of them had cake and coffee on the almost-finished deck. Finn's family was jovial and happy, so unlike the family unit Michelle was accustomed to. As a single mom, Michelle's mother had worked, and growing up all their meals were takeout. Dinner talk revolved around whether Michelle was keeping up her grades and doing extra credit, and after college, what law school she'd get into. After law school, what firm would hire her.

Finn's parents, who obviously hadn't raised underachievers, seemed to already know about their son's life. They didn't ask what goal he'd slayed today but wanted to hear whether he was enjoying working with Noah at Nacho Boat.

They also talked sports scores, documentaries, and the latest bestselling books.

They teased each other mercilessly, Mr. Sheridan over his un-retirement, Mrs. Sheridan over the garden she couldn't seem to remember to water, Finn over his obsession with Lucky Charms.

"He told me he's not lucky at all," Michelle said, turning to Finn. "You're trying to level the playing field with good-luck charms?"

Mr. and Mrs. Sheridan burst out laughing.

"The *cereal*!" Mrs. Sheridan said. "Since he was an adorable three-year-old."

"I think he believed that's where the Irish luck came from." Mr. Sheridan laughed. "And he thought he could do us Sheridans proud by bringing ours back."

"Oh, he was so cute. Remember how he left a trail of them leading from the front door to the pot of gold every St. Patrick's Day?"

"Oh, c'mon!" Finn said, slapping the table.

"I thought you didn't eat breakfast." Michelle smirked.

"It *was* a family secret," Finn said, finger over his lips. "All I eat for breakfast."

"Your secret is out, Finn Sheridan. Now how will I best use this information at my disposal?" Michelle tapped her finger to her lips, getting into the spirit of the marathon teasing.

"For good, not evil I hope."

"Well, we'll see."

And this got Michelle another round of laughter.

Chapter Seventeen

All the way back to her house, Michelle teased Finn about his favorite cereal. It was too easy.

"I can't believe you didn't tell me. Sorry, Finn, but this feels like 'need to know' information for a girlfriend. Thank goodness we weren't trying to convince your *parent*s we've been dating for months."

"I knew it was a mistake to bring you." Finn laughed.

"I mean, do you also look magically delicious in the morning?"

"Wow." He snorted. "You're on a roll."

"Do you pick out the marshmallows, set them aside and save them for last? I used to pick out all the cereal and only eat the marshmallows with milk. I remember as a child wanting to write to the company asking them to please stop putting cereal in my marshmallows."

"No, I'm not weird about the marshmallows like *some* people. You have to enjoy it all together. The parts work together to be the best cereal there is on the market."

"Do you let it soak in the milk for a while until it's soggy?"

"Everybody knows they're better before that happens. It's a carefully timed process." He made a motion with his hand. "See, after you put the milk in you have minutes to spare. No time to waste."

Michelle laughed so hard she got a little weak and was grateful to be sitting down.

"So, St. Patrick gives you the finger, but the leprechaun *likes* you?"

"Something like that." The smile that tugged at his lips was genuine and her heart flopped around in her chest.

"That cereal is filled with sugar and additives. For shame!" She shook a finger at him.

"And a cinnamon roll is so much better for you?"

He remembered. He'd once been behind her at the Green Bean when she'd ordered.

"Okay, so we both love a sweet breakfast."

He quirked a brow. "Something else we have in common."

Something *else* they had in common? They couldn't be two more different people. He'd grown up in this safe cocoon of a family unit, where even if his father was a little over the top, they clearly all adored each other. The love in the room was thick enough to be palpable and she didn't just mean Mr. and Mrs. Sheridan, who were still so clearly in love with each other it was a little embarrassing, quite frankly. Mrs. Sheridan's eyes practically glowed every time Finn spoke. In her mind, he could clearly do no wrong, which was everything you would want in a mother.

"I don't know about that. Our families are very different. Your family, for instance, is great."

"To be fair, Declan wasn't there tonight."

"Does he change the entire mood?"

"He and my father have been at odds lately. Maybe they always were, and I didn't see it. Declan was the rebel. He objected to all the order and rules our father liked to impose on our free time. I can't say that I blame him entirely for that. I was the type to go along and keep the peace if nothing else. As the oldest, I always got along better with adults than he did. I was also willing to work a lot harder than him."

"Does he blame you for getting all the attention?"

"No." Finn pulled in front of her house and shut off the car. "But he should."

"Why?"

"Because he got shafted. It happens in a lot of sports families. One child shows more promise and dedication than the other at a certain point in time and unless there are unlimited funds..." He let the sentence drift off.

She understood because she saw it everywhere and not just in sports. In law school, professors tended to single out and work with the best, as if they understood their efforts would be rewarded faster. Same in law firms. But what would happen if everyone got the same amount of attention? Perhaps dozens of stars instead of just a few.

"You feel guilty."

"A little."

He came around the other side of the car and opened her door. She let him. Together, they walked to the front door, Michelle's steps faltering. She'd planned to invite him inside and christen a perfect day. Unless she was somehow misreading tonight, he wanted this, too. She could almost feel his hot, bare skin on hers, those sensual lips kissing along the column of her neck.

She stood at the door, her entire body facing his. Open and inviting. "Want to come inside?"

"Yes, I do." Finn smiled, then tugged on her chin. "But I better not."

Okay, she didn't understand. Yes, this wasn't part of their agreement. But it could be a side benefit, and she didn't think she was the only one to come up with the thought.

This was simply one of those perks of a job like season tickets to the Astros or a burrito breakfast bar on Fridays.

She was not a woman who was going to walk inside and wonder all night long what happened when she clearly had the ability to speak.

"Is it…because the show is over? What happens in there," she waved to her door, "is not part of our deal?"

"No, that's not it."

"Because, honestly, I'm okay with this. I had fun. Am I misreading you somehow? I thought you wanted this, too. Listen. I don't expect any lifetime commitments from you."

"You're not misreading me." At this, frustration seemed to bubble out of him, and he ran a hand through his hair. "I don't want to take advantage of this situation."

"Take *advantage*? Finn, I was the one who begged you to help me out. I had to throw in a year's worth of your bar tab for you to consider it." She took a deep breath when he stayed quiet. "You know you wouldn't have agreed to play along that night if I didn't offer you *something* in exchange."

"Yes, I would have."

"Really? I clearly recall hearing the words: *Have you been drinking?* Oh, and also: *No, thanks*."

He canted his head, showing he clearly recalled everything. "That's true, but I still would have agreed."

She narrowed her eyes. "No, you wouldn't have."

"Yes, I would have."

"No, you *wouldn't*."

"We could do this all night." He glanced at his nautical watch. "I have time."

"*Why* would you have agreed?"

He stepped closer. "I think you know why."

"No, I don't."

"Think about it." He tugged on her chin.

She finally cracked a smile. "Because...you secretly liked me?"

"I don't just *like* you, Michelle. From the time I first laid eyes on you, I was struck dumb."

Finn gave her a wide grin, and for one second, she thought: okay, this is a joke. He's going to laugh now and stroll inside behind her. *Gotcha!* That's what you get for teasing me about the leprechaun.

But he didn't do any of those things.

"Hello," he said. "Michelle? Did I break you?"

"N-no. I just didn't think... I thought you...you..."

"You didn't think I'd ever noticed you? I can do this, Michelle, I can keep up the pretense that it's all fake for me, too. We can do that if you'd like. If it makes you more comfortable." His warm and callused fingers took her hand, softly caressing it.

"I..." Oh, the glorious strokes of his finger pads on her bare skin. She was out of her mind with desire.

"Look, I know you're jaded, which is not completely un-like me, by the way. But something real is going on here for *me* and you should know that."

"Finn. Just, please..." She reached for him, tugging on his neck, urging him close.

Come inside. Let me show you how I feel.

Finn cupped the side of her face, and the single gesture was so tender that something warm uncurled inside her. "I didn't plan this. Hell, I didn't even see it coming. Not like this."

She shook her head. "But...you said the first time you saw me. Wouldn't that have been when I came to the wharf to see Noah?"

"Exactly. You walked right by and didn't even see me. You were a woman on a mission."

"I did see you," she whispered. "But… I had a plan."

"I know, I get it. *I* wasn't part of the plan." He stuck his arms out to the sides like presenting himself: not part of her plan.

What the hell did a woman do with all that honesty? It was so unnerving.

"But I remember thinking you were handsome. I felt guilty for noticing you, but it's hard not to notice that sort of thing."

"Then we both felt guilty, but we didn't have any reason to."

"I thought you were a little too handsome for your own good."

"How is that even possible?"

"Easy. It's easy to believe that you have your pick of women."

"Is that a fair statement to make? Because *you* think I'm handsome I must therefore be a player?"

"No, it's not fair at all." She came close to press a hand flat across his chest. "And I'm sorry to put you in that position and assume so many things about you. Really."

He took the same hand and brought it to his lips to brush a kiss across her knuckles. "It's okay."

"What should we do with all this?"

"For now, I think you should go inside. And I'll see you tomorrow."

Yes, inside. This was her place. She had the key, somewhere in her purse. Um…yes, here was her key. Put key in keyhole, turn. Open. She turned back to see Finn still there. Not an apparition or a part of her imagination. Yes, he'd just confessed real feelings for her.

No, she wasn't dreaming this.

"Goodnight," Finn said, when she cracked the door open.

Michelle stepped through, disappointment whirling through her. He meant it.

"Goodnight."

She softly shut the door and laid her hand against it. Her breathing was erratic, coming in short bursts of air, then long, deep breaths like meditation. Call her crazy, but she could almost sense Finn on the other side of the door. He hadn't left. Not yet. She tried looking through the peephole in the door but didn't see him. When she swung the door open, he stood there, several feet away from her door, like he'd been waiting for her. Maybe he needed her to be sure. Oh, she was.

He slid her a slow, sheepish smile, like he'd been caught. "How am I still here?"

"You want to be."

Outside, the air seemed charged between them like a live electrical current. Walking inside made no difference. There was still the beautiful energy, that heavy magnetism. Though she would have never admitted it, she'd felt the same sensations from the moment she'd first walked past him. Oh, she'd *noticed* him. He might never know how hard it had been for her to keep walking.

But that was the thing about her, wasn't it? She always had her set-in-stone plans, rarely allowing for deviations. Finn was a twist she'd never taken before. Everything about him felt new, exciting, and equally dangerous. This was a road and a path she didn't know. A plan she had only imagined but never taken.

She crooked her finger for him to come inside, and thank God and all the sweet angels he did.

Finn shut the door, then pushed her up against the nearest wall. One arm was braced on either side of her, pinning her in place.

He smiled against her lips, like she'd given him what he wanted.

Taking Finn's hand, she led him toward the bedroom.

"Are you sure?" Finn asked, and his eyes were nearly black with heat.

"Yes. I am very sure. And also, I have condoms."

"Damn, I love a woman who's prepared."

He pulled her close, and kissed down the column of her neck, the rough stubble of his beard making her moan with unexpected pleasure. Slowly, he removed every piece of her clothing and she proceeded to do the same for him. He unzipped and lowered her dress, and she stepped out of it, kicking off her sandals.

He kissed and licked every inch of bare skin he exposed. "You feel so good."

"I never saw you coming, Michelle."

And it was a long time before either one of them slept.

The next morning, Michelle's entire body buzzed and hummed.

She was lying in her own bed, spooning with Finn. *Finn.* Gorgeous, able, hard-bodied Finn Sheridan. Oh, it was so good to be her right here and now, a strong muscled arm thrown across her, toasty warm and firm.

She didn't want to twitch a single muscle, *ever*, but nature called. Smoothly, she rolled out of Finn's arms, and watched as he moved on to his back, throwing an arm over his face. *Oh no, don't cover that face.* That beautiful face. Without his glasses, he seemed much younger somehow. Otherwise, his face was all sharp angles with a strong jawline that could cut marble. And his body was a monument to male beauty.

Stretching, she surveyed her clothes lying where Finn

had slowly peeled them off last night. She had a surprisingly wicked desire to keep her thrown panties and bra there as evidence of a night of spectacular wanton sexy times. Buck naked, she walked to the bathroom and stared in the mirror at the sex kitten staring back at her. She spied beard burn on her neck and lower, all the way down to the curve of her hip bone.

"Meow," she said, finger combing her messy hair.

Her cheeks were pink as if she'd just gotten over the flu, her mouth bruised, her eyes bleary from lack of sleep and smeared with hints of mascara. She resembled a raccoon who'd had a rough winter.

But actually, she'd never looked more beautiful.

Oh, the things Finn had done to her last night. He'd worshipped her body. There was just no other word for the way he'd treated her like a glass figurine he didn't want to drop. Sweet words, even sweeter caresses. She'd never felt so…loved. Wait. No, not *loved*. Wanted. She'd never *been* so wanted.

Michelle threw on the robe she kept on the door hook and went to make coffee and check to see if she had anything in her cupboard that would come close to his favorite cereal. No such luck. Not even any campfire marshmallows because hello, summer. But it wouldn't have mattered anyway unless he liked his cereal with coffee creamer because she had no milk. She didn't even have any eggs. Studying her cabinets, she found rice, pasta, and canned soup. In her refrigerator were pickles, lettuce and tomatoes. A little bit of cheese. Sad.

"Michelle, get back here," Finn's voice called out. "Where are you, woman?"

"I'll be right there." She hurried back to the bedroom, cheered at least she had coffee to offer him.

He deserved so much more after last night like a...well, another medal.

"Hey," he said from her bed.

Because he was in *her bed*. Under the light cotton sheet pushed down to just below his abs.

"I have bad news for you." She set the two mugs down, then settled on the bed beside him.

Bless his heart, he looked worried. He reached to shove his glasses on like he had to see better to hear what she had to say. Adorable.

"It's kind of serious."

"Tell me." Finn started to mess with her hair, twirling a strand around one finger as he studied her.

It felt so good to be this close to him, his leg pressing against hers, warmth emanating from every cell in his body.

She straddled his hips and cupped his face. "I'm really sorry, but I don't have any Lucky Charms."

His lips quirked in a smile that was equal parts sailor on leave and wicked altar boy. "You brat."

"But is there anything else that I can get for you?" She nudged her chin in the direction of the mug. "I mean, besides the coffee?"

"You're all I need."

Finn covered her mouth with a kiss. The kiss lingered and deepened. He tasted like rich, dark coffee and sweet intimacy. With his free hand, his fingers found the opening of her robe and he groaned into the kiss.

He stared at her from under hooded lids. "You're not wearing anything under this."

"No." She tossed her hair back and removed his glasses. "Oh, and there's one more thing I have to tell you."

"Yes?" he said, pulling apart the folds of her robe.

"It turns out you really are magically delicious in the morning. I would have never guessed."

"Thanks, babe. And I must say I didn't realize you're so religious."

"*Religious*?"

"All that praying last night. Oh God, please. Oh. My. God."

She laughed and squeezed his face between her hands. He had a remarkable face.

"It's better than cursing like a sailor. I haven't heard that many four-letter words in a row since the last time I was at a frat party a decade ago."

He moved suddenly and flipped her so she was flat on her back looking up at all that rangy male deliciousness.

"Time for me to be a frat boy again."

"Oh God," Michelle said.

Chapter Eighteen

Too many times, Michelle felt awkward the morning after the first time with a man. Bumping around each other, wondering when an appropriate time to leave would be, asking to shower.

She and Finn didn't have these issues. When they bumped into each other dressing, it was pleasant. They solved the shower dilemma by showering together. And she never even considered asking him to leave, though there were several new filings from Ted's law firm for her to read. It could all wait until later.

They moved rather seamlessly into their new reality... maybe because they'd been playing at this all along. She was still surprised by how natural it felt.

Because she had nothing to eat in the house, they actually went shopping together. Such a domestic activity that Michelle had to shake her head a couple of times. She was under the impression guys always resisted this kind of "couple" activity this early on. Not Finn.

He had forced her to reexamine her own prejudices against extremely good-looking men. He'd called her on it, too, which was fair.

"Eggs," he said, putting a dozen in the cart.

"Milk," she said from the other side of the aisle, holding

up two percent and whole. "The ever-widening conundrum. Fat is good, fat is bad. Life is hard."

"You decide."

"Smart man."

They were stopped repeatedly as they pushed their cart through the store. She never realized her boyfriend was a minor celebrity. In the grocery store, at least three people stopped him and asked about his parents. Asked about his new venture. Another elderly couple shuffling by congratulated him on "making Texans proud."

"My grandparents," he said mockingly as they walked away. "Lovely people."

"Seriously?"

"Kidding." He cleared his throat. "I know it must seem weird. But it's mostly the older generation. They remember all the articles written about me when I was younger, when I came to train for the Olympics in their town."

"Don't sell yourself short. What you did was a big deal, and everyone knows it."

And she still couldn't believe he didn't have the *medal*.

"That was then, this is now."

Taking over steering the cart, she led them to the cereal aisle. "Ah, here we are."

Methodically, she began shoving boxes of his favorite cereal in the cart until she nearly filled it.

"Stop, you nutcase." Laughing, he stayed her hand and began putting boxes back. "Just one. It's not even on sale."

"Oh, but I want you to have them." She wrapped her arms around his back.

He turned and bent to kiss her right there in the aisle. "One at a time is enough."

"Michelle! Finn!"

The voice was familiar, but it took Michelle a moment

to recognize its cadence. It was out of context at the grocery store where she normally performed the dreary routine of stocking up on food she thought she should eat, like kale and…quinoa.

Lynn Pierce stood before them, holding a box of granola.

"Oh, hi. Hi, Lynn." She disentangled from Finn's arms but held on to his hand.

It was warm and he squeezed hers like: *It's okay, I'm here. Tell her whatever you want.*

"Good morning, Lynn," Finn said, his arm around Michelle's waist.

"Oh, don't stop because of me!" She chuckled. "Love in the cereal aisle. Wait until I tell Arthur I ran into you two lovebirds."

So yes, this was rather convenient. They were very believable.

But it suddenly felt like an incredible invasion of privacy.

"It's…it's nice seeing you," Michelle said.

"I'm so glad to see you so relaxed, dear." She pointed to her forehead. "Those lines will stay permanently, you know?"

Finn coughed slightly, sounding like a muffled laugh. "That's what I keep telling her."

"And, Finn, if you don't mind me saying, that cereal is not likely to help with your digestion." She tapped the box she held. "Try something high in fiber like this granola. Or perhaps some muesli."

Now it was Michelle's turn to cough as she felt Finn tense beside her.

"I meant to tell you." Michelle cleared her throat. "Finn doesn't actually have digestive issues. I was just mad at him when I said that."

Lynn blinked twice but then laughed. "Oh, Michelle, you devil!"

"It was stupid, I admit."

Finn squeezed her hand again. "Don't blame her. I shouldn't have made her mad."

"Oh, Finn, I don't even want to know what you did!" But as she passed by with her cart, Lynn leaned in to whisper, "I once told a friend of mine that Arthur had a little drinking problem. He had no such issue, but you better believe she stopped serving cocktails when she invited us over for dinner. I'd wanted him to stop drinking before the heart attack. Us women can be devious, can't we?"

When she looked back to him, Finn was giving her his slow and easy grin. "What did she say?"

"She said I can be devious, so watch it, Mister." She elbowed him.

"I already am. Have been for a while." He made a motion to look at her butt in appreciation.

She laughed. "Let's hurry up and pay. You're supposed to make me breakfast."

They walked toward the cashiers and Michelle spied an attractive redhead making her way down the aisle next to a guy who was good-looking in that news anchor kind of way. Every hair in place with perfect teeth and a stilted walk. Finn slowed to a stop.

The woman seemed to notice him at the same time. "Finn."

Comically, all four of them stopped in the cereal aisle.

Really, what was it about the grocery store? Why were they running into everyone today?

"Cheryl." Finn nodded, then gave the man a quick glare. "Todd."

"Hello, Finn. So good to see you," Todd said, sounding every bit like a professional weatherman.

Cloudy with a chance of rain, be careful out there, folks. Hahahaha!

"Hi, I'm Michelle." Rather than sticking her hand out, she leaned into Finn's shoulder.

If this was the man who'd broken up their marriage, she wanted them both to see he'd moved on and recovered. Quite nicely, thank you.

"Oh, Michelle. How lovely to meet you." Cheryl gave a frozen smile.

"Same."

Cheryl was lovely, sure, but there was something so disingenuous about her. Her hair was very obviously dyed in a dark red color seen only on a box and her nails were long enough to injure someone.

Finn had once loved this woman.

Give him back the gold medal! You weren't the one who earned it.

Finn was still standing like a statue but as if suddenly waking from a deep slumber, he pulled Michelle close. "We're just getting ready to check out."

"Okay, nice to see you." She gave him a little wave.

"Yeah." Finn pushed on.

It wasn't until they were unloading groceries in her kitchen that she finally brought up the subject.

"Boy, that was awkward with your ex."

"Nah. Thanks for being so great." He pulled her into his arms, his back leaning against the counter.

"Finn." She pressed her head against his chest. "You know I can get that medal back for you."

She felt the rumble of his chuckle, deep inside that granite hard chest. "You think that's what I want?"

"Isn't it?"

She wanted to believe that because if the medal itself

wasn't what he wanted, maybe he wanted *Cheryl* back and Michelle couldn't accept that.

"We didn't have a prenup."

"I'm a skilled negotiator."

He smiled again. "Don't I know it, babe. You put everyone else to shame."

"Remember when you told Tanner that people don't get what they deserve just because it's their turn? That you have to win fair and square?"

"Yeah, but that's not what I—"

"You earned that medal. No one else did."

"Yeah." He nodded and closed his eyes. "I did and no one can really take that win away from me. The medal is just a symbol."

"I don't understand why you just let her have it."

"Maybe I feel guilty."

"Why would you feel guilty?"

"I stopped loving her way before we separated. But I was raised not to give up, and that was the first time in my life I failed in a colossal way. I got selfish when I didn't want to be in a marriage with someone I didn't love anymore."

"But that's fair. You're too hard on yourself."

"I want to leave it in the past, okay? If I ever got the medal back, I'd give it to my dad, anyway. And he's fine." He pressed a kiss to her temple. "But thanks for offering. As much as I'd love to sic you on Cheryl, it wouldn't be a fair fight."

Well, he was right. It wouldn't be fair because one way or another she would leave with his medal.

In a strange switch, like upside-down day, suddenly Michelle's personal life was a thing of beauty, and her work life was a cesspool. A dumpster fire. It was hellfire and damnation. It was the bloody accident on the side of the road you couldn't look away from. It was every zombie horror movie ever made and every Stephen King book ever written.

Goodwill v. Goodwill was going to kill them all.

Arthur checked in daily, pale with worry his friends were going to wind up on *Dateline*.

Ted's lawyers were going through paper with zero disregard to how many trees had died in the process and seemed determined to win at all costs—whatever that ended up looking like. Boxes of files arrived every few days with accounts and business dealings that Ted had all over the world. They were determined to be utterly transparent. Phone calls with opposing counsel ranged from hostile to murderous, and this was all just trying to agree on a mediator. Michelle was already tired when she arrived every morning, and for the past two days, she left the office before Rachel did.

Today, she was determined to enjoy spending the afternoon with Finn on the boat, this time the sailboat he and Noah had recently purchased. Finn wanted to test it out on a weekday when there wouldn't be much traffic. He explained that most owners took their sailboats out on the weekend, those times when the coastline was dotted with brilliant sails and fast speedboats.

She'd wanted to watch Finn in his element for a while now, and this was her chance. Not surprisingly, he looked like poetry in motion as he perched on the bow, then adjusted the sails and steered them into the bay. The late afternoon was unusually cool on this late summer day as they headed into August.

"Come here." Finn beckoned her to join him near the wheel.

She did, allowing him to adjust their bodies so that he'd be right behind her. The sails flapped and unfurled in the coastal breeze. Their speed was comfortable, and they bopped along the waves at a steady pace.

She leaned into his strong arms. "I could really get used to this."

"So could I," he said and brushed a kiss across her temple.

This was sweet because he had to mean the two of them. Finn wasn't exactly a stranger to sailing, or she imagined, days like this when the spray of water was like a blessing.

"Here," he said, handing her a pair of binoculars. "See if you find anything interesting out there."

She adjusted them to her eyes and saw one other die-hard sailboat in the distance, a working fishing boat farther out and a luxury yacht headed in their direction. She supposed rich people could go out whenever they liked. There might even be someone famous on that yacht. She imagined a country music star and his entourage. Though she searched hopefully, there were no dolphins in sight. She handed Finn the binoculars and he removed his glasses and adjusted them for himself.

"What do you see?" Michelle said.

"Lots and lots of water."

She elbowed him. "Funny man."

But she could feel it when he tensed behind her. "Huh."

"What *is* it? A shark?"

He lowered the lenses, squinted, then raised them to his face again. "Well...no, not really."

"What do you mean, not *really*? Either it's a shark or it's *not*. Can't you tell?"

"Not a shark."

"Oh, whew." She breathed out.

"But still…pretty shocking."

She turned to him, giving him all her focus. *"What?"*

He lowered them, and his green eyes were dipped at the edges in that worried puppy dog look.

"I need to show you something, and I don't want you to freak out."

Chapter Nineteen

All Finn wanted today was a calm afternoon sail with his girlfriend.

Now this.

This was going to complicate everything. In the end, it would be for the best. Probably. Although Michelle might not initially see it, and that's what worried him. He couldn't say that he blamed her, exactly. Truthfully, he was in a semi-state of outage himself. Why waste everyone's time like this? All that money, too?

For the past week, he'd had a firsthand look at what the work was doing to Michelle. She never complained but the dark circles under her formerly shimmering blue eyes were a clue. He cooked dinner for her every night, anything she wanted, pretty much spoiling her rotten. She was getting proper nutrition, running every morning, and her libido was certainly serviced regularly. Still, Michelle fell asleep in his arms almost always before the end of *Is It Cake*, which they'd quickly determined to be their favorite show.

She'd started awake in his lap a couple of nights ago, rubbing her eyes, shocked and a bit embarrassed. "Was I right? Was the real cake number three?"

And now this. He would be the one to give her a little bit of good news (he hoped) mixed with bad news, sprinkled with utter confusion.

Why? It didn't make sense.

"I see Tippy on that yacht." He pointed.

"Oh, geez. No wonder she hasn't been returning my calls lately. She must be out of range. Is she with that man again? I warned her about this."

"No, not that man, and this is the tough part."

"Just *say* it, Finn!"

"She's with Ted."

"With *Ted*?" She wrestled the binoculars from him.

He watched as her fingers circled, fast work focusing, and he knew the moment she saw what he had.

Just as he'd seen them, in a tight embrace, looking far from two people filing for divorce.

"Why, Tippy? Why?" She lowered the binoculars and looked at Finn. "They're kissing! Kissing!"

"What?" Now he grabbed them back. Sure enough, the two were in a lip-lock. "I thought these two hated each other. What happened?"

"I've asked Tippy if she was sure this was what she wanted, and the last time we talked she was firm on divorcing. It was over, no chance for reconciliation. Why would she lie to me?"

"It could be she changed her mind, of course."

"When? She couldn't bother to call?" Michelle shook her head. "All the work I've done, all the phone calls and arguing with Ted's Satan of an attorney—"

"I'm still sorry about that, babe."

At the time, he thought he'd done the right thing for Ted. Now, he understood that a contentious divorce was also not the answer to getting what you wanted. Maybe reconciling was the answer, at least for Ted.

"How long have they been pretending? Is this new? Or

should I now clearly understand why she hasn't returned my calls?"

"You would think they'd call it off."

"Or at least let me know to put things on pause. And I'm not the only one who has been kept in the dark. His attorney doesn't know either. I just spoke with him today when he shot down three other calendar dates with the mediator."

"You're obviously going to have to confront her with this."

"Or maybe I should just stop spending so much time on her case and help another couple trying to adopt." She turned to Finn, anger flashing in her eyes. "Let's get back to shore because I have a few calls to make."

An hour later, Finn dropped Michelle off at home.

"I'm going to leave you alone tonight. I have to put together my thoughts on the sailboat and you need to get some rest. I'd only keep you up all night."

"But for good reasons," she said, her voice somewhat muffled as she spoke into his chest. "I'm going to miss your foot rub."

He pulled her face up and stared into her eyes. "I will make it up to you."

"The good news is, I guess I'm going to have a lot more free time now."

"That is good news." He tugged on a lock of her hair.

"Finn, thank you for the sail." She went on her tiptoes and gave him a long and lingering kiss that gave him second thoughts about leaving.

It was on the tip of his tongue, those words he hadn't said in years and possibly never truly meant before. Three little words that could change his life. When he said those words, he would mean them with every fiber of his being because they weren't throwaway words for him.

The night she'd met his parents, something had shifted inside. Like a rearranging of his heart, he'd made room for her. He'd seen Michelle, head tossed back in that yellow dress, laughing with his parents. She fit in with the Sheridans as if someone had cut a Michelle-size hole in the fabric of his family. Little meant more to Finn than family, and he'd always wanted to fall in love with a woman who fit in with his. Who would accept his kooky, overly ambitious father with his dozens of home improvement projects, goal charts and graphs, a somewhat lazy but well-meaning brother, and a sweet mother who didn't know how to keep a secret to save her life.

The thought that had speared him front and center was as surprising to him as if he'd suddenly had a rash of his ancestral good luck. She was it for him. She was everything and he was head over heels in love with her.

She'd been that missing piece of him, lost for years to the wind and other ambitions. But as with everything perfect, there was a flaw. This time the flaw wasn't a difference in sports teams, music, religion, or politics. It was her fundamental lack of faith in marriage that disturbed him. He wasn't going to set out to convince her of the sanctity of marriage. If he wanted her to laugh, he'd suggest they watch John Mulaney. She had her opinions, and they were staunchly based on what she'd seen and experienced, even in her own family.

And his were steeped in what he'd lived with for much of his life. With the right woman, marriage could be a forever kind of thing. Love could last forever.

He tapped her nose. "Get some rest and don't dwell on this too much until you can get some answers."

As he drove home, he couldn't stop thinking about Tippy and Ted. Two wealthy and entitled people were pulling her puppet strings for reasons only they could understand. They had no regard for how hard Michelle had worked on this case, how many hours she'd logged, which were more than just billables. Yes, she'd made Arthur a lot of money, but those had been hours of her life she'd never get back. He could see it in her eyes, too. She had the same thoughts but neither one of them would say them out loud. Those were hours they might have spent together much sooner had she not been wrapped up in winning.

Not surprisingly, at the house, though it was a weeknight, Declan had a poker game going. Again.

It seemed to Finn at times that his brother was the proverbial Peter Pan. That bothered Finn more than the fact he flitted from job to job and wasn't working up to his potential.

"Hey, what are you doing here?" Declan called out. "I thought I'd lost you for good. Michelle finally get sick of seeing your ugly mug?"

Finn ignored that. "She's fine, thanks for asking."

"Pull up a chair." One of the cooks from the bar kicked one out with his foot. "I'm on a roll tonight and happy to take your money."

Finn dealt in for a few hands, folding when his luck was what he'd expected. Horrible cards. Declan, whose luck wasn't any better, lost twice but didn't seem to mind.

"Those are just the tips I made tonight. I'm good."

Finally, everyone filed out of the house. Finn settled on the couch and switched on the TV for background noise mostly.

Declan joined him minutes later, handing him a beer, and staring at Gordon Ramsey as he picked up a pan on fire, threw it into the sink and splashed water on it. Even Finn knew that was a bad move. The flames licked up, nearly singing his eyebrows off.

"Who's the idiot now?" Finn muttered.

"Pretty hot and heavy with Michelle, right? You two have been together longer than anyone since...well, since Cheryl. I mean, you were pretty heavy on the dating scene for the last few months but no one for this long."

"You know I didn't sleep with all those women I was dating every few weeks, don't you?"

Declan snorted. "I wouldn't care if you were. No one's judging you, bro. You had every right to get that witchy ex of yours fully out of your system."

He didn't hook up with all of the women he dated, but people tended to assume he did. People believed what they wanted to believe. And they apparently wanted to believe every athlete, past or present, went through women like garlic through a presser. That had never been Finn.

"I didn't sleep with a new woman every two weeks. Okay?"

"Fine with me." Declan shrugged.

"I liked being married. I just didn't like being married to *her*. There's a difference."

"Really? How would you know unless you try several times?"

The truth was that he knew just from being with Michelle. It would be different with her. They already fit together so well it was almost scary easy. Sometimes he knew what she would say before she said it.

"Just look at our parents!"

"Look, they're from another era. A generation that didn't believe in giving up. You know Dad. He wouldn't give up a race if he had a broken leg. He'd hop and drag himself across the finish line with his fingernails."

"There's a difference between sticking it out to make a point and sticking around because you love each other.

They didn't stay together to make some generational point, Declan. They're still in love."

"Well, they're a rarity, okay?"

It suddenly occurred to Finn that Declan was every bit as intimidated by the lofty standard of their parents as he'd been. The difference was Declan had also watched his older brother fail miserably at marriage. It couldn't have been encouraging.

"Look. There's something I've wanted to say for a long time. I'm sorry that I took your dreams away. You were a hell of a pitcher. If you'd had more training, more resources… I could see you going all the way. You're talented. I mean, you still could go far. You're young and I don't know why you're flitting from job to job when you're a fantastic ball player."

"Is that what you think?" Declan set down his beer and shook his head slowly. "Dude, you've got it all wrong. I was always stinkin' *proud* of you! I never had a problem watching you soar. The thing is, I never wanted it as much as you did, and that much was clear from the start. Watching you, I saw what it meant to dedicate your entire life to something you love. You are the true meaning of excellence. I'm still looking for that *something* in my life. Sorry to say, I liked playing ball but that's not what drives me."

So, Finn had it all wrong. All along, it hadn't been him holding Declan back at all. It also hadn't been his parents, cheating him because Finn showed more promise. They'd seen it, too, no doubt. Finn had the drive and dedication because he had the love for the sport. Declan just didn't. It wasn't anyone's fault.

"Then I hope you find that thing that drives you to excellence. And if ever I can help, all you have to do is ask."

Chapter Twenty

The next morning Michelle opened up the doors of Pierce & Pierce. She flipped on the lights to only her office and didn't bother with reception, the copy machine, or the coffee. There was too much on her plate today. She'd spent a sleepless night wondering why Tippy was avoiding her calls and why she hadn't called off the divorce. Was she getting some kind of freaky delight from sneaking around, her romance with Ted rejuvenated by the forbidden nature?

Michelle decided the minute she got into the office, she would ignore all the work on Goodwill v. Goodwill. She was going to return calls on cases she'd had no time to take. Another adoption would soon be on her docket, a single mother trying to get custody of her daughter back after she'd been through a rehab program, and a father suing for visitation rights. She didn't know why she hadn't taken these cases, except for the fact they weren't the bright and shiny kind that would get her the attention. Get her the partnership.

Maybe this was where she really wanted to be, instead of in the middle of bickering couples who played all manner of games and tricks with each other no one else could understand. Enough already. Divorce or don't, she didn't care anymore!

Ironically, it would seem that at least for the past few days Tippy and Ted were *pretending* to be separated.

The way she'd pretended to date Finn. But she wasn't pretending anymore.

She wasn't sure she'd ever pretended with Finn.

The first time she'd laid eyes on him she'd been walking past him with purpose to talk to Noah. She'd been single minded then, but even now she recalled how her eyes had swept over him, and guilt had pulsed through her at the way she'd responded. His golden boy good looks were not what she was accustomed to. It was a throwback to her college days of tutoring the athlete and her immediate thought was: he doesn't know I'm alive. He'd never notice someone like me.

How very wrong of her. The truth was men noticed her and had since she'd grown out of her wallflower stage. Since she'd allowed her college friend to dress her and tutor *her* on hair and makeup. She'd been shooting for the stars with her career, but she'd settled in her personal life. Settled for relationships that just fell in her lap, but yes, that day at the Salty Dog grabbing Finn for a favor hadn't been all about impressing Arthur.

She could have grabbed her favorite waiter for that matter, someone who was always making subtle passes at her. No, she'd gone to Finn because he was who she'd wanted all along, and it was easier to put herself out there with another reason to serve as an excuse. It took the pressure off the fact she'd been low-key fantasizing about him since the day she saw him on the dock.

Now he was in her bed almost every night making her toes curl and her heart grow. She was going to stay in Charming whether or not she made partner at P&P. She would call a truce with Junior and let him be his man-child self because nothing truly bothered her anymore. Yes, she was in love with Finn Sheridan and hadn't even seen that coming. She might even, someday, take the biggest risk of all with him.

There. Michelle had returned three calls for various cases when Rachel finally arrived. Junior arrived a half hour later, as per the usual and Arthur brought up the rear.

She met him in the doorway to his office. "Good morning, Arthur. I need to talk to you."

He stood. "Dear God, what have they done now?"

"Nothing you'd expect." She cleared her throat. "Tippy won't return any of my calls."

"That doesn't sound like her. But you know how busy she is as mayor. She probably had some commitments. I'll take care of this right away." He sat in his office chair, leaned back, and grabbed his phone. Only seconds later he was already greeting someone. "Hello there, Tippy. How are you? Oh, out on the yacht yesterday? Fine, fine. I was thinking about getting a boat myself, but—"

Michelle crossed her arms and cleared her throat again, lest he forget she was still standing there.

"Well, I'm sure there's a simple answer to this, but my associate tells me she's had trouble reaching you. I explained that I'm sure you...what? Oh, okay. But please do call her back—" He stared at the handset. "She was late to a meeting with the city comptroller. Which was odd because I think I heard *SportsCenter* in the background."

"I'll just bet you did." Michelle closed the door to Arthur's office.

"What's going on?"

Michelle told Arthur what she'd seen yesterday from Finn's sailboat.

Arthur broke into a huge smile. "Wonderful. That's great! They're trying to work things out."

"Then why haven't they called off the divorce?"

"Imagine that. They're pretending to be divorcing. Well, maybe they're still trying to iron out a few matters before they call the whole thing off?"

Pretending. Michelle was familiar with that approach. Far too familiar.

"I've wasted hours on this that I'll never get back."

"But they're billable hours. I'm sure they can afford it. Have we been through her retainer yet?"

"Of course not, it's been what, a few weeks? But at this rate we will be soon. Opposing counsel has delivered boxes of financials to comb through. Rachel has been helping. This is a waste of valuable resources and office time! How can they do this to us?"

Michelle was ready to stomp her foot.

"To us? You mean, how can they reconcile?" He cracked a smile. "If they want to waste their money, what do we care? They're filthy rich, and wealthy people do a lot of *stupid* things. And do you see how lies can hurt people unintentionally? I'm sure they didn't mean to hurt you. You almost sound personally invested in their divorce."

Indeed. This might be a good time to confess her own fake relationship to Arthur, but there was no point now. It had become real, and he'd never have to know how or when it started.

"I'm not invested. I just…maybe I got a little emotionally involved, but that's only because I've spent a lot of time on their case. Time I won't get back."

"What have I been telling you? Were you even listening to me? This is a job. Don't take the work home with you."

He tapped his chest. "It could kill you. It certainly kills plenty of relationships."

"I've wasted time that I *could* have spent with Finn."

He nodded sagely. "Now you finally understand."

"But...okay." She spread her palms apart. "I'm no longer working on Goodwill v. Goodwill. And I want to take more adoption and custody cases, maybe even guardian ad litem. Less divorce. Is that okay with you?"

"Why do you think I hired you?"

"Because I had a ruthless reputation?"

"Yes and no. It's actually because I saw who you were and who you *could become*."

It was a loaded statement. She had no idea how Arthur had seen what she'd been unable to. But it did remind her of another man, one she hadn't seen in years. One who believed in her before she believed in herself. Her father was a special man, and even if he'd abandoned her, he'd left her with memories and sweet words that had lasted decades.

It was something.

"Thank you for believing in me."

Arthur held up his arms in a victory stance. "Wait until we do the team-building activities! That's when you'll *really* thank me."

Later that afternoon, Tippy finally saw it fit to return Michelle's many calls.

"Let me first say that I'm sorry it took me so long to call you back. You were right. I've been avoiding you. See, I guess I was...embarrassed."

"Because you still love your husband? Because you want to reconcile?"

Tippy let out a sigh that Michelle interpreted as a *yes*. "You know I was resistant. I meant every word I said when

I came to see you and filed for divorce. It was a hard thing to admit that I'd had a knee-jerk reaction to something that wasn't even real. I'm a bright woman but apparently not when it comes to Teddy. Still, it wasn't until after that night in the bar when Ted put up such a fuss...well, I realized he cared."

Really? Was everyone secretly a sixteen-year-old when it came to romantic love? Possibly.

"I'm the one who asked you if you wanted to change your mind. Whether you wanted to go to counseling. Divorce isn't something you should file for unless you're sure. I just... I hate to think of all the money and time wasted."

"But time and money are never wasted if the effort leads to positive results."

Michelle sighed. "I'm happy if you're happy. I just wish you'd told me sooner."

"Teddy wanted me to. We were probably each waiting until the other fired his attorney. It's like a dance we played with each other. Don't get me wrong, we still have a way to go when it comes to trust. Without trust, you literally have nothing. But I believe what we have is worth saving. We're going to be doing some of that counseling you recommended."

"I'll have Rachel do an accounting as quickly as possible and return anything unused from your retainer."

"Don't bother. Take it for the pain and suffering."

"That's unfortunately not legal."

"Then let's talk on the phone until I run out of money." She chuckled.

"Sorry, no."

Michelle paused for only a moment. It didn't take her long to think of a way Tippy could repay her for all her wasted efforts.

"What I will take is a sizable donation for our clients who require legal assistance. I have a docket of cases I'd love to take on, but our law firm's services don't come for free."

"Certainly. You've got it!"

"Tell Ted I said hello and I'm happy for the two of you. Contrary to popular belief, not all family law attorneys want a couple to divorce."

"I never thought that about you. Not *you*. You always made me think there was hope and I just needed to accept that."

"Who? *Me*?"

"I'm sure on some level you're very jaded after everything you've seen in your profession. But there was always a little spark in you. When I saw you and Finn together, I finally knew why."

Oh.

Michelle fairly floated through the rest of her day on that happy note. It seemed almost too good to be true that only a few months after the pain of rejection, and without even trying, she could feel so chosen.

But Finn made her feel that way.

Precious and wanted. Protected even when she didn't need him. Her phone buzzed just as she was pulling up to the market where she would buy the ingredients to make dinner for him tonight. For once, it was her turn, and she vowed to make the best tacos her money could buy.

Glancing at her phone, the message she read seemed impossible. It was from Finn, whom she'd given a nickname.

MAGICALLY DELICIOUS: I'm at the hospital. It's my Dad.

Chapter Twenty-One

"Mom, calm down. Please. The doctors know what they're doing."

Finn had been at the marina in the process of tying up the catamaran after a fishing charter when he'd received the frantic call from his mother. His father had collapsed in the middle of caulking. Rather than his knee or some other body part giving out, she feared it was his heart. Never one to underplay anything, she'd dialed nine-one-one. Getting information out of his mother had proved pointless. She couldn't even tell him if his father was breathing, she'd been that preoccupied with getting him help.

Now they were both sitting in the ER waiting room where on the other side of those harmless-looking double doors swinging only one way, doctors were either trying to resuscitate his father or advising him to stop climbing ladders with a bad knee. He fervently prayed it was the latter. If a doctor headed toward them with a grim face, Finn would be living his greatest nightmare. His father, his mentor, the family's rock, his guide. Gone.

"It's a heart attack, I'm telling you. He keeps eating bacon like he's a teenager. Oreo cookies after dinner! Just because he's not fat doesn't mean it's not going straight to the heart, clogging it up like rush hour traffic. Oh dear God. I better sit down." She fanned herself.

"Yes, please and thank you."

The last thing he needed was his mother having a fainting spell. He would like one patient at a time, thank you. Finn slumped into the seat next to his mother and tugged her into his arms. He pulled out his phone to see no reply yet from Declan or Michelle. Not that he expected one from Michelle. If she were wise, she'd go home, wait to hear from him, and stay out of this mess. No one voluntarily entered these antiseptic hallways. Moments ago, a man had been hauled in with a chainsaw injury, which would have been what he'd expected might one day happen to his father. Not this. Not a heart attack. Please, God, not that.

"Maybe you had better ask them again," his mother said, clutching at his hands like a drowning person clutching on to a raft.

He was fully aware he was the raft and had no business sinking. But if something happened to his father, everything would collapse. He was the foundation of their family, and they all knew it. As strong as he'd always been, it was unbearable to think of him as weak even now.

"I asked for the fourth time thirty seconds ago. They will let us know when we can go back. They realize we're family."

At times he wondered if they'd been forgotten, with the bustle and triage of patients coming through. Because his father had come through on an ambulance, no one but the EMTs had been with him. While they waited, Finn drove himself crazy with the "what-ifs." He did the worst thing he could possibly do under the circumstances and googled for possible reasons a sixty-year-old man in great condition (other than his orthopedic injuries) might collapse. The answers ranged from low blood sugar all the way to cardiac arrest. Endless possibilities. He shared none of them with his mother.

The automatic doors to the emergency room flew open and a wild-eyed Declan rushed inside.

Finn waved to him. "Over here."

"What's happening?" Declan ran a hand through his already disheveled hair. "I got over here as soon as I heard. I was at work."

"Oh, Declan." His mother went into her youngest son's arms, weeping inconsolably.

"Oh, shit. Shit. God, no." Declan squeezed his eyes shut and looked ready to collapse on top of their mother.

"Hang on," Finn said, trying to calm what his mother had just stoked. "We don't know anything yet."

"He's not…dead?" Declan seemed to push the words out with the last of his air.

Jesus, Mary and Joseph. "No," Finn said. "*No.*"

But they didn't know, did they? He might have died on the way to the hospital for all they knew. But until they were actually told, he refused to assume the worst. It's what his father would say. Keep your head up. Stay positive even in the face of loss. You can't win if you go in expecting the worst.

Why the hell couldn't he at least get any updates yet?

His mother seemed to finally regain strength when her youngest son was about to fall apart. "We just need to be patient and wait for news."

"Okay, okay." Declan slumped in the seat and covered his eyes.

While his mother explained everything to Declan, Finn decided it had been too long since he'd checked in with the triage nurse. Let her get sick of him. Maybe then he'd get some action.

The doors swung open once more and he glanced up, hoping to see Michelle. He could use her right now.

It was a woman, alright, and Finn sincerely hoped his glasses needed a new prescription. Cheryl. What the hell was she doing here?

"Finn!" Cheryl ran to him. "I heard. How's he doing?"

"What…what are you doing here?"

"I was at the bar when Declan rushed out. I asked someone where he'd gone in such a hurry and…well, they told me something happened to your dad and he was taken by ambulance. I thought you might need me."

He scoffed. "I don't."

"You say that now, but I know how you feel about your father. God, Finn, you're going to need family if he dies—"

"He's. Not. Dying." He leaned in close and said the words slowly, so she'd hear every single word.

"You don't know that. You—"

"Leave. My mother doesn't need your hysterics. You're not welcome here."

The door opened again and this time EMTs rushed in carrying someone on a stretcher. "Move."

Finn moved Cheryl out of their way and that's when he noticed someone else coming behind the EMTs. Someone striding inside like she owned the hospital, wearing a black pantsuit and heels, her hair in an "I mean business" bun.

Michelle.

After that, he couldn't see anything else but her.

On arriving in the hospital emergency room, Michelle did not like what she saw. Cheryl, with Finn leaning in very close to her as if whispering something. She followed the

EMTs and saw Finn pull Cheryl toward him when they needed the room. She told herself, fine, there were old ties between Cheryl and the Sheridans. Of course she'd want to be here to lend support in a possible crisis.

Michelle still didn't like it very much. Her stomach dropped in that way it did before she feared bad news.

Then she locked eyes with Finn and understanding speared her. He'd been *waiting* for her, those eyes told her in no uncertain terms. All while driving over here, she'd worried she'd be intruding. She and Finn were new, and he hadn't even asked her to come. Just relayed information as to why he wouldn't be able to meet her for dinner. In the end, after battling with herself in her car, she'd decided that she already loved Mr. Sheridan and she wanted to be there for him, even if Finn didn't need her.

But he did, clearly. This was…everything.

"God, I'm so glad to see you," Finn said, pulling her into his arms.

In a second, she was pressed into that warm, strong chest that crushed her against him.

"He's going to be okay."

"You don't *know* that," said Cheryl from behind Finn.

When they both turned to look at her, she shrugged. "Well, she doesn't."

"Until we know anything, the best thing to do is remain positive," Michelle said.

"She sounds just like your dad, Finn." Cheryl crossed her arms and smirked.

Finn ignored her. "They haven't told us anything yet."

Michelle pulled out of his arms and marched up to the reception desk. She knocked on the glass partition until a nurse slid it open.

"I'm Mr. Sheridan's attorney, Michelle LaCroix. I need to get back there and speak with him urgently."

The nurse's brow furrowed. "Um, sorry, family only."

"Okay, fine. If you insist. I know there are rules." Michelle tossed up her hands and gestured to Finn. "This is his son."

The magic doors opened for him, and the nurse cocked her head. "Go ahead."

God, sometimes it was good to be an attorney and inspire fear in others.

Finn herded his mother and Declan and all three went in together.

"I'll wait right here," Cheryl called out. "Tell Dad I'm rooting for him."

Really? Tell Dad?

Michelle made her way to the waiting room and noted that Cheryl followed her. So, this would be awkward. At least Cheryl didn't try to make the situation even more awkward by making conversation.

Suddenly she stood. "This could be a while, I'm guessing. There's no need for both of us to be here. Would you tell Finn that I'll wait at our house to hear back? He knows how to contact me."

Their house? It must be the house she won in the divorce settlement. She made it sound like they were still living together. The need for the ex-wife to prove she'd once been important to Finn was something she'd seen before in contentious divorces. Often seen when one party realized the other had truly moved on.

"Actually," Michelle said. "I'm really glad you're here. I have wanted to speak with you for some time."

Her eyebrow quirked up. "What about?"

"The subject is a bit uncomfortable." Michelle stood

to be level with her. Cheryl was still taller, unfortunately. "Why do you want to keep a medal you didn't earn?"

The statement stood between them like a bomb. Michelle hadn't bothered to diffuse it. She'd just pulled the pin and let it go.

Cheryl blinked. "That's none of your business, is it? But Finn wanted me to have it."

"I'm sure you're right. He's a gentleman and wouldn't fight you over a medal. But he should have it, don't you think? After all, he's the one who earned it. Whether or not he wants it is really not the issue here."

"I think it *is* the issue." Cheryl straightened and pulled on the strap of her designer purse. "If he wants it, he can ask for it back. I'm always there. I'll always be there for him. I'll *always* love him, you know."

That might be true, but Michelle refused to be intimidated by the blatant attempt to undermine her relationship with Finn. People like Cheryl loved to poke at uncertainty and insecurity. She wouldn't find it here. Not anymore. Michelle had finally let the confidence of her work life spill over into her personal life. It was about damn time.

Finn did not like this woman and Michelle could see why. She was as different from him as a rat and a rabbit.

"Finn can use a lot of people in his life who love him."

"But I find it interesting that you're so sure of yourself," Cheryl pressed. "If I were you, I'd be careful. Finn hasn't been serious about a woman since *me*. He's dated a lot, sure, but they roll in and out like the tide." She made a casual movement of her hands like the ocean swishing out and in.

Except me, the statement said. *I'm the only one he stayed with long term.*

Michelle had to give it to her. Cheryl was skilled at undermining people and creating uncertainty in her opponent.

She would have made a good lawyer, but it made Michelle wonder how on earth the can-do Mr. Sheridan had ever put up with her for longer than a few minutes.

"I don't care about any of that. All I want is for him to have his medal back. He earned it and he deserves it."

"If he wants it, he knows where to find me."

With that, she turned and sashayed out the hospital doors.

Chapter Twenty-Two

"You did a very good job putting that line in. Way to go! You must be an expert at this."

The minute Finn heard the loud and booming voice of his father, he knew he would be fine. Already encouraging and praising people who were simply doing their jobs. Dad had always said that everyone needed to be acknowledged, from the busboy to the doctor. He never cut corners in dishing out encouragement.

"I see your family is here," the nurse said.

"Sweetheart!" Finn's mother ran to her husband's side.

"I'm okay." He reached for her hand and brought it up to his lips. "You worry too much, my love."

"You collapsed!"

"She's got a point, Dad." This was from Declan. "Don't make it sound like you were just brought in here for some routine bloodwork."

"Del! You're here."

"Of course I'm here." Declan looked sheepish. "You were dying. I thought."

"Good grief, sweetheart." His father shook his head. "What did you tell our boys? I got a little dizzy is all. You made all this fuss. I probably didn't need to come in by ambulance, but some hotshot EMT talked me into a ride. I didn't want to discourage him, even though I knew he was overreacting. Mark my words, he'll be running this hospital someday! A doctor in the making if I ever saw one. How about you, nurse? Did you ever think maybe of going all the way with this medical career?"

"Excuse me?" she said, because she didn't know she was tending to a lifelong coach.

"Dad, c'mon. Take it easy for once," Finn said and turned to the poor nurse. "Any word on how much longer he'll have to be here?"

"The doctor will have the final word on that." She checked the leads attached to his father's arm that were monitoring blood pressure, heart rate and oxygen. "But he ordered bloodwork and tests so not until those come back."

"They wouldn't even let us back here," his mother said. "Not until Michelle showed up!"

"Is that right? That girl, she's so special." His father went hand to chest. "You tell her I said thank you."

"You can tell her yourself once you're discharged," his mother said. "She's waiting outside. Something tells me she's going to be around for a good while."

His girlfriend, the attorney. Sometimes lawyers were good to have around if they were on your side. Especially if the name of the attorney was Michelle LaCroix, with the soft blue eyes and even softer curves.

"She's not the only one who showed up." Declan scoffed. "Your ex-daughter-in-law followed me here. Not that I *told* her anything. Isn't that a violation of HIPAA laws or something?"

"Poor girl." His father slowly shook his head. "If only I'd met her sooner. No one ever encouraged her enough in her life, and she thought the only way she could achieve something was through our Finn."

His mother blinked as though, like Finn, she'd never quite heard it put that way.

But maybe it was true. He'd seen it as devotion at one time. A little bit of celebrity idolatry maybe. The truth was she'd never had anything of her own, as much as he'd tried to suggest interests or hobbies. Being his "celebrity" wife *was* her hobby, along with lording her reflected fame over everyone else. Finn hated that he'd given that so-called status to her, if only for a little while. It's all she'd ever wanted out of him.

"Well, she has zero talent of her own." Declan snorted. "So, there's that."

"Let's not forget that 'poor girl' took our son for every penny he had."

Leave it to his mother to cut his ex-wife no slack. Hers was a different kind of exclusive loyalty, a mama bear to her cub.

"And it's all she'll ever have, honey," his father said, patting her hand. "It's actually very sad. Finn behaved like a gentleman, the way we raised him."

"Speaking of my gentlemanly ways, I'm going to go let Michelle know you're alright. She's the one who got us back here in the first place."

"You do that, son. Tell her I said way to go!"

She hadn't moved from just outside the double doors and his heart squeezed thinking she'd been worried, too. She was already part of his family, and it scared him how quickly it had all happened. He didn't want her to go, but he knew better than to hang on to her too tightly.

"Is he okay?"

She stepped into him, wrapping her arms around his waist, pressing her head against his chest. He already loved the way she did this automatically and without a moment of hesitation, seeming to fit perfectly, her head in a tight space right over his heart.

"He's fine. They're doing some tests, but believe me, I can tell he's going to be just fine. He's back there doing his life coach thing with the nurse. If he has his way, she'll be considering medical school before he leaves here."

"I was so worried when you texted."

"Hey." He tipped her chin up to him. "You were fantastic over there."

"Yeah?" She smiled.

"Thank you for being you."

"A kickass attorney who's on your side?"

"Gotta admit, it's a good feeling. But I needed you even before you came in ready to kick butt and take names."

"You did?"

"Don't think legal services are all you have to offer. You have a nice aesthetic about you, and even though your feet are like blocks of ice, I love sleeping with you."

She quirked a brow. "A nice *aesthetic*?"

"Fine, you're beautiful."

"Why, you charmer. Do me a favor and never enter the Mr. Charming contest."

"I was going to say you're easy on the eyes but that's a cliché, and something the old man would say."

"You have a beautiful aesthetic, too. And your feet are very warm, which is convenient for me."

"Plus, I'm magically delicious."

"Exactly. *Now* you get it."

"Honestly, I am feeling pretty damn lucky these days."

"Oh, I almost forgot. Cheryl said to let you know that she'd be waiting at 'our house,'" Michelle made air quotes. "I wasn't going to say anything, but I wanted to see the expression on your face when I did."

He assumed it was verging somewhere between shock and outrage. And utter confusion.

"*Our* house?"

"That's what she said."

"It hasn't been *our* house for a long time. Michelle, I hope you don't think—"

She shook her head. "I know what she was trying to do. Intimidate me. Make me question you and question us. It isn't going to work. I'm not that easy to get rid of. Especially when I'm wanted."

"Oh, you are wanted."

He'd honestly never felt claimed before, but it was how he felt in this moment. And it was perfect, because she didn't know it, but he'd secretly claimed her the moment he'd laid eyes on her. Only recently had he come to realize that he'd been figuring out a way to make her his all along. When the moment presented itself six long months later, he was ready.

Some people said that luck was merely preparation meeting opportunity. It was the only kind of luck he'd ever had, and he would take it, because she was the affirmation that his type of luck worked quite well. As far as he was concerned, it was all he'd ever need.

He pulled her back into his arms. "Damn it, all that cereal and you're the one who brought luck back to this Sheridan."

After a few hours, the tests all came back. Finn's father had a strong heart, which didn't surprise his family, bacon and Oreos notwithstanding. He did, however, have something called vasovagal syncope. Basically, he'd fainted. After all the scary reasons for a sudden fainting spell had been eliminated, they were left with occasional triggers.

They included standing for long periods of time, and his father had been caulking for hours, hell bent on a mission to finish the bathroom shower stall.

It would likely never happen again.

By the time a doctor officially released him, it was hours later. Finn had sent Michelle home, and it was he and Declan who drove his parents back to the house.

Finn was ready to stay as long as needed, and as it was past midnight, spend the night if required.

"Declan, maybe we should log some home improvement hours over here to lighten the load," Finn said.

"Sure thing."

"You two would help your old man?" His father turned to Declan like the thought considerably cheered him.

"Dad, of course," Declan said. "I mean, all you had to do was ask."

His father stood and beckoned them close. "Then, boys, could I ask something else of you? Would you both leave now, please? Your mother is drawing me a bath and well... *you* know. I think I'd like a little privacy to show her how very well I've recovered from my fainting spell. I can't have her thinking I'm weak. I still have all the stamina of a Kentucky Derby winner."

Declan pulled back, gagging. "You don't have to ask me twice. I'm leaving."

"Right behind you." Finn followed him and once they were outside he said to Declan, "Hey, look at it this way. Our DNA seems to suggest we'll be having sex well into our eighties by all indications."

"Yeah, yeah."

It was a quiet night along the coast, and Finn drove the sleepy curves of the frontage road, the moon splaying rays of light before him. Everything in his life had come together and felt perfect. He'd achieved that elusive goal no one could control or measure in terms of success: finding the woman who would fit with him. No, he hadn't *achieved* a thing. He'd found her, just like a gift. The woman he could build a life with here in Charming, just as his parents had. There was no doubt in his mind he'd still be crazy about her when he was sixty and they both had graying hair and crow's feet. He'd push his grown kids out of the house, too. Yeah, kids. For the first time he wanted his own family. He would love her forever. Of that he had no doubt. And had he ever experienced this feeling before, he would have known never to settle for anything less.

Michelle had said she'd leave the door unlocked and he should let himself in no matter the time. She would be waiting.

But she'd probably be asleep now, her frigid feet wrapped twice under the blanket since she didn't have him. The sounds of the waves rolling in and out behind the cottage soothed him even now. The ocean was his past, and also his future.

He wondered if she'd mind living closer to town. They were going to live together, and soon, of that he had no doubt.

Finding her asleep in bed, he quietly undressed and slipped under the sheets beside her. He pulled her back to his front, and she made a sweet and soft sigh.

"You're here."

"I'm home," he said, hands roaming all over her, dipping under the long and worn *Keep Austin Weird* T-shirt she liked to sleep in.

"Everything okay?" She turned, hooking her leg over his.

"He's fine. I'll tell you everything tomorrow."

"Hmm, okay."

He kissed her, a long and deep kiss that explored possibilities. "How tired are you?"

"Not *that* tired."

Sliding her panties down her legs, he gave her another long deep kiss.

"I love you." The words were said without expectation that she would return them or feel the same way.

They were there, on his tongue, and too important to hold back. He got to this place first and that was okay. He was hopeful and excited in a new way for the first time in years.

"Oh, Finn." She straddled him, and bent to kiss him, her loose and flowing hair cascading around him. "I love you."

Chapter Twenty-Three

A few days later, team-building day for Pierce & Pierce had arrived.

Finn left Michelle in a warm and cozy bed he hated leaving, but he had preparations to deal with on this bright Saturday morning. Everything had mostly been coordinated by the peppy and can-do Rachel, someone else his father would love. She had the heavy lifting for this event with the organizing of games, and she'd ordered a taco bar for lunch. Basically, Nacho Boat would provide the boat and safety while four staff members learned to trust each other.

He reached the marina as the sun was beginning to rise and set up for the day with the help of Noah and Tee.

"You're seriously taking Cheryl's lawyer out on the water?" Noah said. "Isn't this dangerous?"

At this, Tee, who today wore a T-shirt that said, "If you can read this shirt, my girlfriend says you're too close," sounded interested. "Are we getting some drama here today?"

"The man was just doing his job," Finn said.

Noah and Tee exchanged a look.

"Seriously. I mean it."

"So...you're *not* going to throw him overboard and use him as shark chum?" Noah said.

"Hey, what's done is done," Finn said, making a knot.

It was difficult to remember a time when he'd been bitter about the divorce. He was a happy fool these days.

"Not when she took your gold medal, it's not!" Noah said, hands on hips. "You need to get that back if nothing else, if she hasn't already sold it on eBay."

There was a loud gasp from Tee. "She got your gold medal in the divorce? What the ever lovin' hell?"

"Exactly. That was *your* accomplishment," Noah said.

"Really, boss. Where does she get off asking for that?" Tee said.

"She didn't."

Not technically, anyway. It hadn't been listed among the division of assets because the medal wasn't actually valuable, in and of itself. For one thing, it wasn't pure gold as many believed. It should have only meant something to the owner. When he'd come to get the last of his things, the medal he'd kept in the back of the closet had been missing. He'd asked, of course, and Cheryl swore she didn't have it. But medals didn't just grow legs and walk away, and Finn hadn't misplaced it. She must have it, even if she'd never come right out and admit it. She'd only made veiled references to "those things she deserved" for standing by him while he spent all his time sailing and training. No mention, of course, of all the glamorous parties she'd attended at his side or the celebrities she'd met.

In the end, Finn almost felt she deserved the medal for marrying someone who couldn't love her enough to stick it out through the tough times. Who couldn't honor his vows of staying with her for better or worse. His own failure at marriage made him feel undeserving. If he'd failed at the single most important accomplishment in his life, maybe the medal didn't matter. Of course, that was when the whole disaster was fresh and raw. When the failure sat rancid in his mouth and colored his view of the world. A world in which he, Finn Sheridan, bright overachiever, had won an Olympic medal but been stupid enough to marry the wrong woman.

"Okay, look. We're not talking about my medal right now. We have an entire law firm staff coming on board in an hour and we want to be ready for this."

The elaborate taco and margarita bar had arrived earlier, and they were keeping it downstairs in the galley. Tee had offered to play waiter and serve everyone, but the truth was they'd probably all help set up.

Arthur arrived first, this time without his wife. Shortly after him, his son arrived, as if he'd been following in his superfly new silver BMW. Next, Rachel.

Michelle was the last to arrive.

Finn would have known the moment she did, even if he hadn't been turned in the direction of the gangplank. He would have known it by the way the air felt charged and electric because she was in the vicinity.

All four of them walked on to the boat at once. Everyone was dressed casually, the men in khaki pants and both Michelle and Rachel in shorts. They wore staff polo shirts in black, which read, "Pierce & Pierce, When You Need a Friend."

Finn snorted. Even with the ridiculous shirt, Michelle looked so good Finn wanted to devour her.

After a few introductions to the rest of the crew, Noah got behind the wheel and steered them toward the bay. Finn and Tee tried to be helpful, making sure everyone was comfortable and had everything they might need. Funny how effortless his affections toward Michelle were now, as if he'd never had to fake a thing.

She made a move to reach for him, but Junior literally stepped between them.

"So, when are we shoving off, Captain? You remember me, right?" Junior thumped his chest.

Finn nodded. "Good to see you under better circumstances."

"Last time we saw each other I was wiping the floor with you. You should have had a better lawyer. Honestly, it was way too easy."

"Yeah, well, I guess not everyone is out for a gallon of *blood*," Finn said, his jaw tight.

"*Excuse* me." Michelle stepped between them with a voice whose pitch sounded like it had gone up an octave. "We had really better get started with our activities. Rachel?"

"Over here," Rachel called out with a wave.

Sitting portside, Rachel looked a little…green. And had Finn been paying more attention to the rest of his guests and less to Michelle, he'd have realized what was about to happen.

"I don't feel so good," she said, then threw up all over the deck.

"Oh my good God, that is *disgusting*," Junior said unhelpfully. "What did you *eat*?"

"Shut up," Michelle hissed. "You're not helping."

"Well, I can't *be* here. I'm going to be sick." Junior gripped his stomach, then tried to get as far away as physically possible from Rachel.

Which wasn't all that far since they were all trapped on a boat in the middle of the bay.

It was official. Arthur's idea of a team-building event was the single worst idea in the history of ideas. Honestly, being trapped out here on the water with her coworkers felt a little like a punishment. She'd have rather spent the day with Finn. Just the two of them, either lying on the beach or in bed. They were wasting time here with this stupid event, time they could spend lying next to each other watching *Is It Cake?*

She wasn't spending much time working on the weekends any longer unless Finn had something to do. Then she'd pull out the yellow legal pad and start making notes on adoption regulations in Texas. She'd always be an overachiever in her career, and that was okay. Of all people, Finn understood her better than anyone she'd ever known, including her parents. He might be done with the competitive part of his life, but he understood her need for success. Far from being all wrong for her, they were *perfect* for each other. Ironic, since he was her ex's best friend. Her planned fling. Her rebound guy.

He wasn't *supposed* to be the one, but he was.

"I feel terrible," Rachel said now. "Honestly, I thought I'd be fine. A boat. It sounds like so much fun! How hard can it be?"

"It's not your fault. You didn't know." Michelle continued to rub Rachel's back.

"How are we doing, kiddo?" Arthur joined them, tipping back on his heels. "Got your sea legs yet?"

"I'm not so good, Mr. Pierce. I'm sorry about this."

Arthur waved his hand dismissively. "I should have listened to my wife and brought along some Dramamine. She made me take some just in case, even though I was fine the last time."

"Smart." Rachel groaned. "Ohhhhh."

Finn rejoined them, sitting on the other side of Rachel. He'd brought her a cold, wet towel and put it to her cheek. "How are you feeling, sweetheart?"

"Still not good," Rachel said.

Noah had stopped the boat and anchored out, but even with only the rocking of the gentle waves, nothing seemed to help settle Rachel's stomach. She kept saying she'd get better and didn't want to ruin their day. The games were going to be such fun! As soon as she felt better, they'd all see what she'd planned.

"Should we head back?" Finn directed the question to Michelle.

She didn't see any other way. "I think we should."

"Oh, no. Please. Just give me a few more minutes. I'll get better." Then Rachel reached for the bowl she'd been given and wretched.

"*Again?*" Junior said from the other side of the boat. "Oh, Jesus. Oh."

"What the hell is wrong with you?" Arthur bellowed. "The poor girl is seasick and it's not her fault."

It sounded just short of "for God's sake, man up."

"I'm not seasick but the vomiting makes me sick. The smell." He clutched his stomach as his face went from its normal ghostly pallor to scary. "The sights and sounds. Oh God."

Michelle did not miss the hint of a smile on Finn's lips.

"That doesn't sound too promising, got to admit," Finn said to Junior. "Maybe you should lie down. Do you need a wet towel?"

"Get us back to the shore!" Junior shouted. "This is insanity."

Noah approached. "Hate to say it, but I think we better head on back, folks."

"Noooo," Rachel whined. "What about the taco bar?"

"Who could eat now?" Junior moaned.

Michelle had to agree. She had no idea how Rachel could

even think about food right now. Then again, she was probably considering everyone else. She didn't want the entire day and all their plans to go to waste because of her.

"When we get back, I'll drive you home and make you some broth," Michelle said. "You'll be dehydrated soon."

"You would do that?" Rachel's lower lip quivered. "You're so *nice*."

"She is, isn't she?" Finn smiled.

"You too, Finn. You're sweet. I didn't used to like you," Rachel said. "But you're a good guy."

"Thanks, what can I say," Finn said, holding the wet towel to Rachel's forehead. "I try."

"As for two-timing Abby, well, she probably deserved it. I think."

Michelle froze at about the same time Finn did. Both exchanged a look. What were the odds Arthur had overheard?

"I mean, you were dating her at the same time as you must have been dating Michelle since Michelle first started talking about her boyfriend months ago." She patted Finn's shoulder. "I would have chosen Michelle, too."

Arthur's jaw twitched. He was just two feet from them and must have heard every single word.

Why oh why had she lied? The problem was in her field she didn't distinguish between actual lies and harmless ones. This had been a harmless one in the beginning, until she and Finn got serious. Now it felt like everything was riding on this. She could not have Arthur believing this harmful lie about Finn.

"I don't understand," Arthur interrupted, eyes narrowed. "Michelle, you've been talking about Finn and how serious you are for *months*."

It would be alright. She simply had to come clean with the truth and Arthur would respect her. Pulling on every one of her closing statement skills, Michelle prepared for the oration of her life.

"I was dating someone, but it wasn't Finn." Michelle stood, fed up with the whole thing. "When that relationship didn't work out, I still wanted to stay, and I needed this job. You liked the idea of my being in a serious relationship. You seemed to think that it proved I wasn't a flight risk so you could invest your time in me. But honestly, the first time I ever went on a date with Finn was the night I ran into you and your wife. Finn agreed to pretend to date me because he's just that kind of a guy. Helpful. Look, I'm sorry, Arthur."

"I can't believe this! You were the one so upset about Ted and Tippy being dishonest with you. I find this quite ironic, don't you?"

"Maybe, but I didn't waste the firm's time and resources."

"I don't know about that. You wasted my time. All that grooming I did."

Grooming? She required no grooming. She'd come here and hit the ground running. Really, Arthur was quite a bit fonder of the sound of his own voice than she'd realized. Like father, like son.

"Look, I lied to you, but the truth is Finn and I are together now and very much in love. But even if I was single, I'd be fully capable of being a great asset to your firm. I'm not going *anywhere*."

She looked at Finn for support and saw it in his gaze. He was with her and that's all she needed right now.

"You're wrong, Michelle. What I wanted," Arthur spoke slowly, "was for you to have an appropriate work-life balance. You work too hard. If there's going to be a place for you here at my firm, you need to understand your career is not your life. I admire your dedication, but I refuse to take advantage of your work ethic. That was why I was encouraged to hear you were committed to your boyfriend. I didn't realize that you would choose to *lie* about something that serious."

"But…"

"One of the most important things in a working relationship is trust. Just like in any other relationship. That's why we're here today but I can see it's wasted time for at least one of our staff."

"What?" Junior woke from his vomit-trance and seemed to get the gist almost before Michelle did. He was about to lose his Friday girl. "Dad, c'mon, let's not be too hasty."

"I don't think this is going to work out. I'll accept your resignation on Monday, bright and early."

Arthur stuck his hands in his pockets, then he turned in an exaggerated pivot and walked toward his son.

And about that time, Junior threw up all over his father's shoes.

The ride back to shore was the coldest Michelle had ever felt it in Texas. Wind chill factor below zero. Arthur could barely look at her. Junior looked at Michelle, for the first time, with what appeared to be genuine sympathy. Rachel, now miserable for more than one reason, curled into a fetal position on the bench. Tee was making stupid jokes, Noah kept throwing her pitiful looks, and Finn was staying close.

"Did I do the right thing?"

Finn tucked her into his chest. "You did the only thing you could do, and I'm proud of you. He'll get over it. He won't want to lose someone like you."

"He asked for my *resignation*."

"Maybe he'll change his mind by Monday."

Ever hopeful and positive Finn.

If she resigned from yet another firm, hiring managers might see a pattern. But if she left this off her curriculum vitae, that would leave her with six months of unemployment to explain to any prospective employers instead.

What if she refused to resign? Just planted her feet and didn't move? She needed this job, and with P&P being the only family law firm in Charming she didn't have much choice other than starting her own. Facts were, she had few networking contacts in the area, though her mind was already spinning as to who she could call. She'd get started right after she got Rachel home. Old law school classmates, old coworkers, the judge she'd clerked for in law school, maybe even her mother would have a lead. If Arthur refused to reconsider, she'd find work. Being a lawyer might not be who she was, but it was what she did, and it mattered. It also happened to be the only thing she was truly good at.

She'd have to deal with Arthur later. The most immediate concern she had now was Rachel. She'd get her home and settled. They all decided Michelle should drive Rachel home and later she'd get a friend to drive her back to her car.

"I can't believe this happened," Rachel moaned, pressing her head to the passenger-side window. "You wouldn't believe the games I had planned. It was going to be great."

"I'm sure it was, and hey, maybe y'all will do it another time. This time not on a boat."

"I thought the boat was such a cool idea. Next time I'll take anti-nausea meds."

"If there is a next time for me."

"I'm so sorry, Michelle. If only I hadn't said anything about Abby. If only I'd kept my mouth shut."

Michelle had been thinking along the same lines a few minutes ago. But now? She'd had an epiphany of sorts.

"I'm glad it happened. I think Finn hated the lie. He's always teasing me about lying for a living."

"But you don't. You're a good attorney, Michelle."

"I know, but I've at times colored the truth in shades of gray."

"Still, you said you two are in love now, right? So, when did it become real? It's honestly kind of hard to tell. Every single time I saw you and Finn, he was staring at you like he couldn't believe you were real."

It was a lovely thought that he'd fallen before she did. That had probably never happened before. She'd been too busy fighting her feelings for him to allow herself to fall in love.

"I guess...maybe, at least for me, it happened the day I met his family."

It was also the day they'd hooked up for the first time.

"How sweet."

They felt very much like the family she'd always wanted. A supportive father and a sweet mom. She was meant to be part of Finn's family, and someday, well, they'd make it official.

For now, she might need a job and only hoped she could find one in the area.

"I loved having another woman at the firm. You've got to talk Arthur out of this. Make your case. You can't leave."

"I might not have a choice. Arthur is clearly pretty unhappy with me, and I can't say that I blame him. He's big on trust."

"Well, he shouldn't have made you feel like you needed a serious boyfriend to believe you'd stick around!"

But had he, actually? She recalled when he'd talked to her about the firm shortly before officially hiring her, describing how he'd started and built it over the years. He'd seemed to take pride in the connections he'd made with the residents of Charming, deep friendships that were still in place decades later. All the passion he'd put into his life's work had made a difference. The firm mattered to him, he'd said, before adding that it was time to take a step back. Over the years several associates had come and gone only to leave to start their own firms. But what he'd built in Charming felt like an extended family, and he wanted to hire people who cared as much as he did about the importance of work and family. He wanted someone who would be committed to the same goals.

Eager to get back to work, Michelle had volunteered that she was looking forward to making Charming her new home since her boyfriend lived here. In fact, she'd moved here for him and hoped to make a life here. It happened to be true at the time. Arthur took that and ran with it, sounding excited that Michelle had a plan already in place. She saw Arthur's pleasure with that situation and never gave it a second thought, even when things fell apart with Noah. He wanted her to be stable and ready to settle down. So did she, for that matter, but it hadn't worked out.

"I'm really sorry I even said anything today," Rachel said. "It was so stupid and I really blew it for you."

"Well, you didn't know. And I shouldn't have lied."

"There's just something I don't understand. If you and Finn were faking it, why did it look so real?"

Michelle hitched a breath. "It hasn't been faked for a while."

"Finn is one of the good ones. I should have known he wouldn't two-time anyone. He's not like that. Even after his ex-wife cheated on him, he never said a bad word about her. None of his ex-girlfriends have anything bad to say about him, either." Rachel pressed a hand to her forehead and moaned a little. She was still a bit sick, poor thing.

"Look straight ahead until you get oriented. You don't want to get carsick, too," Michelle chuckled.

"Can I ask you something?"

"Sure," Michelle said carefully, wondering if there was really any other answer she could give.

Nope, you can't ask me something.

Who did that?

"What else has changed for you, lately? I mean, besides this fake dating thing with Finn to impress Mr. Pierce. Is there something else going on?"

"Nothing other than Tippy's divorce. It was upsetting to find out they were back together but hadn't told us anything. We put in all that extra work and time because Ted's attorney was a real…um, a really good attorney." Michelle editorialized.

The guy was a demon in human form, but she couldn't fault him for being committed to his client.

"Yeah, but if you don't mind my being honest here, six months ago when you started working, you just weren't very…um…" She seemed to consider the perfect word. "Friendly?"

It was true that she had turned down several of Rachel's invites to meet for drinks at the Salty Dog, game night at her house, or shopping excursions to the local boutique. Rachel had been nothing but outgoing and friendly. But after her office colleague's betrayal, Michelle had drawn some firm lines. She didn't trust anyone at work. Whenever she'd see Rachel privately speaking with Arthur or Junior, she wondered if they could be talking about her.

Was she going to make the cut? Stay? Leave? Ruin their reputation by being too "mean?"

She thought everything was getting better as time went on and she realized not everyone was out to stab her in the back. Even Junior didn't want her gone. Why would he when she took his Friday afternoon appearances whenever he asked? It would be self-defeating.

"I'm sorry. It's true that I've been focused on my work, and I haven't made much time for fun."

"Which was easy to do when your boyfriend was *fake*. But you've changed in the past couple of weeks. You seem lighter. Happier."

"Do I?"

"I think Finn has been good for you."

Falling in love had been good for her. Highly recommended.

"Five bright stars." Michelle smiled. "I didn't think we'd be this good together."

"I bet you two balance each other out. He knows competition and how to excel. You're still winning."

Or *trying* to win.

Winning at what was the real question.

"All I know is that in the best relationships I've ever seen, you each find something in each other that you need to make you a better version of yourself. Not someone else. Just you, but better."

That hit Michelle like a two-ton brick of cement. She'd always tried to improve her boyfriends, without ever realizing maybe they could change her, too, for the better. As long as it was an improvement, that was, and one she wanted to make. And she did want to enjoy her life and not simply endure it.

Finn really had changed her, and she thought maybe she'd improved him, too.

Michelle spent several hours that afternoon with Rachel,

talking books, their mutual passion for true crime, reality TV, and generally having a girls-only afternoon. She left deciding there had always been at least one person at P&P she could have trusted.

Trusting anyone was a risk, but not trusting had worked out to be pretty lonely.

Chapter Twenty-Four

The taco bar was left behind for those with strong stomachs and, well, sea legs. At least they'd had lunch provided after wiping the deck clean.

After Arthur insisted they enjoy the food, and everyone had left, Finn brought the catered lunch up to the deck. The spread included all the fixings: lettuce, cilantro, pico de gallo, tomatoes and several kinds of meat. They'd set it up as per the instructions left for when they originally thought they'd serve this while anchored. Instead, they were tied to the dock and facing the bay. All around them, sailboats were shoving off their unfurling sails, enjoying the day. The expected heat had been tempered by a late-night rainstorm the night before, which left the skyline the bluest Finn had ever seen it.

"Dude, I feel bad for Rachel," Tee said, piling on the sriracha hot sauce. "It could have happened to anyone."

"We should probably keep a supply of anti-nausea meds handy down in the galley," Finn said. "We can't just assume everyone will be like us."

"I admit it's one of the factors I overlooked," Noah said. "We don't usually have a problem."

Finn shrugged. "Don't worry about it, we probably never thought we'd do anything like this before. It just kind of happened to fall in our laps. An entire law firm staff."

"True. Mostly we've been dealing with water aficionados since we took over Nacho Boat," Noah said.

The tacos were helping to ease his state of mind but not by much. When you loved someone the way he did, it turned out, their failures were yours too. He was sure that Michelle was devastated, whether she cared to admit it or not. Later tonight, he'd probably be able to do some good. But until then he was going to worry and wonder what the hell would happen when Michelle had no job. She had an entire career she'd built and wasn't going to give that up for anyone. The thought of her leaving town for a better job, well, it was unbearable. He couldn't think that way. It was time to think positive and only good thoughts.

By Monday, Arthur would have cooled down. Finn understood. No one liked being lied to, and yes, trust was important. But the lie hadn't hurt anyone, and Arthur would understand once Michelle explained the trust situation she'd dealt with at her previous job. Meanwhile, since Arthur had employed Michelle on his staff, she'd been doing free adoptions for gay couples and generally helping Arthur amass hundreds of billable hours. Anyone could see what an asset she was. He'd get over it, Finn was certain. He'd help Michelle come up with a solid argument tonight, and she could bounce it off him.

Funny, Finn always thought he wanted a woman like his ex-wife and the women he'd dated after his divorce, fun and carefree women like Abby. Someone who wasn't particularly ambitious or driven to succeed but simply happy with status quo. Happy where they were, no matter what. There was so much to be said for that attitude. That lifestyle. He had wanted for once to slow down and enjoy his life after years of striving to win.

The last thing he'd ever expected was that he'd fall for

a woman who was just like him. But that only meant that the part of him he thought he'd been able to bury was still alive and well. Maybe he'd been born that way, or trained by his father, but any way he looked at this, Finn still admired and understood ambition. He was pulled to it like a magnet.

It was why he couldn't stand to watch Declan let life happen to him. It was why he'd signed on for Nacho Boat with Noah. It was why he'd agreed to Michelle's charade and accepted the challenge. Though maybe that choice had also been driven by the opportunity to mess with the lawyers who'd made his life so miserable. Who'd beat him on some level.

"You okay?" Noah said as they were closing up the shop later the same day. "I can see you're worried about her."

"Yeah, I'm fine." Finn removed his glasses and wiped the lenses clean. "I'm sure she'll figure out a way to explain this to Arthur in a way that will make sense to him."

"It feels like she just got here. I admit I wanted her to leave, but now that she's here, I want her to stay. For you."

"That's the most Noah-like thing I've ever heard."

"She wasn't the right woman for me, but I don't know why I didn't see it sooner that you two are perfect for each other. Had I realized, Finn, I honestly would have—"

Finn held up his palm. "You tried from the start but you couldn't have helped this along. That's not how it works. She wasn't quite ready for me."

"And you?"

"Brother, I was ready the first day I saw her walking right past me and nearly swallowed my tongue. But she was after you. I came in second in a contest I didn't even enter. She didn't even see me there."

"I highly doubt that." Noah snorted. "Everyone sees you,

Finn. Even Twyla gave you a second look, which made me jealous as all get-out."

"It's the whole Olympic athlete thing. But that's not me, not anymore. I feel like Michelle was the only one who saw me for who I am. She didn't know about the medal. It was refreshing. Remember, for a while, I was the closest thing to a celebrity in our little town."

"Yeah, I remember that. So many women after you. We were all jealous."

"The parties and the attention were okay for a while, but that's not me. I wanted to achieve excellence, and once I did, I felt pretty done with competing. My father had a harder time accepting it than I did."

Finn got through the rest of the day, wanting to text Michelle and check in but choosing instead to give her time. She had some stuff to figure out. He'd do his part and be supportive and encouraging. He'd had a lifetime of watching it done by an expert. Now it was his turn.

When he got to Michelle's with takeout from the Salty Dog, ready to be a cheering section, she was on the phone and waved him inside. He headed to the kitchen and grabbed plates from the cupboard. There were Post-it notes all over her refrigerator with names and phone numbers in her handwriting.

Laura—law school; Megan—Gaus firm; Joe—Boston. Boston? As in *Massachusetts*?

It was the first punch to the gut that she might actually consider leaving. He felt his heart shift and turn like he had just eaten spicy Indian food and rubbed his chest.

She was still talking on the phone, her tone clipped and tense. "Yes, you know me. Strictly family law. A lot of divorce, unfortunately. Plenty of that going around. I've done adoptions, too, and some child custody. Definitely. That's where my heart is. I remember you wanted to be a trial lawyer. Did that work out for you?"

Finn half listened; half tried to compose a five-point argument in favor of Texas. Yes, it was a big state and if she moved to San Antonio, they'd have a long-distance relationship. Face it, those never worked. But at least it wasn't Boston!

A few more niceties and catching up and Michelle joined him. She tore the "Laura—law school" note from the fridge and crumpled it.

"That was my law school buddy. She's in Dallas, which is a distance but not too crazy. I'd get to stay in Texas. She doesn't know of anything available now, but she'll keep me in mind." She wrapped her arms around Finn's waist and buried her face in his chest. "I figured I better start networking."

She'd given it about two minutes. He thought maybe she'd be home wallowing for at least a few hours. Leave it to an overachiever.

"I happened to notice Boston."

"An old employer opened up a satellite office there."

"You realize you might actually die there. It's cold. *Arctic* cold."

She made a face. "That wouldn't be fun and it's my last choice."

"Okay, but you're not giving up, are you?"

"Giving up? Finn, you were there. Arthur was furious. It's not my choice to make."

"Maybe he'll listen to Junior for once. He seemed upset by the idea."

"He doesn't want to lose his Friday afternoon court appearance coverage."

He wasn't the only one who didn't want to lose her.

"Mmm, this looks delicious." She reached for a fry. "I took Rachel home and haven't eaten since I had a waffle this morning after you left."

And here he was, close to losing his appetite. "Do you need help putting together an argument for Monday morning?"

"Look at you, getting all argumentative and stuff. *So* sexy." She reached up to give him a quick kiss.

"I mean it. Don't give up."

"I'm not the one who gave up. After all that talk about how great I am, what an asset to the law firm I'll be, and how he thinks of me as a daughter—"

"He *said* that?"

Damn Arthur. For him to say something like that to someone like Michelle…he was an idiot or just didn't know any better. So now maybe she'd be abandoned by two men. One, her actual father, the other a father figure she'd wanted to please and impress.

She lowered her gaze. "It's not a big deal."

"But it is. He's an idiot if he even thinks about losing you." He tipped her chin to meet his gaze. "Do you want me to talk to him?"

He knew her answer before saying the words out loud. Michelle would fight her own battles because she was a strong and capable woman. And he got it. But sue him if he wanted this woman to stick around. If he'd do whatever it would take.

"No, but thank you. I love that you want to do that. I love *you*."

He pulled her into his arms, held her tight against him. "Hey, you never know. By Monday, this whole thing could be resolved."

He was going to stay positive if it killed him.

* * *

On Monday morning, Arthur uncharacteristically beat her into the office.

Not a good sign.

It was quiet and still as she opened the door to P&P for possibly the last time. Leaving here would hurt, but even the thought of leaving Charming was killing her. She couldn't leave Finn, but she also couldn't give up her career. The law meant everything to her and had for years. It was order and routine. It was the only area where she excelled, and that *meant* something. She couldn't "excel" at being Finn's significant other. The thought of moving away was a rock in her stomach, but the knowledge she'd disappointed Arthur sat equally as heavy.

"Michelle." He nodded as she walked down the hallway. "We should talk."

"Yes."

She didn't bother depositing her briefcase at her desk but hauled everything with her into his office and slumped into a chair. Because if looks could speak, Arthur's said that she wouldn't be here much longer. But like she'd promised Finn last night over hushed whispers in bed, she would try everything to stay with him.

"First, let me just say how sorry I am."

"That's a start." Arthur sat behind his desk and clasped his hands behind his neck, looking up at the ceiling. "I've had to listen to both my wife and son try to talk me out of letting you go all weekend. And I thought you and Junior didn't get along."

"We don't."

He quirked a brow.

"As long as I'm being honest…" She shrugged.

"I get it. He wants you to take the grunt work so he can

spit and polish the place he's set to take over soon enough." He rubbed the handles of his dark wood chair. "I know he hasn't had to work hard, unlike you."

"There's no excuse for lying to you, but let me try to explain. When I came to Charming, I didn't plan on staying. But then…well, I'd like to say I fell in love with the place. I did, but I would have never left my law firm in Austin. As you know, I'm very dedicated and my career is my life…was my entire life." She thought of Finn, how effortless it had been to fall for him. "But I trusted someone I shouldn't have at my previous law firm, and… I was asked to resign. Don't get me wrong, I made a mistake, but the biggest error in judgment I made was trusting the wrong person. That's why I seemed standoffish. All I wanted to do was keep my head down and work hard. I didn't think I needed friends. Rachel was so nice, but until this weekend I mostly ignored her. You've been kind, too, Arthur, and I still kept my distance. Maybe I thought that was the only way I couldn't possibly disappoint you."

"But you did. You made me feel so stupid, believing you two were a real couple, going along with your stupid lies. My wife tells me Finn never even had stomach problems. If trust is so important, why did you—"

"It's what I do sometimes. I tell half-truths. We all do in our business. I accentuate the positive and hide the negative. The truth is Finn has been on my periphery ever since I met him. I think I reached for a truth I wanted to be real."

"It doesn't work that way."

"It did for us."

"You're in love with him?"

"Yes, I am very much in love with him."

"Well, something good came out of this then." Arthur leaned back in his chair and made a somewhat strangled sound. "I know I may come to regret this, but I can't work with someone I don't trust. I have to go with my gut."

"But—"

"I'm sorry, Michelle. Clean out your desk and let us know where to send your last check. It's just not going to work out here."

So, this was it. She'd lost another job due to a failure of trust. Two jobs in six months. She was making some kind of world record.

Until she'd come to Charming, she'd been at the same firm for five years.

Slowly, she stood. Picked up her briefcase and purse.

"But if you ever need anything—" Arthur began.

The echoes of the familiar empty words were a little too much for her right now and she held up her palm. "Please don't. I won't need anything from you."

She was halfway down the hallway when she turned back.

"Would you like a little more honesty? Inspirational Monday is a waste of our time. Those are platitudes for bumper stickers. Want to know what inspires people? Being noticed, acknowledged, and *rewarded*. Rachel hasn't had a raise in two years. Now that I'm gone, maybe you can spread the wealth around and give her a raise. You don't need to hire another associate. Have Junior work harder. He can do it."

Before he could say another word, she was out the door and down the bustling morning sidewalks filled with tourists she'd never noticed before. She bumped into one or two of them and kept walking until she had passed *Once Upon a Book* and realized she'd walked right past her car. Turning back, she headed in the direction of her car, with no idea what she was going to do once she reached it.

She wanted to talk to Finn, and she also didn't. This was a disaster. It couldn't have come at a worse time. They'd just started something real, which meant everything to her, but so did her career. She wasn't going to sit around the house and wait for someone to hire her. She'd take the first job opportunity offered and try like hell to recover from this latest setback.

But Finn. She didn't want to leave him. He'd probably get over her, but she suddenly knew she'd never get over losing him.

"Miss, are you okay?" someone asked.

Only then did Michelle realize she was crying. Dear Lord, how embarrassing. Crying? In *public*? Okay, so this was bad but not worthy of tears.

Telling Finn, watching his eyes as she told him, that was going to be cry-worthy.

"Yes, thank you, I'm fine."

She wiped the tears away and found her car. Slid in behind the wheel. Clicked her seatbelt in place. For several minutes she sat there and let herself cry. Tears she'd held back for so long. About her father. About every failed relationship since then. She'd excelled in her career but failed in her personal life. Until now.

Fumbling in her purse, she found her phone and scrolled to the number. After four rings she answered.

"Hi, Mom."

Chapter Twenty-Five

"Michelle? Is something wrong?"

"Nope. Nothing's wrong."

The last time she'd talked to her mom, Michelle informed her she'd moved to Charming and given her the new address. No big deal. Her mother didn't pry. She never did. Michelle explained that she'd simply chosen a change of pace, a slower one, not that she'd been forced to resign. And now, she was *not* going to tell her mom that she'd lost a job because of a stupid ruse that she'd wanted to be real in the first place.

Her mother would have a few things to say about that.

"Have I taught you nothing? You can't depend on anyone but yourself."

"I had a custody case not long ago and I was wondering. And remembering."

"We've argued this point before, and I won't do it again. Your father left the country."

No need to remind Michelle. She remembered, thank you. At the end of each yearly visit to America he'd said the same few words and to her they'd always been tinged with a salty bitterness.

If she ever needed anything...

She'd needed a *father*. One she could see more than annually. Phone calls didn't cut it. When he couldn't be there for her, Michelle decided she wouldn't ever ask a thing from him.

Distance just didn't work. At least, not for her.

But now after so many years handling divorce and child custody, she'd seen both sides of the situation. She'd seen fathers often denied rights in favor of the mother. And she'd seen fathers who'd done nothing wrong fight to be able to see their children.

"Why didn't...why didn't he ever try to get custody of me?"

A long and heavy pause followed.

"Mom? Hello?"

"You've never asked me this before. Why now?"

"Last year in Austin, I handled a custody case of a father who wanted to move to a different state for a job opportunity. His ex-wife fought him hard, but he never gave up. And I never did, either. I *got* him visitation."

"I remember that. A career highlight for you."

"Yes, it was. It wasn't the first time I wondered why my own father hadn't fought for me."

Her mother cleared her throat. "He *did*. I guess you don't remember that time, but I certainly do. You were ten, so we did what we'd intended to do—shielded you from the vitriol and the fighting."

"Not so much, Mom. I was aware of the fights and I knew you hated each other. But I seemed to have missed the important part. He wanted me."

He wanted her.

He had wanted his daughter. Maybe she hadn't really done anything wrong. He'd left their family because he'd stopped loving his wife. Maybe, like so many flawed people, he'd tried and lost. And then tried to move on.

She sighed. "He did want you. He fought for you, and he lost. It was for the best. He went on to have another family, or have you forgotten that?"

"It's not hard to forget the feeling that you're not good enough for someone."

"Oh, Michelle, for God's sake. Pull up your big girl panties. You are good enough when *you* decide you are."

She had a point, although Michelle wished her mother could add a little gentleness to her wisdom.

When she hung up, she felt calm enough to drive back to the beach. Her phone buzzed at her side in tiny and frequent seizures. It would be Finn, and possibly Rachel once she heard the news. It might be Tippy. Even Junior might call or text.

Or it might be Joe in Boston.

She hadn't told Finn, but he'd phoned later that Sunday night and made her an offer. He'd been the only opportunity after all the calls and feelers she'd put out. Joe wanted to bring her on immediately and was afraid to lose her to someone else.

Boston. For a native Texan, even the name made her cold. But the opportunity was there, bright and shiny and attractive. A large salary unlike any she'd ever pulled (to go with the cost of living, she assumed). A chance to practice law in a major firm very similar to the one she'd left behind in Austin. No more small-town stuff. It was good to know she was still highly employable. People wanted her, and she needed to work. She had to work.

When she pulled into her parking space, she glanced at her phone and the torrent of messages. Finn, Joe and mostly Rachel:

Please call me. I can't believe this! Arthur is an idiot.

Michelle winced. She would warn Rachel to be careful what she put into the ether concerning her employer.

Rachel was the first call she returned, seated in her car staring at the beach just outside her doors. She loved this view and hadn't appreciated it enough. The cottages had a private strip of beach where she'd jogged nearly every morning after first arriving, trying to wrap her mind around her new reality. It didn't seem that long ago, and the most recent changes felt as if the ocean was shifting and repositioning her somewhere she didn't want to be.

"Michelle! I'm so sorry to hear what happened. Are you okay?" Rachel, who'd stepped outside, said. "I just heard. Arthur called a meeting and wanted uplifting verses about moving on and getting through adversity. I almost throat punched him. Junior made no secret of how much he hates Daddy right now."

"I'll bet he does. I'm going to miss you."

"Well, you'll find another job, right? We can still hang out. Screw Arthur."

"He was right, in a way. Without trust, you don't have much, do you?"

"There's also something called forgiveness. You didn't see him getting this upset about Tippy and Ted, did you?"

"That was different."

"It was. They're his friends and they were making him *rich* with their divorce. As upbeat and happy-go-lucky as Arthur pretends to be, he's still a businessman at heart. And divorce is huge business. You haven't answered my question. Are you okay?"

Okay? Theoretically? Yes. In reality? Definitely *not*.

"I'm…going to have to move, Rachel."

"Noooooo," she said. "Why?"

"I have an offer and I can't just wait around for another

one to materialize. I already have six months of employment I'm not going to be able to mention so there's a big gap. I need to work."

"Where?"

When she told her, Rachel made another little squeak, then asked her to please reconsider before she decided. Michelle promised she would. She still had to discuss all this with Finn, anyway, and pose the eternal question: *Can we make this work long distance or would it be too painful?* Did she love him enough to stay? That wasn't even a question. Yes, of course, she did. She just didn't know how. She didn't know *how* to stay without having work to do. She didn't even know how much he *wanted* her to stay.

It was still morning, and he and Noah were on a fishing charter most of the day. He would want to know how it went with Arthur. And she wanted to tell him, to explain she'd tried, but her arguments hadn't been solid enough. Knowing he might not read the text until later, she asked him to come by tonight and she'd explain everything.

In the meantime, she had an errand to run because she wasn't leaving Charming without getting this done. She backed out of her parking spot and started driving. It wasn't difficult to find the home Finn had pointed out to her once before. Situated on one of the loveliest residential streets in Charming, it was set back from the street with a sparkling green lawn leading to the front porch. It hurt her heart to think of all Finn had given up. A home that should have been sold now belonged to the woman who'd once been lucky enough to be married to Finn.

Well, she could have the home.

Cheryl was just leaving the house as Michelle pulled up, right behind her, blocking her silver BMW.

"Oh, hey. I was just leaving."

Cheryl held a mug of coffee in her hand, eyeing Michelle's sedan as if it were a beater. Her car sales agency name tag on her jacket read *Cheryl Sheridan*.

For crying out loud, she hadn't even given him back his name.

Michelle emerged from the car and leaned against it, crossing her arms. This was a common negotiation stance of hers, her "I have all day" look. Ironically, it was actually true this time.

Cheryl approached. "Is Papa Sheridan okay?"

"He's fine. It was a false alarm."

She put a hand to her chest. "Whew. That man means so much to me. He's like—"

"I think you know why I'm here."

"I have no idea."

"The medal."

"Oh my God, you're still on that? I told you, if Finn wants it back, he can come and ask me for it himself."

"Yes, of course he can but we both know he's not going to do that. Finn is too good. He's too kind to ask you to give it back. He could have done so much better for himself in the divorce. You should have been forced to sell this house or at least buy him out."

"Maybe if he'd had a barracuda like you on his side."

"True enough. For now, you can just pretend I'm that barracuda he failed to hire. You can just give me the medal now and I'll take it back to Finn. I'm seeing him tonight."

"Why would I do that?"

"Because I'm not leaving until you do, and I assume you have to be at work soon."

She cocked her head. "Don't *you*?"

"No, actually."

"What is your problem? Why is this so damn important to *you*?"

"Because he's important to me." Michelle sighed and uncrossed her arms. "And also, I know something about you. You're a lot like me, I have a feeling, and you don't cling to things you didn't earn. You're an ambitious and successful woman all on your own. Someone like you is probably on her way to becoming salesperson of the year, judging by that shiny BMW."

She glanced back at it. "It's just a loaner. One of the perks."

"I bet soon you'll have one of your own."

This happened to be something Michelle had learned about people in general.

They wanted to believe the good things people said about them. Sometimes they were even inclined to assist.

Cheryl stood for one last long minute before she tossed her hands up. "Fine! I don't even know where it is, to be honest. This could take a while."

"I have the time."

Michelle smiled, thinking this was at least one thing that would go right today. She'd give Finn his medal, and no matter what else happened between them, she would have given him something for everything he'd given her back. A sense of her true self-worth, the fun back in her life, *love*.

A few minutes later, Cheryl came out of her home with a framed shadow box in which the medal was displayed. It was dusted and clean and had obviously not been found in a corner somewhere. In other words, it hadn't been hard to find at all.

"Here you go. I don't know why I have this thing still lying around. It's not worth much anyway."

Michelle accepted it. "That's the point, isn't it? It's only worth something to Finn."

Cheryl shrugged. "If he'd have asked, I would have given it to him."

Michelle turned to open her passenger door and set it on the front seat then went around to the other side. "I better let you get to work. Sorry for the delay."

"You know, he's not perfect."

"I know," and then more under her breath than so Cheryl could hear, "just perfect for me."

Later that same day, Michelle headed to the Salty Dog to take care of Finn's tab. Even though they'd agreed to this, she still hadn't checked in. She'd left her credit card number for a backup but said she'd come in once a month and pay. How crazy to think it had been only a month and she was already in love. In love and probably leaving. All day she'd felt like a stone was lodged in her throat.

At lunchtime during the week, the bar wasn't usually open, so she approached the regular hostess.

"Hey, there. I'm here to pay Finn's tab."

"Tab?"

"I made a special arrangement with the owner to pay for Finn Sheridan's drinks for the year. I said I'd come in and pay every month."

"Cool." She quirked a brow. "Awfully generous of you."

"Not really. I'll have to make another arrangement now."

Just the memory of standing only a few feet away from this very spot, grabbing Finn and planting a kiss on him seared her. She hadn't any idea that she'd find the love of her life and kiss him for the first time in front of a crowd to make a point. There were so many things she could have known sooner had she paid attention.

"We don't usually run a tab here."

"Yeah, I know. I left my credit card as backup but also said I'd come in and pay cash. The owner said he'd do it for Finn."

A few minutes later, the hostess returned. "Sorry, there's no tab running."

"Maybe it's under my name instead of Finn's?"

"I checked both."

"Are you *sure*?"

She nodded. "I can tell you that Finn always pays cash and leaves a nice tip, too."

So, there it was.

Finn hadn't run up a tab on her account.

She should have known he wouldn't, no matter what their deal.

All through their fishing charter, Finn had a feeling bad news waited for him. It was confirmed the moment Michelle swung open the door that evening. Her eyes were bloodshot and red around the rims, her lower lip slightly swollen from all the biting she tended to do when she was worried. He'd started to learn and memorize everything about her, and she didn't even have to say the words out loud.

Arthur had fired her.

"Not a good day, was it?"

She shook her head and went into his arms. "I'm sorry. I made my arguments, but Arthur said he can't trust me anymore."

He crushed her against him, already knowing the sweet smell of her hair would always be his strongest memory of her. That, and those beautiful, serious eyes of hers, which could be equally playful and naughty.

"Hey, hey. Don't be sorry. It's not your fault."

"Yes, it is. I ruined this for us." She clung to him.

"So, Boston or San Antonio?" He knew the answer before she gave it.

"Boston."

Damn, his Irish luck. Boston, home of the Irish, taking his girl away from him. If that wasn't the last straw, he didn't know what was.

"Yeah, I'm officially the unluckiest Irishman on the planet."

She started to cry, and it was as if someone reached into his chest to slice off a chunk of his heart.

"I'm sorry, honey. I shouldn't have said that." He rubbed her back in slow, soothing strokes, leading her to the couch where he tugged her into his lap.

"It's not that. I have to go, but I don't know how to do this. I love you so much."

He pulled her back to frame her face with his hands. "I thought I would talk you into staying here with me. I had my arguments ready. But the truth is I love you too much to ask you to stay. I know you need to go, and I should accept it. We'll make it work."

"We will, won't we? I'll text you every day and you'll come and visit."

"Sure."

But he knew with a new business venture, with the financial hit he had yet to recover from, it would be impossible to visit often. It would be months before he could see her again. The separation wouldn't be painful. That wasn't the right word. It would be like cutting arterial blood flow.

"Oh, I have something for you." She scrambled off his lap and came back a minute later, holding something behind her back.

"Am I supposed to close my eyes?"

"Only if you want to." She plopped herself beside him and slid over the frame she was carrying.

Inside the frame was his gold medal.

It was engraved with the year of the Olympics, summer games, and the country. He hadn't seen it in so long he'd almost forgotten what it looked like.

"She obviously had it displayed somewhere."

"How did you…?"

"I went to see her today and demanded she give it back to you."

He quirked a brow. "Demanded?"

"You know I have my ways."

"I do know that."

Finn had never expected to get it back, figured it wasn't worth seeing Cheryl again. He'd tried like hell to pretend it didn't matter, but it had. This was the physical representation for him of the commitment and years it took to get where he'd been and it mattered. It mattered it was back with its rightful owner. He'd think of this as a good and hopeful sign that sometimes the things you loved and let go found their way back to you.

With the help of a kickass attorney.

And now Finn knew exactly what he'd give his father this Christmas.

"Thank you."

"Now." She crawled back into his lap. "You didn't run a bar tab."

"Nope."

"But Finn…we agreed. At least in the beginning, before we slept together… I mean, why didn't you when I'd offered?"

"What do you think?" He quirked a brow. "You shouldn't have to pay me for something I wanted to do in the first place. I wish I would have gotten over my damn self and asked you out immediately."

"Well, why didn't you? Surely you knew Noah and I didn't have a chance."

"You walked by me. What can I say? It hurt my fragile male ego."

She lowered her gaze. "I didn't walk by you, Finn. I nearly ran from you. The first time I saw you, I felt such a powerful attraction it scared me. You scared me."

"Damn. I wish I'd asked you to be my fake girlfriend the first day you came to Charming."

"We would have had six months together."

"You mean you'd have said yes?" He grinned.

"What do you think?" She cocked her head.

It might have been even more painful then, knowing how well they fit together, settling into a real kind of domestic bliss. But while he didn't think it possible for her to burrow deeper into his heart, he would have had more time to make himself indispensable to her. Now all he had were a few days so that she'd have a damn good memory of him. They'd had this time together, teaching him that he still had a whole and undamaged heart that could grow and change and…hurt. How great for him.

He knew how this would end. If she moved to Boston, they would not stay together, and he had to accept that. Life would move on for her and she'd meet someone new. Eventually what they'd had would fade into a dulled and pleasant memory for her, while his heart would never be the same.

"I honestly expected you to get all male-pattern grumpy and hurt that I'm not staying."

"I'm a big boy, honey, and I would be the last person to hold you back."

"I know, and it's just one of the many things I love about you."

He took her palm and kissed it. "I know what's going to happen. You're going to meet some *lucky* Irishman and fall in love all over again. And learn how to love a frosty winter."

"First, I will never learn to love a frosty winter. Second, it's more likely you'll meet someone else when I'm gone, someone who isn't career driven. But don't you dare!" She raised a threatening finger.

"It's an already established fact that no one but you is ever going to have my whole heart. You have it all, Michelle. You've ruined my heart for anyone else."

She squeezed her eyes shut and when they opened, they were shiny and filled. And she kissed him, hard and demanding.

They were both going to ignore the hard-pressing fact between them: they could not have a successful, long-standing relationship two thousand miles apart from each other. But it was easier to part this way, pretending they'd work it out. It wasn't as if Michelle was leaving for a few months. She was leaving for the foreseeable future. She was leaving permanently, and his life was here and always would be.

This wasn't going to work.

They weren't going to work. Ever.

But for this moment, she was here, and he'd never been this in love with a woman. So, he took her to bed and made love to her until the sun came up.

Chapter Twenty-Six

The next few days were a whirlwind of activity as Michelle made preparations for her move. Joe wanted her there immediately as they were handling the divorce of a senator and his second wife. The firm was in "all-hands-on-deck" mode and there weren't nearly enough hands.

"The sooner, the better," Joe said. "We have temporary employee housing available for you."

It was all happening so fast, as if it was meant to be.

She could have a nice career in Boston and make new contacts. She'd certainly be far enough away from her past failures to feel like she had a clean slate. Now it was up to her to prove her worth and she knew she could.

But honestly, the thought of another contentious divorce as her first case made her heartsick.

She spent every day and night with Finn, and he was being so grown up about it all. Such a devoted, sweet, and encouraging boyfriend. Everything she'd ever wanted. And she was leaving him here in Texas. There was no doubt they'd try to keep in touch, but they'd both be so busy that she really didn't see how they could make it work from two thousand miles apart. The idea was ridiculous. She knew they were both skirting around the fact that they had to break up. More than likely, they would do it after several weeks of not seeing each other. The loneliness would turn into arguments, the physical distance would become an emotional distance. And then they'd be done.

She cried at least three times a day over this fact, always out of Finn's presence. Sometimes in the bathroom when he was cooking her dinner and she realized how much she'd miss these times. And when she woke up to a cold spot next to her, realizing she had better get used to the single life again.

She finished taping up another box and glanced up at the clock. It was late afternoon and Finn would be by later for a dinner she hadn't planned yet. Her appetite for food was all but gone, and she hadn't eaten well in days. She was on the lovesick diet, and every hour she was apart from Finn now was simply a reminder of how much worse it was going to get, and very soon.

There was a knock on her front door and Michelle thought it might be the sweet neighbor Maribel, whose husband was actually the owner of the row of beach front cottages. Funny how she'd never bothered to tell her that. Michelle opened the door and was shocked by who was behind it.

Tippy. They hadn't spoken since that last time in the office when she had called to apologize for wasting Michelle's time.

Now, she looked angry. With *Michelle*? That didn't make sense.

"I heard."

Michelle waved her inside. "That I'm leaving for Boston?"

"That Arthur fired you! The twit. I'm absolutely *furious*."

"He had good reason. I lied, and having trust with your associate is vitally important in business. I mean, I get it.

He trusted me with valued clients and then realized I'd lied to him for months."

"About something trivial, which was quite frankly none of his business in the first place!"

Well, she had a point there.

"It's okay. I've already got another job opportunity in Boston. A good one."

"You are not going to Boston, young lady!"

"I'm not?" She shook her head. "No, Tippy. I appreciate it, but I don't actually want to go back to Pierce & Pierce. No matter how many strings you pull for me."

"Not what I had in mind." She took a seat on the couch. "By now, after all the financials you had to dig through, you know I'm a wealthy woman."

"I know. But in case you're wondering, I work for a living and I'm not going to ask you for any money."

"How about a loan?"

"That's kind of you, but I wouldn't feel right about it. Besides, the opportunity in Boston came up and if I don't accept it, I'll lose it."

"Not what I meant, Michelle." She spread her palms apart. "Start your own law firm, right here in town. I'll be your investor."

Michelle snorted. "What? Oh, wait, you're serious."

"I don't mess around with my investments. As you know, the lighthouse—"

"I *know.*"

If Michelle never heard another word about that lighthouse again, it might be too soon.

"I invest in people and causes. The last thing I want is for a brilliant woman to leave town because we only have one law firm where she can work. Charming needs people like you."

Her own law firm. The thought was far scarier than being a partner in Arthur's firm because everything would fall to her. All failures. All possible losses.

All the wins, too.

She could almost hear Mr. Sheridan's voice: You can do it, Michelle! You're a champ! Way to go!

"I confess I… I never seriously considered it."

That was a lie. She had. For about two minutes, when Finn looked particularly adorable telling her why he knew cake number two was the real one. If she called her father, if she reminded him: *you said if I ever needed anything…* then maybe he could have loaned her the money to start her own firm. The thought was fleeting because they no longer had a relationship. It was far too late to ask him for anything now.

"Think about it. I don't want you to leave us. Please. I will always blame myself if I let you go. Maybe…maybe if Ted and I had actually divorced, this little lie wouldn't have been a big deal when you won the case."

"Tippy, this didn't happen because of you."

"Fine, maybe not, but he'd never have done this to a man! Mark my words."

Okay. Score another point for the mayor.

Michelle felt a sharp ping of excitement, the kind she hadn't in weeks. Her own law firm. She'd make the rules, hire a staff, decide what cases to take and which to turn away. Open up every morning and close every afternoon, but she did that already. She'd join the Chamber of Commerce and continue to be a part of Charming.

Finn.

Most importantly of all, she wouldn't have to let him go. She could keep him.

"Are you serious? You really mean it?"

She nodded. "Even Ted agrees. I ran it by him, of course. We're in counseling and part of our work is sharing and not holding anything back. So, I had to tell him. If you agree, I'll start the process tomorrow."

"I accept! Make the terms fair for both of us and I promise I won't let you down. You'll make your investment back and then some."

"I have no doubt in you. I only invest with people who I believe in. You're going to take every major case away from Arthur. He should learn *never* to underestimate a woman."

After Tippy left, Michelle practically floated on a cloud the rest of the day. She had a lot of work to do. She knew exactly what she'd cook Finn for dinner, and it didn't even require a recipe.

Finn was having a tough time lately, having to schedule regular calls with his father for uplifting and encouraging messages. He had confessed to him that he was struggling and without even mentioning why, he was getting daily texts of encouragement.

Good morning, son! Whatever you do today, I know you will slay it!

Man, he needed those messages. He was straddling two very different emotions at once: the joy of seeing Michelle every night and falling asleep with her in his arms followed by despair that she was leaving him. The packed boxes were his daily reminder. He was going to lose her. Every day he fought against the selfishness of continuing to see her instead of making a clean break. It would be easier for both of them not to prolong the inevitable. Not to pretend this could work just because they wanted it to.

Maybe he'd bring it up tonight. He'd suggest they start to gradually spend less time together, like a weaning away from each other. But even before he opened the front door to her house, he understood he'd do no such thing.

You are a selfish man, Finn Sheridan.

He stepped inside, hearing a slight crunch under his shoe. Looking down, he saw several bits of cereal on the floor. He discovered after close inspection that one of them was a marshmallow. Hmm.

It looked like Michelle was playing a joke on him.

"Michelle? What's going on, honey?"

"In here! Follow the trail I left for you, Irish!" she called.

He did, following a straight line to her bedroom door.

She was sitting cross-legged on her bed wearing the yellow dress with pineapples, and she looked so bright he needed his shades.

"Here's your pot of gold!" She threw her arms in the air. "I don't have a gold dress so this is the closest I could get."

He rolled onto the bed next to her. "What are you doing, you nut?"

"Look! This is our dinner. Cereal, your favorite."

There were two bowls of his Lucky Charms cereal on the nightstand.

"Today is my lucky day, it would seem."

"Oh, you have no idea!" She bounced on the bed. "Finn, I'm staying! I called Joe in Boston and said, 'Sorry, Joe, it's a no-go.' I'm not going anywhere."

This got his attention, and he allowed himself to believe for one second he was finally getting some ancestral luck. His smile had to be big enough to be breaking his face.

"Did Arthur beg you to come back?"

"No, and I wouldn't go back even if he begged. He wouldn't have fired a man for something so stupid. Tippy was right."

"Tippy? What does she have to do with this?"

"She wants to invest in me, set me up in private practice. I can open up my own firm and take only the cases I want to take."

"Is that what you want?"

God, he hoped so. If she would just stay here with him, it would be all he'd ever need. They'd be a family someday. He could already see it. Little Michelles running around arguing with their stuffed animals.

"Yes. I want to be with you, Finn. Forever. Isn't that what *you* want?" She seemed to deflate a little, a hint of uncertainty in her eyes. "I love you. So much."

"God, yes." He pulled her into his arms. "If it were up to me, you'd never go anywhere without me. I want you near me all the time, next to me in bed, in the shower, on the sailboat, helping me cook. I love you. I don't need anything else if I have you."

"Face it. *I'm* your lucky charm. You finally found me."

"Then I'm the luckiest man alive."

Epilogue

Six months later

Michelle stepped back to admire the shingle on the front door, sliding her fingers over the carved wooden letters.

LaCroix Law Firm

Her new office was located in an older section of downtown in a sweet little converted Victorian home that was one of the many Goodwill LLC real estate holdings. There were green awnings on the windows facing the front, a kitchen in the back, and the old dining room had become the conference room, the walls now lined with law books. Her office was in the middle of it all, with a small reception area in the front.

Though they'd officially opened two months ago, today was the Chamber of Commerce ribbon-cutting ceremony and everyone she knew would be in attendance. For someone relatively new to Charming, that turned out to be quite a few people. Naturally, her fiancé, Finn, would be there, but also his entire family, her own personal cheerleading section. Noah and Twyla, of course, Rachel, Tippy and Ted, and yes, even Arthur and his wife. Things had been tense for a while, as she threatened to take market share from

P&P, but it was Tippy who finally turned the tide with a little raw honesty.

"You wouldn't have fired a man!" she'd yelled. "You men lie all the time. Why, Ted lies at every golf game. But a woman tells a small untruth and you blow a gasket."

Michelle always thought Arthur had a point, but it went both ways. She hadn't been honest with him—but he hadn't been fair to her either. Even though he'd said he saw her like a daughter, she knew he wouldn't have cast Junior out. The trust had to be rebuilt on her part, too, and it had been slowly growing for the past few months. Michelle referred divorces to P&P. In turn, Arthur handed down most custody and adoption cases, where Michelle had chosen to specialize.

She would do a little consulting on divorce but had already decided it would be less than 20 percent of her practice. It turned out there were enough adoption and custody cases to keep her busy for a while. For now, she was the sole partner, but she had a five-year plan. By year four, she planned to hire on an associate.

But for now, she had Rachel.

Rachel, who had decided she'd rather work for Michelle, even if she couldn't pay her as much. Rachel, who had given her two weeks' notice to Arthur along with an earful. Rachel, who was arguably Michelle's first real friend in Charming. Sometimes workplace-based relationships were successful. And sometimes women did support each other in the best kind of ways.

Even Michelle's mother was happy to hear news of her own law firm.

"Now you won't even have to depend on a man to *hire* you!"

Oh, well. You couldn't fix everything.

She'd also called her father with Finn's encouragement. It was the first time they'd spoken in years and while she couldn't tell for certain, she was fairly sure her father sounded tearful. She explained that she hadn't known he'd fought for custody, and that she appreciated the fact he had. She remembered he'd always believed in and encouraged her and explained at times it had been a motivation to excel.

They made plans to meet in Paris, and she and Finn were seriously considering it for their honeymoon.

Tippy had definitely come through as promised. She bragged that she was proud to own a law firm in her portfolio and had also started the legal fund for those who could not afford Michelle's services. Everything in her life had come together, and for the first time since she could recall Michelle was truly happy. She had a family, both a found family and one that would soon enough be hers through marriage. She had her health, career, and the love of her life.

Best of all, she'd discovered how to have fun again thanks to Finn. He'd joked that the whole pot of gold and lucky charms trail meant he'd rubbed off on her.

He was right.

In all the best ways, Finn Sheridan had changed her life *and* her heart.

And all because she needed a boyfriend at the last minute, and there stood Finn, the man she'd wanted all along.

All things considered she highly recommended taking a chance, however impulsive, wild, and public.

It had worked out quite well for her.

* * * * *

Special EDITION

Believe in love. Overcome obstacles. Find happiness.

Available Next Month

A Fairy-Tail Ending Catherine Mann
Their Unexpected Forever Laurel Greer

....

Tying The Knot Brenda Novak
Road Trip Rivalry Mona Shroff